DARKNESS
COMES
at DAWN

ALSO BY FRANCINA SIMONE

GUARDIANS SERIES

The Keeper's Vow

GUARDIANS TRILOGY

❧ BOOK TWO ❧

DARKNESS COMES AT DAWN

WITHDRAWN

FRANCINA SIMONE

CHUNKYCATBOOKS
IDAHO

DARKNESS COMES AT DAWN

GUARDIAN'S: BOOK TWO

ChunkyCATBooks

ISBN-13: 978-0-9977103-1-1
Cover art by Kimberly from KimG-Design
Interior design by Francina Simone
Editor R.A. Weston Editorial

www.Francinasimone.com

For more information regarding this book contact:
thefrancinasimone@gmail.com

Twitter: @francinasimone

First Edition

Printed in the U.S.A

—To Leah and all other readers who asked,

"What happens next?"

"It is by luck of birth that until now you have never seen true hate. The hate that takes comfort in your suffering and salivates at the though of causing more.

But there is another kind that is much worse. The kind of hate that does nothing—that feels nothing."

Jedidah

PART ONE
THE DEVIL

1

FREAK

KATIE'S SHINY, BLACK loafers dragged as she trudged down the hall of her crappy school. She was on her way to the front office to finish out her in-school suspension. She'd spent a week in solitary confinement—a stupid closet in Mr. Carver's office with just a desk, a chair, and an overhead light. Now, she was on her way to be lectured to by the last people she wanted to be in a room with.

The Board. They were the heads of education for junior guardians. What did they want? *Her* to apologize for her behavior? She contemplated giving them the finger instead. She hadn't even started the fight—not completely. If Know-It-All Michael Heckler hadn't asked to see her fangs, she wouldn't have chased him around Practical Applications threatening to sink them into his eye so he could get a *really* good look.

It was a joke. Maybe a joke that had gone too far when she'd cornered him and punched him in the stomach—*after* he'd pushed her. Maybe a joke that had stopped being a joke by the time Tristan and Steve Sensei pulled them apart.

Michael was the one who'd turned it into a fight, the moment he put his hands on her. He's the one who'd made her say, "I'll drain you and your entire family. Just wait."

Of course she'd left out that, to her, blood was absolutely disgusting, the idea of drinking blood from a person was even more disgusting, and she'd only said it to freak him out.

Anyway, it worked. Michael was thoroughly freaked out— but so was had everyone else. By the time Tristan had dragged her to the other side of the classroom, screaming and with a fist-full of Michael's hair, everyone was on Michael's side, gaping at her—the animal freak that escaped it's cage.

Katie walked into the office. Myrtle, the secretary, was too busy shouting at the copier to notice her. She walked back to the main conference room and knocked on the door. This wasn't the first time she'd been here. Before summer, they'd made a special visit to her and Tristan to let them know they were on a short leash.

She heard muffled voices, but nothing to acknowledge anyone had heard her knock.

Katie leaned on the opposite wall, tapping her head against it. She'd spent the last four days of school in a broom closet, staring at blank walls, trying to figure out how things had gotten to this point. *Sure*, she'd spent the last year coming to terms with the fact that she was a descendent of long ago vampire/werewolf hunters, now secret keepers; that she was blood-bound to a boy who, like her, was half-vampire and could read her mind; and topper on the cake, she'd watched Larry—or the ice cream guy who'd turned out to be her pureblood vampire dad—die next to his sociopathic brother who'd tried to kill Tristan and rape/kill her (thankfully she'd never had to find out which would have happened first). But how had she ended up in a broom closet for bullying? When had she stopped being the Katie who stayed under the radar to avoid schoolwork? Where did *this* Katie, the spazzed-out, half-vampire juvie chick, come from?

At least now she had a great boyfriend. The guy who was still serving his in-school suspension because, while "Sensei Steve" yelled at Katie in his office, Tristan had crossed the room and punched Michael dead in the face. It was kind of romantic.

Katie blinked back the lump in her throat—pride, sadness, or whatever—as the door opened. She immediately saw Michael sitting at a round table. He glared at her. The left side of his face still a gross greenish-purple color. A large body moved and blocked her view. Jim Heckler, Michael's dad and a member of The Board.

"Come in, Miss Watts," he bellowed.

Katie peeled her body off the wall. She wasn't going to let him get to her. Not like he did that one night when he'd all but threatened Tristan after werewolves tried to kidnap her. She entered the room surprised. She'd known Henrietta—a stern-faced, gray-haired women—would be there. She hadn't expected Will to be sitting firmly on the left side of Henrietta. Last she'd heard, he was suspended. Apparently letting an undocumented half-vampire stay at your house and attend a school for guardian children without consent from the other board members was a no-no. At least, that's what Lucinda made it sound like.

"Katie." Will shuffled papers on the desk. "Please sit down. Michael, there is no need for all that."

Michael shuffled his chair farther from the empty one meant for Katie. "Yeah? Tell my face that."

"Quiet," Mr. Heckler said to his son.

Katie sat next to Michael, even though he moved another foot away from her.

"Where to start?" Henrietta looked between both Katie and Michael.

"An apology would be nice." Michael's voice lost its usual annoying alto and was now an acid-dripped tenor.

"I'm sorry your face looks like a truck hit it. Oh—and for the bruises."

Michael threw a sling of curses at her, and she smirked, glad to get a rise out of him.

"Quiet!" Mr. Heckler boomed. "You've been shown up by a girl and you let that boy beat you senseless. You don't deserve my last name."

Michael stared at the floor, but Katie knew it wasn't because he was afraid of his father. The way he gripped the edge of his chair said he was afraid of what he'd do if he didn't control every cell in his body.

"Jim," Henrietta warned. "Michael is right. An apology is in order. I believe you had an ample amount of time to think of what you want to say."

All eyes, except Michael's, were on Katie. While they'd kept her locked up, day after day and for hours on end, in that stupid little room, she'd thought of a lot of things. However, an apology wasn't anywhere near what she'd plotted and contemplated.

Will cleared his throat, a frown pulling at his mouth.

"An apology?" Katie half-laughed. "Whatever. Sorry." She folded her arms. The faster she complied, the faster she could get out of this stupid office. At least then she could go back to her little room and listen to music on her phone.

"Katie, that's not acceptable. You and I both know that." Will's voice was all business, but his eyes pleaded for her to do what they wanted. What was that exactly? Sure, she'd crossed the line, but Michael wasn't the only one asking her stupid questions. *"I bet she's like one papercut away from attacking us all." "Look at them pretending to be normal. Why are they still here?"* Her personal favorite and the most frequent: *"I wonder if she eats her period."* It wasn't just the whispers that bothered her; it was that the teachers heard them, too, and said nothing. Steve Sensei was there and heard Michael taunting her during class. Yet, when she stood up for herself, she was the one at fault.

"I'm not going to apologize for what I'm not sorry for. I'd rather stand up for myself than be everyone's punching bag—no offense," she said to Michael.

"This isn't about standing up for yourself. You got physical. You put your hands on another student," Henrietta said.

"*After* he pushed me."

"You were trying to bite me." Michael's alto-ish whine was back.

"Shut up. The thought of touching you, let alone putting my mouth on you, makes me want to vomit. I wasn't going to bite you."

"You threatened to kill me and my family."

"After you kicked me. And what, you find out I'm half-vampire and all of a sudden you think I'm capable of killing you?" Katie's brows furrowed. How stupid was this kid. Everyone spewed stupid, empty threats when they were mad. If anything, he should have been terrified to sit next to one of his best friends, a kid who'd actually stabbed and shot two different people. Katie bit her tongue as Brian's name danced on the tip of it.

"I don't know what you're capable of," Michael spat at her. He turned to the adults. "She's a danger to us all."

Mr. Heckler cut him off. "You're pathetic. You're graduating in a year and you can't even defend yourself. And you—" His gazed shifted to Katie. "—the next time you threaten a student at this school is the last time you attend this school. I will see that you are charged like the *wannabe* adult you are."

Katie growled. "Is this how you treat all the other kids who fight and threaten each other?"

Mr. Heckler opened his mouth and Will raised his hand, but Katie went on. "No, I want to know. Because I've got a list of kids who I've seen fight in Practical Applications over girls, boys. Hell, I saw a fight break out over a spilled soda bottle. Do you charge them with crimes? Are they a danger to society and the school? Why don't you cut the bullshit and tell me what you really want to say." Katie sat taller in her chair. She clenched her sweaty palms. Her nerves bounced around her body, threatening to explode. She'd crossed the point of no return, and the charge in the room raised the hairs on her neck.

"Watch your language, Katie," Henrietta said.

Mr. Heckler grunted. "She can't control her hands, and you're worried about her mouth?"

Will spoke louder than Mr. Heckler. "The difference here, Katie, is you have the power to take someone's life much easier than any normal teenage girl. You have weapons built into your teeth. So, yes, we will take what you do seriously. You have a responsibility to control yourself and be the bigger person. If Michael had chased you around the room with a knife—"

"A knife? Now I've got shivs in my mouth? Screw that, Will. I don't deserve to be treated different just because I was born differently."

A cloud of silence passed between them—distancing them. Out of the corner of her eye, she saw Michael look at her.

Mr. Heckler scowled. "Being born different is being born with blue versus brown eyes, being born with an extra finger, or short versus tall. You weren't born different. You were born a vampire. That isn't as simple as being *different.*"

"How can you say that?" Michael glared at the table. "She's a person. It *is* that simple."

"What did I tell you, boy?" Mr. Heckler's voice grew darker with every word. Michael's breath dragged as he murmured obscenities only Katie could hear. He gripped the edge of his chair so tight his knuckles turned white.

"Stop talking to him like that," Katie said.

"Katie," Henrietta and Will warned.

Katie shook her head. It was wrong. All of it. Sitting in this stupid chair being lectured to about bullying while not only be subjected to it, but also watching it.

"Michael's right. It *is* that simple. I'm a person. He provoked me, and I fought back." She stared hard at Mr. Heckler. "Obviously that's a foreign concept to you. People *fighting back.* You probably treat everyone like your personal punching bag. That's what—gasp—*bullies* do. You'll be lucky if you don't die alone in your own pee and vomit."

Mr. Heckler stood up. Will yelled, but she didn't hear anything he said. She stared at Mr. Heckler and smiled. She would never let him win.

Never.

"Get out," Mr. Heckler growled.

Katie stood up. "I'm sorry, Michael." She meant it. Punching him had been wrong. Chasing him and cornering him and letting him get to her had been wrong. He was nothing more than a product of his environment—but at least he wasn't like his dad.

Katie pushed in her chair and turned her back on them. Before she even opened the door, Mr. Heckler yelled for Michael to get out, too. They both left, not saying a word until they cleared the office.

"You've made my life astronomically worse than it has ever been," Michael said as they walked past the library.

"Well, I spent the last week in a closet because of you." Katie pulled her phone out of her bra. She noticed Michael's eyes lingering on her chest. "Stop perving."

"Whatever." He slowed his pace. "I'm sorry. For saying the things I said about you. I didn't realize I was just like him. My worst nightmare—second only to being eaten alive by parasites."

Katie chuckled even though it wasn't that funny. Her nerves were stuck in free fall. She wanted to go back to her tiny little closet and scream at the top of her lungs. Whatever little victory she'd felt back in the office now seemed pointless. Nothing had changed.

Today was the last day of her suspension, but she'd go back to class a leper. No, worse—lepers were harmless. She would go back to losing her mind as the clock ticked down every second spent sitting and listening to stupid lectures about what vampires were like. What she was like. She'd go back to everyone watching her—the freaky, erratic class pet who was moments away from foaming at the fang-riddled mouth.

Katie sighed. Her canines were hardly fangs.

"And for the record, I didn't get beat up by a girl. I got beat up by her boyfriend—the one everyone knows is like the best in our class because, you know—he's half-vampire."

"Congratulations. You fought a girl and didn't flat-out lose." Katie picked up her pace, remembering why she'd chased him around the room threatening to bite him.

"What's it like?"

Katie knew exactly what he meant. What annoyed her more was the fear on his face.

"You really want to know? Besides the fact that I have to get up like everybody else and go to school, I have to study harder, I have to be polite and smile, and I have to pretend like I love everyone and everything. Because if I don't, people think I'm going to up and murder everyone—even though these same people go to Gray City every weekend and hang out in night clubs and bars with the same thing they fear in me. That's what it's like."

Katie turned a corner, annoyed when he still followed her.

"Are you going to start wearing black eyeliner and smoke outside while listening to emo-music, too? Lighten up, Watts."

"Don't do that." Katie scratched at her ears. He was a little fly. "Don't call me Watts. My name is Katie."

"Are you going to start drinking black coffee and write sad poetry, *Katie*?"

Katie flipped him off.

"Why get all pissy when people talk about you behind your back if you're going to act like this when we actually try to talk to you? I want to know what it's like—what it felt like to have fangs. Your teeth look normal. I just want to know what it feels like being—a vampire."

"And what about what you said about my period? You just wanted to know my snacktime routine. Huh?"

Michael blushed. "Come on. You've never made fun of someone before? Whatever. Yeah, keep walking…I said sorry!"

Katie waved him off, opening the door to Mr. Carver's classroom. A bunch of first-year students stared at her, wide-eyed, as she made her way to the back of the class and toward one of the two tiny closet rooms. They whispered about her altercation with Michael—now more bizarre than a backroad circus show.

"You're back," came a voice. It was soft and sweet. Tristan was the only reason spending a week in a tiny white cell was bearable.

"Yup. Everything went perfect as expected." Katie's nerves climbed into her chest as a girl sitting close to her door whispered that Katie had actually bit Michael out of thirst and lust. Katie rolled her eyes.

"Katalina—"

She heard the sigh in her name. *"Don't. I don't want to talk about it right now. I don't want to talk about anything."* Katie grabbed her headphones out of the desk. She put them in her ears and started a playlist.

⋅☙ ♋ ❧⋅

Lucinda was waiting for Katie and Tristan after school. "You, go home. You, get in. We have to talk." Lucinda opened the car door and waved Katie in.

Katie silently pleaded for Tristan not to leave, but he shrugged, his blue eyes just as cold as his unsympathetic frown.

"I just spent the last three hours listening to your crap music. No sympathy here."

"Way to be a hero," Katie grumbled.

"I'll be a hero when you stop listening to songs on repeat." Tristan adjusted his bag and waved as Katie got in the car.

It was Friday. They weren't supposed to have training on Fridays. In fact, Katie had hoped for a Lucinda-free day as she had been annoyed with Katie for getting suspended.

"Will called me. He's not at all pleased." Lucinda started the car.

"Lucy—"

"I don't want to hear it. I want you to explain to me what made you think what you said today was okay."

Katie stared out the window, avoiding eye contact. Gone was the satisfaction from staring at Jim Heckler's bulging eyes. "I don't."

Lucinda exhaled. "What?"

"I don't think it was okay. But what he said wasn't okay either."

"Katie, Jim is—he's a turd, yes. But you can't go around telling off everyone you don't like.'"

"I don't. He was saying things. He was making it sound like I was some kind of abomination. He said I was weirder than a three-toed giant with one of those eye mutations."

"I don't think Will would sit there and let him say anything that was unprofessional to you."

Katie opened her mouth—and closed it. She smacked her head against the seat and stared at the road. Jim hadn't said anything as much as he'd implied it all. He'd made it clear what he thought without outright saying it. "It's not fair."

"Katie, it wasn't fair of you to get into a fight. You can't tell me none of this is your fault."

"I didn't say it's not my fault. Lucy, stop. Please."

Lucinda glanced at Katie, pressing on the break as a light turned red.

Katie pulled at her seatbelt as it tightened on her chest.

"I'm not trying to get on you. You've missed school. You've been suspended. You just told off a board member. You have to admit all these things aren't working in your favor."

Katie itched to pull her headphones out of her pocket and slip away into her music.

"Are you listening?"

"Yes," Katie breathed.

"You're making this even harder for Will. He's barely got his job back, and he's the one advocating for you."

That wasn't fair. "You weren't there."

"I didn't have to be to know you're making the wrong decisions. What's really going on?" Lucinda started to drive again, but slowed again as traffic came to a complete stop.

"Nothing." Katie said. How did you answer a question like that? It wasn't one thing. It was a thousand things.

"It's not nothing. You haven't talked about—you haven't opened up about anything that happened. Like losing your father."

"He wasn't my *father*. Just Larry."

"Katie, he was. It's okay to admit that."

"Lucy, he really wasn't. He's just Larry. *Was* Larry. Whatever, why are we talking about this? Why do we always talk about this?"

"Because you didn't go to the funeral. You haven't brought it up. You haven't cried about it. I'm worried. You keep acting like you're fine."

"It's not an act. I am fine. Just because I don't want to cry doesn't mean there is something wrong with me. I knew him for like a month."

"A month? *Are you serious*? Katie, you have to get these things out. You're letting it affect your life."

Katie groaned. "You're not making any sense. One minute I'm supposed to be wrecked and the next you're telling me it's affecting my life *too* much."

"That's not what I mean. Don't be smart." Lucinda cursed as the same light turned red for the third time.

Katie waded in the silence. "I hate school. I don't belong there anymore."

"Don't be silly. You belong there just as much as everyone else."

"No, I don't. I'm sick of it. It's beyond pointless."

Lucinda rolled her eyes. "If I had a dollar for every teenager who thought school was pointless…"

"I'm not—that's not what I mean. I'm not saying this because I'm lazy or whatever."

Lucinda laughed.

Katie gripped the seat.

"Katie, keep your head down, study, and you'll graduate. Trust me. That's much more productive than what you're doing now."

"Graduate and do what?" Katie pulled at her seatbelt again. It was locked tight against her chest.

"There are numerous jobs you can choose from. What do you want to do?"

"I don't know," Katie growled and unbuckled the stupid belt.

"So your answer is to cause everyone problems. Smart."

Katie reached into her pockets and pulled out her headphones. She put them on and turned on her music. She didn't care that Lucinda gave her dirty looks or shook her head, annoyed.

Lucinda had trapped her in the car so she could tear her down. Nope, not today. Katie wanted to Hulk-out, rip the car door off, and run down the street screaming like a maniac—but that would only get her locked up in a real white padded cell.

Lucinda dropped her off at home, and Katie mumbled a goodbye that Lucinda pretended not to hear. Katie thanked her lucky stars that she wouldn't be seeing her over the weekend as that was *"family bonding"* time for the Andersons now.

Katie kicked some weeds as she walked across the lawn. She wasn't the same girl she'd been before. No one cared about that, though. They wanted her to go back to being laughably predictable and lazy. They treated her like a bored rebelling teenager.

Yes, she was bored. Yes, she had some serious troubles. But she wasn't turning into an emotional attention-seeker. She wasn't going to start writing edgy poetry or paint her walls black to mirror her soul or wear tons of dark eyeliner and tell her teachers off.

"Uggghhh!" Katie screamed, stomping on the wooden porch steps.

Maybe she should. What if all those kids were like her? Laughed at for telling the truth, for having a thousand problems and no idea how to explain one without the rest tumbling down.

No. She couldn't do that.

Allison would never approve of her wearing anything black.

2

WHAT NOW?

WHAT HAPPENED TO *me?*

The words rolled over and over in Katie's mind as she lay on her bed, in pitch blackness. It was the dead of night on Sunday; a gaping hole sat in her chest and it ached.

It didn't make sense. She was stronger now, a completely different person than just a year ago. She'd *gone through* stuff—*done* stuff. She was a vampire capable of—nothing but being a teenage girl riddled with angst and rebellion.

Katie rolled onto her side as a heavy cloud fell over her. Was it going to be like this for the rest of her life? Never tired, nothing to do, and no one to talk to without sounding like a whiny freak.

She'd tried telling her dad to let her train with Tristan at night, but all he heard was *sex, sex, sex* and the conversation ended before it began. Even Lucinda had laughed at her when she'd tried to tell her she needed to *do* something.

They didn't know what it was like to never sleep, to sit in her head all day and night. She'd start thinking things—things like, what would it be like if she just disappeared? Or she'd hear voices that weren't hers and then realize they *were* her—like her mind broke in an attempt to amuse her. Snapped, like a twig, under the pressure of appearing normal.

The only person who got it was Tristan. Katie smiled to herself and gripped her pillow. He got how much she wanted to punch a wall when Lucinda or her dad said, *"Why don't you study?"* Study what? She wanted to scream. All these things would never relate to her future. She wasn't going to be a guardian. She wanted to rid herself of everything guardian-related. Everyone treated her like a feral cat. Why would she spend the rest of her life around these people when there was a whole city, under her feet, of people just like her?

She just had to hold on to her head until graduation…a whole year. Katie let out a long sigh that turned into a growl. She threw on headphones and blasted music into her sensitive ears. She was tired of not being tired. Tired of being expected to be the same sixteen-year-old she was before she'd met Tristan; been force-fed blood; and found out her dad wasn't her dad, but actually the ice cream guy with a psychotic brother who'd killed her mom and her boyfriend's parents.

Yeah.

If that doesn't change a girl…

Katie blinked.

She got up, turned the music up louder, and danced. She flung her body around the room, her hair flying around her face, whipping across her cheeks, and tangling around her mouth. She jumped onto and off the bed, whipping around and around until light poured into the room.

Her dad mouthed something at her, his face red and fuzzy. She paused her music.

"—I'm trying to sleep—take off those damn headphones."

"I can hear you."

"I said, take them *off.*"

Katie sighed and pulled at her headphones until they popped out of her ears and fell to the floor. "Sorry," she breathed, turning back to her bed.

"What the hell is wrong with you? I have work in the morning and you have school. Go to bed," he barked.

Katie stared at him blankly. Maybe last year she would have been too scared to do anything but hop under the sheets and apologize until her tongue fell out. Hell, last year he wouldn't have had to tell her to go to sleep.

Her dad fumbled over some words, confused by her lack of action.

"I don't sleep," she said.

His expression changed from anger to confusion but settled back on anger. "Well, I do." He stomped out of her room.

Katie pushed the door closed and flung her phone hard against the bed. It bounced off and smacked onto the floor.

She contemplated smashing it to pieces. She wanted to break stuff. All the crap in her room. None of it meant anything. It wasn't as if she couldn't buy more stuff or an even a bigger house to put it all in. Larry had left her more money than she could spend—a fact she still hadn't told her dad.

How could she? Even if it meant he'd never have to work again, it would have just been another thing that made him angry. Katie screamed into her pillow, thinking of the ice cream shop that was still closed and untouched since the day she'd gone with Tristan.

"I told you to hire someone to run the shop."

Katie opened her dry eyes, hearing Tristan's voice in her mind. A smile stretched across her face.

"Where are you?" she asked.

"On a plane to Tahiti. Where do you think?"

Katie rolled out of bed and left her room. She crept pass her dad's room. His light was off, but he wasn't asleep. His breath was too shallow. He was probably trying to figure out how he'd ever forgotten she doesn't—can't—sleep now.

Katie found Tristan waiting on the porch. He sat on the steps facing the street. "You're late," she said.

"Said the most punctual person I know." He side-eyed her. "Lucinda knows I'm sneaking out. She's trying to catch me. *Us.*"

Katie laughed, sitting next to him. "Tristan—sneaking out and caring what Lucy thinks. That's a first. I'm surprised you didn't just waltz out after dinner."

"We both know she'll come down on you if I don't let her think she can control me." Tristan leaned in and kissed Katie on her forehead. All her worry washed away like sand on the shore.

Ever since Lucinda had caught them half-naked in his room, she'd all but banned them from seeing each other without some type of supervision.

"So what? What makes you think I won't tell them to stuff it?"

"How'd that work out Friday?" Tristan studied her, his crystal-blue eyes laughing at her and taking her in. Eyes like that are what got her into this mess. Taunting her on the surface—but yearning below that.

He looked away. "What do you want to do tonight? We don't have that long."

"Tonight I want to bang something." Katie smirked, wiggling her eyebrows.

"Don't be such a pervert, Katalina." The words rolled off his tongue quick, but she heard the husk in his voice.

Katie laughed, too afraid of letting their true thoughts fill the silence. "I want to fight. No running. Just fist-hitting-flesh action. I want these knuckles to bleed."

Tristan grabbed her hands. "We'll fight. But no blood. I'm serious."

Katie yanked her hands away. "I wasn't being serious." She scanned her own hands. What did it matter? She'd heal before anyone would notice. The pain would be more distracting than the nothingness.

"But you were." Tristan stood up and waved her toward the backyard, all the suggestive husk gone from his voice. "Look, I won't tell anyone what you're thinking. I told you that. But you've got to deal with this. Seriously. You're—"

"What?" Katie stood up, feeling heavy again. She just wanted to move. Why did he have to make more out of it? This was nothing like last time. Last time she was angry. Last time she kept seeing that son-of-a-bitch choking her out. Last time she saw Larry showing up a minute too late and caring more about his brother than her. Last time, she'd thought about what would happen if anyone found out Tristan was the one who'd killed Larry.

This time she didn't care. He was dead. Gone. They both were. That had nothing to do with right now.

"Katalina—"

Katie waved him off and put on her best smile. "Let's go. Backyard. Now."

.ഐⒺ☺⊙.

Light crept into the sky before the first bird chirped. Katie and Tristan lay on the grass, covered in dirt and bruises. Tristan, to Katie's satisfaction, wore more and more bruises these days. She breathed heavily and grabbed his hand. Touching him both sped up her heart and calmed it.

"We could skip school," she said.

He rubbed the back of her hand with his thumb. "And do what?"

Katie had a specific thought but stifled it as soon as it was about to give her away. "Stay here. My dad works."

"And do what...?"

"It's better than going to Hell."

"It's not that bad."

Katie swallowed. It was that bad. Maybe he didn't care about everyone judging them and watching them—waiting for them to turn into bats and suck the student body dry—but she was over it.

Tristan kissed her hand and moved to get up. "Come one. I've got to get back before Lucinda notices I'm gone."

Disappointment seeped out of her pores and coated her skin. Nothing took the taste out of happiness like rejection.

"I'm not rejecting you. I'm just not letting you turn into a delinquent. No more than you already are, at least." He offered her a hand and she looked away. "Suit yourself. See you in a few hours."

As much as she wanted him to lay back down and cover her with kisses and suggestive touches, he was right. If she skipped any more days the school would call her dad—again. Apparently missing six days in the first three weeks and spending one of those weeks in suspension put you on a list.

She sighed and closed her eyes, focusing on the nothingness that crept back over her. The silent idleness that waited for her in her room, class, lectures with Lucinda...

Like ice cold water to the face, she felt him on top of her. The slightest pressure of his lips on hers. He ran his fingers over her body and hugged her tight. "Stop," he whispered.

Katie's eyes stung. She couldn't keep doing this. She *hated* living like this. She had everything any normal person could want. A too-awesome-for-words boyfriend, money, immortality, *and* she could heal herself—but the price was steep.

She'd let Larry die in her arms to get the boyfriend she now had.

There was only so much time she could spend idle before she really started thinking about it. Like what if Larry had showed up too late. She still felt Eshmael's hands on her throat... squeezing harder and harder...

Tristan gripped her tighter. "It's over. You can't keep thinking about it. You have to stop."

"And do what else instead?" Katie pushed Tristan away, breathing harder than before.

He looked hurt. She sensed his desperation, reaching out to her as if she was tipping just out of reach. He was right to feel that way. She *was* tipping; part of her believed the free-fall would get rid of the numbness.

"Katalina. You could—" His eyes searched her, and he rubbed a hand over his face, completely lost for words. "I don't know. I get it. You're right. It's a waste of time and energy to go to school. I felt like that last year, but I had you. You were—fun. Now...I don't know. You're gone. I don't know what to do to help you. I don't want to do this either. *I've* already graduated from high school. I've been in the real world. I get it."

Katie gaped in disbelief. "You've *already graduated*? When? How? *When?*"

"I told you."

"No, you didn't." Katie sobered up. How had he not told her that? All this time she'd thought he was just really studious and missed out on the high school life.

"Look, that's what you conjured up in your crazy head. I swear I've mentioned it."

Katie stared him down. His blue eyes glinted back dark in the dim morning light as his eyebrows rose to the top of his head in genuine surprise.

"In the Patrol. It's part of early admission. We finish our high school degree in about two years—basic stuff, plus task force stuff. It's standard practice."

"You made being a *Death Dealer* sound like you were some poor punk kid in the Mafia." Katie squinted her eyes. He'd been calling it "*the Patrol*" more and more lately. As if *Death Dealers* wasn't the more accurate title.

"Well, it is like the mafia. It's volunteer, but each house has to give members to the task force '*for the good of the coven.*' What does this have to do with anything? The point is, I get how you feel."

"No, you don't! *You* can leave. *You* don't have to go to school. You're just hanging around like the kid who graduated but loved high school so much he can't leave."

"Thanks." Tristan crossed his arms. *That's how you think of me? As a loser?* His voice moved heavy through her mind.

"That's not what I meant." Katie grabbed his arm. "I'm sorry. I know you're here for me. I'm sorry—" She sighed. "Maybe that's even worse. I'm holding you back from being something more. This is all so fucked up, Tristan." Katie exhaled. The small version of herself, stuck inside her head, screamed to get out.

"There are other schools in Gray City. Schools just for vampires. Compared to Hamilton, there is more work, especially since our schools are high school and college in one. But you leave ready for a career. It's more focused and the teachers are better."

"So you want me to trade one year of Hell for who knows how many more years at a vampire school?"

"It will most likely be one-and-a-half years—and a lot of studying. But it's not like you don't have the time."

"Oh. My. God. If one more person tells me to spend my time studying, I'm going to blow up the entire city and start World War Three."

"Katalina, it's not the same thing. It's not even that bad."

"Not the same? No, you're right. I'm going to start behind like I did last year and spend all my time catching up on schoolwork I don't want to do. I'll take my chances at Hamilton."

Katie stood up and kicked a rock into the fence at the far end of the yard. She didn't care that it made the loudest *pop* she'd ever heard a rock hitting wood make.

"Whatever. Fine. I was just trying to come up with solutions."

His frustrations welted in her, and she reveled in it. For a moment, his feelings mirrored hers. Helpless, hopeless, and angry.

Tristan locked eyes with her. "Don't. Don't do that. Don't annoy me on purpose." He bit his tongue, but she heard the rest in her mind. *It's not attractive.*

Katie rolled her eyes. "Bye, Tristan." She pushed passed him and went inside, straight to her room to punch her pillow. She cried and screamed into it until her arms ached.

3

BORSAS AND DIRTY HAMSTERS

KATIE OPENED HER notebook as the bell rang. She wasn't surprised by Tristan's empty chair. Beautiful. If he was going to skip school, he should have agreed to it when she'd mentioned it. They could have skipped the fight, and she wouldn't be sitting through a long, boring lecture from Mrs. Barnes on the interrelations of the races. Katie spent most of the class scribbling in her notebook—until Mrs. Barnes said *his* name.

"Coven leader Lawrence from the Borsa House line, as you may have heard over the summer, was murdered, along with his brother Eshmael Borsa. Rumors say that it was an attack from another family trying to take over the coven, but as you all know, I do not like speculation. I like facts."

"Facts like all the people that have been disappearing from the city?" Jenna, a girl Katie had accidentally pelted in the head with paint last year, sat up higher in her seat.

"It does seem to link closely to the death of Lawrence Borsa. Anyway, this is an important moment for history. Lawrence was seemingly tolerant of other races and made efforts to keep the peace. Whoever takes the seat will set a precedent for interrelation policies. These are very dangerous times. We must take care to watch the city below because the tides can easily change out of our favor. Times like this are when power vacuums are made."

Jenna spoke up again. "You have to admit, though, it's already starting."

Katie was well aware that things in Gray City were changing. Lucinda had made it a point to mention it all summer—how there were no other witnesses to Larry's death, meaning Katie and Tristan would have to come clean to the heads of the vampire houses and their judicial system or hope a new leader would be elected soon and stabilize everything again.

The latter wasn't looking so good, and little did Lucinda know, Tristan had been the one holding the knife that killed Larry.

Mrs. Barnes sat on the edge of her desk and took off her glasses. "I'm going to be honest with you. Missing persons reports are piling up faster than I think even our local council cares to admit. The rise in D-ranges last year, the death of a coven leader... I'm afraid it looks like someone is raising an army. Don't look too alarmed. Vampires create armies for one reason—to secure a nomination for coven leader. To be a coven leader, you have to have numbers behind you.

"Now, I don't know if this is true or not, and you *know* I hate speculation, but I fear things aren't moving in a good direction. If Lawrence was murdered by a head of house, it means they weren't happy with the way things were. It means they want change. Change is often…not that good."

Katie knew that wasn't true. But what could she say? She raised her hand. Mrs. Barnes looked surprised but called on her anyway.

"How is the next coven leader chosen?"

The class was quiet, but they were alert and trying not to stare as Katie waited for an answer.

Katie knew, from the little bit of studying she did, that vampire politics were fairly simple. There were houses—not necessarily related people—and they all took their orders from the leader of their house, who took their orders from the coven leader. There were at least twenty houses in Gray City, and because she listened to Lawrence instead of her instincts, they were now all without a coven leader. Twenty vampire houses scrambling to do whatever they wanted.

"Well, we don't know exactly. We do know it's based on the size of the house. The family with the most house members usually rules. We know it's also based on nobility but not much more than that. Lawrence was coven leader to the oldest and most regal houses that we know of. We don't know if a vampire from his immediate family will take over or not. It isn't like it was in the old days when vampires fathered children—well, pureblood children," Mrs. Barnes added with an apologetic look.

Katie blushed. Murmurs around the class picked up.

"Usually coven leaders and house heads are purebloods. They have a protocol in place for who takes the torch when another's light goes out. From what I've read, it's done the same day, if not the following. Never has a coven been left without a leader for months."

Katie stared at Mrs. Barnes. "What is the punishment for killing a pureblood?"

"Death. To spill pureblood blood, even accidentally, is punishable by death. I will refer you back to the death of Maximus Epidus, the barber who accidentally cut his house leader while giving a close shave. I believe that was on last year's final exam. Or more importantly Eric Stall. The man who assisted in his pureblood father's suicide. Though this was over a century ago, I bet the sun would rise in the west and set in the east before that law changes. Suffices to say, when it happens, no one comes clean about it."

"So, if no one comes clean about Lawrence's death…"

Mrs. Barnes shook her head. "Don't worry. They'll pick a leader sooner or later. Let's just hope the world doesn't go to Hell before that. Okay, enough tangents! Interrelation policies." Mrs. Barnes stood up and dusted off her skirt. "Who knows when the Moon Act was passed?"

Katie stared at Tristan's empty desk. There was no way they could ever tell anyone what happened in that room. No one would believe them. Even if it meant the whole world was going to Hell, she would rather live in Hell with Tristan than on Earth without him.

⊰⊱

The only interesting part of the day was Field Study, a momentary escape. There was also a slim chance she might see Allison, as Field Study was after lunch and spent at a community center in Gray City.

Ever since the summer, Allison had been completely off the grid. No cellphone, no email, no snail mail. Nothing. The program she'd joined didn't allow her to have any contact with anyone who wasn't in the program. She didn't even attend regular classes or go home on the weekends.

Katie only knew she was at the community center because she'd caught a glimpse of her red hair once, right after they'd been sorted into groups and led to their workstations. They had different jobs, so Katie had no hope of talking to her during working hours.

Even the Bistro's thick air, filled with the smell of heavenly creamy pastas and warm bread, couldn't block her thoughts about her job: organizing and stuffing brochures and envelopes to be mailed out. It was a crappy enough job, but she was also partnered with Brian, Christi, and Michael. As she got into the elevator, she stood next to Brian, who didn't move away from her like she thought he would. Instead he smiled and nodded.

Katie raised her eyebrows. "Are we friends again?"

"Nod at a girl and now she wants to go out on a date. Take a step back, Watts."

Katie side-eyed him. "Don't be stupid. And why are you calling me Watts?"

"You're charming. I just didn't want to stuff envelopes all quiet and hateful-like. You know?"

Katie nodded as the elevator plummeted. The last time she'd done community service it had been more than a little tense between them, as if he were trying not to show his new friends that he was still friends with the vamp-chick.

They walked to the community center in silence, and Katie exhaled, relieved when Brian caught up with Michael and Ethan, leaving her alone. Gray City was freedom. Even walking to the community center to stuff envelopes gave her more excitement than being at school, home, or even training with Tristan. Bright and busy, life hummed here. People were doing things and going places; they had lives that had nothing to do with the world above. People down here were free to make their own way.

She looked up at the grayed sky (if the underground could have a sky) where the darkness from above met the light of the city. There was something beautiful about it. Katie embraced every moment, up until they entered the brightly colored community center and were sorted to their stations.

Katie shuffled to a little closet-office and sat at a round table with Brian, Michael, and Christi.

She was stuffing her third envelope when the guy who was

supposed to be supervising them walked into their tiny supply room.

"Hey. Don't touch anything not on that table. I still can't find the hole punch," he said. He scratched his scraggly beard and wiped his fingers on a T-shirt that was too faded to read.

"We didn't take the stupid hole *puncher*. We've just been stuffing envelopes," Christi said, folding a flyer and grabbing an envelope from the box. It wasn't a wonder the guy couldn't find the hole puncher; the room was a mess. Between the papers, cabinets, tables with piles of books, and old printers—probably from the eighties—there was only enough room for their three chairs, the two stacked crates Brian sat on, the table, and the box they put the envelopes in.

"Well, it didn't just walk out, did it, Curly-Q?" The guy watched them with beady eyes.

Christi's hair had extra curl and bounce today. It whipped as she looked up. "Whatever."

The guy left, and they continued in silence until Michael stood up.

"What are you doing?" Christi put another envelope in the crate and leaned back in her chair.

"I'm going to touch stuff." Michael wiggled his fingers at the piles of paper behind him.

If he were anyone else besides Michael Know-It-All Heckler, who would touch a pot of boiling water if you told him not to, Katie would have rolled her eyes and continued stuffing, but the glint in Michael's eyes flashed images of imminent disaster.

"Don't, Michael. He's already spastic about a hole puncher," Brian said.

"I'm just going to see what all this crap is. I want to know what propaganda they feed to the newly changed?" He smiled devilishly, waving his hand and knocking over a stack of papers. They spilled onto the table all over the flyers they were folding and stuffing into envelopes.

Both Katie and Christi sighed and glared at him.

"What? It was an accident. Ladies, chill."

"You're such an idiot," Brian laughed.

Katie shared a look with Christi, surprised that they both seemed to be comrades in this moment. As she helped clean up the papers, Katie noticed they were all the same. A flyer of some sort. It was gray, and all it had was a simple question:

Why Stand Apart
When We Can Stand Together?
7

"These are a lot of copies for an inspirational quote," Brian said, looking on the back of the flyer for any clue as to what it meant.

Christi shook her head. "I've seen these before. They're everywhere. They say different things, though—I think. I never paid them that much attention, but they all have the same number on them." Christi looked at Brian. "You've never seen them?"

Katie looked at the font. It was like someone had typed it out on a typewriter. She had noticed it before—maybe?

"I don't think so," he said.

Christi shrugged and shoved a pile of scattered papers at Michael. He put them back—as best he could without knocking over more papers—and they went back to stuffing envelopes.

"So," Brian exhaled. "Do you and Tristan trade off on the days you skip and give each other your notes?"

"No. I'd quit completely, but he drags me back as if—" Katie stopped folding flyers when she saw their faces. "What? I'm not serious."

"You can't quit. They'll erase your memory. It'll probably leave you drooling and eating pistachio pudding for the rest of your life," Brian said.

"I don't think they would. She's half-vampire. What would be the point? They'd have to let you go." Christi's eyes were pensive.

"I wasn't serious. Since when do you guys care about what happens to me?"

Christi scoffed. "It's not that I care—but you know… I don't hate you. You are annoying, but I have better things to do than hate you."

Katie frowned. "Could have fooled me."

Christi turned to face her. "Do you know why I say mean things to you? Or why I laugh when people make fun of you? It's because you're that chick who thinks she's better than everyone else and thinks she's too good for the rest of us. It's nice to knock you down a peg."

"*I* think *I'm* too good? You should meet yourself," Katie snapped back.

"Actually you both are kind of stuck-up." Michael started looking through boxes again.

Brian shrugged.

"No one asked you, Know-It-All." Christi snatched an envelope from the stack and shoved a flyer inside.

"See? That's why no one likes you guys. Well, people like you, Christi, but it's because we can see your boobs and sometimes you're nice."

Katie gripped the table. *She* was stuck-up? She could admit some fault, because sure, sometimes she was a pain to be around. But *needing to be knocked down a peg?*

"You know, last year, I didn't know anything. I needed help and all anyone ever did was laugh at me or make snide comments about how I was trash. The only friends I had were Allison and Tristan." She noticed Brian stiffen. "If you think starting at the bottom deserves to be knocked down a peg, then fine. But that makes you guys the assholes, not me."

Katie stood up but sat back down. She was boxed in by Michael and Brian and the piles of crap-paper and boxes everywhere. She rubbed her temples. She couldn't even make a dramatic exit.

"Whatever, Katie. You've been a pain in my ass since fifth grade when you told everyone I smelled like a dirty hamster cage." Christi folded a flyer the wrong way and refolded it again until the creases became distressed lines, marking up the page.

"For the record, I said I didn't want to sit next to you *because* you were sitting *next* to the dirty hamster cage. I wasn't allowed to go to recess for two days until I apologized for something I didn't even say!"

"Like you didn't throw a cup of mashed potatoes at me?"

"Because you threw corn at me."

"Yeah, corn doesn't *stick* to your hair."

Both Katie and Christi stared at the flyers.

"I wanted to be your friend," Christi said. Her words burned—not because of the acid in her voice, but because of the bitterness in her tone, like biting into an orange rind. "Ms. Lipsmit was going to make you sit next to me, and I thought it was my chance—that you'd have no choice but to get to know me. And you told the entire class I smelled like a dirty hamster. You're a bitch."

Katie didn't want to look into Christi's eyes. There was too much guilt clogging up her throat. The she-devil was making her feel things other than contempt. "Okay. Sorry. I might have said that. I was eleven. And I was mad. And in all honesty, the whole side of that room smelled like a dirty hamster cage. Sorry." Katie held up her hand as Michael opened his mouth. "Shut up, Michael."

"Just saying, you all smelled like dirty hamsters. Like, we kept our door closed because you guys stunk up the halls."

Silence sat in the room while they slowly went back to folding flyers. Katie didn't know what to make of it. She'd apologized—kinda—but she still felt responsible for something she didn't even think was her fault. How could she apologize to someone when the guilt might coil around her throat and choke her if she did? Apologizing would mean she was a terrible person, even if she had suffered, too.

"Ugh," Katie growled. Brian and Christi looked up, and Katie's face burned. "I didn't mean to do that out loud."

They stared at her.

"I'm sorry," Katie said. "I didn't know I hurt your feelings or started this…*thing*…we have. I just knew you were the girl who took every shot at me for no reason. I didn't realize it was because I said that. I *barely* remember saying it, I just remember being pissed that Lipsmit was yelling at me when everyone was talking and made me sit out of recess for two days. That was like the reason I went to school… Anyway, sorry. And for the mashed potatoes and the wig thing—all of it."

Michael turned around from rummaging through another box. "What do I get? I'm missing hair because of you."

"I already said sorry Friday, so shove it." Katie squinted her eyes, but Michael's nonchalant shrug meant he was still bothered by it.

"Okay. I'm sorry *again*. It's really crappy being different. Everyone either makes fun of me or asks stupid questions like I'm not a person with self-respect. So I'm sensitive about it. I shouldn't have chased you or punched you or kicked you back or pulled your hair or threatened to kill you or your family or planted that bomb under your bed—I'm kidding!"

Michael shrugged and nodded. "Fine. I'm over it. Just tell your boyfriend to back off."

Christi snorted. "What'd you expect? You kicked his girlfriend and fought her in class. Any boyfriend worth keeping would defend his girlfriend."

Brian raised an eyebrow in agreement.

"Defend her? I was defending myself." Michael shook his head.

"You started it," Katie said.

"We sound like a bunch of kids. Look at us." Christi shook her curls. "I'm sorry for all the crap I've said or done. Michael?"

"What? I apologized already—fine. Sorry. I'm not making any promises for the future, but we're cool as long as you're cool."

Katie looked between them and nodded. "Yeah." She nodded again. "I almost wish I'd stayed home so I could have skipped this highly uncomfortable moment we're having."

"Do you make a joke out of everything?" Christi's hair bounced as she went back to folding flyers.

"Didn't you just apologize for being snarky?" Katie grabbed an envelope.

Christi shrugged. "Habit."

Katie continued her work in silence. They barely spoke until their supervisor came back and accused them of touching and stealing pens they'd never even seen—they had a few choice words about him.

After community hours ended, Katie hurried out the office and shuffled toward the hotel doors to wait for Mr. Carver to herd them back to the hotel elevator. Brian stood talking with Mr. Carver. Katie avoided eye contact, pretending she wasn't the only person without a friend.

Katie and Brian didn't talk these days. They weren't on bad terms as much as they weren't on any terms. Apparently last year had been too much on their friendship—or maybe it was that their friendship had been a matter of proximity and convenience and not really founded on anything to begin with.

Mr. Carver excused himself from the conversation and went to yell at Michael for picking up shards of glass off the street.

"Hey," Katie said to Brian. They were standing too close to ignore each other, though he seemed to be trying.

"Hey. What's up?"

"Nothing really. You?" This was stupid.

"You know."

No, she didn't. "I see."

"Anyway, I got to go. I have to tell Allan something about class today. You know."

No. She *really* didn't know what he was talking about. *Whatever.* "Cool."

Brian nodded and made his way back to his group of friends. She wasn't jealous. She wasn't angry. She actually felt…relieved. She had enough in her life to work on without Brian being in the mix. She was done working on that friendship. It would just have to be whatever it was. She was okay with that.

Mr. Carver led them back up into Boise and patted himself on the back for being the *"hip"* teacher who wasn't going to make them go all the way back to school. Katie was thankful for that because she had other plans. Plans that involved sneaking back into the city. Plans that involved pretending that her best friends weren't either ignoring her because she was an ass that morning or too busy for her because of some intensive training program.

4

The Seven

KATIE WANDERED OVER to an elevator Tristan had shown her over on Eighth Street next to a hot dog stand. It looked like a door into a dingy apartment complex, but required the same passcode to open as all the street elevators.

She rode back down into Gray City, leaving behind the guilt, anger, and numbness that swayed in the air above ground. She had no idea where Tristan was and wasn't in any hurry to see him. They'd been more careful about concealing their thoughts around each other, especially since most of his thoughts consisted of *"Are you okay?"* and hers often reverberated, *"I'm fine."*

Katie stepped out of the elevator and let out a sigh. Down here, away from everyone and their questions, she really was fine. She tucked a stray hair behind her ear and headed towards the only place she could think of: The Pub.

The streets filled as the work day ended, and Katie stood shoulder to shoulder for a few blocks as she left the inner city for the werewolf district. There was a distinctive disorganized look to the werewolf district that made it less grand than the inner city. Especially compared to the vampire district, it was extremely urban. Graffiti littered the walls like trash littered the streets, and paint chipped off buildings like the cement chipped off the sidewalks and staircases. However, children played in small concrete parks and ran up and down the streets. Two women hung out of third-story windows yelling cooking instructions to each other, as an old man nodded in greeting from his stoop while he watered his plants.

The werewolf district wasn't as refined as the vampire district, but it had life.

Katie stopped at an alley. A bright white light lit up at least sixty or seventy people gathered around a small makeshift stage in the back. The buildings that surrounded them were covered with flyers. The same flyer she'd seen earlier that day.

Why Stand Apart
When We Can Stand Together
7

A stout man with a white shirt and thick jeans waved at the crowd, and the noise level decreased just enough for his voice to slice through. He spoke quietly with another man on the stage. Katie was surrounded by werewolves. The smell of them permeated the air like wetness after a heavy rain. She didn't have to guess to know the man was also part-wolf; his body hunched as he laughed as if he were more comfortable on four feet than two.

He raised his hand before he spoke. "I come here only to ask you one question."

Katie moved closer to the crowd. A woman wearing a thousand bangles handed her one of those flyer.

"Do you like your chains?" He paused, glancing over the crowd. "Do you enjoy living like caged dogs, never allowed to hunt under the moon or make love under the sun? Is this the life you want for your children?"

Murmurs erupted over the crowd, and a few people laughed, making their way out of the crowd and back onto the streets.

"It's all right," he said. "Some dogs like to be leashed. But I am no dog. I'm a wolf. So are you. We deserve the freedom of a limitless sky. Wolves were meant to howl at the moon, not scurry under the earth like rats and roaches. Yes, this city is divine. A great accomplishment of our community. A great show of how well we work with the vampires and—"

The crowd went into an uproar, drowning out his voice. Katie could make out words like *bloodsuckers* and *leech* and *tick*. The man rose his hand again. "I understand your disdain for our fellow neighbor, but they are not our enemy. They did not force us underground. They—like us—are victims of the true oppressor. The human."

Murmurs spread throughout the crowd again.

"Do we not deserve the same freedoms and liberties just because we are a different species? Are we not equal? Do our children not cry and laugh the same? Do we not bleed and suffer and love and hope just like them? You, my brother, my sister—you and I are no less than them. We deserve equality.

"We all do. Each and every one of us in Gray City. We are all the children of earth. We are all equal. It's time we come together on this. It's time we stand for justice. Why stand apart when we can stand together for what's right?" The man lifted up his hands, palm out, to the crowd. "Do you like your chains?"

A woman standing in front of Katie shouted, "I am no slave!"

The man looked out at her earnestly. "No, sister. You are not. You are an equal. You, like every creature on earth, deserve the right to the sun—the moon."

A man somewhere deeper in the crowd yelled and threw his fist in the air. "Equality for all!"

A few others echoed the man until a new chant emerged: "Seven. Seven. Seven." The air buzzed, their shouts falling into unison.

"You shouldn't be here," a voice said behind her. Katie turned around, trying not to look disturbed. The voice was familiar and so was the face.

"Mr. Reynolds," Katie replied. He looked the same as the last time she'd seen him, tall with mud-colored hair. The five o'clock shadow that made him look younger than he was. The heavy British accent.

"Indeed." He grabbed her arm gently and pulled her out of the alley.

"Are you going to tell Mr. Carver?" Katie was surprised by her own lack of fear of being caught in Gray City without a mentor.

"Of course not. That's not what I meant, anyhow. You should stay away from gatherings like that. If anyone had taken the time to sniff you out, they'd have thrown you up on stage and pulled you apart like a chicken."

Katie's eyes bulged as Mr. Reynolds let go of her arm and escorted her down the street.

"You may have the distinct smell of a vampire, but there is this lingering hint of guardian—you know, the slave master of the wolf."

"They're right, though. It's not fair."

"It's not, is it? The humans selling us off at auctions, too? Can't remember the last time a human gave me a good lashing for prowling above ground. There is no law that says a werewolf must live underground. The humans don't even know we exist. How can you enslave a creature you can't see?" Mr. Reynolds beckoned Katie across the street to a small bookstore with comics on display.

"Guardians do. There is no law that says Jim Heckler can treat me like I crawled out of Hell, but he does."

"Jim Heckler is one man. A bigot of a man, everyone knows that. Does Carver treat you that way? Any of your other teachers? You can't condemn a whole race of people for what individuals do."

"They say nothing to stop him. Can't I condemn a whole race of people for allowing individuals like that to exist?"

"Only if you think no one should have the freedom to speak his or her mind." Mr. Reynolds stopped, looking into the window of the bookstore.

"Ms. Watts, while I share and understand your concerns for the treatment of our races, I don't and will never trust a group who preaches inequality in the guise of equality." Mr. Reynolds glanced back across the street. The alley was so bright it made the street look darker. "Equality is about raising people up, not tearing others down. Never forget that. If you do, you'll become everything you're fighting against."

Katie nodded. She watched him as he looked across the street. Something about him drew her in.

He turned his head and caught her staring. "What is it? Spit it out."

Katie blinked, embarrassed and sure of what she wanted to know. Last time she saw him, he'd mentioned that his brother was half—that she wasn't safe with the guardians. "What happened to your brother?"

He studied her, confused. "He died." Mr. Reynolds turned around and stared into the bookstore window.

Katie feigned interest in a comic on display. "I'm sorry."

"Don't be. He died fighting for something he didn't believe in. He was a guardian. The best Level 0 you could find—until the day he wasn't."

"If you think guardians are so bad, why do you hang around them? I mean, you told me before that what I am is like a disease to them. How can you be around people like that?"

"I'm not around people like that. I'm only around the one I—Ms. Watts." Mr. Reynolds looked up into the gray, searching for the words. "You're a smart girl. Don't always take everything at face value. Don't trust what I say or what you hear from radicals. Trust what you know. Question what you know until you're sure you can trust it. That's the only way you'll survive in this world. The worst kind of people aren't the ones who do evil—the worst are the ones who can't think for themselves."

Katie raised an eyebrow. "Did Mr. Carver send you down here to lecture me?"

"I do rattle off like a well-bred prat, don't I?"

Katie laughed. "I didn't mean that. It's just—I've been getting a lot of lectures lately."

"That kind of girl, eh? I better get on before you ruin my pristine reputation." He winked and smiled.

Katie smiled back and crossed her arms. "See you around, Mr. Reynolds."

"Where are you headed?" He moved toward the crosswalk.

"The Pub." Katie silently cursed herself for not lying. There was no way he'd be cool with a minor going to a bar.

Mr. Reynolds cursed out loud and laughed. "Lovely. Do me a favor, yeah? Don't wear your school uniform. If you're going to be a rebel, rebel in regular clothes so I don't feel guilty for not selling you out." He flashed a smile and jogged across the street.

.⊛⊛.

The door to The Pub creaked as Katie dragged it open. Mercedes was behind the bar, leaning against it with her slender smooth brown arm. Her long braids spilled around her shoulders. She was yelling at Clyde, who Katie had grown to like. He had a rough charm.

There were a few guys at some of the high tables, and a group of women sitting at a booth, eating chicken wings and laughing.

"Hey, spitfire. Haven't seen you around here in a minute. You should leave and never come back," Clyde said, nursing a beer.

Katie sighed. Charming.

Mercedes side-eyed Clyde. "Katie, hey, I thought you were banned from coming to the dark side."

It was true. She'd been kept on a short leash all summer. School almost seemed like a vacation—almost. Between her dad and Lucinda, doing anything outside of training or staying in the house was impossible. But nearly dying and not telling an adult where you are, when you are coming home, or what happened will do that. Apparently *"I just watched my boyfriend murder my real dad on accident but on purpose after I was lured in by my creepy chester-molester uncle"* wasn't enough to warrant time to process alone—or with said boyfriend.

"I've decided some rules are worth breaking." Katie sat next to Clyde and smiled. It was nice to see faces that weren't pitying her, judging her, or scanning her over for red flags.

"Hey!" Clyde pointed his beer at her. "That other bloodsucker said something like that before he came in and tore up the place. Then you all went off and—she really shouldn't be here. We can't afford for anyone to notice."

"Shut up, Clyde. Where is Tristan anyway?" Mercedes held up her hand and told Katie to hold on as her phone rang. "It's Frank." The entire bar quieted. Even for Katie's sensitive ears, it was quiet. Frank was—at least Katie thought—Mercedes' boyfriend. He had helped them get into Eshmael's house to save Tristan. Why Katie felt tension edging off each person now, she didn't know. Mercedes answered the phone, and Katie made out the sound of a hoarse voice on the other end.

"What's going on?" Katie asked Clyde, but he didn't answer.

Mercedes spoke and the entire bar went deathly still. "Again?"

Clyde's hand wrapped around his bottle tight, and Katie swore she heard glass cracking.

"Who? Can you tell who it is? Is he from—thank god." The tension in the room eased, but no one went back to talking.

"Someone has been killing werewolves." Clyde frowned into his beer.

"Who?"

"If we knew, they wouldn't be killing them anymore, would they?"

Mercedes hung up the phone and grabbed a set of car keys. "I've got to go. This one was in our territory, but Frank can't tell which pack he's from. You two come with me." Mercedes pointed to the booth with the four women eating.

Two girls with straight dark hair slid out. The one built like a roller derby player chugged back a glass of whatever she was drinking. "That was the shortest break ever," she said to the other girl before leaving with Mercedes.

Clyde must have seen the confusion on Katie's face; he looked her over before saying anything. "She's got to get ahead of this or whoever that wolf belongs to will come after us for his death. An eye for an eye."

"They can't prove you did anything."

"Wolves don't need proof. We need strength. You have to make someone pay when they take from you, otherwise you look weak." Clyde finished his beer before standing up and moving behind the bar.

Katie thought back to Mrs. Barnes lecture, about uncertainty for the future causing power vacuums. "Does it have anything to do with Lawrence's death?"

"Of course it does. Bloodsuckers are taking forever to pick their next leader, and one of them is falling out of line, attacking our kind. They'll pay when we figure out who." Clyde's eyes flashed at her, and she saw the animal behind them. "They're still trying to investigate Lawrence's murder. Especially since he died under his only known next of kin's collapsed house."

Katie winced as he dropped a crate of bottles onto the bar.

"No offense, kid. If anyone finds out it was our pack leader with you that night, everyone will think we are at fault. That we were the ones who killed them. Somebody is on to something because every pack has had a member murdered out in the streets except ours—now a body turns up in our territory." Clyde's eyes narrowed in on her. "And you just so happen to show up out of the blue on the same day."

Katie sat up tall. "I didn't do anything. Back off." Her muscles tensed as she could see Clyde's pupils got smaller and fur appeared on his hands. The guys sitting at the high table watched her, and she didn't have to look behind her to know that the other girls were watching, too.

"Calm down, spitfire. I'd be able to smell the blood on you if you did. Besides, you don't have the personality for it. Whatever has been killin' those wolves—they've got blood lust. And you can feel that before you smell it."

Katie got up, wondering how it was possible to go to a place looking for an escape only to need to flee again. Whatever was going down in werewolf territory had nothing to do with her—at least not directly—and being a part of it was the exact opposite of what she needed.

"What are you doing?" Clyde scratched at his beard.

"I'm getting the hell out of here. You just said so yourself. I can't be seen with you guys. Not until stuff gets settled."

"There's a dead body a few blocks over. You think *now* is the time to sneak out unseen? There are going to be patrols crawling the streets looking for any and everyone who doesn't belong. Make yourself comfy."

Katie groaned. "What a day."

"Yeah, tell that to the dead guy." Clyde wiped the counters but paused and cursed just as Katie heard a familiar voice in her head.

"What are you doing here?" Tristan opened the door to the bar.

Clyde let out a few more curses. Most of which a few people agreed with. "I can take her. Not you. Out. Go back from the cave you crawled out of. *You're* the type they're looking for."

Tristan sucked his teeth, but didn't say anything to Clyde. "Of all the days to slip out and come here, you picked the worst day ever."

"Tell me about it." Katie half-smiled. *"You're not still mad at me?"*

"We're only young once." Tristan leaned in and held out his hand. *"Actually, for forever, but saying that doesn't work in your favor."*

Katie took his hand. The tension in the room weighed down on her, but holding his hand made it easier to bear.

"Let's go. Lumber Jack Joe is right." Tristan nodded at Clyde.

Clyde glared. "Just don't come back." He looked at Katie. "Seriously. Not until it's over. You'll only cause problems for us."

Katie nodded. A pang of hurt pulsed in her heart. They weren't exactly her best friends—Clyde wasn't a friend at all— but they had a thing. This was the first place she'd thought of, the first place she'd felt any connection to. And now she wasn't welcomed here.

"See you when the dust settles." Clyde waved her off before turning his attention back to the bar.

Tristan gripped Katie's hand as they left the bar and whispered in her ear, "Hold on tight."

As soon as they were out of the door, he scooped her into his arms. She grabbed onto him and—to her horrid surprise— he raced them down the street. It was the first time she'd done this since he'd carried her bleeding body to Lucinda's house. Before, she'd thrown up on him and passed out. Now, she saw the streets and people and cars and lights meld into one as he ran at a speed too fast even for a vampire.

Her eyes burned with dizziness. She couldn't breathe. Her lungs had stayed back at the bar, even though the rest of her was headed into the middle of Gray City and toward the vampire district.

When they stopped, she gasped, bent over, trying to breathe and telling herself that her organs weren't coming out of her throat. "What—the—" Katie gagged.

"Sorry." Tristan rubbed her back.

She couldn't see anything. Had she gone blind? She couldn't breathe or see—he'd done it. He'd killed her.

Tristan let out a short laugh. "Katalina, your eyes are closed. Jesus, you aren't dying. It just takes a minute to adjust."

Katie sat on the cool ground and leaned against the side of a building. It took her a minute to realize she was leaning against a movie theatre. "What *is* that?"

"Eclipsing. I learned how to do it during Academy." Tristan knelt down next to her. "Took me two years to be able to get the length of the room."

"Why does it—I feel like you g-forced me. I could have died."

"Not really. Might have killed you that one night, but it was either that or let you bleed out and die while I ran down the busy streets with you in my arms. Can you imagine how that would have looked?"

Katie stood up, and Tristan helped her. "Enough with the romantic talk."

"Actually, it might have looked kind of romantic. You know, if I was crying hysterically and cursing God on my knees. With the right lighting and the right words, it could have worked."

Katie's mind flashed to that horrible night. Being shot. Watching him rip the guy apart with a knife. Watching him beat up Brian, then panicking and force feeding her blood from a bag until she'd blacked out. All the screaming.

"You were crying and it wasn't romantic," Katie thought, still hearing Lucinda's hysterical pleas for him to stop.

Tristan's face went white, and they both stared at each other. "You brought it up," he said.

"No, you did. I was leaning against this wall trying not to spit out my kidney."

Tristan reached out and tousled her hair in all the ways one should never tousle loose curls. "Your hair looks like crap. It's all over the place. Use a brush once in a while."

Katie glared. "It's a cardinal sin to screw up a girl's hair in public." She ran her fingers through her hair, glaring more as her fingers snagged and pulled.

"You're still cute."

"Mylanta." Katie sighed—why did she even know that word?

Tristan laughed. "Mylanta? Who are you? And why was that—slightly attractive?"

"Just let me catch my breath. I'm feeling a thousand things at once, so excuse me if I'm all out of wit." Katie laughed at herself and pulled at the hairband on her wrist. She scraped her hair into a bun. Thousands of things swirled around inside her—in addition to her liver dropping into place, her quick breaths growing faster because of how he looked at her, and her embarrassment because her bun kept sagging to the side.

Telling her she was cute and attractive was overkill. The best possible, most awesome type of overkill.

Tristan leaned in and kissed her. People were walking by and looking at her with her hands on top of her head as a boy leaned in, smacking his lips against hers and—she let it kill her.

Overkill accepted.

Katie closed her eyes and wrapped her arms around his neck. His kisses were warm and sweet. His breath, his skin, his hair—everything about him was right. His body chemistry was the perfect makeup to attract and please every part of her. He squeezed her against him, and she let his calm wash over her.

When he pulled away, she held onto him a little bit longer. Right here, in his arms, everything was manageable.

"You never had wit. I don't think your head works that way." He smiled, his eyes darting back down to her lips.

"Seen my life lately? I'm lucky if my head works any kind of way with all the crap clogging it up." Katie slouched back against the wall.

"You've got to let stuff go," Tristan whispered.

Stuff? Katie wished it was just stuff. At this moment, they were supposed to be with Lucinda so they could train, as if they still needed to do *that* every day. They'd already passed all the material in Lucinda's mentor manual. When she'd tried taking them on field trips to Gray City, Tristan knew more accurate information than she did, and then she'd pretty much put their trips on pause when "vampires only" or "werewolf only" signs started to pop up in windows. She'd said it wasn't safe, even though the school thought it was safe enough for their community service class.

What else was there? Oh, they were now banned from Mercedes' pub for being directly involved in the murder of a coven leader. A murder that even affected the werewolves; not to mention the missing people who were probably kidnapped and brought to Gray City for who knew what—but she could guess a few gruesome things.

Oh, and she just found out her arch nemesis was really a girl who'd been scorned by her in the fifth grade.

What else? Maybe the best one: "*My dad all but refuses to accept that I'm a vampire.*" He wouldn't say it, but it was in the little things he did: like bringing home takeout for two, forgetting she didn't sleep, and yelling every time she left a cup with blood residue in the sink.

Her *stuff* went with her everywhere.

"Okay. Then let's just give everyone the finger and do what we want."

Katie looked up, searching for the hint of sarcasm on his face. It wasn't there. His eyes bored into her, his thoughts clear and echoing a need to make it better. She wanted it to be better, too. Every time she tried to stop and sort it all out, her mind reeled, a madhouse with reflecting mirrors and monkeys nipping at her heels.

She just wanted peace.

"It's about time we had a movie do-over," he said.

"You mean, a do-over because last time you asked me on a date to the movies you asked Allison, too?"

"It wasn't a date—don't ruin the do-over." Tristan smiled and squeezed her hand.

A weight lifted off her shoulders. She smiled back. Could they do it? Just skip training with Lucinda and go to a movie? Lucinda would be livid. She'd tell Katie's dad and he'd probably ground her. But—ground her from what? What life did she have now that he could take away?

"I pick the movie." Katie led him toward the door. She could feel the hesitation in his mind, too, but the more she thought about it, the more the invisible leash her dad and Lucinda had on her ripped and pulled until—it snapped.

It was a real date. Tristan paid for tickets to some sappy-looking love story he kept rolling his eyes about. He'd ordered her a small popcorn so she could taste it in her mouth—because what was a movie without popcorn? They cuddled and kissed when the movie got boring...

However, if Katie was honest with herself, she could feel his hesitation. His concern that they were making the wrong choice. She pushed that thought into the back of her mind until they were getting ready to leave and she came back from washing popcorn butter off her fingers and heard him on the phone.

"Stop yelling at me. I told you. I took her to a movie. ... No. Luc—*stop yelling at me. I'm not your kid.* Look. She's going to snap if you keep trying to control her every move. Hell, *I'm* going to snap. ... Yes, I get that. ... Yes, I know. ... No. ... Fine. Give me a break. I know how to say no to drugs—at least the bad ones. The good ones, that's a whole different story. ... Yeah. ... Yep. ... See you when the crack-house runs out of crack. Or nine. Whichever comes first. Bye." Tristan hung up the phone, but Katie distinctly heard Lucinda's voice screeching on the other end.

Tristan stood still for a moment before he sighed. It was long, and with it came what he'd been hiding from her. A tiredness. It was heavy and bleak. He rubbed his face and let out another fast breath, shrugging his shoulders, trying to shake off the dreaded weight. He turned around, stunned to see her. "Hey." His voice rose, and he cleared his throat. "Ready?"

He was smiling.

"What's wrong with me smiling?"

"Don't do that," Katie said. The *stuff* was creeping back.

"Do what."

"That. Pretend like you don't know that I felt it. That I heard you on the phone."

"Christ, Katalina. I feel like this because I just got done talking to the biggest pain in my ass. Stop reading into everything."

"I'm not. I know what I felt. It wasn't that. It's me."

"Look, if you want to make a big deal about it, go ahead. I'm going to go home. If you want to feel happy, then just be happy."

"And ignore everything?"

"There is nothing to ignore. You're—I am not doing this."

Katie's eyes stung. Was she making it all up? Was she really the only one feeling the tension everywhere she went? Was she crazy?

She wasn't crazy.

"I never said you were crazy. But…I can't take the constant black cloud. You're Eeyore on a bright, sunny day. Just let me enjoy the sun without all the negativity."

Katie frowned. It stung. It hurt like a bee sting to the eye. "I'm sorry," she said, pulling all her thoughts into herself.

"Don't. Don't do that." Tristan's eyes shined under the bright lights.

They broke eye contact as a crowd of people exited a movie.

"No. I'm sorry. I'll try to let stuff go. I'm sorry. You're right."

She was getting better at apologizing. The pride that made her want to defend herself grew smaller and smaller these days.

It was true. She *was* the one with the problem. At school. At home. With Tristan. It always led back to her.

"Katalina?" He watched her and searched for a way into her mind.

"You're right. Seriously." Katie rubbed her hands on her skirt, focusing on the smooth worn fabric. Anything to keep her from crying or giving in to the truth of her feelings.

Tristan gave up. "Okay. It's eight. I told Lucinda we'd leave Gray City by nine. What do you want to do?"

"Let's just go. I'm not trying to be a downer, I swear. If we leave now, she'll worry less, and my dad will start calling if I'm not home by eight-thirty." Katie smiled like the world's biggest liar.

Tristan didn't return the smile. Even if he couldn't read her thoughts, he could probably tell she was lying. Whatever. She just had to smile long enough for him to believe it.

For them both to believe it.

5

SOURCING

KATIE SAT AT the kitchen counter as Lucinda dried a plate and coffee mug. Katie listened to the words coming out of Lucinda's mouth, but didn't really believe them.

"You mean…" Katie leaned on Lucinda's freshly wiped kitchen counter. She could see her reflection in the granite. It was almost impossible not to admire the impeccable way Lucinda left everything spotless. "…you're letting me do nothing for the next week?"

"I'm not letting you do *nothing*, Katie. I'm just giving you a break. I know school is a drag, and despite your best efforts, I know you and Tristan have been doing something in the middle of the night—nope, I don't want to hear it. I hope to God it's not sex, but with all your progress in training, I'm going to stupidly believe Tristan when he says you just practice." Lucinda rolled her eyes and let out an irritated grunt.

"Lucy…"

"Nope. I don't want to hear a thing. Just listen to me when I say your virginity is a precious gift. It's like…like a pretty little white flower. Sex is a big can of red spray paint. Once you spray that little flower red, there is no getting it to go back to white— let me finish. Red might look pretty, but soon it will look like three kids and a minivan and that red starts to turn brown. Then everything will start to go."

"Why don't I know normal people?" Katie rubbed her eyes, trying to get the image out of her mind. "I'm not having sex, I swear. How many times do I have to tell you people? I just want to go on a date sometimes. Or talk to him without one of you breathing down our necks."

"Back in the day that *was* dating."

"You aren't that old, Lucy. Don't pretend you and Will weren't doing it in the back of Will's truck so your parents wouldn't catch you—yeah, your third glass of wine is your weakness." Katie shuddered, trying hard not to think about *that*.

"That's different. We were older and—do as I say, not as I do." Lucinda wagged her finger at Katie.

Katie laughed. "Well, for starters, Tristan doesn't have a truck."

"Katie."

Katie laughed harder. "I'm just kidding."

Lucinda ran a hand through her dark curly hair. It was cut short these days, in waves just above her shoulders. It suited her, and from the way Will lingered on his goodbye kiss (the kind where you hear spit being swapped even without sensitivity to sounds), he must have thought so, too.

"Katie, you don't think I'm hard on you, do you? You know you can talk to me about anything. Even if you are—or want to—have sex. You can tell me."

"That's so not on my mind, but thanks," Katie kind of lied. Not only did she think about it, she wanted it.

"Then what *is* on your mind? You've been so moody lately."

Great. Was Lucinda going to call her Eeyore, too? Katie's welted heart throbbed, even though Tristan had said it five days ago. Five days of smiling and pretending. She was tired. She walked around with bricks of guilt, anger, lies, and much more on her shoulders; they toppled down her back—it was a wonder she could still walk upright.

"Period?" Katie offered. The truth was too complicated.

Lucinda stared at her, apparently aware she didn't get those anymore.

Katie smiled. "I'm just moody. I'm a teenager. Angst. Hormones. God! Can't I be moody?"

Lucinda smiled back, but she studied Katie. Katie was really getting sick of people doing that. "Is that it?"

"Yes."

"How are you feeling about…you know…"

Here it comes.

"…your dad passing."

He didn't pass. Tristan stabbed him while trying to kill my lunatic uncle. Then my dad made me watch him die because he wasn't man enough to kill his own brother. He made us do it—even though he knew what that would mean for Tristan.

"*My* dad is very much alive. Larry—well, it was sad. Like I've said a thousand times before. I don't know what you guys want me to feel, but I'm telling you I just feel like…he's dead. I didn't know him all that well. He was here, now he's not. It's not like he took me to little league or was there for my first skinned knee."

Hell, my actual dad wasn't even there for that.

"You have to feel more than that. He was your father whether you want to admit it or not."

"Lucy…"

"Katie, I'm serious. You were just laughing as if nothing has changed. It's okay to be sad if you feel sad. He can't mean *nothing* to you."

"I didn't say that. I didn't say he was nothing."

Lucinda crossed her arms. "That's what it sounds like. I should hope we raised you better than that."

Katie wished she could molt and leave her shell for Lucinda to tell how it should and shouldn't feel.

"You're right," Katie surrendered, but was it enough to get Lucinda to stop chastising her about it?

Lucinda studied her, waiting. Katie quieted the angry and put on her best calm and serene face. Lucinda bought it enough to change the subject. She went on, rattling off her to-do list and what she'd do with a week free of her mentoring duties.

Katie seethed. When she wanted to talk about how she felt, they complained about her being lazy or moody. They told her what a drag she was, how she needed to focus on other things like school. Then, when she stopped, they probed. It was... unfair. Why wasn't she allowed to be happy and laugh or be quiet and sad when and how she wanted?

Of course it bothered her. It might have been all her fault—

Katie froze. She felt *him*.

She turned around and saw Tristan standing in the kitchen doorway with two black plastic bags in his hands.

"Sneaky bastard." She smiled and pulled her thoughts back into herself. He'd been out buying blood when she came over, and now he was standing in the doorway like a little spy. How long had he been standing there?

Tristan frowned.

How much had he heard?

"You're back. Here, I made some room in the refrigerator." Lucinda waved him over, but Tristan's eyes never left Katie.

That was all she needed to know he'd heard *enough*. Katie rolled her eyes. She wasn't going to deal with that. She got up and grabbed her phone off the counter.

"Wait," Tristan said, putting the bags on the counter.

"I have to get home. I've got shows to watch, books to read, dreams to write down in my dream journal."

"See you, sweetie." Lucinda barely looked up from stocking the fridge with blood.

"Stop. We need to talk."

"We don't."

Tristan followed Katie all the way to the front door. "Why won't you talk to me?" he whispered, as if Lucinda was the one sneaking around.

"We talk all the time. Were we not talking this morning at my house? You know, in-between the kissing?"

"Katalina," he said, unamused. It had been a long time since she'd seen those blue eyes in the midst of a storm.

"Look, I'm fine. We're fine. You can be fine, too, if you chill out. Okay?" Katie kissed him on his cheek and smiled. It was numbing how easy this was becoming. "Now, I'm going home. I'm serious, I've got three shows coming on today. The good ones." It wasn't a lie. In fact, she watched more TV now than she ever had.

"I'll watch with you," Tristan conceded.

"Nope. Dad's home early. He'll just fuss until you leave."

"Then I'll walk you."

"Okay, you know some people would call this behavior stalker-ish and borderline obsessive." Katie opened the door and waved him forward.

"I'm just… Can I not want to spend time with you?"

"Not when you're looking all beady-eyed and lusty. Lucy said you wanted to spray my little white flower red and ruin me."

Shock, mixed with disgust and curiosity, twisted across his face. Perhaps he hadn't heard as much as she thought. Either way, he finally left her alone, and they walked, talking about silly things that didn't matter.

Katie relaxed. Masking her thoughts and smiling when she really wanted to close her eyes and zone out was hard. It took a lot of concentration and control. When he finally left her on the doorstep, she breathed out, relieved to go inside, slide down onto the leather couch, and lose herself in someone else's drama.

Her dad brought Chinese takeout, and as usual, he'd ordered her old favorite like she was going to scarf down sweet and sour pork and fried rice at any moment. At least that was all she had to worry about with him. He didn't mention her attitude and had only mentioned Larry's death a few times before dropping it completely. He seemed to like all the time she spent watching TV with him. It was nice. They had shows and bonded over toilet humor and impossibly interconnected medial dramas. It wasn't so bad sometimes.

Sometimes.

♋

At first Katie didn't know what she'd do with the free time after school. She'd have at least four hours guaranteed to herself. Monday morning, she decided to triple that time by skipping school. It meant lying to Tristan, but Katie took the risk. She spent two days exploring Gray City. She made sure to stay clear of the werewolf district, but walked everywhere else imaginable.

It really was something amazing. She had never realized there was a river between the inner city and vampire district or a lovers' bridge that people tied notes to. A magic lingered on the streets of the city, making lamps sparkle and roads shine with artistic smoothness.

Katie walked up and down the sidewalks, sometimes sitting outside a little cafe—if she could call a place that only sold blood, a cafe—and people-watched.

On Thursday, when she sat in front of a little blood cafe that also sold books and magazines, she realized she felt oddly out of place in the vampire district. From the buildings to the people, everything oozed expense. She could always tell a vampire by looks alone; they had that high-fashion aura Allison always tried to give Katie.

Katie watched a girl wearing a loose blouse, a tan skirt, and high socks with heels stand across the street. She had the vampire look. A careless finesse.

Katie watched her cross the street, and they locked eyes. The girl smiled and Katie waved—then stopped, then immediately started again, stuck between not wanting to look like a weirdo and not wanting to be rude. The girl looked behind her and tentatively waved back.

"Do I know you from somewhere?" she said as made her way to the cafe.

Katie laughed, embarrassed. "No, I'm just weird."

"Oh. Ha. Are you waiting for someone?" She pointed at the cafe.

Katie blinked, wishing she were, because suddenly being alone at a cafe staring at strangers made her feel closer to the crazy side than she liked.

"This might sound weird, but do you want to join me? I have a fifty-percent-off coupon, but it's only valid if I bring a friend. I'll pay."

The last thing Katie wanted was a girl watching her make faces while she chugged back blood, trying desperately for it not to come back up. Then again, she'd never been inside a blood cafe and the girl snapped the coupon in front of her like it was *the* golden ticket.

"I—I don't know…"

"Please. It's for one of the nicer rooms, too. Come on."

"Rooms?"

"I knew I'd get ya with that." The girl scooped up Katie's arm and lifted her right out of the seat. "They only give out these coupons once a year, and the date is almost expired. Thank you. You are a godsend."

Katie smiled, walking into the cafe. The girl led her past the bar and the books to the back where there was another door.

It wasn't a fancy door, but the place behind it was. Nowhere had the cafe said "spa" in its title, but here one was, warmly lit with classical music playing in the background. The waiting room had the softest and comfiest couches Katie's butt had ever had the liberty of sliding onto. The girl went up to a sleek, dark wood desk and handed a man the coupon. He looked at her, then Katie, and nodded.

The girl came back over, smiling and full of giggles. "You've completely made my day. I swear this is *the* nicest place. And we are going to get *the* second-best room they have to offer. I've needed this all week. Work has been nothing but stress and—haha, sorry, I'm just chatting away."

"So what exactly have I gotten myself into?" Katie asked jokingly, but she was seriously confused. They'd bypassed the café, and this girl was talking about a room. Had Katie just gotten a free massage? From the looks of the place, it wasn't the kind that left you feeling violated or with burn scars from a chemical mask gone wrong.

"It's like any other except… Well, you'll see. The service here is top-notch. It's *the* most relaxing one I've been to. And they don't time you either. Some of those places are so cheap and dirty, you don't know where they get half the staff they do. I can't stand the 'grunge' thing. It's gross."

Katie nodded. "Not to mention a little prostitute-ty." Katie thought about one massage parlor that always made the local news at least four times a year for their "*happy endings.*"

"Right!" the girl said. "I went to one once because my friend said it was 'cool.' I could literally hear the—" she lowered her voice so the clerk couldn't hear "—sex."

Katie half-frowned and half-smiled, and they both laughed. Before Katie could ask any more questions, a woman in a sleek, black, two-piece uniform waved them forward. "Your room is ready." They followed her down a dimly lit hallway and to an elevator. They went up ten floors and out into a hallway with dark wooden floors and the same classical music from the waiting room. There were at least ten rooms on this floor; all except one had a beautifully painted sign that read: Occupied.

"No sex sounds," Katie whispered and laughed nervously.

The girl laughed and nodded, looking giddier the closer they got to the only door without a painted sign hanging on it. The woman looked back at them. She didn't seem to find Katie's comment as funny, but opened the door without saying anything.

The room was really nice. A sectional divided the room into two separate spaces. A large window over-looking the city was all they shared. Each side had a massage table and big leather chairs next to them. Katie squinted in the dim light as her eyes darted to the speakers playing ambient sounds.

"Please wait while our staff prepare. They will be in shortly to start." The woman left.

"Thanks again," the girl said.

"No, thank *you*. I—I've been really stressed lately, too." Katie marveled at the view. She had to be the luckiest person alive—no school, no training, a whole day in Gray City, and now this.

"Then it was meant to be." The girl disappeared to one side of the room, and Katie went to another. She looked for a robe to change into and wondered if she even had time to sit through a whole massage—it was already close to six.

She turned around, startled, when a girl and a guy came into the room. They were dressed in all black, looking more like upscale yoga instructors than massage therapists. The guy went to the other side, and the girl came to Katie's and introduced herself.

"Hi. I'm Portia. Would you like me to lay down or…you're kind of short. We can sit and use the chairs, unless you have something specific in mind."

Katie stared at Portia, completely confused. "Um…"

"First time?" Portia smiled and gestured for Katie to sit on one of the chairs.

"Yes." Katie sat and wished she had something half as comfortable as this leather chair at home.

"Okay. We can start off sitting, and if anything else feels more natural for you, we can do that."

Katie stared at Portia again. "Don't massages usually happen on the table?"

Portia snorted. "We're not that kind of place."

"Then what kind of place is this?"

"The respectable kind." Portia raised her eyebrow and chin. "Wait. Is this your first, *first* time? Like…ever?" Her face relaxed.

"Yes," Katie said, noticing something strange about Portia. Strange, yet familiar. Something she was so used to.

Portia smelled human. There was no mistaking the slight metallic smell. "What—"

"I wish they'd told me, but don't worry. I'm a beginners' guru. It's kinda my thing. I take it you've never sourced before."

"Sourced?"

"The first time is always a little awkward, but I hear it's also the best."

Portia unzipped her black jacket, revealing a black, spaghetti-strap shirt. Katie's ears twitched at a low shallow breath behind her. She looked at the divider separating the two sides, hearing a sucking sound and little gasps.

What the…

She looked back at Portia and saw tiny little holes all over her body. They were really small and looked almost like freckles, but Katie put two and two together.

"Most newbies go for the neck, but I recommend the wrist. It's less intimate and way more comfortable."

Katie sat in her chair, dumbfounded. "You want me to suck your blood?"

"Well…you paid to do it. I get paid whether you do it or not, but the high and all-I-can-eat buffet after is really nice."

Katie blinked. "Um." She looked back at the sectional, glad some guy wasn't getting a blow job next to her, but so, *so* not ready for the actual blood-sucking that was happening. Katie lowered her voice, sure the girl next door was going to hear her anyway. "I totally thought this was a spa. Big misunderstanding. So I think we can just skip the…yeah."

"Suit yourself, but you know, I hear it's a thousand times better than harvested blood." Portia relaxed in the chair next to Katie.

"How do you know this? I mean, you're human, right? How are you even down here right now?"

Portia smiled. "Yeah, that's a long story. But the pay is really good, excellent breaks, and free food. It's like *the* best job I've ever had. Well, besides the fact that if I talk, they'll hunt me down and erase my memory or something equally horrific. I signed some papers. Pretty sure I've signed my soul over to the devil—beats corporate America."

"Right." Katie still heard sucking. It was growing more intense, and she thought she heard pawing, too. What was that girl doing over there? Portia turned her chair and told Katie to do the same so they could look at the view.

"So what's your story? Just recently changed? Let me guess—love gone wrong?"

"Not exactly. Long story." Katie fixed her gaze on the sky. Lights sparkled above the gray, twinkling throughout the darkness. "What's that?" she asked in awe. It was beautiful.

"The elevators. Nice isn't it? From this view, it's dark enough that you can see them. Not like in the Burrow."

"The Burrow?"

"Yeah, the inner city—you know where everyone kind of mixes." Portia made a weird gesture, but Katie got what she meant.

"Hey." Katie and Portia turned around and saw the girl peeking around the corner. She wiped blood from her mouth, and the guy held a piece of gauze to his shoulder. "My good money wasn't spent so you could chat up the help—no offense. I meant that as a joke." She looked between the guy and Portia.

The guy excused himself, looking pale, and the girl came closer.

"It's her first time and she's not into it," Portia said.

"What? Why didn't you say anything?" The girl looked shocked but was comfortable enough to sit on the arm of Katie's chair. "First time is *the* best. You have to do it. But the wrist, anything else might feel too...you know...carnal."

"That's what I said." Portia held out her arm and walked her fingers up her wrist.

Katie frowned. She didn't want to be judgy and knew this was a thing—but gross.

"At least try it." The girl nudged her toward Portia. "When you finally do, you'll regret that you wasted this great room. Instead it'll be at some cheap place where you'll have to take your own hand wipes to make sure what you're about to suck on is clean."

Katie and Portia looked at the girl, both clearly judging.

She shrugged. "I've been through some things."

"She's right. You might as well try it while you're here. If she paid for it, it's free and sourcing is expensive—well, unless you go to places where you need to bring your own hand wipe."

"I think I'm good," Katie said, trying to figure out how she ended up sitting in a room with two people trying to convince her to suck on the other one's arm.

"You're a vampire. It's what you do, girl," Portia teased.

"Even if I wanted to, I can't just bite you. That's...weird."

"Just put your mouth next to her wrist. You won't even realize you're biting until you've done it," the girl said.

Katie opened her mouth to decline when Portia rubbed her wrist against her lips. Katie inhaled, and her eyes fluttered.

Portia and the girl laughed. "See?" they said at the same time.

"Here." Portia fumbled through her jacket pocket. She gasped a little, and Katie smelled it. The blood. "You won't have to bite, just suck." Portia brought her wrist back to Katie as the blood beaded.

It smelled much different than the harvested blood she'd grown to hate. The perfume was both savory and sweet.

"Yep. Just taste it. You'll be glad you did," the girl said.

Katie knew she was succumbing to peer pressure from a girl whose name she didn't even know. But they were both right. She was a vampire, and if it smelled different than the harvested blood…maybe it tasted different…

Katie looked at Portia.

"Just do it, girl. I promise it won't hurt."

Katie glanced back at Portia's wrist, and before she could change her mind, Portia put it to her lips. The flavor, mixed with salt and saliva, burst, glazing her tongue. Something deep inside Katie clawed its way forward and she went for a second taste. Like inhaling a sweet perfume while lying in the warmth of the sun, she basked in the sweetness of the blood. It was better than when Tristan lay on top of her and explored her body. It was all that and more.

Katie opened her mouth and bit down. Her eyes rolled as she sucked. She knew what it was like to be a lion gripping the neck of gazelle, clamping down and tasting the blood between the fur. It was natural. The bite was no different than biting into a peach. A slight pull and release. She wanted to feel it again—

the slight snap of the first bite—but she didn't dare pull away. Not when heaven was just at the tips of her fingers. Right there on her lips…

When Katie finally released Portia's wrist, Portia was smiling but getting paler by the second. She reached into her pocket and pulled out a piece of gauze.

Katie saw the holes, two deep red bubbles threatening to boil over. Shame coated her skin like greasy lotion. She'd just bit a girl. Yet, she felt good in so many ways that were wrong.

"I know that look." Portia laughed. "It doesn't hurt. It feels kinda cool and relaxing." She leaned back in the chair. "But I'm probably going to need some help down to the cafeteria. Do you mind?"

"Sure." The girl walked over to a phone and called up a medic like she was asking for another pillow or the lunch special.

"Look," Portia said, "don't be embarrassed. There is nothing to be ashamed about. I'm not going to feel bad about the steak I'm about to eat or those weird baby carrots they keep serving. It's the natural order of things. As long as no one gets hurt, it's okay. What's the difference between this and me going to a blood bank?"

"I'll tell you the difference," the girl said, fixing her lipstick in the window reflection. "A clean fresh meal versus that month-old bag crap. Anyway, mind if we get going? I have to get back to work."

Katie nodded, feeling a new sensation, a high she hadn't felt in her entire life. She felt…good.

They left Portia in the room and passed a medical attendant with a wheelchair as they headed to the elevator. "Is she going to be okay?" Katie wasn't completely buying it.

"Did you see how many holes that girl had? Not her first rodeo. I wouldn't be surprised if she let people bite her—you know—*anywhere.*"

Katie blushed. She couldn't make jokes like that. Not after what she'd just done. Even still, she cracked a smile. The warmth running through her shined too bright to be dimmed.

"Hey, since it was your first time and all, make sure to source again by the end of the week. That bag crap slogs through our bodies for weeks, but getting it from the source is so clean you metabolize it like nothing. You know the saying—'*source smart*' or something like that." The girl pulled out her cellphone as they passed the clerk's desk. He bid them a good day, and they were back out on the street again.

"Hey, cool meeting you. See you around maybe." She waved and disappeared across the street.

"Wow…" Katie laughed to herself. What had she just gotten herself into? She laughed again, louder, letting the vibrations fill her entire body, until her stomach ached with a sweetness she hadn't felt in a long time. She smiled, and for once, it felt real.

It *was* real.

Katie walked back toward the inner city—or the Burrow, as Portia had called it. Sourcing had done something to her. Life coursed through her veins.

A slight hum buzzed in her ears, but she couldn't figure out where it came from. The closer she walked to the Burrow, the louder she heard it. Beneath her feet, she felt the ground pulse, really felt it. Like for the first time, she was connecting to gravity and feeling its pull on her body. As people walked past her, she smelled instantly who was werewolf, vampire, guardian, or neither.

She knew fates and omitters existed, and Portia had just made her privy to an actual human population other than guardians— but she sensed something else. Something not quite human, but very much like one. Maybe they *were* guardians, but whenever she made eye contact with one, she got the feeling they were something else entirely.

Katie saw one now—an older guy taping fliers to the side of a building. The fliers were the same as the ones from the community center. The ones from The Seven.

Katie had stopped in the middle of the sidewalk, watching as he covered the walls, overlapping one flier over another, when something heavy hit her back.

Katie caught herself on one knee before completely face-planting onto the ground.

"Are you okay? I'm sorry, you just got right in front of me and—here, let me help you up."

"I'm fine," she grumbled. She turned around to find a purple-haired woman kneeling down and scooping dirt back into a large potted plant. Katie helped her and apologized.

"No. It was meant to be. You know the stars—fate—all that." She gestured to the sky, and Katie realized she was one of the nondescript people she couldn't identify. Katie's eyes moved from the woman with the purple hair to the plant sprawled out on the concrete. It was a pretty thing—the leaves green with deep purple, bell-shaped flowers. Katie helped the woman put it back in the pot.

"Yeah. Nightshade," said the woman. "The lady who sold it to me said it wasn't the poisonous kind, but I'm pretty sure it killed my neighbor's dog. Now it's dying on me, and there is a cat that won't stop peeing on my porch."

It drooped limp and sickly. Katie held the base of the plant as she helped scoop the dirt off the concrete and back into the pot.

The woman gasped.

Katie looked up. Right before her eyes, the plant began to perk up.

"You're good," the woman said. "Are you an herbalist? I've got a hydrangea that won't keep no matter where I put it."

"Uh. No. I'm like the opposite of a green thumb. My dad's rose bushes are all but dead." Katie watched as the leaves lifted higher, looking more alive.

"Then stop touching my plant. Who knows what you're doing to it." The lady hoisted up her pot. "And watch where you're going. It's busy this time of night."

Katie pulled her phone out of her pocket. It was almost eight, and she had three missed calls from Tristan. She put her phone back in her pocket and looked around for easiest way back toward the elevator she always used.

She'd think about Tristan later—now, she wanted to know why she'd been able to heal that plant. She knew she could heal herself, but she'd never been able to heal anything else. Not like that. There was that time with Tristan, after they'd escaped Eshmael's house, but it was after she'd drank two whole packs of blood.

"I'll be damned." Katie smiled to herself. Sourcing. The world had just opened up to her—a gift straight from above. She'd been able to heal another living thing instantly when it always took minutes for her to heal herself from minor things like paper cuts or scratches. Anything more than a bruise took more than an hour, and that was right after drinking.

Katie neared the elevator and rolled over a thought in her mind. She didn't have anything sharp, but she could bite herself and see how long it took to heal. She waited for the elevator, letting three people go before her and waiting an extra two minutes for it to come back.

She got in and took three breaths before tentatively biting her own arm. It didn't feel anywhere near as nice as biting Portia...

Katie pulled her arm away. Two little beads of blood puddled on her wound. She wiped them away to see—nothing.

"Holy. Shit." Katie tried it again to be sure, but the result was the same. She healed before she wiped the blood away. A thousand ideas popped into her mind of how she could test it, but she lost the nerve to do anything more than bite herself.

⁂

Tristan was waiting on her porch when she got home. He sat under the light, even though her dad was home.

"What are you doing here? You know he'll make a big deal. What's wrong?"

Tristan's face was neutral, but she heard the debate in his mind. *"How do I say this without sounding like a nag?"*

"Oh. God. Not this again." Katie tossed her head back. She'd walk to the end of the Earth before listening to him ask what was wrong with her again. "So I didn't answer my phone. I was busy. I was joking before, but now I'm serious. Stalker tendencies. I don't do obsessive boyfriend well."

"I'm not obsessive. I haven't seen you in three days. That would be fine if teachers weren't asking me where you are like I'm your keeper."

"How is that my fault?"

"What, that they care? That we *all* care?"

"Care about what, Tristan? You're treating me like I'm—like I *am* sick. Like a little fragile thing. So I skipped school. You should have met me two years ago. I only went the minimum amount of days necessary *not* to fail. I've missed what…" Now that Katie thought about it…

"Yeah, eleven days. We haven't even been in school a full month, Katalina."

"Okay. I won't skip—for a while." Katie nodded and moved for the door. As far as she was concerned, the conversation was done.

"That's not the problem." Tristan grabbed her hand. He

looked at her, rubbing her hand like she was a child. "I'm concerned. You've been so…"

Katie looked him in the eyes and nodded, though she wasn't listening. She was tired of this same damn conversation, but if she got defensive, it would only get worse. So she nodded and focused on the humming in her mind. It had gotten louder now that she was out of Gray City. She wondered what it was. Maybe it was the heartbeat of Earth itself…

"Katalina? What the hell is that noise?"

Katie focused. "What?"

"That static. Were you even listening to me?" Tristan dropped her hand. "Whatever."

"Just leave me alone, Tristan."

He flinched. The hurt on his face cracked through her numbness.

"I don't mean it like that. I mean…" She scrambled for the right words because the look on his face felt dangerously close to something she'd never want to see again. "…I mean, the touchy-feely, tell-me-what-you-are-feeling crap. I'm telling you I'm fine. I actually feel good today. I had a lot of fun, but you keep asking me the same thing. You're making me feel like I'm crazy."

He studied her, suspicious. "Then why are you hiding from me?"

"I'm not hiding."

"You're hiding right now. I'm so used to hearing everything you think. You know I've spent an entire year fine-tuning the crazy that is your mind so I can actually have room for my own thoughts and now... Nothing."

Katie laughed. "Oh, cry me a river. You're mad because you can't read my thoughts? Welcome to the real world. If I remember correctly—" Katie smiled and patted his cheek. "—when I complained about the same thing, you said something like, *'Goo-hoo, little girly can't hear my thoughts. Go suck on a lollipop and tell someone who cares,'*" Katie said, imitating Tristan's voice.

"One, I've never used the phrase, 'go suck on a lollipop.' Two, I don't sound like that."

"*I don't sound like that.*"

"Stop."

"*Stop.*"

"You're so annoying."

"*You're so annoying.*"

Tristan looked at her for a minute. "*My name is Katalina, and I like kitties and bright colors, even though I'm a short, little pervert. Do you want to eat ice cream with me?*"

Katie's mouth dropped, and she laughed until she couldn't breathe. "What the hell was that? You sound like an old lady gargling acid."

Tristan raised his eyebrows.

"I don't sound like that," Katie hissed between laughing.

"*I don't sound like that. Now who wants MeMaw's butterscotch kisses?*"

Katie hit his arm and covered her mouth. "Do I really have butterscotch kisses?"

Tristan smiled, showing his white teeth. His face was open and honest, and his lips curved into a grin. "I don't know. Let me check."

The front door opened. "You two idiots are going to wake up the whole neighborhood," her dad said.

Tristan rubbed his lips together and rocked back.

"It's not even nine yet, Dad." Katie rolled her eyes, wishing he'd go back to his couch and just turn the TV up like a normal person.

"Well, it's never the right time to announce to the neighborhood that my daughter is a kitty-loving pervert." Her dad frowned. "Why don't you come inside like a man instead of skulking out on my porch like you're trying to steal a pie off my window sill?"

Katie blushed and murmured. "As if we have a window sill. Or bake pies. It was a joke."

"Sure, I used to joke when I was his age, too." He watched Tristan for a second and then went back inside without closing the door.

Katie waited until she could hear him messing with the remote. "Why does he have to be so embarrassing?"

Tristan exhaled. "You think he'd hate me more if he knew it was his daughter's pie I was hoping to steal?"

Katie slapped Tristan's arm, bursting into giggles, both mortified and flattered.

Tristan stole a kiss and his lips lingered. "I'm sorry. I believe you. Just send a guy a text every now and again."

Katie nodded. Guilt burned in her, but she stomped it down. She was fine. She'd just needed a few days to—to breathe.

They kissed again, deeper, until her dad called her inside. The guilt came back as she watched Tristan walk down the street. She hadn't been fine—but she was going to be. Katie listened to the hum. More of a thump now. Earth's heartbeat. It was soothing, and she focused on it and repeated to herself: *I'm going to be okay.*

6

SHADY PLACES AND STRANGE FACES

S HE WENT TO school. The only people who mentioned her absence were her teachers during class and Brian and Christi, during their new community task of addressing envelopes.

"You're totally going to fail," Brian said.

"And look at you. You could do your hair once in a while," Christi said, making little hearts over the i's.

Katie subconsciously fingered her bun. It was tight and not a hair out of place, but to Christi that meant underdressed. "I'm not going to fail. I have plenty of time to do makeup work." Katie wiggled her fingers. "Vampires. We don't sleep."

"This isn't just about schoolwork. You're missing time in the classroom. We do have things called lectures and demonstrations.

We had three guest speakers last week. How are you going to pick your focus if you don't even know what jobs are available or what might fit you?" Christi went on. Brian nodded his head in agreement, like he had any room to talk about being studious.

Michael had taken to snooping through the boxes. "Look at all this junk. I think this is a typewriter."

"Stop touching stuff," Brian and Christi said at the same time.

He sat down and picked up a pen.

"What *are* you going to do?" Brian asked Katie.

Katie looked at him. Something was different. "When did you start wearing glasses?"

"I always do when I'm reading. You'd know that if you actually looked at me once in a while. Answer the question."

"I do look at you. Well—wait, did you know he wore glasses?" Katie asked Christi.

Christi looked up. "No, I didn't." She went back to writing.

"See?"

Michael chewed on the top of his pen. "Why are you avoiding the question?"

"Because I don't know."

"There is the vampire thing to consider," Christi said.

"Exactly." Katie really hadn't given anything much thought these days. Thinking was overrated and overwhelming.

Michael hunched over an envelope. "Well, that's not a plan."

Katie shrugged. "Who needs plans when you have youth?"

Brian laughed. "You're screwed."

Michael and Christi agreed.

"Well, if you could do anything in the world, what would it be?" Christi asked, putting her pen down for the first time.

Katie thought—and drew a blank. "I like painting. But...not really. Before they died, I really liked breeding hamsters."

"*They?*" Michael asked. "How many did you kill?"

"I didn't kill them. And just two—three, if you count Squeaks. I didn't feed him...properly."

"Okay...." Christi thought for a second. "Why not do something with animals? Like be a veterinarian or an animal researcher. You could work on a reservation or travel around the world building animal sanctuaries. Or you could work at the zoo as a keeper and manage the animals or staff."

Christi pulled out her phone and rattled off a number of other things Katie could do with animals, what colleges she could go to, and what research facilities she could work at.

"You could finish your degree super-fast. You could study around the clock. Or..." Christi put down her phone and picked up her pen again. "...you could show up to class more often and listen to some career options you might find more interesting than your dead hamsters."

"That's a plan." Michael waved his pen at them, getting some of his spit on the table.

"You're right. I should get a new hamster."

Christi shared a glance with Brian. "That's not remotely close to anything I said."

Why did Christi even care? Katie rolled her eyes.

Michael shook his head. "No. She's crazy."

"I'm not. I'll get a hamster and try my hand at being a responsible pet owner. If it goes well, I could try doing something with animals. I like them well enough—okay, stop looking at me like that, I'll do the school thing, too. Jesus, you're worse than Tristan."

"I have no idea what he sees in you," Christi murmured. "Save the laser eyes. I mean, you guys don't seem to have any common interests. He's all studious, and you're one letter grade away from being a dropout. He's super-calm and normal, and you're kinda irrational and crazy. That's all I'm saying."

"Well, say it to yourself next time," Katie snapped.

"You've got nice boobs," Michael said "Maybe that's what he sees. You know, instead of your face."

Katie threw her pen at him.

"I'm kidding. Chill out. I'm kidding." Michael peeked out from his arms, flinching when she threatened to throw another pen.

"Well, at least I have a boyfriend." Katie wished she didn't sound as sore as she was.

"I do, too," Christi said, turning red.

Katie noticed the way Brian's cheeks favored that of a peach.

"Brian asked me out this summer," Christi said slowly.

Katie tried not to show her surprise. If she said anything, she knew it would come off as jealous, even though she wasn't the slightest bit interested in Brian.

Still, Brian had crossed over to the dark side.

"And you have the nerve to question me and Tristan? You've got plans, and Brian's as bad as me, if not worse."

"No, I'm not. Not anymore," Brian said, his cheeks going back to their normal color.

"And the difference is he wants to be better. You don't. You're betting your future on a hamster."

"It's a plan!"

"Whatever, Katie. It's your life. I really don't care. But apparently Brian's parents are really worried you're going to turn into a degenerate."

Brian's eyes opened wide, and he stared at the table.

"How do you—why would you tell her that?" Katie felt betrayed—by her no longer friend, but *still*.

"I didn't."

"He didn't. We heard his parents talking." Christi's voice tapered off like she knew she'd messed up by saying anything.

"And my dad wants you expelled," added Michael. "I think the teachers are fudging your absences. I'm pretty sure nine is the max per semester before you get called in for review."

"Can we just change the subject?" Katie focused on the low thumping, trying to quiet the anger swirling in her, but even that didn't work. The thumping and the thoughts sloshed in her mind. "Actually, I need to use the bathroom."

Brian looked apologetic as she climbed over boxes and crates. When she was finally free, she walked to the lobby and sat in a chair. All thoughts, words, and breath caught in Katie's throat when she saw Allison sitting across from her, staring at her phone.

"Allison? I think I'm seeing a ghost right now."

"Huh? Oh, Kay. Hey." Allison looked up from her phone and smiled before finishing a text.

"I haven't had a single text message from you in three months and all you say is *hey*? What's that about?" There was more bite behind her words than she meant.

"Sorry. Also, work phone. They confiscated my personal one. I've been really busy. I—you know, I was looking for you the other day, but Brian and Christi said you hadn't shown up in a while. You okay?"

Even Allison, who hadn't even had the slightest clue what was going on in her life, had joined the Let's Check Katie's Mental Health Club. Katie stared at Allison, her best friend since grade school, the one person who she told all her secrets to. She thought about telling her the truth. But what was the truth? She wasn't fine, that was easy to say. It was the question of *why* that she couldn't, and didn't really want to, put into words. Katie looked at the circular patterned carpet and lowered her voice.

"Where do I start? It's been…I've been…lost. I don't know how to feel about Larry and it's eating me alive. I keep thinking that, if he'd loved me, he would have fought to stay alive or he would have been there from the start. And it's not that I needed him to love me. I just…it's all my fault. If I hadn't of said what I said to Tristan, he never would have left, he never would have looked for Eshmael, and Larry would be alive. I wouldn't see them every night…. I can still feel—I just…

"I want to move past it all, but there is nothing for me to

move toward. I've never known what I wanted to do with my life, and now being what I am changes things. I'm at a guardian school, and that's the last thing I want to be. I don't know where else to look. Every time I try and talk about it, the words don't come out right or Lucinda or my dad don't get it. It's like they're trying to fix the problems I don't need fixed, and I need help... but I don't know how I need them to help..." Katie looked away from the carpet and back at Allison, expecting to see pity or that look Tristan gets when he would rather it all be fine— but Allison was staring at her phone and texting.

Her fingers flew across the screen of her phone like lightening.

After a minute, she looked up. "I'm sorry, Kay. You said you've been—okay, I know, shoot me. I wasn't listening, but I swear that was urgent. Like, I get yelled at for five minutes straight about how worthless I would be to someone who is now dead because I missed a call kind of urgent. Anyway. You've been?"

"Fine. I've been fine." Katie pushed back the tears welling up in her eyes. She'd thought she was finally free, finally letting it out to someone who was the best at listening and not just hearing. Someone she'd missed like crazy for the last three months.

She focused on the hum. The thumping steadied her. "I was just being regular old me. I get handed one too many assignments, and I'm suddenly allergic to school." Katie laughed, but it was forced. Allison didn't seem to notice.

"Yeah, I wish I could take a break. This program is Hell. I mean, it's good, I wouldn't leave it for the world. But even now, my CO knows I'm at school and yet he's asking me to check in about my results on a report that doesn't even matter because it was solved fifteen freaking years ago. But you know, if I miss out one detail, I'm the reason three kids get killed or a building catches fire or the whole human race gets wiped out." Allison ran a hand through her hair.

Her phone buzzed, and Katie never saw someone scramble so fast to check it. Allison's red eyes flickered across the screen. Relief washed over her as she exhaled. "I can breathe for the next three hours. Wait until Jamal hears about this one." Allison looked up. "Sorry. Anyway, how are you? I asked that, right?"

"Fine. The question is, how are *you*? No offense but—you look a little on edge."

"Because I am. Technically, I'm not even supposed to be talking to you. I can only talk to people on my team or my CO. Everyone else gets to stay back at the dorms, but I have to come here and look like I'm on vacation even though I'm not, and everyone hates me and thinks I get special treatment because I'm the youngest, but I don't. It's really worse for me—but whatever. Enough about me. I shouldn't have even said all of that. How are you?"

"Allison. You've asked me that three times now. Maybe you should lay down."

Allison looked around. "Don't patronize me, Kay."

"I'm not. You should hear yourself. If it's that bad, you should quit."

"Quit? And waste all the time and effort I already put into it? Disappoint all my teachers? What would I do? This is the career I want to go into. This is a once-in-a-lifetime opportunity. Not everyone can or wants to quit just because things are hard. Ugh…"Allison looked at the front desk. "I have to go. They're doing another tour. I'll see you later."

Katie said goodbye and wondered if Allison meant that last part about her. Of course she did.

Katie sat in the chair for another five minutes, trying to focus her thoughts. Allison hadn't heard a word. She didn't care—didn't even notice. Katie's world was crushing in around her.

Her head pounded and she thought back to the last time she'd felt the bliss of sweet freedom. Her throat ached at the thought of blood, flowing down and into her body. Freedom like she'd never felt before.

Katie went back into the supply room and grabbed her book bag.

"Where are you going?" Brian asked, his eyes looking up at her from beneath his glasses. He looked boyish under them.

"None of your business," Katie said.

"You can't just leave." Christi looked from Katie's book bag to Brian and back to her.

"Well, I am."

"And what are we supposed to tell Mr. Carver?" Michael looked up from a box in the back.

"You know. I don't care. Tell him whatever you want." Katie pushed back her tears. She was drowning under the pressure of the thoughts that pushed her deeper and deeper into the dark corners of her mind.

Her phone buzzed, and she pulled it out of her pocket. She nearly laughed when she read Tristan's text: *Is everything okay?*

Peachy. She texted back.

She shoved the phone in her pocket.

"Real cool, Katie. Just leave us to cover for you," Brian groaned.

Katie opened the door. "I'm not asking you to."

"Well, I'm not a snitch either," Brian called after her.

Katie hurried past the desk and out the door even as the desk clerk called for her to stop. She was wearing the stupid junior guardians black T-shirt with bright yellow letters. She stopped a few blocks over and pulled her white button out of her bag and put it on. She knew where she was going, but she had to stop by the one place she'd only ever seen twice, since her Gray City adventures: Larry's bank.

She'd kept the bank book and card that was issued to her after Larry's death in her wallet. She'd put it there thinking she'd never use it, but knowing she was just a little bit curious. Was the money really hers?

She ran to the bank, trying to outrun what she'd left at the community center, but it grasped at the back of her neck and clawed its way up into her skull. People stared as she ran past, but she pushed their disapproving eyes out of her mind and focused on the one thing she needed.

She was too chicken to go inside, so she tried the ATM card. It didn't work. She turned around to leave, but her throat burned, like an ache after a long and hard run with no water.

She went inside and regretted it the moment she stepped onto the marble floors with her dusty loafers. Banks shouldn't have columns. They shouldn't have gold-stained artwork and pristine marbled arches. All it was missing was a giant marble statue of a Greek god or some other symbol of superiority.

Her throat burned, but feeling like a fraud who'd be tossed in jail pained her more.

"Can I help you?" A man wearing a tailored suit stepped forward and gestured for her to step to one of the counters. He didn't make any outward acknowledgment that she didn't belong, though it was clear she didn't. The other clients looked refined and affluent in their suits and expensive fabrics.

"I...I was left... I think I have an account here." Katie glanced around and then stilled herself. Last thing she needed was a bunch of vampires thinking she was about to rob the place.

"Can I see your bank book and photo ID please?"

Katie handed him what he asked for and the debit card she'd tried at the ATM. He typed some things into the computer, stopped and looked at her, and then typed more. "It looks like you need to activate your card. Please create a passcode of four numbers and type them in here."

Katie did as he asked and keyed in four numbers on the keypad. After a few moments, he printed out a receipt and handed it to her. "Would you like to withdraw any money today?"

Katie took the paper, and her heart dropped. It was true. She'd seen the number before, but now it was true. She had over twenty million dollars in an account with her name on it. She cried. Right there in the bank. She held her hand over her mouth and tried not to make any noise.

The man behind the counter cleared his throat and handed her a box of tissues. "Ms. Watts, you also have a box down in our vault with various effects. Would you like to go into one of our offices? We can continue from there."

Katie shook her head. She didn't want to be trapped in an office crying all her ugly tears.

How could Larry leave her that much money? How could he have known that she'd struggled her entire childhood and not have done anything? They'd almost never had money for anything, not after paying for her tuition at Hamilton. How could a man who didn't even care about her leave her that much money?

She had—she was... How would she tell her dad?

"Can I take out five hundred dollars?"

"Of course," the teller said, pretending she hadn't just snorted out a huge glob of snot.

Katie took the money and left. She focused on the thumping. *Thump. Thump. Thump.* Earth's heartbeat. It wasn't strong like back at the community center or even in her room, but she listened to it all the way to the cafe. She walked all the way to the back door where the spa was and met a new face at the desk.

"Hi. How much is a...session?"

"Depends on the room, number of sources you'd like at one time, and blood type." The woman smiled, ignoring Katie's puffy eyes.

"Can I…can I request a specific person?"

"Yes, but we cannot guarantee availability." The woman handed Katie a price sheet, and she picked what looked like what she wanted. A single room with just one source. She left blood type empty.

"Well, you wrote down Portia. She is O-negative. Is it okay if I circle that?"

Katie nodded. Jiminy Crickets—she had a type.

"The total is three hundred and twenty-five dollars. Please wait there while I put your information into the computer. Someone will be with you shortly."

Katie paid, shocked and relieved. She sat down in a chair, tapping her feet. It wasn't long before she was sitting in a room with a nice view like before, this time on the fourteenth floor, and waiting for whoever would walk through the door.

"You're back. And so soon." It was Portia, and Katie was relieved and embarrassed. "Okay, same as last time?" Either Portia didn't care that Katie looked like a mess or she was too polite to comment. She pulled out a device with two sharp prongs on the end. "Should I? Or do you want to just dig right in?" Portia smiled and winked.

It didn't make Katie feel any more comfortable, and though her throat thumped like the sound in her head, she was still hesitant.

Portia waved her off. "It takes a few times." She pushed the prongs into her wrist and sat next to Katie. "Bottoms up." Portia relaxed in the chair.

Katie took her hand, feeling sheepish, and sucked. The heavens opened up and took her away, far above the clouds. A warm blanket right before drifting off to sleep, that stage between alert and awake. She hovered there, soothing her throat and feeding her soul.

৵৹৻

Katie sat in the chair, amazed. Portia snacked on a cookie and a juice box, smiling in the same weird, goofy way she had after their last session. Katie looked at the time. If she left now, she could make it back to the community center in time to make it seem like she'd never been gone.

Katie thanked Portia and left, refreshed and less embarrassed as she passed by the clerk. The humming in her mind was louder now, highly tuned and steady.

She made it back to the community center and slipped back into the supply room just as Brian, Christi, and Michael were leaving.

"Look who's gracing us with her presence." Christi scowled. "You're lucky I don't have to explain to Carver why you're missing."

"Sorry, I—"

Brian pointed at his lip.

Katie wiped at the corner of her mouth. She could smell the blood on her hand without even looking at it. She had to stop herself from licking it.

"Did you leave to—oh. Why didn't you just say you were going to eat? Or get blood or whatever." Christi adjusted her book bag.

Katie stuttered, embarrassed and too panicked to reply. So far she had never really let her worlds mix. They knew, and she knew they knew, but this was the first time it was real. This time she was caught.

"What's it like? Is it good or is it—wait, is this one of the questions I'm not supposed to ask you because you'll get pissy and hit me?" Michael said.

"Yes." Katie looked at the ground.

"Don't be such a drama queen." Christi walked past Katie and left the supply room.

Katie followed her out and breathed. She relaxed her shoulders and acknowledged that there was nothing wrong with what she'd done. She wasn't surprised to see Tristan in the hall, waiting for her.

"Don't make me say it." Katie smiled at him. She found it a little easier to hold onto her thoughts after sourcing. Everything was easier. Breathing, thinking, not thinking—it was all easier.

"I'm not stalking you. Funny how you say that after I catch you acting strange."

"How am I acting strange?" Katie looped her arm around his, willing him to be fine about her being fine.

"What's that noise?" He watched her, confused and annoyed. "Every time I hear you, there is this static. Do you hear it?"

Katie thought he meant the humming, but it didn't sound like static at all. More like a soft, slow beat of a drum.

"No," she lied.

He stopped her.

"Did you just drink? You smell different. Like…I don't know, but it's kind of familiar."

"And here comes the obsessive," Katie joked, but Tristan frowned.

"Fine." He dropped his arm from hers.

Katie let him walk ahead. She was tired of them being like this, one step away from an argument. It didn't matter what she said or how she said it. If she let him in, she was a dark cloud. If she shut him out and kept all the cloudiness to herself, she was acting strange and being secretive.

Enough already.

∘⊕ ♋ ⊕∘

Katie spent the next month not quitting. She went to school. She studied and did everything except train with Lucinda. Lucinda kept extending the break, and Katie didn't complain.

After school, she'd go home and watch TV with her dad on the nights he got out early—but on the nights he was out late, she slipped into Gray City.

At first, she told herself she was there to explore. It was fun finding little shops or standing in front of the giant glass station that broadcast local news for the city. Often, it played footage of the werewolf district and the mystery behind the growing number of deaths.

It was speculated that a lone alpha was trying to gain influence by turning the other packs against each other. Two reporters discussed the decline in tolerance for werewolves in the vampire district because of the violence and the growing number of missing humans.

The vampires blamed rogue werewolves, and according to Clyde, werewolves blamed a rogue vampire family. It was ridiculous.

One evening she stopped to watch the news when coven politics dominated the report. They showed a picture of Larry and talked about the main issue over his death and the succession of the next coven leader. He'd apparently left the coven house to his next of kin and not the next coven leader. To the other house leaders, it smelled of suspicion. To her, it was eerie to be talked about on the news like she was a part of some coop. The next of kin—not his daughter.

She stopped going to the news station all together after Larry's face started appearing more often than not. The last time, they were interviewing the people closest to him. She didn't want to know how giving he was, how he loved the park and sponsored the annual Festival of Lights, or that he was the biggest supporter behind the merging of the Burrow.

She didn't care that he'd done a lot for inter-race relations. She definitely didn't care that he was reported to have no children—except his people.

It was around the second week, when the exploring waned, that she started going to the sourcing spa every time. At first, she always saw a different clerk and she'd usually ask for Portia. But after a while, she noticed that when she checked in, they would check her profile and mark down how often she came in. From the look on their faces, it was too often.

She couldn't help it. Her throat burned when she didn't. It would start to ache only hours after she sourced. She needed the blood like she needed air. That was what drove her to finding other sourcing spas. She asked Portia if she knew of any places, and Portia gave her the names of three.

Two of them were decent. They weren't anything like the one at the cafe, but they also weren't as expensive. She didn't mind sacrificing the comfortable chairs and the classy view. She was there for the blood.

The third place was shady. The lights in the room she had flickered, and she'd thought about the hand wipe advice she'd gotten from the coupon girl. The upside was, they didn't care if she came once a week or once an hour. They just wanted her money. It was around the third week—or maybe the middle of the second week—that she started going to each place every day.

One morning, the thumping in her head grew. She was sitting in class, and the thumping turned into twenty different beats, all pounding at once. No matter how hard she tried to quiet it, it clouded out all other sound. It didn't matter where she was; she heard the beats, louder and louder, until she finally realized they weren't coming from the Earth.

They were heartbeats. She was hearing blood pulsing through people.

On Thursday, it drove her mad. Her throat burned, and she'd gone to school early because she'd caught herself thinking about her dad's pulse. It was pumping and her throat was getting dry, and as soon as she thought about how his blood would ease the burn, she felt queasy and left the house.

Katie sat in an empty classroom, listening to all the thumping. What made her think she would be any better off at school? Her head smacked down on the desk. The throbbing made her neck and shoulders stiff with pain.

A girl passed by the door, and Katie looked up. In the midst of the pain, with complete clarity, she smelled her. O-negative. She just knew, somehow, that the girl was O-negative, and Katie's throat begged to be soothed. She yearned to feel that moment of bliss in the eye of the storm.

She needed the relief…

A hand grabbed Katie's arm. She pulled away and backed up into a locker. When had she left her desk?

It was Tristan.

"Where have you been going?" Tristan's eyes poked at her like little icicles.

"Nowhere."

"You can't be serious. You can't be serious." He clenched his fist and let out a controlled breath. "You've been sourcing?"

"What? I don't even—"

"Quit lying to me. All you do is lie, Katalina. I can smell it on you. You smell like a—God, how have I been so stupid?"

"So what? It's not a big deal."

"It's not a big deal? Look at you. You were just…" He lowered his voice so only she could hear. "You were just about to *bite* that girl. '*Suck her dry*.' I heard you." His words cut through her, and she pushed him away defensively.

A few students stopped and watched them, but most kept going, looking back a few times until satisfied nothing else was going to happen.

"I wasn't," Katie said between her teeth. Did he really think she'd off and attack a girl? She was just hungry. Just—when *did* she leave the classroom?

Katie smoothed the hair in her perfect bun.

"This is why you've been fine? Because you've been sourcing? Of all the ways to solve your damn problems, you do *that?*"

Katie growled. "*Shut up*. I'm sick of you judging me. Everything I do you criticize. Just back off. You get your shit from a disgusting bag, and I like mine fresh, so what?" Katie started to walk away.

"I'm done." He said it aloud. He wanted it to be heard by her, everyone around them—the world. "I can't fix this. It's you. Not me. You can't ask me to fix this. I… You can't ask me to save you from everyone *and* yourself. Jesus, Katalina. I'm done."

Katie's throat burned, and the thumping nearly drowned out his voice. She turned around and stared him in his eyes as a weight lifted off her. "I don't need you to save me. I'll save myself." She turned back around and kept walking until she was out of school and headed toward Gray City.

Katie went up and down the elevator four times. Her throat burned. She coughed and cleared her throat—anything to get some relief, but none came. The only thing stopping her from entering Gray City was the way Tristan had looked at her and the fact that she was rubbing on her throat like… like she was…

Katie stared at her reflection in the elevator door. The circles around her eyes were dark, making her normally gray eyes shine like silver.

She was addicted.

The longer Katie stared, the more she saw herself fade into…nothing.

She blinked until she was whole, but in just moments she saw herself fading again. Her arms, her face, her entire body was disappearing into a shadow with only two silver slits staring back at her. Katie backed up into the wall and screamed.

The door opened, and she ran out of the elevator.

She walked to the closest blood cafe and ordered a drink. They didn't have O-negative so she just told the guy to give her whatever they had.

It was disgusting. Not as bad as a bag, but it wasn't what she wanted. It did nothing to soothe the burning or quiet the thumping. She heard them everywhere—the pulses. It was all she heard. She walked up and down the streets for hours.

She wasn't addicted. She could *not* do it if she wanted to. She could resist the urge, drown out the pulses, ignore the shaking in her hands…

Katie waited in the cafe until eight. She thought about waiting longer, but her dad would be angry if she wasn't home by eight-thirty. She found an elevator and ignored the thought in the back of her mind—the one that wondered if she could ask him to bleed a little into a cup.

Katie pressed the button and felt the pull as it went up into the sky above. She dared a glance into the elevator doors. Her eyes glinted silver. The only times she'd seen eyes like this was the night Tristan had killed the guy who'd shot her. That time he'd faded into a kind of shadow she'd thought was just her imagination.

Katie held onto her arms. When had her whole body started shaking? Maybe she could go back down into Gray City. Source just one more time so she could think clearly. Plan her next move.

Yeah.

The elevator doors opened into the night. If she had been standing in front of an amp at a rock concert, the blast would have been kinder than the hundreds of pulses that hit her. She stumbled back into the elevator, hearing nothing but the heartbeats—pounding, calling to her.

She couldn't breathe. Her eyes blurred, and she grabbed at her throat, falling to her knees. Everything went black.

7

DETOX

HER MIND BUZZED with life. She heard and felt it all. Their pulses like musical beats drumming against her skull.

She slid into the darkness where no light could reach and let the euphoria ride over her. The one she wanted was coming. They stumbled closer and closer down the street. Seconds stood between her and the one who would ease the ache in her throat—the thought sent a ripple down her spine.

She breathed fast through her mouth, taking in the metallic taste mixed in with alcohol, street, and thick air. Their pulse grew louder. She looked around the corner and saw them. Holding onto the wall for support, they made their way closer and closer to her watering mouth.

They were almost there.

She breathed in their scent. O-negative. A taste like no other. Velvet to the throat, like warm broth to the stomach—like a soft caress on the lower back.

They were one step away...

She reached out and grabbed them. She held their mouth tight with a fierce grip and dragged their shocked, but lazy, body to the back of the alley, where only darkness could see. She pinned their body against her and the wall and clamped down on their neck as the fear of never having another taste wracked her mind. They struggled and jerked against her, but she sucked deep.

There, mixed in with salty sweat, was what her body ached for. She sucked deeper and deeper, afraid she wouldn't get enough. She bit down harder, her teeth tearing through muscle. There wasn't enough. No matter how much she swallowed or how fast, it wasn't enough.

They jerked and scratched at her, trying to get away. She would have to do something about the resistance. She needed every drop they had, and she couldn't risk them running away or spilling.

She'd snap their neck.

As she reached for their head, something grabbed her and pulled her away.

Her eyes blurred, and she saw the outline of her most prized meal falling to the ground.

The assailant pulled her back as she ran to grab her fallen

food. She ripped her arm away and faced them. They didn't pulse like the others. They were like her, and they wanted her food. She'd kill them before she let the O-negative go.

They fought. She punched and kicked, and they dodged. They weren't fighting back. She took the opportunity to pull out her pocketknife and swipe at them.

On and on, as precious blood spilled out onto the ground, they went back and forth. Her opponent trying to grab her, and she trying to slice it. In a fit of rage, she ran at her opponent, stabbing at the damned thing.

They grabbed her wrist so tight she thought her arm would snap under the pressure. They smacked her elbow hard, and she dropped the knife. The pain pierced her, and she gasped, blinking back tears.

Through her tears and blinks she saw fragments of blue eyes staring back at her. She saw a mouth yelling at her, but heard nothing except the weak pulse of her O-negative spilling out onto the ground. She swung her other arm around and punched her opponent in the face. They took the hit and grabbed her, wrapping their arms around her so tight she thought she'd snap in half.

A bolt of fire ran through her body and out through her skull.

Katie fell to the ground, writhing in pain. Her breath caught in her throat, and her skin burned. In a panic, she looked up at whoever had done this to her, knowing they'd surely kill her. She held up her hands in defense and skidded back into the wall behind her.

Tristan stared back, moving toward her. "Kat—Katalina, can you hear me?"

"Don't touch me!" Her head pulsed. She gasped, still shaking. The cold of the ground crept onto her skin, and she knew where she was and who had burned her. She looked down at her skin, the piercing hot turning into a slow burning numbness. There were no marks. Just her bare tanned skin. Tristan had used his power to burn her.

She eyed Tristan as he stood above her. He looked as afraid as she felt, but he wasn't looking at her. He stared into the darker part of the alley where a body lay, barely moving. Katie heard the faint pulse.

"I…I didn't—"

"Yes, you did." Tristan cursed and ran his hands through his hair. He cursed again.

"I could never—He wasn't—" She could see the man's face clearly. He looked to be in his late twenties, Latino, cleanly shaved…blood all over his neck and white shirt. His neck—it looked like an animal had bit into it.

"Fuck. I—" Tristan's eyes turned from anger to panic.

"Tristan, I—it couldn't have been me—I—I swear I didn't know it was…"

She couldn't really say it. It had been her. She'd attacked this man. She'd killed a man. She felt it. Deep in her stomach and in her throat.

She screamed. When her screams turned to sobs she didn't know, but she collapsed on the floor, sobbing into her bloody hands.

Tristan took deep, audible breaths. "Listen to me—stop, Katalina!"

Katie looked at Tristan. He knelt down, his face close to hers. "I have to call this in. A Death Dealer is going to come. You have to get your shit together or else they will take you and kill you. Reel it in or we're both dead."

"Don't. Don't call them."

"I have to or they will find you. They will find a way to figure out who did this. The Fates will know. Pull it together."

Tristan walked away and pulled out his cellphone. He spoke fast, and all Katie caught was their location, the words *west*, and *D-range*.

Tristan disappeared and left her alone in the alley without a word. Katie would have panicked, but she could hear his mind searching for water and clothes. He came back with a man's light jacket and a half-empty bottle of water. He washed her hands and face with the water and helped her put on the jacket. He zipped it up, covering her bloody white blouse.

When he looked into her eyes, she didn't have to reach to feel his anger and disappointment. It was inside of her, swirling around her, written all over his face. He blinked and sucked in a breath.

"He's almost here. Don't say anything." He turned away from her, but she heard him clear as day. "*I love you. Just trust me.*"

Katie heard what Tristan must have heard before her—a speed, so quick she almost missed it.

A guy with light brown skin, older than them, wearing a black jacket and black pants stepped into the alley. "Tristan— who's that?"

The guy raised an eyebrow at Katie. His dark curly hair sat disheveled on his head, bags hung under his eyes, and he stretched as he walked closer to them.

"I didn't call you to meet my girlfriend."

"Nice to see you, too. You're as cuddly as ever. I haven't heard from you in almost a year and when I do… Whatever, T. What we got here?"

The guy's eyes glanced over Katie again, and she looked away. He walked between her and Tristan—though there was plenty of room to walk around—and toward the body lying in the alley. The pulse was almost gone. Katie listened to it fade. She smelled the blood. It was being wasted.

Tristan took in a sharp breath. "We were walking down the street when I smelled him. Looks like a fallen bit him and took off." Tristan sounded nonchalant.

"Oh?" The guy surveyed the body and smelled the air. "O-negative—she must have a fancy appetite."

"I don't know if the fallen was a man or woman," Tristan said. Katie felt both their tensions rising in her.

"Why'd you call me here, T?"

"Because I have to report it."

"You could have called anyone. But you called me. Damnit, I know she did it, T. Why call me if you're going to lie?"

Tristan grimaced. "She didn't do anything. I already told you what happened."

Katie braced herself.

The guy crossed his arms and planted his feet firmly on the ground. "Fine. We'll do this the hard way: She's still got the silver in her eyes; she's shaking like the wind might blow her over; I can smell the blood on her—hell, she reeks like a fallen; and the fact that you didn't tell her to run, lets me know you want her in *your* sight, like you're afraid she might do it again in the time it takes for us to take care of this."

Tristan moved in front of Katie.

"I told you, West. We—"

"For fuck's sake, T. I'm not stupid." West sighed and moved toward them.

Tristan pushed Katie back. "I won't let you kill her. You'll have to kill me—"

"Calm down, Hulk Smash. We don't do that anymore." West looked back at the body. "But he's going to die. She can't just walk away free from this. At the very least, she has to go through detox."

"I won't let you take her."

"T, she bit him, and from the looks of it, she was going to tear his neck off to get every last drop. She's fallen."

Katie's head pounded with guilt and pulses. She grabbed onto Tristan. She couldn't say anything. How had she become— how had she turned into something that could do this? She'd murdered a man. A man who could have a family—children... And still she wanted nothing more than to lick his blood off the asphalt.

Katie turned over and gagged. Nothing came out, but her body wrenched and heaved, trying to get rid of all the blood that was now coursing through her veins. The blood she'd stolen. The blood she needed and wanted.

"Do you know the position you're putting me in? I can't *not* report this—don't look at me like that." West ran his hand through his hair in a way she'd seen Tristan do a thousand times.

"Make your choice then," Tristan said darkly.

"After everything, you think I won't find a way to help you?" West pulled a wallet out of his back pocket. "You realize, if we do nothing, she will only hunt again. Whether you find her or one of us, she'll be lost—for good."

"I'll handle it."

Tristan's resolve and fear rolled around her mind, making her hands shake. How had this happened? How had such a simple thing led to two guys haggling over her like she was something to be handled? How?

West laughed. "Yeah, I bet. That might be good enough for you, but not when my ass is on the line. I still have to report this body, and if they find out I let her go, I'll be put out to burn. From now on, I keep tabs on her—if she makes it out of detox."

He reached out his hand to Katie. In between his fingers was a single business card.

"Take it," West said irritably. Katie took it and looked it over.

There was an address on one side and a handwritten phone number on the other side. "That's the address to an SA meeting and my phone number."

"SA?" Katie's voice croaked.

"Sourcers Anonymous. It's for people with addictions. You'll fit right in." West put his wallet back into his pocket and looked at the body.

The body convulsed. Katie clasped her hand around her mouth. He was dying. Right there before her eyes.

"And here is the moment of truth." West got behind the man and lifted up his head. "You're going to feed him your blood. If he makes the change, you'll feel a little less shitty about killing a guy. If he doesn't, well then you fucked up royally and I'll feel shitty about letting you off."

Katie gasped. She looked at Tristan, but his eyes were on the man. What did she expect—him to do it for her?

Tristan pulled out his pocketknife and handed it to her without looking.

Katie took it and pulled out the blade. "What are the chances he'll change?" She kneeled at the man's side.

West looked her deep in the eyes. Even in the dark, she could see they were bright, almost amber in color—and angry. "How the fuck should I know?"

Katie stared back into his eyes, knowing he'd never be as angry in his life as she was with herself right now. She slit her wrist without a second thought and held it over his mouth, pumping her hand open and closed to get the blood to flow fast and free. She cut her-self over ten times, but her skin healed within seconds of it being sliced. It wasn't until she cut deep into her wrist that enough had flowed into the man's mouth.

Tristan covered her arm, tears in his own eyes.

She deserved every bit of pain. She would have kept going if Tristan hadn't stopped her.

West shook his head. "Cutting yourself to escape the pain of what you did won't make it better. It makes you worse."

Tristan punched West hard, and West fell onto the asphalt. Katie looked at her wrist covered in blood, completely healed. He was right. She was a monster. Even hiding in the pity of herself wasn't going to take away what she'd done.

Tristan wiped at her wrist with the bottom of his shirt. He wiped away her tears, but they wouldn't stop falling.

"I'll put this on the list of things you owe me," West said, brushing dirt off his shirt and scowling. He grabbed the body and threw it over his shoulders.

"Where are you taking him?" Katie panicked. She didn't know what she expected, but it wasn't for him to take the body.

West looked away from Tristan and let his anger fall on her. "The next meeting is Friday at six. If you don't show up, you'd better be dead…" He looked at Tristan before turning back to Katie. "…or I will find you and kill you."

West stared between them again before disappearing from the alley.

⋅⊗☙⊗⋅

She couldn't go home, and Tristan didn't take her home. They walked deeper into downtown. She had become the thing she'd seen in her reflection. The black shadow. And now someone was dead because she'd given into it. She'd let sourcing take control of her every thought. Even now, all she thought about were the pulses she heard in her head. How could she ever trust herself again? How could she go back to who she was?

Tristan didn't say a word as they walked, but Katie soon guessed he was taking her to Gray City. As the city swallowed her, the pulses grew weak and the need to feed was less. Tristan held her hand tight.

"I'm angry. At you and myself. I compromised my friend and put you above a life. But...I have no regrets."

Tristan gripped her hand tighter as he took her deep into the vampire district. The pulses were almost nonexistent. He stopped at a black car and pulled out keys. She didn't ask where he'd gotten the car.

She would have rather walked to wherever they were going, just to move her muscles, but she got into the car and Tristan drove down the street. Everything blurred between her tears.

"We'll stay somewhere until you're better." He grabbed her hand and held onto her while he drove. An hour went by as he curved around roads before he slowed the car. All she knew was they'd gone through darkness, then a tunnel, and back into lights. Old-fashioned lanterns lit up the streets and a rolling countryside of rock. She could make out giant houses in the far distance, burning light off into the darkness.

"Where are we?" Katie stared, wondering how far away from

home they were.

"The alcove. It's away from the city—we're under the foothills," Tristan said.

They drove on, and Katie squinted as they passed by grand houses, each just as barren as the last.

"Where are the people?"

"In the city. This is a fallback for each house. The way it used to be in the old times—except underground."

He pointed ahead to the biggest one they'd seen yet.

A stone wall surrounded it, as well as a steel ten-foot wide gate. It was just as desolate as the others. The main house stood regal and tall, and behind that, even in the darkness she could see the silhouette of more buildings. It was probably the closest thing to a castle she'd ever see in her life.

Tristan got out and opened the steel gate before getting back in the car.

"It's the only place we can go."

Katie shook her head. The answer was there in her mind, and Tristan wasn't denying it. It was the last place she'd ever want to go. She saw Larry's face in her mind and knew this was punishment. Tristan was punishing her for what she'd done.

"Katalina, I'm not punishing you. I'd never—it's the only place we can go. We can't stay at Mercedes's bar. A hotel is out of the question."

She accepted what he said, but in her heart, it still felt like a punishment and she'd take in silence after what she'd done.

They parked around the back of the main manor. Katie

expected to go through the front door, but Tristan broke a kitchen window. He shrugged. "You have the only keys since he died—except the house staff, and they're probably in the staff quarters all the way at the back of the property. Unless you wanted to go introduce yourself and ask for a tour?"

Katie looked away, pretending his sarcasm hadn't bit her as hard as it had.

They stepped into the biggest kitchen Katie had ever seen. It was without a stove or cabinets; only refrigerators lined the walls with a few sinks and pantries with glasses. Tristan led her down a hall and up some stairs. At the top left was a door and another staircase leading to another story.

"These are servants' quarters when the house is in use. In here—" he opened the door, "—is the hallway that leads to the different rooms. The study, library, drawing room, dining room, and the entrance." He closed the door and pointed toward the staircase. "Those go to the bedrooms." He grabbed her hand again and led her up, staircase after staircase, and down two hallways. He stopped in a room and grabbed a set of keys before taking her to one of the bedrooms.

Tristan flipped on the light, and Katie took in the wooden floors, queen-size bed covered in down bedding, real lambskin rug, wooden tables, and dressers older and finer than anything she'd ever seen in person. The only thing missing was a window.

"The window is boarded up. They're boarded up in all the rooms no one sleeps in."

Katie eyed Tristan. "How do you know that? How do you

know this house?"

"Because it's exactly like the one in New York. I had a lot of time to explore that one. And servants came twice a month to clean and stock the fridge. They didn't talk much, but I watched everything they did. Wait here a moment." He left and closed the door behind him.

Katie touched the bedding. It was smoother than silk and softer than anything she'd ever touched before, let alone owned. Technically, she owned this bedding and the whole damn house. She realized she was stepping on the lamb rug and moved off, afraid to be caught dirtying the place up. There was a fresh pad of white decorative paper on the desk and a fancy looking pen.

She picked up the pen and pulled off the cap—fine point. She leaned over the desk and let the ink stain the white paper.

I never said I wanted this, she wrote. Katie grabbed the paper and balled it up. She looked for somewhere to throw it away but found nothing.

The door opened. Tristan walked in with a cooler and a glass.

"I'm not…" Could she ever eat again without feeling like a murder?

"I know you aren't hungry. But you will be." Tristan set it down on the desk, looking at the pen cap. "You have to detox. You'll feel fine at first, but sourced blood burns faster than harvested. As it burns out, you're going to go through withdrawal." He pulled the keys out of his pocket. "There is no way out of this room. Not unless you rip the locks off the shutters covering the window. I'll get to you before you can do that."

"What do you mean? Why would I... You think it will get that bad?" Katie looked at the boarded window and thought back to a documentary she'd seen about people detoxing from heroine and meth. They went into fevers and shook a lot and seized...

"I know it gets that bad. I've seen D-ranges kill themselves for the chance to source. My old commander used to chain them up and let them walk out into the sunlight to try and feed." Tristan grimaced. "No matter how bad it gets, know that I love you. I'll protect you."

Katie could almost smell the fear pouring out of him. "What aren't you telling me? What's going to happen to me?" Katie shook, already faintly hungry. "The girl said a week. Why am I always hungry? What—what's happing to me?"

"Do you have any other weapons on you?"

Katie handed him his pocketknife back and the pocketknife she'd used in the alley. Her heart plummeted. She'd used it on *him*.

"Where is the pen?" Tristan looked at the empty cap.

"What—" Katie pulled it out of her pocket. She must have put it there unconsciously. Or maybe she'd done it on purpose... "You have to leave. I'll try and kill you again." It came out a whisper. She'd actually tried to kill him. The pain gutted her.

"I can't," he said, and Katie watched him steel himself. She heard him chanting over in his mind, *"We can get through this."*

The hunger crept back, and her ears strained to listen for a pulse. "Then tie me up." Katie looked around the room for anything that would hold. She tugged on the curtains.

Tristan stood there solemnly. "I can't."

Katie turned on him, feeling angry for the first time instead of just disgusted with herself. "You can. You have to."

"No. I can't. I can't bind you or you'll rip your limbs off. I can't leave you alone, or you will awake from your thirst and kill yourself to escape the pain. I have to stay. I have to bring you back—"

Katie dropped to the floor. What had she done? She looked at Tristan. He spoke, but she couldn't hear his words. Just the pulses. Faint—maybe not even real—but they were there in her mind, drowning him out. Then he was gone, throwing out the knives, the pen, the dresser drawers, the curtains, the bedding. And before it all went black—she heard him lock the door.

⚬⚬

Katie threw herself back into the wall. Her body burned in flames. She convulsed as glass shards dug into her back. He came toward her, and she screamed until sound came back to her and she heard him yell her name.

Tristan.

"Katalina. It's me." He knelt down to pull the glass shards from her back. He had scratches on his face, and tears fell freely from his eyes.

As the burning slowly subsided, she saw the blood splatter on the wall. Her eyes grew wide, and she cupped her hands over her mouth.

"Shhhh, it's okay. It's not yours—or mine. It's from a packet."

He smoothed the hair out of her face.

She gasped, afraid his hands would burn her again.

"I'm not going to hurt you," Tristan said. His eyes reflected her fear. "See?"

She flinched as his fingers brushed her skin.

"It only affects you when you're in shadow form. It is the only thing that brings you back. I'm sorry."

Sweat coated every inch of her. She grabbed at the jacket she didn't know she was still wearing. It was torn around the hood. She took it off, letting the cool of the room crash against her wet skin. Her throat burned and she couldn't make out the words. *"I'm so hungry."*

"I know. Do you want to try some from a pack?"

The thought made her stomach knot. Her head pounded with one giant pulse. It made her dizzy. She needed to sleep.

.ₒℓℰℊℴ.

Pain shot through her chest like she'd been stabbed with a branding iron. She saw his blue eyes before she heard his screams. Or maybe they were her screams. Both in the same high, tortured pitch. He held onto his neck, blood pouring between his fingers. She was both repulsed and tempted to eat it. She hated how bad she wanted to taste it.

He was still screaming. Why didn't he just kill her and be done with it? Katie sobbed. If she were strong enough, she'd kill herself and set him free from her and set herself free of her burning throat—the burning of hot, scorching sand grating back and forth between every breath.

She clutched onto her chest and the pain slowly subsided. She grabbed onto her throat, but the need to feed only got stronger. The pulsing thudded in her mind. She should do it. She could find the key, and salvation was just beyond the door in the form of a blade.

Katie crawled to Tristan's body. He rolled onto his side and faced her. He grabbed her arms with his bloody hands, and she saw his missing flesh—a chunk pulled out of his neck. He mouthed something.

"Tristan. I—I didn't—I—"

For a moment, she almost believed what she thought. But she'd done that. *She'd* done it. The pulsing stopped, and she heard him.

"Come back, Katalina. Come back. I can see you. I can hear you. Come back to me."

His words blew away the fog that had settled in her mind. She grabbed onto his neck, willing any ounce of healing she had for herself to pour into him. As it did, she felt the burning return to her own chest, but she saw the relief in his eyes.

"I'm…sorry," she croaked. Her eyes grew heavy.

"You have to drink a pack of blood. If you don't, you'll never come back." He looked terrified.

Did he hear it, too? The pulsing that seemed to come from nowhere, like a blood red sun creeping over the horizon. He shouted, shaking her and burning her—but even as her flesh burned, nothing hurt like her throat.

The scream woke her up. It came from her body. She couldn't move her arms or legs without screaming. Tristan sat next to her, sobbing. His eyes were as red as the scar on his neck.

Her arms and legs—they were broken. And all she heard before he held her down were the same words over and over.

"I'm. Sorry."

The blood went down like hellfire. She choked, and her broken body convulsed as she drowned in an ocean of blood.

PART TWO
THE FOOL

8

ROCK BOTTOM

A S SOON AS Katie's eyes flickered open and adjusted to the light, she panicked. She looked around, waiting to take in the carnage…waiting to feel the pain.

It took a few seconds to see she was in a new room—one with bedding, drawers in the dresser, a large window with dim light pouring in. Tristan sat at the side of the bed, watching her through puffy, bloodshot eyes.

He looked both terrified to see her and relieved. Yet he said nothing. They stared at each other. When she thought he'd stay stone-still for hours, a scene of him breaking her arms and legs flickered into her mind, followed with enough heartbreak to weigh down her own heart and shatter it.

Katie tried to sit up and reach out to him, but her entire body felt both heavy and brittle.

Tristan sucked in a loud breath and cried into his hands.

Katie reached for him through the pain. *Please.*

He tentatively grabbed her hand and spilled all his grief onto the bed with her. She remembered him grabbing her shadow form and burning her until she convulsed and changed back. She remembered how sometimes it didn't work and he'd have to settle on breaking something. A finger. A wrist. Each time worse, as if she'd been breaking pieces of him.

How had she done this to him? For blood. He'd warned her. Katie rolled into herself. *"I'm sorry. I did this. All of it. Not you. Please. I'm so sorry."* Her throat burned, but it was bearable. Even as she apologized, she was hungry and wanted just a taste to get her through it.

She shut her eyes. What was wrong with her? She scratched at her face and pulled at her hair until Tristan held her down.

She screamed at the top of her burning lungs.

"Shhh," he said.

She didn't want him to touch her. She wasn't worth it. Tainted. He should've just strung her up and left her. And then she realized, even if he'd wanted to, he couldn't. How could she have been so careless with *his* life? She'd not only murdered one man, but in her pity, she might have even tried to kill herself, which would've resulted in his death, too.

In the end, she hadn't changed at all, only gotten worse.

"Shhh. It's the addiction. You can't help it."

"I could have helped not being an—"

She still couldn't admit it to herself. She was an addict. Tristan lightened his grip on her. He smoothed her hair out of her face and stared into her eyes. She was broken. She'd broken him, and now he was picking up her pieces. The guilt and shame were enough to kill her.

"I didn't stay for me. I'm not here because I feel like I have to be. I'm here because I love you. I'm just so—"

Katie saw a flash of his memory. Him breaking her arms behind his wavering eyes. She wrapped her arms around him. "I'm sorry, Tristan. I'm sorry. It's my fault. All of this. I'm so sorry."

Her throat burned, and in the back of her mind, she wondered—how much would she have to beg for him to bring her someone? She just needed some relief.

He moved back and stared at her with a fierceness. Katie looked away.

"Open your eyes, Katalina."

She couldn't bear to see his face. Either because she knew he'd say no or because he would be disgusted by her and leave her.

"Open your eyes. I'm not going anywhere."

She looked at him and saw his relief.

"The silver is gone. You're over the worst of it." His eyes softened, and he kissed her forehead. Tristan stood up and wiped his eyes while clearing his throat. "You're past the physical addiction. Now it's just mental." His shoulders dropped in relief. "We made it."

Katie didn't feel like she'd made anything but a mess so big she'd never escape it. Never be clean or clear of it. There was no coming back from this. Even now she wondered if she could sneak past him to find someone. Anyone would do—it didn't matter the type.

"It's normal to feel that way."

"No." She cried, crippled and pathetic on the bed, hoping he'd take pity and just give her one last taste.

Tristan closed his eyes and breathed. "You need to drink another packet. You can't get hungry or the mental addiction will drive you insane."

Katie shook her head, on the verge of vomiting at the smell of stale blood.

"I love you, but I will force it down your throat before I let you get hungry." Tristan's eyes and voice were hard.

She saw a vision of her covered in blood, on blood-soaked sheets, as he readied the second packet.

He softened again. "I'm sorry."

Katie shook her head and cried. She was sorry because she was sure he'd have to kill her before she put any of it near her lips.

⚘

He didn't. But he did have to lock up the window again. The good news, he said, was she was in the flight stage, not the fight, though the scratches on his arms suggested that she was still willing to fight.

There was blood everywhere again. All over the richie-rich bedding. Some of it had gotten on the walls, but most of it, Tristan made sure, went down her throat.

Katie shook, freezing, as he carried her weak body down a hall to another room. She heard the sloshing of the cooler below her. She wanted to slice open her veins and get the disgusting blood out. The putrid smell was all over her. Blood on her face, all over her shirt and legs. She didn't know when she'd lost her skirt.

The new room had a tub. Tristan set the cooler down and brought her to the tub. "This is going to hurt." He turned on the faucet, and the sound thundered in the empty room. Behind his steady tone, she could see him breaking.

"Nothing hurts as much as what you've done." she said to him. She waited for him to cave. "Just bring me someone. Anyone. I will only drink a little. I—"

He put her in the ice-cold tub. A thousand knives jammed into her eyes would have hurt less. He held her in there until everything went black.

.₀ℰ℈₀.

She came to while he was wrapping her in a thick towel. She laid her head down on his body. She just needed to feel warm.

.₀ℰ℈₀.

He was singing. The room glowed with light as she lay cradled in his arms. Katie had never heard Tristan hum, let alone sing. It was a sad tune, and his voice broke off as he looked down at her.

Tristan ran his hand over her arm. "Sleep," he whispered.

Her eyes closed before she could hear the words to the song he'd started up again.

♦♦♦

The lights were off. They lay on the bed. She was still wrapped in a towel, and Tristan's arm was around her. She turned to see his eyes open and watching her. It would have been creepy if she hadn't seen worse over the course of the last...twenty-four hours?

"Seventy-two." Tristan answered.

Three days. It had been three days. Katie closed her eyes and imagined her dad wracked with fear, anger, and horror, thinking his daughter was either dead in a ditch or—well, she was much worse. She was withdrawing from an addiction. She'd never be able to explain herself.

It wasn't like someone had come up to her and asked her to buy a bag of drugs. She'd only done what she thought was natural—no one she'd run into at the sourcing centers had looked strung-out.

She shook the thoughts away and focused on the warmth at her back. How sad—she'd wished for them to be this close and alone a thousand times. Now, when they'd spent three days trapped in a multitude of rooms, she'd wasted it feigning for the next bite.

Tristan laughed.

It sounded familiar, yet foreign, as if she'd never expected to hear it again.

He held her tighter. "You're back. That's all that matters. I've got you back."

Katie turned into him, drinking in his sweet familiar smell, letting it momentarily comfort her.

"My throat doesn't burn…but I still feel…like I want it." She couldn't say it out loud; that would make it true. She didn't want it to be true.

Tristan rubbed her back. "We'll work on that. For now, you're back."

For the first time since the night Larry died, she saw Tristan close his eyes and sleep. He was pale and his breaths were shallow. When was the last time he'd drank? After all the fighting and the wounds she inflicted, he'd have needed to drink. Katie looked around the room for the cooler. There were three packets left. She opened one and flinched.

"Tristan?" She shook him awake.

He opened an eye and took the packet. She looked away and focused on her stained white blouse and missing skirt. She'd never felt so needlessly embarrassed. He'd seen enough of her true self naked over the last three days; some bare legs wrapped in a towel might as well have been a burka.

"It ripped off when—never mind." He shook off the thought as she saw him pulling her away from what looked like a chunk of sharp, splintered wood. "Come back to bed."

"I'm okay." She braced herself against a smooth cherrywood desk. The floor in this room was cool and wooden, but brighter than the first one.

"I know," he said, getting under the covers and holding them out for her. *"I'm not."*

She slipped in, and he pressed his face against the nape of her neck. She could feel him memorizing her smell, her warmth, and the way she breathed until he fell asleep again.

She waited an hour until his breaths grew deep and then slipped away from him. She needed to walk—to get away from the smelly blood packets. She made her way downstairs.

The grand hall was beautiful. Katie found a light switch and that made the chandelier sparkle with light. She moved to the parlor, where most of the furniture was covered with white sheets. She could see the layers of dust stacking up—it never occurred to Katie that people did it to keep dust from collecting on them. She thought it was just a fancy thing to do. When fancy people leave their houses, they put white sheets on everything. Now that she thought about it—she was stupid.

Larry really had a thing for the old-style dramatics. Katie found the study embellished with studded leather and wooden furniture, each piece having the air that only comes from being crafted by hand, and then the library—the only room with another widow. It overlooked a garden like none she'd ever seen. Tristan had said they were in the foothills, but she would never have guessed from the view of the garden—luminescent plants and trees growing in darkness and lighting up the sky. Most beautiful was the pond, lit-up from beneath the water to show big, neon fish swimming between luminescent plants.

She walked the length of the room, stopping at a curtain pulled over what looked like double doors. Light poured out from the thick fabric and Katie pulled it back. A wide balcony jutted out into the edge of the garden and over the pond. She tried the door handle, and it gave way, clicking as it opened.

The coolness smacked her in the face, and though she had that thick towel wrapped around her legs, she felt the cold almost immediately. She hadn't felt the effects of temperature since she was human. Sourcing must have affected more than just her mind.

She stepped out onto the terrace. With each step toward the edge, she saw farther out into the glowing garden. It was still, yet it moved with life.

A firefly—or what she thought was a firefly—zoomed past her face and toward the pond, blending into the glow. A fish jumped out of the water, catching the fly and taking it back down into the blue water.

Katie caught herself scratching at her neck. She didn't notice the growing pit in her stomach until it was climbing into her throat.

She dug her nails into her arms, feeling instant pain and relief from the growing hunger. She needed to go back in and find Tristan.

She couldn't be what she had been. She needed...

Katie turned around to run back to the darkest room and lock herself inside—but stopped. Tristan stood in the door, looking better than he had since they'd been in this house.

They were quiet for a while. "I think this is the only house in the alcove with a garden like this," he said.

Katie's eyes moved to the pond.

"Even in this house, only the rooms for nobility have a view of it—and the library, obviously."

"Great, so I just covered some aristocrat's room in blood."

Tristan frowned. "You have to drink again. Flush out the sourced blood and fill up until you are back at you max with harvested blood. Otherwise, you'll stay on the edge between fine and nearly empty." He held out his hand, and she could feel his worry and hope bundled in one.

Just the idea of harvested blood made Katie flinch. It was like a whip lashing into her flesh. A part of her looked at the edge of the terrace into the pond, wondering how deep it was. But she had to be stronger than that. She owed it to Tristan— and most of all, the man she'd murdered—to be stronger than that.

Katie turned back to Tristan and took one step forward and then another until her hand was in his and he was leading her back to the kitchen.

His relief washed over her, and Katie held onto it because she didn't think she'd ever feel it herself again. Especially when he pulled out the packets.

She went through three before she could keep one down. Blood covered the sink and the side of one of the refrigerators. She, again, was covered in it, her white blouse and towel nearly drenched, her legs streaked. How was she going to clean all of this up? She still thought the real owners would come in at any moment and think a massacre had occurred in their absence.

"There are servants on staff. You just have to call them back."

Katie couldn't stand the idea of someone seeing what she'd done, let alone trying to explain what had happened in each room.

"They've probably seen worse. Most of them are as old as Lawrence. They worked in the days where getting rid of bodies was normal."

Katie wanted to be repulsed—but she done just what he'd eluded to.

"I didn't—" Tristan stopped short, and Katie turned as she heard it, too.

Tires on gravel.

Someone was coming, and Katie knew they weren't expecting anyone. As the sound grew closer, so did another.

Pulses. Katie took deep breaths. They were faint, like a whisper, but she knew what that meant. They were going to get louder. Panic filled the air between them. Tristan's eyes grew wide, and Katie found her hand at her throat. How could she be hungry after swallowing down a disgusting packet? One that would have normally lasted her a week or two?

"Listen to me. You aren't hungry. It's in your head. Breathe. I'll go get rid of whoever it is. I—"

They both froze as he heard it, just as clearly as she did. Distant, yet distinct, were the voices of people they knew all too well: her father and Lucinda.

"You have to make them leave. Tristan, you have to make them leave."

Tristan was gone before she finished. Katie screamed, knowing she'd tear the flesh off her B-positive father just to calm the burn. The pulses grew louder, but she could hear the car stop and the screaming start.

"Where is she?" her father yelled, slamming a car door.

"You have to go. If you go in there, you'll kill her."

"I'll kill you before that." She heard a gun cock. Lucinda yelled at her father. Her smell was A-negative. Not Katie's favorite, but it would do as a top-off.

NO! Katie opened a fridge and ripped at one of the packets. She chugged it down and threw it back up in the sink. She tried another.

"She's detoxing."

"You got her hooked on—you made her *source*?" Her father pulled the trigger, and the sound thundered through her ears.

No pain. He'd missed Tristan. Katie ripped another pack open and forced it down and breathed until it stayed down. She wasn't hungry—but she still wanted to taste. She dug her nails into the flesh of her arm, lifting the cloud in her mind. She could still hear the pulses thumping in the back of her mind. She ran to the door and put up her hands.

"Stop. Don't." They all looked at her. She was covered in blood and in a dirty T-shirt. Her towel snagged on the door and fell, revealing her bloodstained underwear. She knew what it looked like. And she didn't have to hear her dad's thoughts to know she'd broken his heart.

Lucinda took a step toward her but stopped when Katie screamed.

"Don't. I can hear your pulse. I can smell you, and I can't stop the burning."

"What have you done…" Her dad dropped his gun to his side. The words hung in the air, broken and cracked.

The thumping grew. Or maybe she was focused on it. She shook her head, as if she could shake it out.

Tristan grabbed her arm. "Look at me. Focus on me. You're not hungry. Breathe."

His voice was starting to disappear in all the sound. Katie's eyes drifted toward Lucinda, then her father. Only steps away. Only steps away…

"Look at me!" Tristan screamed in her ear. It sliced through the heartbeats until they faded away. "There's no silver, Katalina. No silver. *You* can control this." His hand rubbed against her face hard, his eyes searching hers for any trace of the silver she'd once seen staring back at her.

Katie screamed, feeling at once split apart and put back together.

"What did you do to my… What did you do?" Her dad braced himself against his scratched-up truck.

Lucinda's face tightened.

"You have to leave. I'll call you. I swear. Get in the truck and I'll call you. Just drive away. Far away so I can't hear or smell you. Please, Daddy. Please." Katie sobbed.

"I'll be damned if I—"

"Get in the truck, Drew. She's detoxing. You know as well as I do what that means." Lucinda tried to take the keys from her dad, but he grabbed them back, staring for a moment longer.

"If you don't answer on the first ring, I will come back, kill him, and drag you out of this god-forsaken house. Do you understand?"

Katie nodded, wishing he knew just how much she needed him to still love her.

"Who can I send with clothes?" Lucinda's voice had an edge to it, threatening but calm.

"I'll get a friend to come." Tristan eyed the ground, a look and posture she was only used to seeing on Brian.

"Text me their name and number. I'll make sure they get the clothes. Let's go, Drew." Lucinda opened her truck door. Her eyes sliced through Tristan, and before she got in, she looked at Katie and then him again. "You asked me to trust you once. I never will again."

The engine roared and the gravel kicked as they sped back down the lane and into the darkness.

When their pulses had faded into complete nothingness, Tristan spoke. "It might have gone better if you'd stayed inside. You look like you just walked out of *The House on Haunted Hill*."

Katie didn't find comfort in his attempt at humor.

"I'm being serious. You're in your underwear and covered in blood. How did you think that was going to go?"

Katie wiped her tears and wrapped her arms around herself. "Do you know where my phone is?"

"Maybe it's in the car. It was the last thing on my mind when all this started." He was angry. He had been blamed for all her mistakes.

"That's not why I'm pissed. Stop fishing and look in the car."

Katie found her phone, nearly dead and littered with notifications, missed calls, text messages, and alerts. That's how they'd found her, using a GPS tracker.

Tristan turned the car on and handed her a plug to charge her phone.

They waited in silence as her phone charged. She turned up the sound to its maximum level to be sure to hear when her dad called.

"I know it's not an excuse, but I didn't know this would happen. I—I had no clue. I mean, I thought it was something everyone did and I'm not excusing myself. I'm just saying I had no clue."

Tristan was quiet, blocking her from his thoughts, calculating his words carefully. "I know. I didn't either. I should have guessed it. I should have known you couldn't handle it. But I—I didn't think…a part of me was glad you were…" He didn't say the rest, but he let it slip from his mind. "…*giving me space.*"

"It's not your fault. I'm the one who turned into a crack fiend. I'm the one sitting in my underwear covered in blood. I'm the one who will never come back from this." Her eyes were too dry to cry, but it was true.

She'd hit rock-bottom and there was no way back. She could never face anyone, let alone herself. Maybe that's why she'd gone outside and stood in front of her dad and Lucinda. To see if it was true. If they would look at her like she was still the Katie they knew or some gutter rat looking for her next hit. Now she knew. Their eyes didn't lie, no matter what their words said. They'd never look at her the same.

Tristan sighed, confirming what she felt. She'd turned into a monster, and now she'd never be clean again.

"Katalina—"

The phone rang.

Katie answered before the ring finished. "Hello," she said, so quiet she wasn't sure her dad heard.

The line was silent, but she could hear the road as he drove.

What should she say? What could she tell him that he hadn't already figured out? She opened and closed her mouth a few times before he spoke.

"Lucinda's waiting on the name and number of your *friend*. We'll let you know when they should be coming with the clothes."

The line ended. Katie crumbled into herself and cried until her eyes burned more than her throat. The door opened, and Tristan got out. She could hear him on the phone and Mercedes on the other end. She could hear Mercedes' no-questions-asked, can-do nonchalance.

Then she heard a familiar, angry voice. It was West. She had to strain to hear as Tristan was moving farther away from the car.

"I told you not to call me again, T. Seriously, what the fuck do you want now?"

"Katalina…" Tristan was silent.

West voice softened. "Is she…did she make it?"

"Yeah." Tristan sounded grim.

"Okay. That's good news. Now explain to me why you can't bone a vampire like the rest of us. Why the fuck would you change a human girl?"

"I didn't. That's not what happened. I—I don't know—I can't—where do we go from here?"

There was a pause, and Katie could feel the door shutting on her. There was nowhere she could go from here. Here was the last stop in her life. No more family or friends. Just her and her demons.

"You're lucky my shift ended two hours ago. Where are you?"

Tristan said nothing. Katie could feel his suspicion.

"For fuck's sakes, T. They don't do that shit anymore, I told you. And you know I *never* did any of it. You need my help? I'll give it to you, but not if you're going to keep treating me like I'm the one who disappeared without a trace."

"Hill Crest Manor."

"Hill Crest? Full of surprises. I feel like you're going to get me killed. You know, now that Lawrence is dead, his successor is going to show up and wonder what a D-range and lovestruck shadow boy are doing in his place."

"They won't. Trust me."

"Trust—haha. I'll be there in an hour—if there's no traffic."

Katie released the clutch she had on the seatbelt. She hadn't realized she'd been straining so hard. Why had he asked his friend to come? What was he going to do with her? Whatever it was, she deserved it.

Katie left the car and went back into the kitchen. She cleaned the sink and found a rag to clean up the side of the refrigerator and the floor. She made a mental list of the things she would clean and fix. First the kitchen, then the bedrooms. As she scrubbed the countertops, she knew she'd never be clean again. She'd never get the sludge off her soul.

9

THE SPONSOR

IT ONLY TOOK thirty minutes for Katie to finish the kitchen and do one of the bedrooms. She stripped the sheets and straightened up the room. She didn't know what she should do about the bloodstains on the mattress. She took the sheets, folded them, and brought them to the last bedroom.

She couldn't get to the door if she wanted to. The curtains, dresser drawers, bedding, and broken bits of wood and fabric were spewed about the hallway. Katie got to work stacking up the drawers and folding the bedding and curtains that weren't ripped.

She stopped and picked up the pen and looked for the cap. She noticed the knives were gone—she'd probably never see those again.

Katie pushed the bedroom door open and winced. It would take her an hour just to scrub the blood off the wall. The mattress was torn, and she found half her skirt soaked in blood.

She started with putting the drawers back in the dressers. The wood bore blood-stained scratches, and she pretended not to remember her own nails digging across them.

"You don't have to do this." Tristan leaned against the door frame. He might have looked better than the last time he was in this room, but his mind was exhausted, angry, scared, worried—the list went on.

"I do." It came out curt. She didn't have the right to be angry, but it wasn't anger directed at him. She picked up fractured pieces of wood and caught a glimpse of her filthy shirt.

Rock-bottom had never felt so damn unforgiving. Glass broke under her foot, and she flinched. Shards littered the ground, glinting like angry glitter. She pulled the glass out of her heel.

They both looked up at the faint sound of a car door slamming. "I think that's Mercedes." He said it as if Katie was going to run down stairs and offer her a tour of the place.

"I told her you were sick."

She wanted to thank him, but it stopped in her throat. What was the point of hiding her shame if it was laid out so obvious and blatant?

A car horn sounded in the distance.

"I'll be right back."

Katie focused on the glass pieces and fixing the bloody lambskin rug back into its place.

When Tristan came back, he told her he put the clothes in the bathroom.

She nodded but waited for him to leave before putting down a broken picture frame and finding the bathroom. It wasn't hard as it was the only room with a light on.

As every sober moment passed, she wished he wasn't there, seeing her like this. She knew he was somewhere close by, lurking, waiting for her to freak out again.

She stripped, careful to fold her dirty clothes before running a hot bath. She left the faucet on to stamp out the sound of her crying.

She scrubbed her skin and her hair. Tristan had only been able to find a pale purple bar of soap that smelled like lavender. The scent suffocated her.

She took her time drying her hair and getting dressed again. The clothes were new and very plain. A pair of straight jeans; three black T-shirts; two bras, one a size too small; and a pack of white socks and underwear. Five each.

Her hair crinkled around her as she got dressed, her locks stretching and hanging as they dried. She used the twine from one of the clothing tags to tie her hair out of her face.

Katie let her eyes find the mirror. She didn't look like an addict. She looked like herself, clean and attractive at the right angles. She didn't look like someone with a demon dark enough to drag her to the depths of Hell. She didn't look like a murderer.

Tristan knocked on the door. "Can you come to the parlor room?"

Katie stacked the extra clothes on a shelf. She took her old clothes and hid them in a basket.

When she opened the door, Tristan looked up, surprised, as if he was relieved she hadn't come out looking like a freak.

"Katalina—"

Katie avoided his eyes and found the main staircase. She stopped at the top, staring down at the guy from the alley. West. She hadn't expected him to be standing in the great hall, admiring the chandelier. She'd expected to have time to ready herself.

He looked at her and Tristan, and his eyebrows flew to the top of his head. "You clean up quick." He looked at Tristan suspiciously. "I thought you said she detoxed."

"I did." Katie wanted to take responsibility for herself. No more going to Tristan. She climbed down the stairs, breathing deeply with each step.

"You'd look much more... You heal freakishly... Hill Crest Manor—how did I not put two and two together? Lawrence had a kid? Of all people, I wouldn't have thought of him as... the fatherly type." He looked at Tristan. "That explains a lot."

"Where are you going to take me?" Katie wanted to get it done with. She had thought about it. They might have some kind of prison for people like her.

West raised an oddly mobile eyebrow. "I'm not taking you anywhere. What did he tell you?" West looked at Tristan. "I told you we don't do crazy crap anymore." West dug into his jacket pocket and pulled out a badge. "We're STAR now." West smiled slowly, letting it sink in. "Special Tactics and Assistance Regimen."

"You've got to be kidding me," Tristan said.

West laughed. "I like it. I'm a STAR." He gave them another STAR-worthy smile.

Katie stared blankly, still wanting to know what he was going to do to her.

"Right," West said. "As far as I can see, you've already detoxed. And I can't take you in on charges for attacking *and* changing a guy, not after I covered it up. Plus, you're a half-born. They'll just ban you from the city—then again, Lawrence is dead. They might try to make an example of you, bind you to servitude until you die or grovel for forgiveness. Azezel is kind of a freak about penitence and punishment."

"Azezel?" Tristan and Katie said it at the same time.

"I guess you wouldn't have heard. We have a new coven leader. He took Lawrence's place. You'd know that if you weren't a twat." West directed the last bit to Tristan. "Anyway, figured I might as well start off with good news. Emanuel made the change."

Her victim had a name. Of course he had a name. And probably a family and a life—he was alive. A part of her felt relief; the other part knew that she'd condemned him to a life in the shadows. He'd never feel the sun again.

"You look like a decent kid."

Kid. It was borderline offensive.

"Didn't like that? Okay. You look like a decent chick. You have to be either a special kind of crazy or extremely tolerant to put up with Tristan. Given our last meeting, I'm going with crazy—but that's beside the point." He pulled out a necklace from under his shirt. A round coin hung at the end of his chain. "I know what it's like to be in recovery. I mean, *I* didn't completely destroy someone else's life like you...but addiction is addiction. We all have demons. You know the saying? There are two wolves, one is evil and one is good—which is stronger?"

Katie shrugged. "The evil one."

"No. The one you feed. You're a dark one, aren't you? Black soul and all, Christ."

Katie winced. He was blunt. He saw right through her clean skin down to the sludge that lay right beneath.

"West..." Tristan warned. Katie could fell Tristan having second thoughts, wanting West to leave.

"He's right." Katie held back a tear. *"He's right."*

"Of course I am. Let's sit down and talk. I need to sit. I've been on my feet all day—and driving doesn't count as sitting."

Tristan showed them to the parlor, but West stopped him at the door. "Sponsors only past this point. You're just going to get in the way." West stared Tristan down.

Tristan's eyes went dark.

"It's okay." Katie knew he was right. She needed to talk to someone who wasn't afraid to break her spirit and strip her to the bone.

West put his arm around Katie. "See, T? It's okay."

Katie cut him a look and flung his arm off. She might be a junkie but that didn't mean she wasn't a person. "I might be lower than the scum of the earth, but I'm not your toy. Whatever crap you two have going on, leave me out of it." She stalked into the parlor.

She pulled the sheet off a chair, careful not to disturb the dust, and folded it into a neat tiny square.

"Fixating, eh?"

She looked at West. He didn't look much older, but there was something deeper to him than his act.

"People often fixate on something they can control when they start recovery. You seem to be pretty focused on everything looking neat and tidy. Look at how you're sitting."

Katie looked at her crossed legs and straight posture. She'd never sat like this in her life. She folded her legs under herself, her back still straight as a board.

"I've never met anyone after detox who looked so…neat. I'd say it's not all that bad, but you don't seem like the type of person to do things in moderation. And fixating on perfections can be just as bad as having imperfections."

"You said sponsors only. Are you sponsoring me?"

West nodded. "Mostly to get under his skin." He tilted his head to the door. "But also because I'm responsible for you being *here* instead of where we take everyone else who falls off the edge." West sat on a long couch and propped his legs on a coffee table.

Katie cringed. It didn't feel like her coffee table, but the gesture was still offensive. Who knew where those shoes had been?

"So how did it happen?"

Katie looked up into his eyes. He reminded her of a tiger. It was like he saw every little thing she did and didn't do. He was taking it all in. He was like Tristan. No wonder they were at odds.

"I don't know. A girl had a coupon but needed a friend, and I tried it. I—I kept going back and…I couldn't hear anything but their pulses after a while. Next thing I knew…" She trailed off, staring at the alternating red and green lines on her cream-colored chair.

"One of those fifty-percent-off coupons the fancy places pass out once a year? There's always a rise in sourcing when those go out. You know, he should have told you sourcing was dangerous for your kind."

They locked eyes.

"I found out T was half when he ran out into the sun to save this little girl. You halfs aren't like the rest of us. We don't lust like you do for sourced blood. It's easier to go in and out of shadow form and control it. When we were training back in Academy, Tristan couldn't do it. Not at first like the rest of us. It was…well, one hell of a week, and I saw some things I'll take to the grave." West smiled. "And that's saying something." He laughed at his own joke. West looked at the door and then back at Katie.

"He had to have known. You reeked that night. He would have known before that, that you were sourcing. And your eyes. They're gray, but there's nothing like the sliver glint after someone's hit the tap." West relaxed back and spread his arms out along the sofa. "He should have known that, if you sourced, you wouldn't be able to handle it. Something about sourcing is just so much more alluring for you than it is for the rest of us. We do it to survive. You do it to...feel alive." West cocked his head to the side. "You know exactly what I mean, don't you?"

She did. She closed her eyes, feeling it, the freeness and euphoria. She'd chase it until there was no more life left in her.

No.

Katie gripped the edge of her seat and pushed the desire deep down.

"Don't. Don't run away from it. It's part of you now." West shifted in his seat. "I'm going to be straight with you. It never goes away. That want. You'll always hear the pulses in the back of your mind." He let it sink in. "It will only control you if you let it. You can hear Tristan outside pacing the hall, right?"

Katie nodded, but left out the fact that she heard him cursing himself and West. She left out that she saw his thoughts of her, of him catching a whiff and suspecting, of him thinking he saw a glint in her eye but preferring the space she'd given him, preferring the time away from her crazy instead of the questions that were starting to pile up.

"You can hear the hum of the lamp-light up there, right? You can feel each fiber on that chair you keep rubbing on, like you're OCD, right?"

Katie frowned.

"Those are all things you've learned not to fixate on." He looked at the sheet she'd folded into a perfect crisp square and rubbed his shoe against it, ruffling it up until it fell off the table and into a slump. "The wind, the gorilla shuffling out there in the hall..." West gestured to the door and raised his voice as if Tristan couldn't already hear every word. Tristan did sound like an animal, like the big cats at the zoo pacing the glass.

"Get out of my head." Tristan growled, annoyed that West was getting to him.

"What's with you two?"

Tristan grumbled and left the Great Hall, pulling his thoughts away with him.

"Finally, I thought he'd never leave. Eavesdropper." West rolled his eyes, frowning at the door.

She'd killed a man—damned him for forever, just been told she'll live her life forever addicted and haunted by pulses—and here they were, squabbling like...like kids.

West looked at her, almost offended that *she* was now studying *him*. "Look at me like that all you want. At least I didn't nearly kill a man and ruin his life."

Ouch.

"Sorry." He looked sincere. "It's mean, but it is true. You have to remember that. Don't punish yourself. Just remember what it does to you when you let it control you."

"How do you...go back... How can I be who I was before?"

"You can't. This is your new reality. The thing is, you have to stop thinking there is something to go back to. Life moves forward. Either move or get left behind to be swallowed whole by it."

His words had a kind of nostalgic feeling. It brought back some of the courage she thought had been stripped away.

"How do I do that?" She looked at him, desperate for the answer.

"One day at a time."

West answered her questions for another hour: how to help with the burning in her throat and how to tell between her mental hunger and her physical hunger. He got her to do something she felt was both strange and full of hope.

Laugh.

"If you think that's funny, you should meet Zuri. She does the best impression of Tristan—oh, don't look like that, he hates her. He's barely ever said two words to her and never will." He smiled to himself. "You'd like Zuri. She's got the same crazy look in her eyes as you do." West winked, and they both looked at the door as Tristan's pacing returned. "The old Tristan wouldn't have asked me to do what he did. He would have put duty above his girlfriend. He wouldn't have asked me to come here after punching me in the face—unless he was desperate."

Katie wondered if West would have thought the same thing if he knew that Tristan's life depended on hers.

"Sitting in front of you now, I can't tell."

"What?" Katie looked at the door, feeling Tristan's patience run thin, but underneath the annoyance, his relief that she seemed better.

"Who's the dangerous one. You or him."

Tristan opened the door. "Shut up, West." His voice was full of aggravation, but Katie felt his gratitude.

"Shall I add this to the list?" West stood up, brushing nothing off his pants.

"Do whatever you want."

West half-smiled. "I gave your girlfriend my number. She's instructed to call me whenever she *needs* me."

Katie rolled her eyes. That wasn't exactly how he said it before, more like, "*If you feel like you're about to snuff someone else out, call me or punch yourself in the face. That's worked for me a few times.*"

Tristan gave him a side glance. "We'll see who gets there first."

"More like we'll see who finishes."

Katie stood up and sighed. "I'm not a chew toy. If you guys are going to fight it out, don't use me as bait."

Tristan looked affronted, but Katie ignored him.

Before she left the parlor, West called her name, "Katalina."

Katie froze, feeling Tristan's heart squeeze. *Katalina* was his. Maybe West could sense that, maybe not, but Katie didn't want there to be confusion. "Call me Katie."

"But Katalina sounds a lot cooler. Old school, but, you know, fancy and kinda dangerous." He said it again like it was a roller coaster ride: "*Ka-ta-lina.*"

"Katie," she said again, never realizing just how much she wanted it to be Tristan's and his alone.

"Can we settle on Kat? Katie sounds like you live in the suburbs and go to a prep school and have a hundred stuffed animals on your bed."

"I do," she said, thinking the number was more like three and they were all from Tristan.

"Gross. Well, that was the old you, and if there is ever a time to reinvent yourself, it's now. You know, killing a guy and all..."

She sighed. This guy was exhausting.

"Anyway, take this." He pulled a chain out of his pocket and tossed it to her. It had a coin like his on it. He had explained earlier that it was iron, and he'd touch it or press it against his skin when he needed reminding that the pulses were just white-noise.

She put it around her neck, feeling the weight of it even as it lay on her shirt, waiting to burn her. "Thanks." She hoped like hell it would work. Even now she felt a tingle in her throat. She was already breaking one of West's rules.

Rule number one: Stay Ahead of the Hunger.

"Look, I'm giving your girl jewelry."

"Shut up, West." Tristan leaned against the far wall, watching her, echoing her words in his mind.

Katalina is his.

Katie waved and thanked West again.

"Friday at six. Don't stand me up." Despite his smile, he was serious. And despite his brashness, he was a hand helping her climb out of the pit she'd fallen into. She shared one last look with Tristan before steeling herself and heading to the kitchen. She swallowed back her disgust for what she was about to do.

Rule Number Two: Don't Be a Punk Bitch.

৵ঙ 10 ৯৵

INTERVENTION

GOING HOME WAS hard.

She kept imagining all her stuff would be out in the yard in black plastic bags and the locks would be changed. Or her dad wouldn't be there. Or worse, he would but would never talk to her again.

Tristan held Katie's hand as they walked down the street. "I feel like we've been here before. Me taking you home and you scared what your dad might say or do."

It was true. Last year, when her dad saw her with Tristan and found out she'd known about being a guardian, she was so scared he'd ground her and blast her memory into oblivion. That seemed like a long time ago now. Now, she knew—*her dad knew*—that grounding her or erasing her memory wasn't an option.

But kicking her out of his life was.

Tristan held on tighter. "He won't. I, on the other hand, probably have to find a new place to stay."

Katie exhaled. That had been her fault. "Lucy can't blame you for what I've done."

"I told her to give you space. I told her you were getting better because we were leaving you alone. She wanted to do an intervention, and I stopped her. I told her you'd run away and join a circus before we saw you again, and she believed me."

"A circus?"

"You weren't that far from it."

"Still. She can't put the blame on you. It's me. I'll tell them. I'll make sure they know." Her heart sped up, and she breathed heavily.

When they rounded the corner, she could see her house. No trash bags. It was one scenario she could cross off, but there were plenty more to add. Will's truck was in the driveway next to her dad's, and as they got to the house, the door opened.

"So much for any last-minute pep talks or escapes."

Her dad stood in the doorway, staring at her. Katie tried not to cry, but she could see it in his eyes. No matter what she was wearing now, he still saw the strung-out girl covered in blood.

"Stop standing on my grass and come inside." He let out a breath and nodded at Tristan. "You, too."

Katie looked at Tristan, and they started, together, inside.

"*No matter what. I'm here,*" he said to her.

Inside, Will and Lucinda were sitting on the couch, her dad in his usual chair, and there were two empty kitchen chairs waiting for them.

Katie didn't want to sit down, but she did anyway, trying not to fixate on their pulses.

"I can't say how absolutely, positively disgusted I am with the both of you." Lucinda's voice was dry, and her hands shook. "I...I've tried talking to you. I tried giving you space—I—I don't know—how could you?" Lucinda stared at Katie. "I've raised you since—how could you sneak around this whole time behind my back and not feel an ounce of guilt?"

"You don't know what she feels," Tristan said.

"Don't even start. You. *You* made me believe she needed space. That I was smothering her. You made me doubt my instinct."

"Lucy." Will's voice boomed in their living room. "This isn't about placing blame. It's about moving forward."

Her dad sighed, sitting forward in his chair. "What...what happened, Katie?"

Katie stared at her father. His voice was surprisingly calm. He looked disappointed but also determined. Not angry or done. Determined.

Katie started to shrug, but stopped. "I...I got lost." There was no point in hiding anything anymore. There was no point in sparing them the sob story or denying the pit in her heart constricting every time she thought about Larry.

"Do any of you know what it feels like—" She stopped thinking about the best way to say it. "You know when someone says *'tell me about yourself'*? Most people would tell their life story or even say their hobbies or something special about them. I'd say, *how can I tell you about someone I've never been allowed to be?*"

Everyone looked at her, probably trying to figure out how that had anything to do with her being a blood-sucking psycho.

"I don't know who I am. A few months ago, I got a glimpse into who I was, where I came from, why I am here. On this Earth. And then, right before my eyes, that answer chose a sociopathic murderer over me. I—" Her voice was getting hoarse and her vision blurred, but things were finally starting to ache the right way. Like when a bullet was yanked out. It hurt, but it was almost over.

"I know I shouldn't care because he's not my dad. But for a little while, he was *something. We* were something, we were figuring it out. You know, painting a bunch of dumb pictures, talking about my mom. I saw her. In so many different ways. Did you know she was a dancer?" Katie looked up at her dad. "She danced for a long time and...I have grandparents. I've never met them, but I know that my grandmother made me a quilt when she found out about me. He was going to bring it to me, and now I'll never know where it is. Or I'll never see the picture he promised to paint of my mother dancing. He—for a moment...sometimes he sounded like he loved me."

Katie laughed, even though she was crying. "I hated that. I hated when he did that. Made it seem like he cared. Because I could handle being weird and never really acting like family, but he'd always tell me those stupid fucking stories and, goddammit, I don't know why I even fucking care."

Tristan reached out to hold her hand, but she pulled away. She didn't want the sympathy. She was stupid. Stupid for feeling anything other than traumatized because he had the nerve to die in front of her.

"Who does that? I mean, who makes their child watch while they die? I've—as if—how could he not choose me over his batshit-crazy brother? Why do I care?" She was screaming. The pulses thumped in her mind or maybe it was her own heart beating, furious and angry—and throbbing.

"What am I going to do with for the rest of my—my *never-ending* life? No. No, I get it people die and life goes on. But my life is going to keep on going and going and I can't even see to the end of tomorrow, so how am I supposed to plan out the rest of my life?

"And then, to top it all off, he pretty much sentenced Tristan to die if anyone finds out what happened. An entire coven was left in chaos because I can't tell them that there was no suspicious activity. Do you know what it's like to know you've completely destroyed everything?"

She ran her hand over her stiff jeans and stood up. She needed to get out. This was too much. Everything was starting to look very bleak again. She was trapped. There was no out. No way out of the past that was very much still her present. Katie rubbed her arms, trying to ignore her throat.

Tristan grabbed her arm as her dad stood up and embraced her. She sobbed and fought it. She didn't want to be held, and she didn't want to be loved because she didn't deserve it. Not after everything. Not after being sad that a man who wasn't her father didn't want her. She had a dad, and she had no right to feel the way she did.

Her dad rocked her, and she lulled into a quiet sob, feeling like a stupid little girl.

Katie couldn't figure it out. It's not like she'd wanted him to love her or be her Daddy Warbucks. She hadn't wanted him to be there for her. She hadn't wanted anything from him—so why did she feel robbed? Why did she feel like something had been taken from her, like he'd taken something from her?

"I felt like that, too." Tristan's voice drifted in, and she didn't know if she wanted to hear it or not.

"He left me in that house, and for years he'd come and visit and I thought he'd stay. I didn't want a new dad. I didn't want some cozy uncle. I just…I just wanted him to stop coming and leaving. Every time he left, I felt like that stupid kid who gets jilted on his birthday. It's what he did. He was the worst kind of parental figure. It wasn't just you. I get it. I do, Katalina. I mean… he made me kill him. He could have let me stab Eshmael, but he made me stab him instead. A pureblood. He's the worst kind of selfish person I've ever met. Seriously. Look at me. I'm not the easiest person to get along with. It's probably because I grew up feeling rejected." Tristan's voice was flat, like it was something he'd accepted and spent too many emotions over.

Katie moved away from her dad, telling him repeatedly that she was okay and he needed to get away from her because she was starting to hear his pulse and all the touchy-feely crap was really sending her mind to darker places.

"Why didn't you say anything?" Lucinda asked her after a long pause.

"I don't know. I—I didn't know how. I didn't know what to say. How do you say something you don't even want to believe?"

"Well, if you'd told me, I could have helped you, Katie." Lucinda was still mad, but there were tears in her eyes and she sniffled.

"I'm sorry."

Will shifted in his seat. "What about school? Do you want to be a guardian?"

"I don't know. Not really. I don't want to be something that doesn't even accept me."

"Katie," Will said. "I'll fight for whatever you want to do. Not everyone is like Jim."

"What if I don't want to fight? I'm so tired and numb. I just want to be free of it all." She didn't know what she meant, but Tristan seemed to.

"I'm withdrawing from school," he said.

"Tristan!" Lucinda scolded.

"I never planned on finishing. I was just going to stay long enough to help Katalina. She was pathetic when I met her. No offense."

"Thanks."

"And just what do you plan on doing?" Lucinda looked like she was going to lose her mind, but Katie's dad didn't look surprised.

Will spoke next, cutting Tristan off. "That's probably best. We'll find you a school in Gray City."

"I've already finished high school."

Everyone looked up except Katie. They still didn't know that he'd been a Death Dealer. It was a secret she'd kept for him because she didn't want them knowing just how dark Tristan's past had been.

"How? You *lied* to me?" Lucinda laughed. "Why am I surprised?"

"Went to the Academy—look, it doesn't matter."

"Yes, it does," Lucinda fought back.

"It doesn't! You're just going to yell at me. If I told you I'd been to space and solved world starvation, you'd yell at me."

"That's not fair, Tristan. This is what you do. You lie to me. You've lied about going to Gray City, about Katie needing space. You've lied about sneaking out at night to see Katie after I forbade you two from seeing each other without supervision."

Katie's dad looked up. "What? What were you two—why am I even surprised?"

"We weren't having sex," Katie said, exasperated. "We were practicing in the backyard."

Her dad eyed Tristan. "Yeah, I practiced once."

"If I wanted to bone your daughter, I'd have done it by now," Tristan spat. Katie could feel his anger rising. He was always the subject of blame and anger. Her dad stood up quicker than she'd ever seen.

"Stop," Katie said as Lucinda geared up for lecture mode. "This is what has been driving me crazy. God, what did you think I did at night? Sleep? Why can't we train? Why can't we be *trusted* not to have sex? Why can't I be trusted to do anything? I've had to sneak around doing everything I've wanted to do because no one cares about what *I* want." Katie was trying to catch her breath and ignore the growing pulses. She was even hearing the neighbors now.

"Because when I give you a little room to breathe, you go out and get yourself addicted to the local street drug," Lucinda snapped.

Katie felt the sting. She was right.

Will cut Lucinda a look. "That's not even remotely fair."

But it was, wasn't it? She was the worst of the worst. She got an inch, and she took the whole damn Grand Canyon. And now she was on the set of an intervention, crying about her daddy who didn't love her.

The throbbing pulses were driving her insane. How had she ever found it comforting?

Tristan stood up and grabbed Katie's hand.

"Sit down!" Lucinda yelled.

"Where the hell are you going?" her dad growled.

"Tristan?" Will boomed.

"If you could hear what she was thinking, you'd back the fuck off." Tristan was losing it. Katie hated that. He was never like this. Another thing she was responsible for.

"Don't talk to me like that!" Lucinda yelled.

Will put a hand on Lucinda's arm as Tristan gently shook Katie. "Stop. Stop blaming yourself for everything. Yes, you fucked up, but what I do is on me. Got it?"

"Just sit back down." Her dad held his head like he was getting a massive migraine. Katie could empathize.

Tristan sat down, but he didn't let go of Katie's hand until she reassured him she was fine.

"God, of all the things… A boy who not only steals my daughter in the night but can hear her thoughts. This is too much. I can only handle one thing at a time." Her dad stared at the ceiling and leaned back in his chair.

"It's not like that's news, and I'm not getting stolen in the night. I'm a person with my own mind and my own feelings. Stop treating Tristan like some criminal. I asked him to come. He lied because Lucinda can't handle the truth. None of you can."

"I can't handle the truth?" Lucinda laughed, standing up. "This is beyond ridiculous. What is the point of me being here if you aren't willing to accept any responsibility and stop blaming everyone else for your problems?"

Katie sat, dumbfounded. Lucinda searched around for her purse and rattled off about how Katie needed to grow up and how she couldn't be trusted. Katie had never blamed anyone for anything. In fact she had tried to handle things on her own.

"Lucy, you're not helping," her dad said.

"No one can help anyone who doesn't want to be helped."

"I'm here, aren't I?" Katie yelled. Why? Why was Lucinda of all people making her feel worse than she already did?

Lucinda shook her head and put on her jacket. She looked up, and her eyes landed on Tristan, who was holding back a slew of curse words and trying to think past his own anger. "Find somewhere else to sleep tonight. I don't want to see your face or hear any more of your lies."

Will hissed. "Enough, Lucy."

Lucinda stormed out of the house without another word.

Katie sat in her chair, trying to figure out what she had done wrong—besides bottling up her emotions and resorting to being a junkie to cope. She was here looking for help, facing it, owning it…and now she felt stupid.

"Don't," Tristan said to her, still fuming in his anger.

"I'm sorry, Katie." Will shook his head. "She's just upset. That's not how we feel."

Tristan rolled his eyes.

Katie nodded, but inside she felt the mix of guilt and anger building up again.

"Looks like you and me are walking home," Will said to Tristan. "And I'm probably going to have to make my own dinner."

"You heard her," Tristan said. Under the anger, the disappointment and hurt spilled out from his mind to Katie's.

"She's in a mood. You heard her kick Brian out three times in the last month for not cleaning his room."

"I'm not her son."

"But you are *our* family," Will said. For something that was supposed to be a good thing, it sounded more like Will was laying down the law.

Tristan and Will locked eyes, and Tristan conceded with his silence.

"I don't know about you—" Will looked at her dad "—but I'm starving. Pizza?"

"Can't you eat at your own house?" her dad asked. It was mean, but she could tell he was complaining to complain, not because he wanted them to leave.

"You met my wife? She's probably burning my favorite shirt because I didn't back her up."

Her dad laughed. "We're not getting anything with that bell pepper and broccoli crap you like."

"Let a dead dog die, Drew. That was ten years ago and I only got it once."

They went on back and forth until Will called and ordered a pizza and Katie and Tristan were able to slip out of the room.

"Katie," her dad called. "This isn't over."

"I know," she said, glad to be able to walk away for a moment. She was already in need of another drink. It had been like this for the last three days they'd spent at Larry's manor. She'd never drank so much blood in her life as she had in the last few days. Then again she'd never puked up as much blood as she had in the last few days, either.

"It's going to get better." Tristan rubbed her back as she opened the refrigerator. She had to dig into the very bottom to find the pack. Her dad always moved them back there if he saw them.

"Does it?" Katie was tired of waiting for things to get better. Always waiting. She was stuck in this waiting place.

"I don't know." He was getting aggravated. "What do you want me to say?"

"You don't have to say anything. I don't need you to say anything. Just be here."

"I am."

"I know. I'm not saying you aren't."

"Sounds like it."

"No. I'm—why are you picking a fight? Why is everything a fight?"

Tristan rolled his eyes and sighed.

"Seriously?" Katie was doing everything in her power not to focus on the pulses throbbing and banging around in her head. She just wanted to drink and puke up her disgusting pack of blood in peace. The throbbing, the yelling, the passive-aggressive jabs—they weren't helping.

"I'm trying," Tristan said between his teeth.

"I know. Thank you. Thank you for trying." Katie was trying to offer peace. She was begging for it.

She could feel Tristan's anger building up, and as she caught a snippet of it, he pulled his thoughts away. What could she do? She knew she deserved it. There was nothing left to say. Sorry wasn't worth anything these days.

"You have the SA meeting tomorrow, right?" he said, changing the subject.

"Yup. West texted me the address."

"Do you need a ride?"

"What SA meeting?" her dad said, walking into the kitchen and grabbing two sodas from the fridge.

"Sourcers Anonymous. I—I have to go." She didn't know how she was going to explain she bit a guy and it was either go to this meeting or be arrested for real.

"Oh." He nodded. "I was reading about some of those."

Katie hoped he didn't see her surprised face.

"What—did you think I just came home and sat here waiting for you to waltz in and everything would be fine? I know what having to go to detox means. You changed and you couldn't change back. You got lost in blood lust. We're lucky you didn't kill anyone. If you had… Anyway, I got some information from a friend I used to work with. He found me a list of places that do meetings. I'm glad you're set up. I'll take you." He looked at Tristan pointedly and then sighed like his headache was back again.

Will and Tristan left before the sun sunk deep into the earth. Katie told Tristan she'd call him after the meeting to let him know how it went. The truth was, he looked relieved. He looked like he was getting a break from her crazy and she didn't blame him.

She envied him.

❧ 11 ❧

ZURI

KATIE'S DAD NOT only dropped her at the meeting, he went inside and spoke to West. Katie was surprised at how taken her dad became with West after only ten minutes. Then again, West had the strange charm of a used car salesmen. After they exchanged numbers and West promised to keep him updated on Katie's progress, her dad left and the meeting began.

Katie didn't know what was worse—that SA was exactly as she imagined or that West volunteered her to share her story first thing.

She sat up in her chair, staring at the circle of people looking at her. It was a small group of eight people—vampires. At the head, if a circle could have a head, was a hipster wannabe in a Rastafarian hat with fake dreads. When Katie first came in, he'd offered her a drink and a rubber bracelet that said: *"I am not my past."* She'd taken both, wishing that instead of blood there was enough alcohol in the cup to help her forget the humiliation she was up for.

When she sat down and West nominated her to share first, she knew exactly what he was doing:

Rule Number Three: Deal With It

She cleared her throat as the others waited for her to speak.

"If you're not gonna talk, Barbie, I've got baggage I need to unload." A skinny guy with thick glasses and a Hitler-mustache scowled.

"Remember, this is a place where sharing is caring. And where caring is listening to others sharing," said the group leader. His smile stretched across his long face, and he held a clipboard close to his chest. "Go ahead…" He paused, looking down at the clipboard and frowned. "…you didn't write your name, sunshine."

Katie looked at West. This was SA? This crowd? How could she share her lot with this crowd of crazies?

"Kat—Kat," she said when West offered no help.

"Okay, Kat. Share. Anything you want. It can be about what brought you here, how you're feeling right now, or even something you've written—like a poem. You look like the poetry type."

Katie blinked. *Barbie. Sunshine. Poetry.* What she thought

was that they were a bunch of judgy weirdos, but she held her tongue and took a deep breath.

"I have a sourcing addition. I did it a few times, got addicted, nearly killed a man, then tried to kill my boyfriend while detoxing, and now I'm here."

They all stared at her, wide-eyed.

"This chick's crazy," said a girl with orange bangs.

"Shouldn't she be locked up or serving time?" Hitler-Stache said, a little bug-eyed.

"I don't feel safe." A porky woman frowned before eyeing up West and flashing a toothy grin.

He smiled back and winked.

"It's not like I'd eat you." Katie was confused and feeling like West had placed her in the wrong group.

"Bitch," Porky spat.

"Settle down. Calm down. When you're feeling mad, like you wanna yell, take a deep breathe! And ring a bell!" Rasta reached behind him and rang a small bell. "Time out, said the kitty."

Katie side-eyed West. "Seriously?"

"They'll grow on you." He stretched back in his chair. "Speaking of kitty, what happened to your cat, Elma?"

A girl with big eyes and a black bob looked at West. "He… ran away."

The group groaned in unison. "You can't keep eating cats, Elma, it's not right," said Hitler-Stache.

Porky, siting next to Elma, rubbed her back. "Honey, you've got to get a grip. That's the third cat this month."

"I know. I know. I just really like petting their fur when I feel anxious…but the last one didn't like being pet and he scratched me and—I got angry—I put him in a shoebox in my closet. I'm scared my landlord will find out…again."

Katie didn't realize her mouth was open until West closed it. She sat in awe and silence at the dysfunction in the group. Porky had taken to eating steaks raw, and they'd caused her to bloat to a horridly unhealthy size. Hitler-Stache was in love with a guy he used to source and had now taken to writing angry hate poetry to express his feelings—except it was full of a lot of graphic sex. The girl with orange hair didn't really have a sourcing problem as much as she liked getting humans to let her bite them in inappropriate places, which creeped out the people at some sourcing establishments, getting her banned. And one guy in particular sat on the other side of Katie and stared at her the whole time. West explained, during one of Hitler-Stache's epic poems, that the guy hates change and would stop staring once he was used to her.

Sooner than Katie expected, the hour was up. She got up to leave, but Rasta wanted them to hold hands and read one of the motivational posters on the wall: *"Feel blue? Use a tissue! Feel mad? Dance till you're glad! Feel a rumble in your tummy? Reach for the rummy, then grab a glass and swig with sass."*

Katie left as soon as the chanting was over. She'd gotten a text from her dad asking if she was okay to walk home—he'd gotten tied up in "business," whatever that meant—so she waited outside for West.

"That was some looney shit, West." Katie put her hands in her sweater pocket and took in the street noise. A group of guys walked by, laughing as they jay-walked across the street.

"Yeah, they're all pretty fucked up. They've all been kicked out of the regular groups."

"Why didn't you sign me up for a regular group? I'm not crazy—what? I'm not."

West laughed. "Not like Elma, no. But they'll accept you here. The other groups won't."

"How do you know that?"

West looked her dead in the face. "Because you fucked up a guy's life and didn't have to serve any time for it. You're lucky no one in this group will report you."

Katie panicked. She'd *told* them. Maybe she could backtrack and lie… "How do you know they won't?"

"Kat. Elma eats cats. I think Roger used to feed on corpses at the local hospital before he got caught. They're crazy. They've all got shit to hide."

"Who's Roger?" Katie thought of the guy sitting next to her.

"The group leader. The one with the Rastafarian hat."

Katie could do nothing but blink.

"What are you doing after this?" he asked.

"Going—nothing." It wasn't a lie. She'd told Tristan not to come by her house after. She didn't know what it would be like and didn't want him thinking he had to pick up her pieces.

"Come on, then," West said, putting his arm around her shoulder.

Katie shrugged it off.

He put it back. "Don't worry, I'm not hitting on you. I only do that when Tristan is around. *We've* committed a crime. We're friends now."

Katie frowned. "After what I've done, my dad isn't keen on me being anywhere besides school or SA."

West smiled, showing a row of milk-white teeth. "Don't worry about Dad. I sent him a line."

"Don't call him *Dad.*" Katie shrugged off his arm again. "Where are we going?"

"To meet some more friends, grab a drink, get our mind off of the one thing we aren't supposed to fixate on."

Rule Number Four: Fuck the Pity Party

They walked out of the vampire district and into the Burrow, where all species mixed and melted. West checked his phone and grabbed Katie as she walked past the door to a restaurant.

"We're going in here."

It was a Bohemian nook, packed with bodies and chatter. Eclectic centerpieces embellished small tables, and thick red and purple curtains hung over the windows and walls. Spices and thick sauces wafted and filled her nose.

West led her to a table in the far back where small floor tables were surrounded by pallets covered in multicolored pillows.

Katie saw the girl before she even knew West was taking her to that exact table. She was hard to miss—lithe, and built like a dancer with a small round face and short, bright silver hair. Her eyes found West before they landed on Katie. The girl smiled wide and waved them over.

"Guys, West has a date," She said in a voice way too loud for her body.

West grunted.

There were two other people at the table. A guy and a girl. Dark black hair, brown skin, dark lashes. They looked too similar not to be related.

"Make room, Salem, so I can hit on your sister," said West.

The boy ignored him and grabbed a menu. His sister laughed, shooing West away.

"Who's your date?" the silver-haired girl asked.

"She's not my date. She's my new partner in crime."

The girl frowned. "I've been replaced."

"Snooze, you lose, babe." West gestured for Katie to take a seat next to Salem, the black-haired boy, as he sat next to Silver Hair. "This is Kat. Kat, that's Salem, Mariam, and the cheeky one is Zuri."

Katie remembered the name. "Hi." She felt like a new kid at school. She wished she'd done more than throw her hair into a lopsided bun.

The siblings mumbled over their menus, and Zuri watched her, smiling. Her eyes were big and wild, and something felt off about her. Her smell. Katie could tell the boy and girl were werewolves. Something about them smelled…wild, like the river in spring. But this girl… Katie couldn't figure it out. She had a pulse, but it was mute and uninteresting—mysteriously inhuman.

Zuri smirked. "You look like trouble."

Katie half-laughed. "That's all I've been lately."

"Can I read your palm?" She grabbed Katie's hand as if her question was more of a statement.

Katie felt oddly okay with this bizarre girl running her perfect finger over the lines on her palm.

"You're…" She stopped and gave Katie her palm back. "Interesting." Zuri picked up a menu and browsed over it with the same intensity.

Katie looked at West and then Zuri and back at West, then the menu. What was she doing here?

"Zuri's a witch," said West. "Like most witches, she's coy and you never know what's brewing behind those eyes."

Katie tried to look nonchalant. She didn't want them knowing she'd never known witches existed.

The waiter came over with his pad and pencil. "What you chumps want this time? You're new." He looked Katie over and scribbled on his pad. "Let me guess—a glass of A-negative with a shot of B on the side?"

Katie hadn't even brought money. "Uh—I'm fine."

"O-negative," said West. "Straight, don't add shit to it. I'll take AB."

"O-negative. Spending that fancy money and she's not putting out?" Zuri looked between them over her menu.

"What can I say? I'm trying to make a good impression." West leaned back against the wall.

The waiter wrote down Salem's and Mariam's lamb—lightly warmed—and Zuri's Cesar salad. Katie watched them talk and banter back and forth. When the food came, Katie cupped her glass between her hands, unsure if she should subject these people to her gags in-between chugs.

West nudged her. "Rule number five, kid."

Katie looked at him, skeptical.

Rule Number Five: Fine Dine. Don't Drink That Shit From a Bag.

West had told her before that drinking blood from the banks was like eating meat from a can. *"Just because that shit says blood doesn't mean you should drink it."*

Katie gripped the cup and sipped. It—it wasn't that bad, but it wasn't that good either. It was like craving a fruit smoothie and getting hit in the face with kale and carrots. She was sure, however, that it was better than the packets she'd been drinking. After the third or fourth sip she realized that, for the first time in a while, her throat eased.

"All food is not created equal." West grabbed his glass and swigged it down in one go.

"No, it's not." Mariam pushed away her plate of pink lamb. It glistened with red blood.

Katie frowned, smelling the cooked blood.

Mariam pulled out a notebook and started writing.

Salem grabbed his own. "It's not that bad. But I like the idea of the rub they put on it. Maybe something not so tangy."

"The tangy has got to go. I'm thinking something more basic, letting the natural flavor pop. And a side. We need a side, even if it's just for looks." Mariam scribbled wildly, her straight black hair moving with her head like a silk sheet.

"That's a waste of money," Salem said. He side-eyed Katie. Katie looked away, embarrassed but not sure why. She hoped she wouldn't be known as the weirdo girl with a staring problem.

"They're opening a restaurant," Zuri said, picking out the sandwich-sliced tomatoes from her salad. "My Cesar is missing the Cesar. I just have…olive oil. How does this place stay in business?"

"Atmosphere," both Salem and Mariam said, without looking up from their notebooks.

"How's your O-negative?" Mariam asked.

Katie looked at her, confused. "Bloody?"

Salem looked at Katie through his dark lashes. "Is that a joke?"

"I don't know. It takes like…well, cardboard cereal with a lot of sugar. You know, so you don't notice it's cardboard until the aftertaste."

Everyone looked at her.

"I paid top dollar for that," West feigned outrage.

Mariam took Katie's half-full glass and dipped her finger in Zuri's olive oil and tomato Caesar-less salad. She delicately ran her finger around the rim of the glass. She grabbed the salt shaker from the middle of the table and tilted the glass, rotating it as she sprinkled salt on the rim. "Try it now."

Katie took the glass back, skeptical about putting her mouth on anything someone had rubbed their fingers all over.

When in Rome, she thought, bringing the glass to her lips and giving it a go. The salt mixed with the olive oil and hit her tongue first. When the O-negative followed, she was flashed back to the first time she'd put her mouth on someone's skin. A slight oily salty mix before the warm blood. It was gone as soon as it flashed before her, but she held on to that second, savoring it before the guilt and stale aftertaste settled in.

Katie cleared her throat. "Much better," she said, not wanting to give away her thoughts.

Mariam smiled and scribbled down more notes.

"They want to start the greatest fusion restaurant in Gray City. I think they're going to be the best in the country." Zuri smiled, her teeth big and white. Zuri had strange features. Her head looked a little big for her size, her eyes were large and round, and her mouth seemed small but her teeth big. All abnormal features but—uniquely beautiful. Mariam, like Salem, was the opposite. They were perfectly symmetrical, though Salem's short hair was much thicker than Mariam's. A thickness Katie would have both loved and hated.

"That's the best blood I've had not from a—" Katie stopped, embarrassed. She could feel her cheeks burning.

"I'm hoping to recreate the sensation of getting it from the source," Mariam said. "You'll have to be my guinea pig. West is horrible at describing taste. Everything is either 'good' or 'shit' with him."

West rolled his eyes, but he was watching Zuri and poking her under the table.

An hour rolled by, and Katie found herself laughing and opening up and telling them about how she had no idea what she was doing with her life. How everything seemed to come to a halt and she was living day-by-day.

"I don't know what that's like." Salem offered Katie a pen and paper. They had started playing a game, and it was her turn to draw something based on a word he'd written in the corner: *clown*. The image was supposed to represent the word without being a direct or obvious representation.

Salem continued, "I've always known I wanted to cook. My dad really wanted us to have a passion. I guess we're lucky." He watched her sketch and laughed when he recognized a compass with only the letter *W* drawn boldly. "Nailed it."

Katie wrote the word *passion* and passed it to West. He scowled at her interpretation of clown and gave her the finger.

"I'm surprised." Zuri cocked her head. "You have such a set path. I would have thought you were the planned-out type."

Katie laughed. "A set path? Never. It's worse now. Everything in my life since last year has been…" She wanted to say a mess, but Tristan popped into her mind and despite all the chaos, she felt right. She laughed again and settled on one word. "Weird. Why do you say that?"

"Your palm. It's all there."

"Well, it's wrong." Katie looked at her own hands as if the lines would rearrange themselves into words and spell out the answers to her questions.

"It's never wrong."

"Zuri thinks she's psychic." Salem rolled his eyes. "Don't let her fool you. She's only good at casting and potions. She told me when I first met her that I would die two days later. That was three years ago."

"So I'm sketchy." Zuri stood up and moved West to her seat so she could sit next to Katie. "Give me your head."

"What?" Katie glanced around, nervous, but everyone's eyes said they'd seen this before and it was nothing to take serious.

Zuri placed her fingers on Katie's temple and closed her eyes, breathing deep. "This might pinch a little."

Katie flinched at the pressure Zuri's tiny fingers inflicted. "How can someone so small cause so much—"

"Ruckus? It's one of her many charms," West said, still sketching in the notebook. Katie could make out two bodies intermingled as one. He was a good artist. Maybe too good.

Katie flinched again. It was strange. Like she could feel Zuri in her mind, digging and pulling and—

"Ouch!" Katie pulled away.

"Oh my stars." Zuri looked at her hands.

Mariam tilted her head concerned. "Are you all right, Kat?"

Katie nodded, but it was a lie. Her head hurt.

"You. Holy stars. *You?*" Zuri's eyes widened, and then she looked away.

"What this time? Will she drown in a puddle of water or turn into a mermaid?" Salem took a drink from his glass of water.

"No. I—I don't know. I'm sorry, are you okay?" Zuri massaged Katie's temple, but avoided eye contact.

Katie started to ask Zuri what she'd seen and what she meant, but Zuri shook her head.

"It was nothing. I just wanted it to sound mysterious." She smiled, but Katie knew that Zuri had reached something deep in her mind because it was burning and sending tingles down her body.

Katie left it alone, but everyone else goaded Zuri until she stuck out her tongue.

West lifted his head. "Your psychic powers are piss-poor. I think some humans are more intune than you."

"I know you'll be alone until you die," Zuri snapped back.

He frowned. "Funny, babe. Real funny."

"Anyway, the thing about readings is they can easily change. What someone might have read once can change in the future." She looked at West. "It's not set in stone any more than a person's choice to be who they want to be is set in stone."

West dropped the notebook in front of Zuri and stood up.

"I'm going to take a piss."

"Classy," Zuri shot at him.

Katie looked down at his drawing. It was graphic—a naked man and a woman linked together in the throes of passion. They were staring into each other's eyes, and it looked blissful. It also—Katie leaned in—looked like Zuri and the guy could have probably passed as—well, with the rippling muscles and all, it looked like a *wishful* West.

Zuri grabbed the notebook and covered it, but not before Katie saw the word scribbled on the corner: *heartbreak.*

◦◦◦

The atmosphere was back to its light and fun banter by the time West came back. Katie looked at her phone, and her heart panicked a little. It was already eight. Her dad would be home by ten-thirty and no doubt would expect her there. Or maybe he didn't. Maybe he'd given up on her and didn't expect anything. Either way, she wanted to show him that she would never be the girl he left in front of Hill Crest Manor ever again.

"Need a ride?" West offered as she excused herself. Katie declined and nearly bumped into the waiter as she turned around.

"I hope you're all leaving. Order something or get out, leeches." He put his hand on his hip and spun away.

"Put something good on the menu and I will," Zuri called after him. The waiter patted his butt and blew Zuri a kiss. "What are you doing this weekend?"

Katie looked behind her, but realized Zuri was talking to her.

"Oh, um…nothing." Her life *really* was empty.

"Come with us to the Festival of Lights tomorrow. We're going around noon."

Katie looked around the table. She didn't expect their faces to be as inviting as they were. Her eyes burned. She nodded, afraid that saying anything would bring on the waterworks. She felt so stupid. If she cried in front of these people, they'd realize that she was a crazy.

Katie nodded. "Okay."

Zuri took Katie's phone from her pocket and sent herself

a text message. This girl really had no boundaries. Katie didn't mind; it was better to have someone intrude than to make the first step.

Zuri smiled. "I'll send you the details when I get home."

Katie took her phone, smiling back.

It was a silly thing to feel wanted.

She waved and rushed out of the restaurant before her face gave her away.

12

FESTIVAL OF LIGHTS

IT WASN'T A long walk home, but she had to run halfway to get there before eight-thirty. Her heart sank when she saw her dad's truck in the driveway.

He was sitting in the kitchen when she walked in. A pile of brochures and papers covered the table, and he hunched over them with his reading glasses. His hair was neater than usual, and he wasn't wearing his work clothes. Instead, he had on a pair of his nicer slacks and a button-up shirt. He looked up and did a double-take when he saw her.

"Hey." He put down one of the papers. "Come sit down. How was...the meeting?"

"Interesting." Katie thought it better to leave out the details.

"That's better than nothing." He smiled.

Katie had half-expected him to be distant, like he usually was when he was disappointed. Something other than *this*. She looked down at the table and glanced over the brochures. They were full of kids reading books and smiling. They were school brochures.

"After I dropped you off, I visited a few schools in Gray City. I think…I think a lot of this is my fault."

Katie shook her head.

"Let me talk." Her dad held up his hand. "I'm the parent. You're my responsibility, and I let you down. I kept you at Hamilton, thinking you'd finish out and do what? I've ignored everything about who you are for a long time. I mean, sometimes I'd get takeout and it wasn't until I was here unpacking the boxes that I realized you can't eat any of it. I'm still buying you cocoa puff cereal. This problem started here because I couldn't accept that you'd changed."

Katie stared at the table, not seeing anything really.

"It was a red flag when you were skipping school. Anyone could see you weren't dealing with what happened to… Lawrence. I guess I just wanted you to be a regular kid, rebelling like kids do. I didn't see… I *believed* you didn't need help. I'm sorry for that." Her dad cleared his throat and picked up one of the brochures. "I think it's time we look at your options. I've got to say, you have many. You can go to a regular public school and finish out the year. You can enroll in a school for vampires only. Here is a mixed school for vampires and werewolves and…it says *other* but I have no idea what that means."

Katie looked at the one her dad held. In bold letters it said vampires, werewolves and witches.

"It says witches, Dad."

"What?" he said, looking at her, confused.

"*Witches.*"

Her dad stared as if he couldn't make out her words. "Yeah, others. Maybe it means half like you and...the boy." He rolled his eyes at the thought of Tristan.

Katie blinked. Had he really not understood her? Could he not see the word printed in bold letters?

"This one has optional boarding. I don't know about that. Coeds mingling in the middle of the night."

"Jesus, Dad." Katie laughed and picked up the one for vampires only. They were talking and it was calm—they were really talking. Something they hadn't done in a long time.

"That vampire one you have looks kind of intensive. Could be a good option because you have a lot of time and you *have* missed a lot of school lately..."

It was called Camden Academy, and it was strictly a boarding school with no option to go home on the weekdays. They looked it over together and found out it was a six-month program. A school day lasted twelve hours, four days a week.

"Well, that's out of the question." Katie tossed the brochure in the pile.

He smirked. "You know, you could do with a new attitude toward academics."

"Or I could pick a school that won't kill me." She picked up the mixed school: Burberry Contemporary School of Arts and Science. Something about it really intrigued her. Going to school with people who were all different. No one would think anything of her.

"So you like this idea?" Her dad said, peeking over his glasses.

"I do," Katie said honestly. Hope glimmered in her. The new possibilities opened in front of her.

Her dad moved the papers and found the matching catalogue to the brochure she had. He flipped through the pages. "They have a tour on Sunday. You want to check it out?"

Katie nodded as that hope opened up wider. Her dad found a twenty-four-hour line and made an appointment for Sunday morning. The cost of the school was less than Hamilton High, and he hooted how that alone made it better than Hamilton.

They looked over the courses offered, and Katie took the catalogue to her room when her dad turned in for the night. She lay on her bed and read every word. Even though the school was mixed, there was a different track for witches. They had more specific classes on witchcraft.

Katie had no idea what she'd do, but she knew she'd rather do it at *this* school than at Hamilton—or for twelve hours a day at Camden Academy.

Katie rolled to the edge of her bed and grabbed her phone. She scrolled to Tristan's name in her call log. Her finger hovered over it before she locked the screen and put it back on her night stand. She hadn't talked to him since yesterday. How could she call him now and tell him that today had been a good day? A day without him there to help had been the best day she'd had in weeks. Guilt swelled up in her like a balloon, threatening to burst and spill out its poison.

How could she call him and tell him the idea he had two months ago, that she turned away and all but spat on, was now a glimmer of hope on her long dark road to recovery?

If he called or came to see her, she'd tell him.

.ↄℓℐↄ.

He didn't.

By the next morning all she'd gotten was a shout goodbye from her dad and a text from Zuri with a thousand emojis and a meet-up location for eleven-thirty. Katie changed her clothes three different times, trying to figure out what anyone would wear to a festival of lights. She gave up trying to look cool and nonchalant and threw on a knee-length white corded sweater that used to be a dress four years ago and the only flats she had without holes. She closed her closet door, hating that she needed to go shopping and hating that she knew she wouldn't.

Shopping was a thing her and Allison did together. Allison knew what was a good buy and what would fall apart in the machine after the first wash. Allison knew it all, and Allison was gone. Katie didn't need a shopping trip to rub that in her face.

She pulled her hair into a neat ponytail and grabbed her only purse, a cute brown leather satchel Allison got her last Christmas, and threw her phone and wallet inside. She pulled her wallet out again and opened it.

A card fell out.

The one with Portia's number and the names of three different sourcing spas. Katie grabbed it, acutely aware of the pulses she'd been hearing since last night. The neighbors. All ten of them beating healthy and strong. Not counting the fat cat across the street. Katie grabbed the necklace West gave her. It never left her neck, and she embraced the slow burn, thinking of Elma and wondering if she'd eaten anymore cats.

Katie breathed until the pulses were back to their normal murmur. She ripped the card in fours and ran to the bathroom. She felt disgusted that, even now, a piece of her hesitated before throwing the pieces into the toilet. She could actually see herself taping them back together.

She flushed.

"One day at a time," she said, leaving to grab the house keys.

When she got downstairs, the doorbell rang.

Tristan was already sitting on the front step when she opened the door. He looked at her silent. Obviously silent.

She smiled. "The Wall. That's original."

"You never called." He stared straight ahead at a fat calico cat lounging on the neighbor's porch.

"Neither did you."

"I didn't know you wanted me to."

"I wanted you to want to." Katie was surprised at her honesty. She felt a flash of his annoyance. "What do you want, Tristan?"

"Really?" He stood up, shoving his hands in his pockets, still not looking at her.

"You came all the way here to ask why I didn't call? You could have called me for that."

"Or you could have called."

"Why are we fighting?" Katie closed her eyes, settling the anger building up inside of her. The guilt.

"I'm not fighting with you." He said it more as a statement than a response.

Katie let silence settle in before deciding her next move. "SA was okay."

"That's it?"

"West said I'm not supposed to talk about it to people outside the group."

Tristan rolled his eyes. "Yeah, I guess that's fair. It *is* anonymous."

Katie wanted to move in and hug him like everything was all right between them. But it wasn't. He wasn't saying it and neither was she.

"Where are you going?"

"Stalker," she teased, desperately wanting for it to be all right.

Tristan moved in and kissed her. It was soft. "It *is* all right," he said, but she could see him convincing himself behind his eyes—or maybe he just wanted to convince her.

"I'm going to the Festival of Lights. With—"

"Really? With him? Katalina…"

She'd never seen Tristan like this before. Jealous, and over nothing.

"I'm not jealous. I'm annoyed. He's weaseling his way into everything."

"He didn't invite me. He's just going to be there with the people who invited me."

"Now you're hanging out with him *and* his friends?"

"Whatever. Stand here and sulk or come with me. I'm going to go see some lights—or whatever is at a festival called *the Festival of Lights*." Katie left Tristan standing on the porch. She was going to be late if she didn't get going.

He jogged behind her and pulled her around, kissing her again, but harder. She felt this one in the pit of her stomach. One kiss, then another—and another. Her sane self knew they were starting to border on indecent, but the part of her that he completely possessed with his touch wanted nothing but to turn back to her house and melt into him.

But in the back of her mind, she heard another voice:

Rule Number Six: Stay Away From That Bitch, Temptation. She'll Fuck You.

She knew this didn't count, but as soon as the voice was in her head, Tristan pulled away.

"Seriously?"

Katie gaped, speechless.

"Buzzkill, Katalina. Good God. West can go fuck himself."

"I don't know why I thought that. It just popped in my head—"

"Nope. Nope. Let's go." He grabbed Katie's hand, and they walked to the city.

He relaxed a bit, and Katie told him the meet-up location. She snuck in a text to Zuri, asking if it was okay if she brought someone. Zuri respond with another obscene amount of emojis and a single letter: *K*!

They took an elevator she'd never been through before. It was in the back of a pet shop, and she thought of Elma again.

"Who's that?"

"A girl in my group."

"The one who eats cats?"

"Tristan!" Katie cursed herself.

"You thought it."

Katie punched him in the arm, and a bunch of parakeets fluttered in their cages. They went to a door marked with a hazard sign, and one of the assistants unlocked it after Tristan paid him ten dollars.

"Was that a bribe?"

"No, some elevators cost money. The ones on the streets are free, but the ones inside of shops usually cost. This one is expensive because it's in the middle of downtown."

Katie nodded. She wondered if the ice cream shop had an elevator.

"If I remember correctly, it does. They make a lot of money. This one probably gets hundreds of customers a day."

They rode down and found the meeting spot between a frozen yogurt shop and a gaming center. The Arcade stood four stories tall; the noise and flashing lights filled up the entire street. She expected to see only kids, but most of the people in it were adults.

"That's not an arcade. It's a casino."

"Tristan." Katie shook her head. "That's a basketball hoop. And there is air hokey and—slot machines?"

"Yeah, where else would you see an old lady with a bucket full of coins?" He pointed to a row of them—old women with little buckets filled to the brim.

A familiar voice sliced through the noise. "Look what the Kat dragged in." West laughed at himself.

Katie turned to see West and Zuri. Their arms were locked, and Zuri waved at Katie. They both seemed to have a bounce in their step.

Tristan side-eyed Katie. *"Pervert."*

"That is not where I was going with that," Katie retorted, waving back and genuinely glad to see Zuri. Something about her made Katie feel…good.

Tristan turned back to the casino, ignoring both of them. Katie blushed. He was so embarrassing.

"Always uncomfortable seeing you, Tristan," Zuri said, leaving West to link arms with Katie. "You're soft." She rubbed her face against Katie's sweater.

"Thanks?" Katie was caught between feeling uncomfortable, and yet like it was an opportunity to break away from who she had been. "You're sparkly."

She smiled. "Just for you. I sparkle just for you."

"We had the best time with Kat last night," West said in his usual insinuative voice.

"I bet. It's hard not to." Tristan still pretended to be interested in the casino.

"You come to kill the fun?" West shoved his hands in his pockets like Katie had seen Tristan do a million times.

"Only if you think a punch in the face kills the fun."

"Fuck you." West stared at the casino, too.

"They're like girls." Zuri scrunched up her face. "Vulgar, big-headed girls."

Katie laughed. It was true. There was a lot of history swirling around them, and Katie didn't know if she'd ever get to the bottom of it—or if she even wanted to.

"Mariam," Zuri shouted, waving to Mariam and Salem. Katie joined in the waving as Mariam and Salem jogged across the street to meet them.

Salem's eyes lit up when he saw Tristan. "Hey, T."

Tristan turned around, and a smile crossed his face. The kind where his teeth showed and his eyes creased. They did a weird handshake-hug combo and talked over each other.

Salem introduced his sister, and Tristan nodded and asked how he was, to which Salem rattled off a few words mixed with profanities. When he reciprocated the question, Tristan answered similarly.

Katie had never seen Tristan shake a guy's hand before, let alone hug one. In fact, she'd never seen him with friends. It was slightly unsettling—and amusing.

West rolled his eyes. "Can we go already?"

"Don't be so sore." Salem hit West in the arm.

The three walked off, talking fast, leaving the girls to catch up.

"Is that what we look like?" Mariam asked.

"Only if there's a classy version." Zuri linked Mariam's other arm, and they started down the street.

The Festival of Lights, according to Zuri and Mariam, was a once-a-year event for only two days. The biggest park in the city was decorated and bewitched with light shows.

"Different sections are sponsored and decorated by different sects of witches. I did one with the chick who lives across from me. Nutty as a screw, but she's got an eye for things. You'll have to guess which it is," Zuri said.

As they neared the park, Katie could see the glow rising to the top of Gray City. The street lights were off, but the streets here shined brighter. Katie thought she felt the warmth of the sun.

As they neared the entrance, they pulled out their wallets, but Zuri and Katie found out they'd been paid for. Mariam rolled her eyes. "I need a boyfriend."

Zuri laughed and opened her wallet. "Call me Zurich," she said in a deep voice.

Katie opened hers, too, and pulled out five dollars. "You can call me whatever you want. Just be gentle."

Mariam smiled and took their money. "I'll take you two over any of the guys my dad has lined up."

Zuri and Mariam chatted behind her, but Katie stood planted to the ground, taking in the sight before her. Lights wasn't what she saw.

It was magic. The kind that swayed, illuminating flowers and trees from the ground up. The kind that transformed the living into beauty so breathtaking she couldn't do anything but take it in and hope it never left.

Tristan's hand wrapped around hers, and his voice danced on the back of her neck. "None of it compares."

Katie pulled her eyes away from what looked like a pixie handing out flowers to see Tristan looking at her. He held her hand tighter, and they joined the crowd moving slowly from one display to another. She couldn't tell the difference between what was real and what was magic.

She knew that, in the world above, it was high noon and the sun was beaming down. But here, the stars were out. A galaxy opened up before her and she swore if she reached out far enough, she could grab a star. As they neared one display, deer pranced, running through and around the crowd. When one ran through Katie, it was like a ray of sunlight leaving behind its warmth.

Zuri's was easy to spot. An ethereal glow centered over a pond. In the middle, a small island hovered, only big enough for a silver cherry blossom tree, taller than any display around. Illuminated pale, pink flowers drifted from the tree and fell into the pond, where the water—clear as clear could be—showed a translucent reef. A moving painting of perfection—fish swam to and fro, flying in and out of the water, disrupting nothing.

At the end of Zuri's display was a large field were people sat like dark blots, staring up at fireworks shooting off into the galaxy and exploding into more stars. Katie had been so engrossed in the displays she hadn't realized she and Tristan had been separated from the others. They found a spot under a thick tree, momentarily lit-up by the exploding stars above them.

Katie leaned against Tristan. She could feel him watching her, and she turned to look at him, knowing he wanted something. She could feel his anxiety rising in his chest. It rose in her own until he kissed her.

It was hard and deep. Not the kind of kiss you'd expect in a public place. The kind you did behind closed doors, the kind that made you feel naked and exposed to the very depth of your being.

Every explosion was an escalation. He was slow and tender, but aggressive. Katie moved her hands into his jacket and under his shirt, feeling his warm, bare skin. He kissed her neck, and his hands found their way up her sweater and to her bare stomach, to her hips, pulling her closer to him.

With every burst in the sky, she felt his breath grow heavier and his grip and caresses grow hungrier.

The thought came to her and she knew it was honest: She didn't want to lose her virginity in a park with hundreds of people around—no matter how literally magical it was.

Tristan stopped, his body pressed tightly against hers. She could feel his lust; it was heavy and dangerously alluring. He steadied his breathing, and she could hear him plotting. Wondering if her dad was working late. Wondering if they could leave now.

It scared her how quick his mind worked. He stiffened, but

softened when she kissed him. He moved off her, leaving his hand on her upper thigh.

Tristan stared at her lips and down at her rising chest and back to her lips. She felt herself wanting to feel the euphoria, wondering if it would be better than her first time sourcing—

She blinked.

She blinked again, not believing that it was there in her mind like it had been waiting since she'd flushed it down the toilet.

A wave of Tristan's thoughts hit her. He was stuck between feeling repulsed and wondering if she would think he was better than sourcing.

It hurt—knowing in that moment he felt repulsed by her.

"I didn't... I don't..." He cursed. He did.

Katie swallowed, feeling dirty and sick to her stomach. How quickly his feelings for her changed. She pulled her sweater down past her knees and got up.

"Katalina." Tristan cursed again, but he didn't move.

She brushed off her legs and held back tears. She pulled herself from him, all her thoughts and her mind. She hugged herself and walked away, picking up speed when she heard him getting up.

"Katalina!" he yelled into the crowd. She stayed in the cover of the darkness, momentarily exposed with every explosion as the sky fell into tiny lights.

She walked in circles until she caught a glimpse of Zuri, sparkling even in the dark. Katie didn't want them to see her. Even in the dark, she was embarrassed and exposed.

It was useless. Zuri spotted her after the next explosion and started to wave her over, but stopped and got up to walk over instead.

West looked up, but the darkness returned quick enough for Katie to hide again.

"What's wrong?" Zuri pulled her out of the bodies scattered across the field. "Sweetie, you're shaking. What happened?"

Katie shook her head. The last thing she wanted was this girl to think she was crazy. But she was, wasn't she? Katie raised her head and wiped her tears. She stood as tall as she could and shook her head again.

Zuri stood next to her and put her arm around Katie's waist. The simple gesture was enough to help her stand there.

"Stick with me." Zuri watched the magic fall from the sky. "They're horrible—boys."

Katie nodded.

"Don't give him your heart." Zuri's voice was calm and steady, not her usual light bounce. "Guys like Tristan, like West—they'll never give it back. Even if it means tearing you down."

Katie looked at Zuri's profile in the flash. Her silver hair shimmered, and her smooth skin glistened.

"Stick with me, and even if the sky falls, we'll stand tall together. You and I." In Zuri's eyes, Katie could see a sense of conviction, a sense of security. "We girls are stronger than they'll ever be."

They sat and watched the display together, and Katie caught a glimpse of Tristan sitting with West. Every now and again, they'd both look over. She could feel Tristan prodding at her cautiously.

Every time Katie let a tear slip, Zuri would grip her shoulder. It was bizarre. Katie had met this girl all of a day ago. Now she was leaning on her.

Zuri took off her flats, dug her toes into the grass, and rested her head on Katie. "You know, my mother told me once, '*Zurina, that pretty little face of yours is a curse.*' She was the biggest bitch I knew, but afterward she'd always say, '*Use it. Don't let it use you.*'"

"Was your mom Russian?" Katie asked confused because Zuri was definitely Asian.

"No, but saying it with a Russian accent sounds better than her Oklahoma drawl."

Katie laughed.

"Do you think our mothers can see us?" Zuri paused and Katie stiffened. "I saw it. That you were orphaned at a young age."

"I'm not really. I have my dad—adoptive dad. Anyway, I hope so."

"I don't."

Katie said nothing, and when the show finished, they took their time getting to their feet.

West called to Katie. "How was it, kid?"

"Magical." Katie meant it.

"Where are Salem and Mariam?" Zuri looked around, peering into the dimly lit, star-covered field.

"They're checking out the food stalls." West and Tristan put their hands in their pockets at the same time. The resemblance was creepy. They even stood the same, like they didn't care what was around them or who was watching. Arrogance.

Katie checked her phone. It was almost four-o'clock. She needed to get back home before her dad. She'd never mentioned she was going out—or asked permission, for that matter.

"I have to get going." Katie only looked between Zuri and West. Mariam and Salem walked up with their hands full of something that smelled like chili and cheese.

"You're leaving?" Mariam said, handing Zuri her plate of chili cheese fries. "Let me pay you back for the ticket. We're going to go restaurant-hopping tomorrow morning. Just Zuri and me. Want to come?"

Katie nodded but stopped. "I can't—I'm going to look at a school with my dad."

Tristan's eyes found her, but she refused to meet them.

"Oh? What school?" Zuri said

"Burberry Contemporary—"

"You're trying to go to Burberry? I graduated from there. I live two blocks from it." Zuri twirled like the stars had aligned and pooped out unicorns and rainbows.

"We do restaurant hops all the time. I'll let you know when we go again." Mariam smiled. Katie and Mariam exchanged numbers, and as Katie said her goodbyes, Zuri glanced at Tristan and gave Katie a wink.

Katie walked backward, waving and not missing that Tristan was saying bye and following after her. She kept her thoughts hugged tightly to her and walked fast to the exit.

"Katalina."

She walked faster, slipping between people.

"Katalina."

She steeled herself.

"Kat—Katalina." He grabbed her hand, and she pulled it back.

"What?"

Tristan said nothing, but she heard all this thoughts. Apologies filled with annoyance and guilt and anger.

The truth was she didn't want his apologies. She wanted him to have not done it. To not have hurt her. Not to have admitted he wanted space from her.

She wanted him to not have been repulsed by who she was now.

She covered ground faster and faster and didn't really know where she was going.

"I'm trying," he said behind her.

She stopped. "Trying what? To love me? To accept me? To accept that you're tied to me? To accept that we probably shouldn't be together?"

"I didn't say that!" he yelled.

"You didn't have to." Tears clouded her eyes because she knew the truth. "You didn't have to *say it*. Remember?"

His silence was more hurtful than if he had tried to lie to save her feelings.

She kept walking, the breath blown out of her. This was the end. The ground beneath her shook as her heart burst. She clutched her chest, willing the pieces to fall back together. She held her head up, though the tears streaked down her face.

"It's true," His voice drifted in.

She shut him out, clenching her fist.

"Katalina." She heard his anger. He grabbed her arm, pulling her back. "You can't blame me for being human!" he yelled.

She punched him in the face.

Tristan cursed, grabbing his nose. The people on the sidewalk around them scattered faster than roaches.

"But you're not." Katie turned her back on him, realizing that he was the only reason she was standing on this very sidewalk, able to be normal. He'd been the one with her in that room. The one fighting for her to come back. But that's why she had to walk away. Because even though he was fighting for her, he couldn't accept what he'd fought for. He couldn't even decide if he'd fought for her or for him.

Either way, she could never be with someone who was repulsed by any part of her. Even the parts that repulsed her.

13

Untangling

EACH STEP AWAY from him was heavier and heavier. Her heart weighed her feet down, but she pushed forward. She found a familiar street elevator.

When the door opened to the city above, the pulses pumped in and out of her mind. She ran home and locked herself in her room. Each beat was a reminder of why she was crying in the corner of her room. Counting each pulse, she rocked and rocked to the thumping.

When she realized she was no longer in her room, but on her neighbor's porch, petting their cat while clutching her necklace and pushing it against her skin, she got up. The burning of the iron helped her breathe and walk away, but it didn't ease the burning in her throat.

She had to go back to Gray City, where the pulses were dull and quiet. She went home and left a quick note for her dad saying she was out shopping. Inside she knew the truth. She only wanted to buy one thing: a cure for her ache. The one in her throat and chest. She needed to feel the ease.

⁖⊷⊶⁖

Standing in front of the sourcing spa, where it had all started, she gripped the door, ready to feel the slow slip into paradise.

Katie let go and walked across the street. Her hand rubbing over her face, she breathed deep and bent over, heaving, her breath just out of her reach. Spots dotted her vision as she focused on the cracks in the ground. She leaned against the cool brick of what sounded like an electronics store.

She reached into her purse and pulled out her phone. Ten missed calls from Tristan. She ignored them and found the number she needed.

It rang for a while before the line connected. "Hey, Kat?" West's voice rose in question.

"What happens when…when none of it works?" Katie stared at the bright blue sign: *A Taste of Paradise*

"Where are you?"

"I just need…help." Katie choked back her humiliation.

"I just started work. Can you—wait, where are you?"

"I'm in front of a cafe—Paradise. A Taste of Paradise."

"Don't move. Hold on." He shouted at someone, saying he needed a cover. "Kat?"

"It's okay. I'll just go back home. You're at work."

"I'll be there in a few minutes. Don't hang up."

She heard him open and close a car door. "I'm sorry."

"Nah. I was doing patrol duty by a strip mall. Most action here is getting to catch a peek under a few short skirts. Hey—don't judge me. I can hear you judging me. If they didn't want me to look, they wouldn't advertise."

Katie exhaled in an attempt to laugh.

"I'm probably going to get another graveyard shift for ditching, though—I don't want to hear any apologies. That's not going to stop me from scratching out my own eyes in boredom." West paused. "Did I ever tell you about the one time I chased a naked guy for five blocks? He kept trying to pee on the stop signs and...well, I didn't want to grab him because he looked loaded as hell and it's hard to get the pee smell out of leather pants—don't ask how I know that or why I was wearing them—yeah. Graveyard shift. Either you're waiting for the silence to end or trying to get a crazy lady wearing a hospital gown to stop yelling at imaginary rabbits." West went on, telling her stories he'd collected over the years, until he pulled up in a sleek black car.

He opened the passenger door. "Get in."

Katie slid onto a smooth leather seat. His dashboard lit up her face aqua-blue and silver. She hadn't noticed the burning in her throat was almost gone.

West's brow settled into a serious line. "What happened?" His voice was calm and concerned. She had expected some anger.

"My throat was burning. I tried thinking about SA and how I didn't want to…well, next thing I knew, I was petting the neighbor's cat and…I ended up here. I didn't mean to come here. I just had to get away from all the pulses and…I'm sorry."

"That's not what I mean. I know why you're standing outside trying to tap up. What happened before that? What got you here?"

Katie stayed silent.

He turned off the engine, and they sat, right there, across from Paradise's pretty blue sign.

"If you don't confront the problem, you'll always end up right back in this position. Why'd you start sourcing?"

Katie looked out the front windshield at the occasional car passing by. She told West about her life at school, home, and how coming to Gray City had seemed like the only escape, until she'd tried sourcing.

"Yeah, I knew you were an escaper that night you were slicing at your wrist. So you were depressed?"

Katie looked at him. "No, I was just…I don't know, sick of my life. I just wanted some change."

"People who *just want change* pick up a new skill or a constructive hobby. They don't look for escapes. Escapes are what you use when you're depressed and ignoring the problem."

Katie shrugged. Maybe she had been depressed. She wasn't now, not really. She was just…trying to make it to the next day.

"So what triggered it today? You seemed fine—until the fireworks."

Katie hoped he couldn't see her blushing.

"If you're going to be coy, I can't help you." West reclined his seat. "I'm not going to tell anyone what we talk about. I won't even tell anyone we talk if you want. I'm your sponsor. I won't judge you and I won't tell your dad or your boyfriend about what demons you've got locked away—as if T hasn't seen them already."

Katie exhaled. "I…I broke up with him. At least, I think I did. I punched him in the face and left him on the sidewalk."

"Well, you broke something."

"I…I shouldn't have."

"Probably not. That's pretty fucked up."

"Thanks."

"Truth hurts. Get used to it."

Katie sighed, pulling her hair out of her ponytail. Her head hurt. "Do you have sex?" Katie asked, wrapping her hair in a low bun, undoing and doing it over and over until she realized she was fixating again.

"I'd never do that to him."

"I'm not asking you to have sex with me." Katie scoffed and rolled her eyes. "I mean, do you think about sourcing when you're…getting really into it?"

West gave her a long side-eye. "Um…usually I'm thinking about a lot of other pressing things."

Katie opened her mouth, but thought better of saying anything else.

"Do you?"

"No... Kind of. I've never... When I'm..." She looked at West. "This is getting weird, isn't it?"

"Got weird when you told me you were petting the neighbor's cat. But I'm not trying to think about T's junk, if that's what you mean."

Katie smiled despite feeling her face burn. "We've never gotten that far. So no junk to talk about."

West side-eyed her again. "Just say what you mean."

"When we're kissing and...stuff...I start to think things. Like, will it be like sourcing? You know, euphoric. Or will it be better or worse? Then Tristan...well, he got grossed out by me. I don't blame him. I can't leave my crazy behind long enough to...I don't know."

"Sex is way better—but don't take my word for it."

Katie looked up, thinking she didn't exactly know what she was asking.

"I think your problem is you use sourcing as an escape. Maybe when you're getting all hot and heavy, you're using that as an escape, too. I think once you fix what started the problem, you'll be able to get a handle on yourself. But I don't see why it would matter what you're thinking. Just keep it to yourself and bump nasties, you know?"

"Bump nasties?"

"Grind it out. Pound the flesh. Make the beast with two backs."

"Okay."

"I got more." West smiled, staring at the street light changing from green to red.

"I'm good." Katie sat in silence, feeling openly exposed and comfortable with someone who didn't have access to her thoughts.

"You should apologize."

"Huh?"

"To T. For punching him in the face. I imagine the guy who would go to such lengths to save his girl, even if it meant putting his life in danger, would be hurting real bad right about now."

Katie nodded. "I shouldn't have done it."

"You shouldn't have sourced either, but it is what it is. You have to deal with the consequences the right way or you'll never get out of the hole you're in."

"Truth hurts," Katie mumbled.

"You can take it." West shifted. "How are you feeling?"

Katie absently touched her throat. "Normal...as can be. Thanks."

"Yeah, I'm magic like that."

Katie thought he was a few things, none of them magic— but she was thankful nonetheless.

"Where do you live? I'll take you home." He started the engine.

"I live in Boise."

West looked surprised. "I forgot. You're half. Soaking up the sun like an original gansta." He turned on the radio. Commercials.

"You can just drop me off at an elevator."

"Nah, sun's going down. I'll just drive up."

They were quiet for some time, listening to overplayed hits. Katie watched the underground streetlights zip by. "What happened between you and Tristan?"

"What happened between *you* two?" he said.

"Touché."

"He's not like you and me. He's the kind of asshole who doesn't say shit. He's all cryptic like it's cool. Unless he needs something, of course, then he calls you and expects you to do whatever without asking any questions. Dick."

"How do you know I'm not like that?"

West looked at her. "You think I've never tried to have a conversation with T about his issues? He's got plenty. But he just sits there like a moody fuck saying as little as possible." West rolled his eyes and gripped the steering wheel.

"Why are you still his friend?" Katie asked.

"I'm not his friend. I'm his brother. You have family you can't pick, and when they're gone, you have the family you pick. Though these days he feels more like the family I didn't pick. Dick."

"Well…" Katie always knew there were parts of Tristan she didn't know, but one part was driving her home and painting a picture of him that she both knew and didn't know.

"What?"

"Sounds like you guys need therapy."

"Look who's talking. Need I mention why you're in my car?"

"Asshole." Tristan and West were more alike than he knew or cared to admit.

West pulled into a large lot with a line full of cars. The line led to a building Katie assumed was an elevator.

"Rush hour," he murmured

They filled the waiting time with music until finally it was their turn and they rose into the above world. The evening opened up in front of them as the sun glowed just under the horizon. Katie gave West directions, and he drove in silence, rubbing his chin and staring beyond the traffic.

It wasn't until they pulled in front of her house that he said something. "This is going to be awkward."

Katie looked at her porch and knew he was referring to the blue-eyed boy sitting on the steps. She felt Tristan's curiosity and jealousy penetrating the car.

"Thanks, West."

"Anytime—but try not to wig out between now and Tuesday afternoon. I'm not off until Wednesday."

"I'll keep that in mind," Katie said, getting out of the car.

West rolled down the window. "And stay away from the cat, Elma," he said, before driving off.

Katie's stomach dropped and twisted at the sight of Tristan. A red bruise formed under his eye.

"I'm sorry," Katie said, disgusted with herself. All she did these days was apologize. The words really meant nothing. She could add abusive to her list of issues. "I should have never punched you."

"It's fine. I grabbed you. If I taught you anything, it's reflexes."

"It's not fine. None of this is fine." Katie breathed, ignoring the pulses next door. "I'm not fine."

"I called you."

"I know." She sat next to him on the steps and stared at the sidewalk.

"I'm sorry about how I reacted."

"I know."

"I'm sorry I don't understand. I'm trying." He was being so candid, and Katie wasn't used to that. It made her feel like he knew what was coming and was trying to stop it.

"I know."

"I make mistakes. I'm not perfect. I've never been in love before. I've never had to deal with anything like *this* before. And both at the same time? I'm trying." His voice rose. He knew what she was thinking, what she was preparing herself to say. "I love you. I'd do anything for you. Not for me. For *you*. I'll… Katalina."

She looked into his eyes, his desperation breaking her nerve.

"I know," was all she could say. She couldn't put the rest into words. She couldn't say it.

Tristan moved in front of her and cupped her face. "Don't. Don't say it, then. We can make it work. *I* will make it work. I—I'm still figuring out how… Don't." He wiped her tears.

"Tristan…" The rest caught in her throat. Her throat that, for the first time, didn't burn—not for blood. "I have to make myself better. I can't do that with you—or anyone else." She stumbled on the words, each one tearing out her chest. "I have to do it by myself. For myself. Or I'll never get better."

It was the truth. It wasn't his job to fix her crazy. It was hers.

He searched her eyes with tears falling down his face. She heard him searching for a way out of this, a way to turn it back. A way to make her feel whole again.

He pressed his head lightly against hers; they stayed there, wrapped in pain and regret and guilt. How could they ever have a chance, when the truth was, they needed to figure themselves out before getting tangled up in each other again?

He kissed her. Hard, then soft, before he pulled away. He held her shoulders and looked her in the eyes. His eyes glistened, but the tears were gone. He ran a thumb over her cheek and stepped away and down the stairs.

She moved to take it all back. Panic burst inside of her like tiny fireworks, until he turned around. "I'll be waiting. Just... don't cut me out. You're my best friend."

Katie ran to him, unable to say anything. She wrapped her arms around him a final time, his arms warm and strong around her. He kissed the top of her head. Breathing deep, he let her go and put his hands in his pockets.

Katie wiped her eyes; the finality sunk in.

"Let me know how the tour goes tomorrow," he said, looking down the street as her dad's truck turned the corner.

"Yeah." She sniffed and wiped the tears that wouldn't stop.

Her dad's truck pulled in.

"I love you, Katalina." His voice drifted in and took her breath with it. He greeted her dad with a nod before taking off down the street.

Her dad slid out of the truck with a bag of takeout and looked after Tristan. "What..." He looked at Katie. "Nope. Don't even want to know. Do I need to know?"

Katie shook her head, still watching Tristan. *"I love you, too."*

Her dad glanced at Tristan again. "He wasn't trying to get fresh, was he? He didn't...you know..."

"Jesus, Dad. No. I... We broke up."

Her dad shrugged. "I don't like him anyway. Damn him, the little punk."

"Dad, I just need time to work on myself. That's all." Katie breathed deep, not caring that her dad looked at her strange.

"I get it. It's all part of growing up." He put his arm around her and led her inside.

If this was what growing up felt like, she wasn't sure she saw the charm in being an adult.

She looked back again before going through the front door, and clear as day over the low hum of the pulses, she heard him.

"I'll be waiting."

ᴔᴔ 14 ᴔᴔ

BURBERRY

KATIE SPENT THE evening going over the catalogue for Burberry with her dad. He suggested she take some film classes, and she circled them as an option to ask about. Despite the gaping hole in her chest and feeling like tomorrow would never come, she couldn't wait for the tour. In all honesty, she couldn't wait to have an excuse to call Tristan and hear his voice.

Breaking up was a strange thing. Her body felt like there was a death, and her mind perpetuated it.

After her dad had gone to bed, she spent a while listening to some of Tristan's old voicemails. She gripped the stuffed animals he'd gotten her. The bear was from the summer fair.

The lopsided rabbit was because she'd wanted one as a pet and Tristan said she couldn't kill a stuffed one. And the small felt monster—it had funky stitching and one big eye, one little eye, and a scrappy looking eyebrow. He'd said it was weird-looking and reminded him of her—in a good way, whatever that meant. But he was right. It did look at home in her room, all mismatched and crazy.

⊶❦⊷

Her dad choose to drive into Gray City using the same lift West had. There was no line and they were down and pulling into Burberry in the time it took her to regret breaking up with Tristan, deciding it was best, and then having a mini pulse attack and telling her dad to pull over so she could breathe it out while jumping up and down like a maniac. People stared… but whatever.

It was a long ride.

"You sure you don't want to go home and do it another day."

"Positive." Katie pressed her face against the cool window. *Get it together. Get it together.*

"Well, fix your hair, it's a little…off." He was being kind. Her ponytail had snagged on the door when she'd jumped out of the car to get away from his nagging pulse.

"Yeah. Hair—check." She pulled it down, then up again. Then down.

"Christ, Katie. You look like a PSA for meth. Stop twitching."

"I'm not twitching, I'm… Thanks, Dad. That really boosts my confidence."

"Would it make a difference if I said, all that aside—" he gestured at her untangling her hair in frustration "—you look nice? Just relax a little."

Easy for him to say. Katie settled with a messy bun. It would have to do.

"Look. They have uniforms, too. Bit more color to it than your other one, eh? That's stylish."

Bless his heart. He was trying to be hip and excited for her.

"They are nice." She took in the purple, blue, and gray plaid skirts and grey cardigans. It was defiantly more up-to-date than the Hamilton uniform. "I'm ready." Katie took another breath, unsure why this was such a big deal. A tour. Maybe because she wanted this to work badly. A place she could fit in and find herself—the part of her that could plan for a future. It was a lot of hope to put into one tour. A lot of hope to put into a school.

They climbed the stone stairs, and her dad admired the pristine architecture, a mix of modern design with classic arches and columns. They walked inside and the place beamed much brighter than could be seen from the outside. She looked up at a star-studded ceiling, reaching up three stories. It glowed throughout the balconies that bustled with kids in uniforms. A girl stopped and looked up to see what Katie stared at.

"I know. Gets me every time." She smiled and disappeared up the staircase.

"I wonder how they do that," her dad said, mesmerized.

"Magic."

"Ha. I could almost believe that."

She still couldn't figure it out. How could he not know witches existed? Let alone not see any sign of them, even when it was in bold letters or lighting up a room.

They found the front office, and her dad spoke to a woman wearing a gray suit and a classic French braid.

"Oh, yes. I'm Denise. I was waiting for you. It's nice to meet you, Mr. Watts." She grabbed a folder off her desk and a tote bag. "You must be Katalina. It's always nice to see a new face."

Katie shook Denise's hand, and a surge of energy ran up her arm.

Denise let go and waved for them to follow. She took them through the main hall, with the celling, and talked about the history of the school, built in the early 1900s and recently expanded to include an above-ground astrology center. "Hence the decor," she said, leading them up a grand staircase as a bell rang nine times. She showed them the library, which was much bigger than the one at Hamilton and packed with students, and the front of the cafeteria, where she informed Katie that the blood was freshly delivered three times a day, though the types weren't always plentiful. They passed by classrooms. Most were empty, as they should be on a Sunday, but a few classes had students—some kids sleeping, some talking while the teacher scribbled on the board, and a few Allison types raising their hands and talking at the same time.

They walked across a catwalk encased in glass over the city street. Images flickered to and fro on the glass—a clock counting the seconds, the weather and sun position, the lunch menu, and a few animated characters winking at her as she passed.

"Wow. That's... funky," her dad said.

"It's magic," Katie said again.

Her dad continued as if she hadn't said it at all. He stopped and moved in front of the character that looked like a squirrel with cat ears. It followed him and danced back and forth.

"He can't comprehend what you're saying," Denise whispered. "He's a guardian. They aren't allowed to know witches or witch magic exists."

Katie's brows furrowed.

"Try not to think too hard about it. But no matter what you say, he'll never understand you. You wouldn't have either, but you're vampire now. Vampire blood can't be hexed like humans can."

"Hexed?"

"To the dorms." Denise waved them forward to a four-story building, split in two. Girls on the right, boys on the left.

"She has the option to come home, right?" Her dad fumbled for the brochure in his pocket.

"She does, but that's for werewolves, special cases in Gray City, and vampires who live in coven-sponsored homes. All the other vampires have to stay in the dorms. It's important that they learn how to schedule their immense amounts of time. A person without the ability to sleep the night away can get lost. We have strict guidelines, curfews, and scheduled activities. However, Friday nights, weekends, and holidays are always free to the children with parental consent."

"I see." Her dad paused, looking at Katie like she was, yet again, his Katie Bug. "Well, how can I be sure no boys are getting fresh?"

Denise laughed. "Oh, Mr. Watts. I can assure you. There is no coed freshness in these dorms. As an example, would you please follow me?" She went to the dorms on the right and walked through the glass doors. Katie followed, but the door shut on her dad.

Denise turned around. "To get past these doors you have to meet a certain criteria, or—" She moved her hand to the wall and pretended to push buttons on a screen that told the time and weather. "—have the right tour guide." The doors opened and her dad stepped through.

"I see. Some kind of scanner, or...how does this work?" He studied the door, looking for any clue.

"If I told you that, it would compromise the system." She winked at Katie. "For now, we'll just say...magic."

They walked through the dorms. The rooms were two to a room except for a few single rooms. There were resident leaders on each floor available twenty-four hours a day—not shocking as they were vampires. There was a common area on the main and second floor where both sexes could mingle, play games, and study. The common areas had modern decor: bright, simple, and clean.

They were about to go back to the main building when a boy—maybe younger than Katie—came out of the boys' dorm in his pajamas.

"Shi—taki mushrooms," he said, looking at Denise. "I swear. My alarm didn't go off."

"Three Sundays in a row? Preston, if I see you again today, I'll duct-tape the thing to your face. Get dressed and go to class."

He considered Katie and nodded.

"Preston! Get dressed. This is not the time to flaunt your stuff."

He laughed and ran back into the dorms.

Denise sighed and rubbed her temples. "I'd like to say we are perfect and all our students are the example of excellence but…"

"Kids," her dad said in agreement.

"So? What do you think?" Denise escorted them out and crossed the street back toward the main building.

Katie's dad looked at her, and she took in the sight again. As much as she hated school, she kind of…loved this place. There was magic for crying out loud. This was as close to Hogwarts as she was going to get. She smiled.

"I like it. A lot."

"Well, we have an opening. Bad news is only a single-occupancy room is open right now—but that can be a good thing. If you both need to talk it over, you can sit in the cafeteria and have a refreshment or give us a call."

"Where's the cafe?" her dad asked, patting Katie's shoulder.

Denise smiled and led the way.

Atmosphere is what came to mind when Katie stepped under the stone arches and into a warmly lit restaurant. It was miles away from the circular white tables with the plastic blue chairs she was used to. A stainless steel lamp hung over an empty buffet table. Dark brown leather booths, cream-colored table cloths, and some standalone tables with fine wooden chairs covered in cream-colored cushions graced the hardwood floors.

"Can I get you something to drink?" Denise asked, leading them to one of the circular tables overlooking a view of the city street.

"Water would be fine."

"Katalina?"

"O-negative?"

"I'll be right back."

They looked around the room as Denise disappeared into the kitchen.

"This place is impressive. Don't know why I didn't think of this sooner." Her dad checked out a large chandelier made of antlers.

Katie's stomach twisted with guilt. Tristan had.

"I want you to be happy. I think you'll be happy here. I haven't seen you tug and straighten out your sweater since we left the car."

"I'm not that—okay, I've got twitches."

He laughed.

"I do like it. But…how much does everything cost?"

"Don't worry about it." Her dad looked at the tablecloth, running his hands over its softness. "Can I get my meals here, too? This is nice."

"I have money from…"

"No. You're my daughter. I'll pay for your education. Got it? Whatever he gave you, save it. Buy yourself some of those ugly purses girls carry around or useless junk to clutter up your room. Your education is my business."

"How…how long have you known I had money?"

"I'm not as stupid as I look. You wanna go to this school or not?" He looked at her as Denise came out with their drinks.

"I'll be back at the office when you've decided. Take your time."

When she left, Katie picked up her glass, immediately panicked with a thought. What if she had an episode? How could she stay here and hide her problem? What if she drank some blood, but spit it out in one of her fits? What if it all ended in blood-stained tablecloths and people scattering around her? What if she brought all her crazy here, too? What if she ruined the only place left?

"I asked around and found out that fresh blood is better for recovery." He nodded at the glass. "Fresh three times a day. I'd hate to know how they get it or how expensive it is, but I think it's worth a try."

Katie brought the glass to her lips and sipped. It wasn't bad. It was…good. She drank more and waited, expecting an aftertaste. None came. It went down. She finished it.

"I never see you on the weekdays anyway. I can put in for a shift change and get weekends free." He was already making plans. He was willing to make this work for her despite anything and everything. "I can pick you up on Friday nights. We can catch a movie, or I hear there's a new arcade in the Burrow, by the city park."

Katie smiled, twisting the glass in her hand. "It's a casino, Dad."

"Really? I thought it looked more...you know..."

"Besides, I have SA on Friday nights. What if I fall off the wagon?" Katie needed to know he was thinking it, too.

"I'm thinking we should tell them. The more people who know, who can help you, the better."

Katie burned with humiliation. She thought about West.

Rule Number Two: Stop Being a Punk Bitch.

"What's the worst that can happen?" Katie stood up, a flash of horrible scenarios rolling through her mind like a horror movie trailer, all ending with her being thrown out on the streets and doused with holy water.

"What's the best?" He grabbed her glass and looked around until a guy came out to collect them. "You'll look nice in purple. Your mother always dressed you in purple. She said it complemented your eyes." He held her close, and they walked out of the cafe and toward the main office.

Katie held her breath as her dad explained her situation to Denise. She waited for the look of disgust or pity or a "*sorry, but you can't stay with our normal kids,*" but it never came. Denise nodded and smiled.

"I'm glad you've decided on staying with us. Now, given your situation, your curfew and meal habits will be tracked more strictly. And we ask that you always notify us when you return to the surface, where you are going and when you'll be back, unless you've been signed out by your father for weekends and holidays. I know it seems overbearing, but it's with your best interest at heart." Denise opened a file cabinet and flicked through some papers. "We also have a group at the school. I'll ask that you join. The kids meet once a month at night in one of the classrooms. It's after the dorms are closed for the night. This groups counts as a special activity."

"There are other kids who…source?" Katie took the flyer. It was very discreet, with information about meet times and a classroom number.

"No. Our campus has a no-source policy. But many of these students have at some point sourced and found it hard to stop. I think you'll feel at home here, Katalina."

"Katie." Katie suppressed a smile.

"Katie." Denise returned the smile.

They talked about registration, transcripts, and payments. It was surreal. She could move in and register for classes tomorrow. When they got back to their car, Katie took another look at the school. She had to hold back tears. It could work.

She could start over here.

∘◦இ◦∘

Katie paced her room, stopping every now and again in front of her window to feel the late afternoon sun on her face. She held her phone, trying to figure out why it was so hard to call Tristan. She was so nervous. What if he didn't pick up? What if, instead of saying hello, she just cried like a freak? What if he'd decided she was the worst? What if she just waited to see if he'd call?

No.

She pressed his name and stared at the phone as it dialed.

Big breath. Breathe. Breathe the crazy out.

The line connected.

"Hey," he said. His voice was low, but it rose like a wave. "Katalina?"

"Hi."

He sighed. It was light and almost like a laugh. "How are you?"

"Okay. You?"

Tristan paused, and she heard him rustling. "I've been…I'm okay. How was the tour?"

"It was good. I like it. I'm going to move on-campus tomorrow. I'm sorry I didn't listen to you before. It was a really good idea."

"Yeah, what's new? You're thick-headed." He exhaled as if he were reclining or stretching. "You're doing it again."

"What?"

"Analyzing everything I do. Do you want a play-by-play?" His voice was playful. It eased her heart. She wanted—no. She *needed* to stop thinking about what she wanted.

"You don't know that. I know you can't hear my thoughts over the phone."

"I can just tell. I'm in my room, avoiding Lucinda and Will.

They're trying to redo the backyard. I think it's supposed to help them bond."

"Oh?"

"Yeah, it's not working. Lucinda's being a control freak, and Will keeps putting everything off-center to annoy her." She heard the smirk in his voice. "They'll probably take it out on each other in the bedroom."

"Gross." Katie smiled. Even if she was completely grossed out by the thought of Will and Lucinda doing it, his voice made her smile.

"So tell me about the school."

Katie lay on her bed and gave him the playback in extreme detail. She didn't want to stop talking to him—and they didn't stop for hours. They had never talked like this before, over the phone, unable to hear each other's thoughts or know that thoughts were being hidden.

"Katalina?"

"Yeah?" Instinctively she knew he wanted more than the light banter they'd been sharing.

He exhaled and said nothing, but she knew what he meant. She'd heard him say her name that exact way too many times to not know—and she loved him, too.

They sat quiet on the phone for a stretch of time. She studied the catalogue, every now and again mentioning a class she might be interested in. Mechanical engineering looked better in the catalogue than it sounded. Tristan would ask a few questions and say, "you should try it" or "you might want to stay away from anything dealing with animals—at least small ones" when she mentioned the animal health class. She heard him turning pages and found out he was reading a book about a space station on the verge of destruction by some warlords—she'd never known he liked science-fiction. In fact, she'd been sure he thought space operas were the worst.

"Beats *Othello*," he said after she voiced her suspicions.

"I thought you loved that play?" Katie felt a bit burned. She'd gotten him the book for Christmas.

"Yeah, in the context of class. You know, it's not like teachers give us a choice between Shakespeare or everything else much more interesting than that—don't suck your teeth at me. I still love my copy. You—" He paused. "I love it."

"I love that you love it." Katie's stomach flopped and twirled, and Tristan quickly started rattling off all the books he could name that were much better than school books, until they were laughing because Katie said books were only good for looking pretty on shelves.

Neither of them had the desire or the courage to hang up. She even packed up a few things while he finished his book, making sure to take everything he'd given her or that reminded her of him. The stuffed animals and the purple shag rug he always made fun of when she'd lived at Lucinda's took up a box of their own.

"Who are you talking to?" her dad asked, opening her door while she argued that her baby Pokémon bedsheets did not make her look like a tween.

"I'm on the phone with—I'm on the phone," she said, not sure why she was even packing bedsheets. It's not like she needed them.

"Are you really taking that rug?"

Katie looked at her rolled-up, purple, fake-fur rug. "What?"

"Nothing." He picked up the box. "I'll take these to the car if you're finished."

"Yeah."

Tristan turned a page, and the sound scratched across the speakers.

Her dad looked at the phone and rolled his eyes seeing Tristan's name.

Damn speakerphone.

When he left, she took the phone off speaker and held it to her ear.

"Getting ready to leave?" he asked.

"Yeah." She didn't want to hang up. When would they talk next? She took the phone from her ear and smacked her head. *Get it together. Get. It. Together.* She brought the phone back to her ear.

"I've got to tell you something," he said.

"What?"

"Well, you're about to leave, so maybe you can call me when you're settled in? Later tonight?"

"That isn't going to drive me insane…"

Tristan laughed, low and silky-like. "I know the feeling."

"Sigh. I better go," Katie said, glad she had a reason to call him again. Another reason to hear his voice. Something to look forward to at the end of the day.

"Katalina…" He stopped, letting it sit in the air. "Call me," he said finally.

"I will." She wondered if she was allowed to say it if he didn't. She chickened out. "As long as you pick up."

He exhaled. "Always. I'll be waiting."

"Tristan—"

The line disconnected.

She sat on the bed, staring at her phone. This was going to be hard, but she had tonight. She just had to make it to tonight.

Rule Number Seven: Don't Give Up Because Shit Always Gets Better.

PART THREE
THE TOWER

15

FANCY WORDS

THE MORNING BLURRED by. They went to Hamilton High to get her old transcripts. She wanted to wait in the car but knew she had to apologize and say goodbye to her old life.

She walked through the quiet halls while her dad waited in the office. As she walked by each classroom, voices rose and lowered as teachers or the students talked. She stopped when she got to Mr. Rhineheart's class. If it was empty, she'd go in and apologize. If he had class, she'd just leave a note in his school mailbox.

Katie sighed with relief when she saw him standing in front of the class, reciting a passage from a book he held in his hand. That relief balled up like a dead spider when he glanced up and saw her.

He motioned to the class, and Katie heard them rustle and groan. She cursed, moving away from the door and wishing he hadn't seen her. Even if she knew the right thing to do would be to apologize, she was still a giant chicken who wanted to sneak away with some of her dignity.

The door opened. "Katie? How are you?" He looked concerned and relieved at the same time.

"Hi, Mr. Rhineheart. I'm…okay. I wanted to say goodbye… and apologize. For skipping and causing so much trouble."

"You're not the first student to ditch the books and take up arms—sorry, I'm still in my medieval mindset. Anyway, don't worry about it. We were really worried when you stopped coming to school altogether. We missed you."

Katie was tired of crying. She must have spent the majority of her day crying. She wiped her eyes, and Mr. Rhineheart patted her back.

"It takes a lot of guts to apologize. Thank you. I owe you an apology, too. We all saw the signs, but none of us really knew how to help. Not in a way that mattered, anyway."

"No." Katie shook her head, some of those weights falling off her shoulders and turning to dust.

"Are you coming back?"

"No. I'm going to go to a school in Gray City. Burberry."

Mr. Rhineheart nodded. "You'll be happy there?"

"I hope so."

"I'm glad to see you before you go. I'll tell the others you came by." He paused and smiled. "For what it's worth, no matter where you go, if you really apply yourself, you'll shine brighter than all of us."

Katie didn't know how to respond. All her life she'd been an average student...until she'd become the school delinquent.

"I really mean it. You just have to let go and allow yourself to shine." He grabbed onto the door and gave her a firm nod before going back inside.

Katie exhaled, blowing out all the stress. That was one less guilt rattling around in her head.

She said her goodbyes to Hamilton as they drove off. She'd miss it—Steve Sensei and his fake Japanese accent, Mr. Carver's unique checkerboard suits and ties, Mrs. Barnes's stern nodding of her head when someone answered a question correctly, Even Mr. Right's lame math jokes.

Katie gazed at the building one last time. She'd never imagined leaving it would be so sad, so...final.

❧❦❧

The day blurred by with uniform fittings; filling out paperwork and getting rules and guidelines about dorm life; meeting her floor resident assistant, Patty; and registering for classes.

The counselor was a short guy with a messy desk, and he talked endlessly. Katie mentioned she wanted to take some of the veterinarian classes. She thought she could put her healing powers to use, and animals were cute enough to work with. He informed her that she'd have to take extra classes because it was an eighteen-month program. That tidbit of information alone was enough to send her with open arms to some easier program, but she thought better of it. It was time for her to get serious.

By the end, she had a class schedule, a cafeteria card, her uniforms, and a half-unpacked dorm room. She hung up her new uniform in her closet, along with her purse, a few bras, and her shirt ties. She had ties now—she'd stepped up in the world of uniforms.

Her dad looked around her room and out her window down at the street. "You can see the park. It'll be nice when they light it up for Christmas." He was stalling. He'd already said that thirty minutes ago.

"Are you going to be okay, Dad?"

"You think I need you pacing the floors in the middle of the night? Ha." He looked down at his watch.

She hugged him. She didn't want him to leave either.

"Okay, kid. You'll be fine." He was saying it more for himself than for her. She could tell in the way he hugged her back tighter. "I'll see you Friday. Call me if you need me to bring you anything, but I don't know how I'll find it in that room of yours."

Katie smiled. "Bye, Dad."

He left.

The click of the door behind him was all it took for her to tear up. She sat at her desk and cried like a baby. She wasn't sad—but wasn't exactly ready to be on her own either. After thirty minutes, she pulled it together. After all, she wasn't really on her own. She was up the street, around the corner, a few blocks down—and underground.

She slapped her cheeks a few times. *Get it together. No more tears.*

She looked at her white walls. She had put her stuffed animals up on a shelf by her closet door and rolled out her purple rug on the hardwood floor. Once she made the bed, got her desk set up with her laptop, and decorated with other furnishings, it would feel more like home.

Her eyes flickered to the window, and she did a double-take. She could see a silver bob bouncing down the street with a bag of plants. Zuri. She did say she lived two blocks away. Katie watched her cross the street and disappear out of view.

She thought about what Zuri said about not giving her heart away. It was too late for that, and that approach didn't seem to be working for her and West—whatever was going on there.

Katie checked her phone. It was almost seven. In some homes, that counted as night. She waited until one minute after seven before calling.

"Hey." His voice was a warm blanket.

"Hi."

"How's the room?"

"Cozy. Needs some more color, but it'll get there."

"I bet it will."

"What'd you have to tell me?" Katie wanted to play coy, but it really had been bothering her all day.

"Can I meet you?"

Katie's heart flipped. "Yeah," she said before the responsible her made her think it over. "My curfew is at ten, so I can't go too far."

"That shouldn't be an issue."

"Where are you?"

"In front of your school. It's nice-looking. I'm jealous."

"That was quick. How'd you know I'd say yes? How'd you know I'd even call at seven?"

"I didn't. Just come down." His voice was like it was when she first met him—impatient and curious.

She jogged—ran—down the four flights of stairs and attempted to fix her hair before going into the main room. There was a mirror—likely put there by a girl who, like her, never remembered to check herself *before* leaving the room.

"Got a date?" a curvy girl said, coming down the steps. Her hair was thicker than her Southern accent. "Me, too. You look new. Here's a tip: if you have any issues, don't tell Pat. She's all *rules, rules*. Tell one of the other RAs. They'll cut you some slack. How do I look?" She fixed a curl in front of her light brown face. Katie had never met anyone who pulled off freckles—this girl made freckles the *it* thing.

"Good." Katie tried to smooth out her eyebrows. She attempted to fix the hair spilling out of the bun on top of her head.

"Don't. The messy look works for you. You know, makes you look really confident. Confidence is hot." The girl opened the door, and Katie followed her out.

The main common area had four ceiling-to-floor glass windows, and Tristan turned to see her as soon as she saw him. A million thoughts ran through his mind and hers. He looked so…impossibly perfect. Katie understood what the girl meant. Tristan had it. That messy confidence. It was hot.

"Messy, eh?" He smiled, his hands in the pockets of a light jacket he wore.

Katie let the door swing closed behind her. She pulled her thoughts away from him and held them close. "We shouldn't…" She didn't know how to say it.

He stilled his mind and pulled his thoughts from her. "So wanna walk?"

Katie let him lead and matched his slow pace. Being next to him was enough for the moment. Holding his hand would have calmed the itch in her fingers, but it wouldn't do anything for the low burn in her throat.

"I'm going back," he said.

"Where?" Her voice cracked with panic.

A crooked smile played at his lips. "Calm down. I'm not going anywhere. I mean, back to the Patrol. They hired me back today."

"The Patrol? You mean you're going to be a Death Dealer again?"

"That's not the official name. The reputation is changing. Back to what it was before people like Darren corrupted it. Now it's STAR." He rolled his eyes and smiled.

The memory of the vampire who'd stalked and shot her in an alley sliced into her mind as if it had happened yesterday. The way Tristan had turned into his shadow form and killed him in cold blood. Katie stopped. "Tristan. I saw your memories. I know what you went through."

"It'll be different. *I'm* different now. Lawrence is dead, and someone who can actually lead is in charge. I hear he's already weeded out the others like Darren."

"I don't know."

"There is nothing to know. I've already decided." His voice hinted at agitation.

"Then why are you telling me?"

He opened his mouth. "Because..." His shoulders relaxed. "Because I want you to know."

Katie wished she could hear his thoughts. He looked like he wished he could hear hers. He watched the street and nodded for them to keep walking. Clearly he didn't want her to chastise him about it—maybe he wanted her support.

"When do you start?"

"Tomorrow. I have to retest since I've been gone for a year, but then they'll rank me and issue me to a squad."

"I hope you studied," she said, imitating him.

He smiled. "Of course I did. I'm not you."

"Is it going to be dangerous? The job?"

"Sometimes. But anything can be dangerous. It's what I went to school for. It was—it *is* my path." He glanced at her, his arm brushing against hers as they walked.

"That's not going to keep me from worrying."

They turned, heading down a tunnel of little trinket shops and sweet shops. Tristan's hand touched her back, and he pulled at her sweater, making her backtrack. A girl on a bicycle sped by. Katie noticed the way his hand lingered before letting her go.

"Thanks," she said.

He nodded. "What did you decide on? For classes."

She recounted the day and complained about the hours she was going to have to put in. He teased her, but showed no signs of letting himself cross the line. The line she'd put between them. The line she wanted to—and would have—crossed if he'd gotten anywhere near it.

As the time neared ten, they sat on the front steps of her dorm building. Far enough apart not to touch, but close enough to give the accidental brushing.

It was nine-fifty-five, and she didn't want to move. Couldn't. She needed something to make the moment last.

His blue eyes soaked her in, memorizing every part of her face. He reached up and touched her bun. "How do you get all your hair up into this small bun? Well…" He tucked a small piece behind her ear. "…not all of it."

The time flashed on the glass next to the door: 9:57.

Their time was coming to an end. He looked out onto the street and stood up. He offered her a hand. "You'd better get inside before they send the dogs after you. That'll look bad on your first day."

Katie took his hand and let him pull her up: 9:58

He looked at her, on the verge of saying something—or maybe waiting for her to say it first.

"You'll have to tell me how your test goes. My classes finish at four tomorrow. So any time after that…"

"Yeah. I'll call you." They both smiled. Four couldn't come sooner.

9:59.

She looked at the clock and back at him. Tristan leaned into her, resting his forehead on hers. He gazed into her eyes. "Pay attention and read what they give you. Don't flunk out on the first day. Okay?"

She smiled, and he closed his eyes before pulling a way and heading down the street. Katie went inside and watched him from the window. At the corner, he turned around and smiled.

Strange…she felt like she didn't know him, like the distance between them had made him unfamiliar. Or maybe it was her—she was a stranger to herself without him. Either way, he was a stranger she loved to the moon and back.

⸙

Katie took Tristan's advice and read over the papers she'd collected that day. She looked over the syllabi and highlighted everything she'd missed. She'd have to read a lot to catch up on most of her classes. Luckily almost all of them were science classes and half of them were labs. She'd never liked science, but she'd never hated it either. It was—as far as she knew—another obstacle in living her life carefree. However, she always enjoyed lab time. She'd get high marks on her lab reports and one of those motivational speeches from the teacher when she scored less than satisfactory on the test.

This time she was going to be different. She'd learn the material because she had to graduate from high school. She'd take this program seriously, because she wasn't sure there would be a second chance at figuring out what she wanted to do with her life. Everywhere she looked, the people around her knew what they wanted. Maybe they didn't have a plan, but they were at least on some kind of path to figuring it out.

Even Tristan—though she didn't fully agree—was on his path. He was actively doing something. She was behind in this *"get your life together"* business, and it was race and catch up or eat exhaust.

When she was done going through her paperwork, she put the rest of her things away, put head phones on, and danced in her room until she felt like she was flying.

.இஉ ஓஒ.

The classes were what she expected: work. She'd gotten her past-due assignments and a schedule for their expected due dates. The teachers were nice enough; most of the kids in class seemed serious. They kept their heads down and worked. The other kids slept, either from exhaustion or laziness. Katie couldn't decide, but from the look of one kid's bookbag, either he never turned in assignments or he had more work than she'd had her entire sophomore year.

She went back to the cafeteria just to feel the fancy. It was still pretty sweet. She bought a ticket for a drink from a vending machine and handed it to the barista behind the designated "drink" counter.

"O-negative? I'mma hook you up, girl." He poured blood into a glass and shook it like a martini. He added sugar, salted the glass, and other things Katie didn't know—she just hoped it wasn't eye of newt and beak of crow.

She tried to say it was fine plain, but he waved her off and told her if she didn't like it, she could throw it in his face. She smiled politely, knowing that if she didn't like it, she'd chug it down anyway and never order from him again.

The blood touched her lips and exploded in her mouth. "Wow."

He smiled at her and nodded. "You let Cosmo fix you up from now on. I'll take care of you, baby." Though he was way too friendly, she counted the day as successful. She'd almost forgotten she could hear the dim thuds in the back of her mind. She'd almost forgotten to worry.

When four o' clock came, Katie was in her room, phone in hand and trying to be cool. When four o'clock passed, she collapsed onto her bed, ignoring all reasons that expecting him to call at four-on-the-dot was crazy and obsessive.

He called a few moments after and told her the test was easy and he was offered a job above the rank he left at. She congratulated him, though she still worried. He had policies to catch up on, and she had homework to read. They stayed on the phone working silently. It was ridiculous, but she wouldn't have had it any other way.

❦

The end of the week came, and Katie signed out, packing two bags with homework and—more homework. She had to go to her SA meeting, which was a short way into the vampire district. Tristan had offered to take her until he got his schedule and found out he was working. It was for the best; she'd have never gone inside if it meant she could steal some time with him.

West caught her before she headed into the less-than-cheery community center. They really could do something about the sign.

"You can't go in there with all that crap. You'll mess up the Zen of the circle, and Roger will twitch until the end of the meeting. Seriously, put it in my car."

"Nice to see you, too."

"What?" West was more irritable than snarky. Katie put her bags into his car. "What's all that crap anyway?"

"Schoolwork."

"Oh, god. How old are you? Twelve?"

"What's your problem?" Katie closed the door and blinked, not taking the bait.

"Who says I have a problem? You're the one waltzing up in your stupid sweater. Why are you always wearing that sweater when I see you? Jesus. Get more clothes."

"Screw you." She hadn't worn it since Saturday.

West rolled his eyes. "Fuck this." He started walking away.

Katie followed him. "Where are you going? West! Where are you going?"

He stopped and frowned. "Why do you care?"

"Um, because you're my sponsor. You're supposed to support me. And I'm *not* going in there with those crazies without you." Her eyebrows jumped to the top of her head. She stood in a more threatening position than she meant. "You don't get to walk away. Not now. Not while I'm still dragging myself out of this hole. You *will* get your crap together and go inside with me." Katie's eye twitched.

"Back off, thug life." He sucked in a breath between his teeth. "Let's go. If we're late, Sugar will start asking where we were and she won't stop until the end of the meeting and everyone will be pissed."

Katie unclenched her fist and nodded like she even knew who he was talking about and followed him inside.

They sat in the circle, and Elma had a new cat. It was black and kinda skinny-looking. Roger wore a top hat today and had a cane. A comment about his striking resemblance to Willy Wonka—the original—was made by Hitler-Stache. Porky, whose name turned out to be Queenie, looked a little thinner. Katie could see her natural curves. Before, she'd looked like a blowfish—round in ways the human body shouldn't be.

Queenie spoke first, telling everyone that she was dating again and, even though he was human, she had no suspicious intentions. Dave, the guy who kept staring at Katie, stared some more, and Katie shared when everyone looked at her expectantly. She didn't know why they expected her to talk, because there were at least two people she'd never heard talk, but she spoke anyway.

"I started school. Here in the city. It's been good so far. I haven't had any temptations in six days. That's the longest I've gone—so. Yeah." To her astonishment, everyone clapped. Pride and embarrassment sloshed inside her, but she was thankful.

"West, you've been quiet. Sugar ain't talking if you don't have to talk." It was a lady wearing a jean jumpsuit and pigtails. Last week she'd had orange bangs.

West stayed quiet. He ground on his teeth with his hands in his jacket pockets. Katie had seen that look too often on Tristan. "Then don't talk, Sugar," West said.

Roger put his hand on Sugar's shoulder. "You okay, West?"

He snorted meanly. The room was quiet, but conversation picked up again when Elma showed everyone that she'd taught her new cat how to sit.

When the meeting was over, they did a chant, and West halfheartedly read the words of the same poster they'd recited last time. He was the first one out the door.

Katie hurried after him so he wouldn't pull off with her books in the car. His engine was already roaring when Katie knocked on the window. She heard the locks click and pulled at the door, hoping he hadn't locked it.

The door opened.

"Just get in and stop staring at me like that."

"I wouldn't stare if you weren't being all manic. I don't know if I want to get in the car if you're going to drive angry."

West sighed, not taking his eyes off the road. Katie got in and closed the door. He started to say something, but stopped and sighed again loudly.

The third time he did it, Katie turned to him. "Spit it out or shut up." Then she added more politely, "Thanks in advance for the ride."

"She's back with him." West flicked his blinker on and turned.

"Why is it a problem that *she* is back with *him?*" Katie could guess he meant Zuri, but she didn't want to push it.

West glared at her.

"I wasn't under the impression that you guys were together— or getting together."

"Yeah, well, apparently neither was she."

"Maybe that's the deciding factor of why she got with whoever *he* is?"

"What do you know? You've known her for all of five minutes. I knew her before she knew herself."

"Doesn't mean you own her."

West stopped the car, and Katie jerked forward. "Do you want to walk?"

"All right. Just saying. Geez." Katie buckled her seatbelt.

He drove down a few side streets, trying to avoid traffic. It wasn't working. He pressed his head against the car seat as the red brake lights in front of them shined on his face. "I don't think I own her. If anyone owns anyone, she owns me."

Katie really didn't need to be wrapped up in someone else's drama. Her life was borderline abysmal. She wasn't qualified to help anyone—but she could listen. She owed West that much after how much he'd helped her.

"I don't know why I keep doing this to myself. I let her reel me in, even though I knew she was going to change her mind."

"That has to suck." Katie thought back to the festival when they'd first walked up together, looking happy.

"It does." West glanced at Katie. She was holding her bags just in case he decided to throw her out of the car again. "I don't know why I'm telling you. You're, like, seven, and you thinking kissing is going all the way."

Katie sucked her teeth. "How old are you anyway?"

"Old enough to know a square when I see one. You and your grandma sweater."

"For your information, I got it when I was thirteen and it's technically a dress. Can't tell you the last time I saw any old ladies rocking a mini sweater dress."

"Ew."

"And it's corded. Those never go out of style." She'd made the last part up but thought she sounded confident enough. West turned up the radio and didn't talk for the rest of the way to Katie's house. She mumbled another thanks before getting out and watching him disappear down the dark street.

She'd survived her first week—kinda. Six days. The more she thought about it, the less proud she felt, but it was better than nothing.

Six days turned into two weeks and two weeks turned into six. As the days grew colder, she felt more like herself—no, a *new* version of herself. The pulses were always there to remind her she would never be her old self again, but the new her was in control of it.

The SA meetings helped. The group made her laugh longer and harder than she'd ever thought she had in her life. Most importantly, they helped her laugh at herself. When she mentioned that some days she would give up her old Beanie Baby collection to lick the blood off a freshly tossed Band-Aid, they nodded in understanding and cackled *with* her—sort of.

Her crazy was a part of her. Another color on the white wall of her life. She was slowly starting to accept that. After all, everyone was a little crazy, and if the group taught her anything, some were crazier than that.

Six weeks after starting at Burberry, Katie sat in the cafeteria next to a large window watching a girl fill her glass with ice. The clinking reminded Katie of a poem Hitler-Stache had written about winter. It had been full of sex and ice cubes.

She shook it from her mind and stared out at the busy afternoon traffic. Spicy fumes of tomato sauce and fresh garlic bread stretched from the kitchens to her nose. Though her table was full of homework papers and two textbooks, she couldn't concentrate. Not until she got a plate of mozzarella cheese sticks and scarfed one down.

It was amazing—and absolutely uncomfortable—but it didn't solve her restlessness. She packed away her homework as the cheese stick clunked through her body. She contemplated going to the bathroom and throwing up, but thought better of it. She didn't want people thinking she was a vampire with an eating disorder. That would be odd enough to actually make for good gossip.

Throwing herself back into her seat, she looked out the window and saw West walking toward her. He hadn't actually seen her and was about to pass by.

Katie knocked on the window, making the group of werewolves at the next table glance at her.

West looked up. "Kat?" His voice was muffled through the glass.

Katie waved. She didn't know why she'd actually stopped him.

"Are you coming outside or do you expect me to go in?" West looked between her and the plate of cheese sticks. "You pulling a Queenie on me?"

Katie laughed. "I'll come out." She collected her things and returned the plate of food to the window for dirty dishes.

Outside, West leaned against the brick. He looked more pleasant than usual.

"I swear I only ate one. I love cheese sticks." She rubbed her stomach. "Loved."

"Sure. I bet you've got a stash of them up in your room somewhere. I think I'd like you better with a cheese stick addiction rather than this OCD thing you've got."

Katie stopped smoothing out her hair in the window. "Screw you. It's not OCD. There's a fine line between fixating and actual compulsions. What are you doing in the Burrow anyway? Aren't you working?"

He wore the Patrol-issued uniform: black pants, shirt, and a jacket. It was extremely nondescript, but the tell-tell uniform of STAR.

"Going to work. I just left Zuri's." West smiled. An ambulance blared past them, lighting up his beaming face.

Katie proceeded with caution. "I take it you're not mad at her anymore?"

"Nope. Nothing to be mad about." West wiggled his eyebrows.

Katie took the bait. "So you guys friends again?" Katie had seen Zuri twice since the Festival of Lights. Zuri always avoided conversation about West when Mariam brought him up, going on at length about her new boyfriend. A *"refined gentlemen"* she'd put it.

"We're…patching things up." West paused. "Don't you own any other sweaters? If I gave you money, would you buy a new sweater?"

Katie rolled her eyes. This was the first time she'd worn it since the last time he'd made a comment about it, over a month ago. "Don't be a jerk."

"Then burn that sweater."

"What do you have against my sweater?" Katie adjusted her bookbag and looked down at the cream, woolen cords as another ambulance roared by. She thought it looked cute over her uniform.

"Let me count the ways." West laughed as his phone rang. "You must be bad luck. I'm not supposed to start work for another hour, and yet my supervisor is calling me." West sighed and answered the phone. "Boss Lady. What's up?"

Katie tried to pretend she wasn't listening, but it was difficult to ignore the loud voice on the other end.

"There are some causalities at a community center. The one on Second Street. Some kids got slashed up by a fanatic. Our unit's been assigned to show support or some PR crap like that. Meet us there."

Katie's stomach dropped. The community center? She knew right away which one it was. She'd been avoiding it ever since she left Hamilton.

Her feet slammed against the pavement as she ran faster than her lungs could take.

West was beside her in no time. He pulled her to a stop. "Hey, what are you doing?"

"Let go. Those are my friends." Katie took off again. Her insides hurt more now that she had said it. Her *friends*. Seven blocks never felt farther.

West grabbed her arm again. "Stop. If you really want to get there, hop on my back. You're slow."

Katie climbed onto West's back, took a deep breath, and closed her eyes. Air whizzed past her ears as sirens and shouting grew louder, filling her ears with panic. West put her down, and she stumbled forward into a crowd of people, like her, trying to see what was happening.

West grabbed her arm, pulling her along and waving his badge around. "STAR coming through," he repeated.

Katie moved through, bumping into body after body as no one wanted to make space. No one wanted to take their eyes off what she was finally smelling. Blood. West looked back at her, obviously smelling it too and debating whether she would be able to control herself.

"I'm fine," Katie choked, pushing him forward. It was a lie. She wasn't fine. Her throat went straight to burn mode, and the idea that that blood belonged to the people she'd known her whole life squeezed and knotted her stomach into impossible forms.

Her mouth dropped open when they finally broke through. Ambulances lit up the crowded street as guardians shouted orders and carried out bloodied bodies from the center.

Christi lay on the ground, her face covered in blood. A medic pressed gauze to her leg, wrapping a long gash.

Katie held her breath and ran past the barricade to Christi.

"Back up," the medic snapped.

Katie ignored her. She pressed her hand on Christi's face.

The woman grabbed at her hand.

"I can heal her!" Katie yelled. Katie took another deep breath, inhaling the scent of Christi's blood with it.

"You need to get back. I have this under control."

"I can heal her." Katie pulled her hand back and placed it on Christi's face. She looked into Christi's eyes, ignoring the pulses thumping madly like starved demons. She ignored the screams coming from the building, the crying and wailing each time a gurney was rushed to an ambulance.

Christi blinked through tears, wide-eyed and silent. Katie focused, feeling heat pull from her stomach and warm her hands. She didn't dare look up, ask who else was hurt or what had happened. She focused through the panicked running around her and the medic watching her like a hawk while still patching Christi's leg. She tuned out Christi's O-negative and concentrated on the gash across her face.

Christi exhaled loudly, and Katie moved her hand away. Her cheek was healed, but left behind was an angry red scar and blood. Katie scrambled for her necklace and let the iron singe her flesh. She tried to think past the sirens and calm the hunger.

"What the hell was that, Katie?" Christi winced as the medic gasped, staring between Katie and Christi's face.

"What happened?" Katie watched as Michael was put into the back of a wailing ambulance. He kept taking off his oxygen mask until a medic threatened to tie it to his face. Mr. Carver carried Jenna screaming out of the building, and two medics grabbed her and placed her on a gurney. The smell coming off her body was heavy and thick. Katie gripped the necklace tighter, her hand aching.

The medic finished Christi's leg. "Stay here. Someone will be here shortly to get you into an ambulance. You're fine, but you'll need stitches." The medic studied Katie again before running back toward the building. Katie's heart skipped as West came out, with Allan limping next to him.

"Brian!" Christi yelled through the wailing sirens.

Brian ran toward them, his shirt streaked with blood. He dropped down and hugged Christi, his eyes wide and his breath ragged.

"Thank god. Thank god." Brian let her go and looked her over.

"I'm okay," Christi said.

Brian stroked her hair while catching his breath. He glanced up and saw Katie for the first time.

"I came when I heard," she said.

"It was crazy. A guy went psycho right after we got here. First people started screaming, then he started screaming."

Christi cut in. "He said '*no more chains*' over and over."

"Then he was cutting everyone. It was like he didn't care about anything but cutting as many of us as possible. There was nowhere to run. And we didn't know what was happening. It all happened so fast. We were all trying to get away, and Michael fell on top of me and I fell on Ethan—he broke his leg."

They all looked up as another body came out. It was covered in blood. Katie coughed as the smell smacked her.

"That's the guy," Brian said, breathing a little harder.

Even under all the human blood, Katie smelled the wild. "He's a werewolf." The words "*no more chains*" rolled over in her mind. "He was from The Seven."

Christi looked at her, confused, but her confusion quickly turned to understanding. "From the poster?"

"Yeah. I saw one of their rallies. The guy speaking said something about breaking the chains of slavery."

"That's ridiculous," Brian spat.

Katie watched as they put the body in a bag. Her eyes drifted up and into the crowd—she saw a familiar face.

Clyde.

As soon as he saw her, he turned and walked away. Katie jumped up and ran between an ambulance and a few patrol cars, the red and blue lights flashing in her eyes. She didn't know what she was going to say to him, why she was even chasing him, or why he was running away, but she knew she needed to stop him.

"Clyde!" she yelled.

He wasn't running or walking fast; his pace was steady and normal.

"Spitfire," he said.

"Who was that guy?"

"I'm a werewolf so I must know every other damn werewolf in Gray City?"

Katie didn't let up. "Why'd you run?"

"I'm not running. You're the only one panting like a dog. I left because I saw you. Where you go, trouble follows."

Katie tripped on the pavement. "I didn't have anything to do with that. I wasn't even there."

"No. But now you're here, walking with me down the street with your hands covered in that girl's blood, and half the people on this street are wondering why a werewolf and a vampire covered in human blood are walking away from a crime scene."

"I doubt that—" Katie looked around them, and he was

right. They were getting a lot of nervous looks as they passed people moving toward the scene they'd just left.

"I have nothing to hide," Katie said

Clyde eyed her darkly. "You don't?"

She deflated a little. "Fine. That guy was from The Seven. I think. What do you know about them?" She rubbed her hands on her purple and gray plaid skirt. The second uniform in two years to have blood stains that weren't hers.

"Bunch of second-rate alphas and outcasts. I doubt he was from The Seven."

"Why?"

Clyde stopped walking and opened the door to a deli. "I've got to pick up an order."

Katie walked in. The stench of stale blood seeped out of the walls, the floors, and the ceiling. Katie breathed low and held back a gag.

"When there are two alphas in the pack, one has to submit or go. It's unnatural and dangerous any other way. What do you think a group of alphas are like when they are all outcast because they refused to submit?"

Katie shrugged as Clyde passed a receipt to the man behind the counter. "Maybe they'd elect a new leader?"

"No. We aren't like you delicate, blood-sucking bats—no offense—we don't elect leaders. Our leaders come out of the ring as the last man standing."

"Or woman."

"Don't be annoying."

Katie scowled.

"If all those alphas form a group, they have to have a leader, but what are they going to do? Fight each other for it? There would be no one left standing. The Seven is a myth. It's just some loser giving out pretty speeches, trying to snatch up some weak omegas. A wolf slashing up kids? It stinks of weakness."

Katie agreed, but something bothered her. There was something missing. "Why stand apart when we can stand together?"

"What?" Clyde grabbed two large paper bags full of meat.

"It was on one of their fliers."

"Fancy words, kid. That's all it is." Clyde nodded for her to open the door.

"Well, somebody believes them."

Clyde stopped on the street. "Stop following me."

Katie rolled her eyes. "Bye, Clyde."

"Hey," he called after her. "I'll tell Mercedes I saw you. That you're still alive. It's good to see you're still alive." A toothy grin flashed through his mustache, but it fell into a frown. Stay off the streets and be careful.

"Some of us aren't so delicate."

Clyde let out a low laugh before walking away.

ᴂᴂ16ᴂᴂ

The White Rose

KATIE HEARD FROM Brian that the community center program had been shut down pending further investigation. She also heard that the missing people reports were still growing, despite a new coven leader being elected and tightening the reins on the vampire community. According to Brian, who had texted her all of two days before their communications died off again, everyone was okay—but parents were calling for justice.

It wasn't just them. Before her meetings, Katie would stop by the news station and listen to reports on the giant screen. The heads of houses were giving interviews and publicly speaking out against the werewolves, saying they had turned into a pack of unruly hell hounds. The coven leader, Azezel, was quoted saying only one thing: "In times of turmoil, righteousness prevails."

As the days passed, more guardians patrolled the Burrow. They prowled the streets, never stopping anyone, but watching nonetheless. She stayed at school when she could, finding that she didn't feel safe on the streets with guardians stalking. Their presence was an open threat, daring the werewolves to do something else.

Today, though, she didn't find it hard to stay indoors. As winter break neared, her schoolwork kept her too busy to do anything else.

She nudged opened her dorm room door, trying not to drop her books or splatter her notebook papers everywhere like she had yesterday. She had caught up and surpassed what she was doing in her classes. There was a lot of time for studying since Tristan usually worked evenings. They talked between her classes and his breaks, sent texts, and called to ask each other pointless questions or give silly updates that had nothing to do with anything. Once, he had been called off the phone by his trainer and the words had slipped from his mouth right before he hung up. *"Love you."*

They'd never mentioned it afterward, but she held those words closer to her than the scarf wrapped warmly around her neck.

She thought about them now as she flopped down on her bed and let her feet dangle off the side. She giggled, grabbing one of her notebooks and flipping through her notes. There was a lab tomorrow with live animals. She needed to focus so she didn't end up killing the rabbits, but it was so hard to concentrate with his voice in her mind and the word *love* caressing her ears.

Focus.

Most the kids in her class were werewolves, and they often joked about eating the lab animals. However, Katie would definitely stick out if all the animals started dropping dead around her. She'd have to visit Cosmo before class and fill up her tank. Full tank. No dead animals.

Katie's phone buzzed.

Emojis, followed by an invitation to watch a movie at Zuri's house.

Buzz.

Immeeediatly—and more big, red exclamation point emojis.

Katie could use a break, and the last time she'd seen Zuri was by accident on the street, which had led to impromptu shopping. Katie had been hesitant, holding on to the idea that Allison would text her out of the blue and they'd go shopping together and talk about all the things they'd gone through this year. But it was a pipe dream. The last she'd heard about Allison, she'd left school altogether not too long after Katie to finish her program.

Katie grabbed her phone. While she texted back a reply, the phone rang. It was Zuri.

"Hello?" Katie said. "I was just—"

"Kat. I just had a vision!" Zuri was theatrical as usual. "You and a white rose."

"Oh?" This wasn't the first time she'd texted or called about having a vision, but this *was* the first time it was about Katie. Last time was a turtle dying of thirst on the side of the road. The time before that was a volcanic eruption—or, at least, that was the conclusion they'd come to because she kept seeing ash falling from the sky.

Katie grabbed her keys, not sure if she knew which apartment building was Zuri's. She'd only seen it in passing once.

"That's not all, though. It was pristine and falling into a sea of red roses."

"Sounds…dramatic," Katie chuckled. Zuri had a way of making everything sound magical. Maybe witches oozed magic and Zuri's came out through her words.

"It is! I'm going to read your cards when you get here. Are you busy? I rented a movie. It's about Christmas. We should bundle up and cry because it's touching."

"I'm leaving now." Katie locked her door and jogged down the stairs. "It's not even Thanksgiving yet."

"It's next week. Close enough. Mine's the white brownstone next to the red one with a giant French flag hanging in the window. Apartment 4B." Zuri hung up, screaming about cocoa.

Katie smiled. It was nice being around someone with their own brand of crazy.

Finding the building wasn't easy. Katie walked up and down the street twice. Zuri had failed to mention hers was the *red* one *next* to the white one with a giant *Brazilian* flag.

Katie knocked on the apartment door. The door opened, but no one was there. She peeked in, looking for Zuri—and saw everything but Zuri. Plants, everywhere, hung from the ceiling and watered themselves. A large navy blue and silver quilt folded itself along the side of the comfy-looking white couch. A white cat hissed and ran past Katie, followed by a squirt bottle.

"Bad, Sylvester. Scratch the drapes again and I'll end you— Kat, come sit down. I just found my cards." Zuri walked out of the kitchen wearing pink slippers and bunny ears.

Katie followed her back into the kitchen, careful not to bump into a book placing itself back onto a bookshelf. She sat down at a small round table with a deck of Tarot cards. They shuffled and reshuffled until Zuri sat down and took them.

"You know, the white rose is a symbol of spirituality. Are you embarking on a new spiritual journey? Not going to India to find yourself, are you?"

Katie snorted. Did battling addiction count as a spiritual journey? Probably. "Who isn't?"

"Let's start with your present." Zuri put a card down on the table.

The Fool—a card with a man walking with a napsack and a dog. Great. She was a homeless idiot. Kinda spot on if she really thought about it, but better suited for last year.

Zuri studied Katie. "The Fool isn't what he seems. Not to most, at least. Most think he is silly or stupid, but really he possesses the greatest secret to life—blind faith. He lives simply. Every start with him is a new beginning. He's innocent, like a child, full of potential. But if he is too carefree…he might lose what little he has." She flipped another card. "Your future."

The Tower—a card with two people jumping from a burning fortress. Zuri's brow furrowed, and she stared at the card. "It means destruction is coming, and with it, change. Ever since last month, I get this one, too. Apparently we're both in for a little remodeling. It's not always a bad thing—from the ashes, a phoenix rises. It depends on how you look at things." She grabbed the last card. "Your past." She flipped it onto the table.

The Devil. It couldn't have been a good sign. When was the Devil ever a good sign?

"You are far more interesting than you let on. The Devil represents bondage, addiction, sexuality, and all things tempting." Zuri's eyes twinkled.

"I look cursed."

"You aren't cursed. I saw you, clear as day, and then a white rose as it fell into a bed of red roses. It could mean…any number of things. The future is changeable. Your present is a new beginning. Your past—" Zuri cocked an eyebrow "—full of temptation." She looked at The Tower. "Your future could be a kind of rebirth. Something has to die before it is reborn." Zuri's eye's gleamed with seduction. "A white rose amongst red ones. Temptation. Rebirth. Usually that means one thing—sex."

Katie knew her cheeks were flaming red tomatoes. "Well, I hope it doesn't end in me jumping out of a building that caught fire."

Zuri laughed and put away the cards.

They watched *Meet Me in St. Louis*. At first, Katie was against watching anything in Technicolor, but the movie won her over, filling her with a longing for Christmas lights.

She remembered when Tristan helped her decorate Lucinda's house during Christmas. How they'd teased each other, how he'd looked at her in her dress. The rest of the night might have been a disaster, but in that moment, the world had stopped. Maybe their relationship was destined to be like that, full of little moments that stopped time itself, but fated to end in flames—like The Tower.

Her phone buzzed, and his name appeared with a message. It was a picture of him smiling mischievously while West pointed angrily in the background. They were both wearing their black uniforms. Under the picture, it read:

I just passed my training. Guess who's going to be the new assistant of West's unit?

Her fingers rushed across the screen. *Congrats. He looks thrilled.*

Her phone buzzed. *But it will never match how thrilled I was to tell him.*

She started to type when another message appeared.

Get off the phone and go back to playing with your Barbies, kid.

She smiled to herself. *Go away, West.*

Zuri eyed her. "You're missing the best scene, Kat."

Katie looked up. The credits scrolled up the screen. "How is this the best scene?"

Zuri smiled. "I'm just trying to distract you from falling into womanhood—I hope that's not a penis pic."

Katie laughed. "Gross."

Zuri looked at the phone, nosier than ever. "Sure, I bet you and Tristan are sending only the most innocent kinds of messages. Been there, done that—it ends with you spread eagle, painting your sheets red."

"Jesus, Zuri." Katie showed her the messages.

"I'm just saying." Zuri frowned at West's message. "He's so childish." She turned back to the TV.

Katie glanced around. Everything in the house had stopped. She'd gotten used to the random movements of books righting themselves or the cat running from the hovering spray bottle, but now plants drooped, books hovered in the air, and as Zuri exhaled loudly, a dish broke in the kitchen. "Stupid cat," she said, even though Sylvester was hiding under a chair.

Buzz.

Sorry, Tristan texted, and a picture followed of West holding his arm and giving the bird to the camera.

There was a knock on Zuri's front door, and Katie looked up, startled.

Zuri shared Katie's surprise and excused herself.

Katie sat up and stopped the DVD from looping the intro screen for the third time.

A man's voice cut through just as the TV turned off.

Zuri giggled. "I have company."

"We'll be quiet," he said softly.

Katie heard the distinctive sound of lips separating. She took it as her cue to excuse herself and head back to the dorms. She could stand to brush up on…anything that wasn't the sound of two people making out next to her exit. She folded the quilt, waiting for a break in the lip-smacking silence, and noticed that everything in the apartment had stopped again.

"Please?" the voice said. It was a deep voice. A man's voice. Definitely not West.

Zuri whispered and appeared around a large plant.

Katie beat her to it. "Hey, I have to get going."

Zuri winked. "Not before you meet Hugh." She waved, and a man wearing an expensive-looking suit appeared from behind the plant.

He was older, much older than Katie would have thought normal. Not old-man-with-gray-hairs old, but five-years-added-you-could-be-my-father old. "Hugh, this is Kat. Kat—Hugh."

Hugh leaned in to shake Katie's hand. She tried so hard not to stare. He was a good-looking guy, but…wow.

Not going to judge.

He let go of her hand, and she thanked Zuri for the movie and left. The door hadn't completely closed when she heard them back at it.

Katie smacked her forehead. Why was she such a prude, letting a little bit of kissing get her flustered? Maybe it was because she'd never gotten past the kissing and the touching herself. Or maybe it was because that guy had his lips all over someone her other friend was definitely in love with.

Christmas was getting closer, and Katie finally understood what her dad meant about having a good view of the park. It wasn't anything like the Festival of Lights, but it was enough to make her feel the magic of Christmas. Literally. The trees sparkled, and translucent sprites danced up and around, playing a homey melody on trumpets every hour. After the song, they'd disappear into sparkling dust and rain down like real Christmas magic.

One evening, Zuri and Mariam called her out to ice skate in the park. It was her first time skating, and she felt it. Every fall was harder than the last. Linking arms made it worse because Mariam was no better. Just when Katie got the hang of it, Mariam would drag them all down and they'd disrupt the traffic flow in a fit of pain and laughter.

Katie wished her and Tristan could go to the park and see the tree, but with his work schedule, they were never free during the same times and, to her surprise, she didn't want to skip class. She enjoyed her classes. They weren't like the ones at Hamilton where she sat and was lectured to. The teachers spent a few minutes telling them the objective of the day and then they actually had discussions and experiments. She didn't kill one animal—except a chicken, but the teacher, Ms. Luggs (being a witch), zapped it back to life and mentioned it had already died three times that day and was two clucks away from visiting the cafeteria.

Other than the chicken, the animals liked her. Perhaps they sensed she had the power to heal them—that or they knew she could sap the life out of them in the blink of an eye. Maybe Penny, the chicken, spread the news before Ms. Luggs turned her into soup.

Katie sat on her bed—thinking about Penny and how the cafeteria had suspiciously served chicken potpie a few days after her disappearance—when her phone alarm sounded. It was a reminder that she had her SA meeting in a couple of hours. She took a deep breath and closed her notebook.

As much as things were really starting to change—*had* changed—she couldn't believe how far she had come. Her throat still burned every now and again, and she definitely had to remind herself not to focus on the pulses—even now as she listened to the *thump, thump, thump* of the girl next door whose room always smelled like swamp water. But the pulses didn't scare her as much as they had in the beginning. She was an addict. She'd accepted that—but she also was starting to accept that she was more than that.

Katie put away her textbooks and stacked her papers on her desk. She wasn't going to take any homework home over the holidays. She'd changed—but not *that* much. Her phone rang, and she picked it up, expecting Tristan was either bored of chasing kids away from tagging the art museum or West's constant teasing.

She answered it, a second after registering the name.

Damn it.

It was Lucinda. "Hello? Katie? Hello?"

"Hey." Katie hadn't talked to Lucinda since the night she'd stormed out after calling Katie a selfish, guiltless junkie.

"Did you get any of my voicemails? I've called a dozen times. You haven't called back. How is your new school?"

Katie didn't know what to say. She didn't want to talk to her. It still hurt. It might have been close to the truth, but Lucinda had been the closest thing she'd had to a mom. She'd wanted Lucinda to understand and love her no matter what, but what had Katie expected? Lucinda wasn't her actual mother. That wasn't her job.

"Yeah. Sorry. I've been really busy studying."

Lucinda sniffled.

Crap.

"Oh. I understand. I'm glad you picked up. Are you coming to the Christmas party?"

"I didn't know you were still having one. After last year and all." Brian, drunk and angry and yelling about how Tristan was half-breed scrum flashed across her mind.

"It's going to be a lot smaller than usual. Just family and friends." Lucinda sniffled louder.

"Yeah. I'll be there." Katie wished she had never picked up the phone at all.

"I'm sorry, Katie," Lucinda cried.

Katie looked up at the ceiling, wishing she could have avoided this. She didn't want to cry. She didn't want to get sad. Being sad made her throat burn. Being sad reminded her of why she was where she was.

"It's fine, Lucy. Really. I'll be at the party. I have to go. I have a lab to make up. I'll talk to you later." Katie hung up and headed straight to the cafeteria.

Did this count as avoidance? She'd ask West later. For now, she was going to hit up Cosmo to make sure the burn in her throat didn't turn into her massacring a crowd of people and then leave early for her SA meeting.

⚜

The deeper she walked into the vampire district, the better she felt. She stopped by a small park and watched as two men polished the head of a statue. She sat down on the bench, enjoying the ethereal light the place had. It hadn't occurred to her when she first arrived, but as she really started looking around, she realized she was in a cemetery.

Morbid. Vampires didn't really die, not naturally, yet there were tall statues everywhere. As the men finished the one they were working on, her breath caught in her chest.

It was Lawrence, his face carved perfectly in stone.

She sat, wondering who had commissioned it and wanting to leave, knowing how cruel she had been to never even think about his body after she'd left it in the house. How cruel she had been for missing the funeral…

When the men left, taking their supplies with them, Katie moved closer to the statue until she was touching it with her bare hands.

The cold, smooth stone shined between her fingers. There was already a pile of red roses at the base of the statue. People who had missed him—and not one from her. She knelt down, unable to think or move. "You are a shit person, you know that?" she said aloud. "I didn't want anything from you. I just wanted…I wanted to think you cared."

"What we think and what is right in front of us are often two different things," said a strange man standing only inches behind her.

Katie jumped ten feet out of her skin. She hadn't heard him, and a quick glance around told her no one else was nearby. She wondered if anyone would hear her scream if it came to that.

He whispered a prayer, all but the last part in Spanish. "May your soul be pure again." He threw a single white rose into the pile of red ones. His eyes pulled away from the flowers and landed on Katie. "You look like him. I am guessing you are the one he left behind." The man put his hands behind his back. He had shoulder-length, thick white hair, an olive skin tone, and a thick Spanish accent. It was his green eyes that made her feel uneasy. Not because they looked threatening—but because they were attractive. The kind of attractive old guys shouldn't be.

"I'm sorry," he said. "I've been rude." He held out his hand. "I am Azezel."

Katie hesitated before shaking his hand. "The new coven leader."

"Yes. I am going to be frank with you…" He waited.

"Katie."

"Katie." Azezel looked back at the statue. "I usually only visit these once a year on Remembrance Day. But today I am here because you are here."

Katie blinked. "I—I don't know what I'm supposed to say to that or what I'm supposed to think. To be honest, you are giving off a lot of creep factor right now." She began to back up.

"Please. I am a busy man. If I wanted something done to you, I would have summoned you. Also, I do not deal in the transgressions of the flesh, so do not insult me." Azezel looked back at the statue. "I am here because God wanted to show me something."

And this was Katie's cue to leave. She had nothing against religious people—in fact, she had her own feelings and ideas about all that—but when someone started talking about her in the same sentence with *God* and *purpose*, someone she'd never seen before who'd already creeped up on her once…

The signs were all too clear. *Crazy*—the dangerous kind.

"You do not believe me?" He unbuttoned his collared shirt, and Katie turned around and walked away.

"Nope. Not doing this."

"Look," he said.

Katie ran. She didn't want to see anything this crazy had pulled out for her to look at.

He was in front of her before she even had a plan.

Katie skidded to a stop and saw a familiar, glowing tattoo. The mark. It shimmered right over his heart. "Please. As I have said, I am a busy man." He gestured toward the benches.

"Okay, I'm going to level with you, pops," Katie said, not missing the look of offense on his face. "I haven't had a lot of luck with older men lately. One turned out to be a jerk. Another tried to rape me. And there was that one guy three years ago on Main Street who flashed me while he peed. If you're going to talk, talk. I'm not going to sit in some creepy shaded corner so you can…whatever. You get it."

Azezel held up his hand. "Fair enough. You know what this mark means?"

"Yes." Katie thought of her own, now completely visible on the back of her shoulder. He'd showed his for a reason. "What can you do?"

He looked affronted. "I have a gift, Katie. A gift. Not a parlor trick. I do not *do*. I—I see the future. I see what God wants me to see. A month ago, I saw you before that statue was even finished. I saw you touching the face of your father."

Katie stared, waiting for the part that mattered. The part where he told her why that gave him a pass to be a creep about it. When he said nothing, she spoke. "And?"

"Before, I could not see your face. Just your hand on his face. I did not know why God would show me such a thing. But now I am beginning to understand." He eyed her. "I have a witness who saw a boy and a girl climb out of the rubble after Eshmael's house collapsed. I bet, if I were to bring you to him, he would say it was you." Azezel's eyes bore into her.

She made her face as neutral as possible. What was the point of lying? "It was.'"

"Did you kill your father and his brother?"

Katie frowned. "No. Eshmael—he… It's complicated."

Azezel clinched his fist. "Little girl, if you killed a pureblood vampire—my oldest friend—and you do not tell me the truth, complicated will be the least of your problems."

Katie had never told anyone exactly what had happened. Not the full truth. She had never wanted to—never could put it to words and send it out into the universe. But she told Azezel. She told a complete stranger every detail of what had gone on in that room. A stranger with the power to sentence Tristan to death.

"And the boy? Where is he?"

Katie cut him a look. "If you want someone to blame, blame me."

"I am not looking to blame. I have a feeling I have seen this boy before. God has shown me both your faces, and the boy will change the world as we know it. There will come a time when everything seems lost. The only thing that will save you is if you tell him something: *Let go.* Can you remember that, Katie?"

Katie frowned. "What?" She rubbed her temples, the pulses in her mind thumping louder ever since she'd thought about Eshmael's hands around her neck.

Azezel looked to the sky and whispered something in Spanish. "I will do everything in my power to protect our kind. But you must remember."

"I'm going to need more specifics than 'when everything seems lost' because I've had one hell of a summer."

"There will be no mistaking this darkness. It will engulf us all. When it does, do not forget. And…" His eyes softened. He peered past her and saw only something that existed to him. "…be brave." He walked past her, but Katie called after him.

"Nope. You can*not* walk away after that. I'm trying to get away from crazy. Excuse me."

"I am a busy man, Katie. I will see you at the world's end."

Katie stopped following him and stared at his back. Nutcase. Whack job. Screws Loose McGoose. Those were all the things she wanted to shout at him, but the fear dropping into her chest reminded her that what he said was probably right.

"What about Lawrence? What about how he died?" she called after him. Would he tell others? Would they come after her and Tristan? Would the vampire world know Larry died a coward, unable to stop his crazy brother?

"He is with God now. Let us hope it is a long time before any of us meet him again," Azezel said over his shoulder. He was gone in the blink of an eye.

Katie's mind raced over what had happened, and she texted the entire encounter to Tristan. It might have been a novel, but she didn't want to forget anything. She waited five painstaking minutes for a reply.

Creepy, Tristan replied.

"GAAHHHH!" Katie nearly choked on her own built-up anticipation.

Seriously? That's all you have to say? Creepy?! She clutched her phone, getting up from her spot and leaving so she wouldn't be late for the SA meeting.

Buzz.

Can't text a novel. Some of us work.

The nonchalance spilled out from the words and soothed her goosebumps.

Buzz.

Are you safe?

Katie texted back that all was safe and sound.

Buzz.

Then stop using so many ! You're making me nervous. Talk to you soon.

Katie sent three lines of exclamation marks and a heart. Her own heart did a flip when he sent her a heart back. He never used emojis.

⋅இ⦿ஓ⋅

Katie tried to focus at the meeting, but despite everyone's usual oddities, they all seemed to be doing fine—except Hitler-Stache, whose name was Melvin had some pretty explicit poetry because the guy he loved was now dating someone else. At the end, West pulled Katie outside.

"What's up with you?"

"Nothing." Katie stared at the building across the street. Did Azezel know she was in recovery? What had all that "be brave" stuff been about? At least the white rose vision was all cleared up.

"Hey." West snapped his fingers at her. "You're not going to fall off the wagon, are you? I'm not going to have to shoot you, am I? Don't do that to me. Don't make me put you down, Kat."

"I'm not a dog. And I'm not falling off the wagon. I'm just... How much do you know about Azezel?"

"Oh. It's worse. You're crushing on the old man. What is with you chicks?"

"What? No, I'm not. I—never mind." Katie waited for West to unlock his car door. He always drove her home after meetings. She wondered how much was habit and how much was because he didn't trust her to be alone after spending an hour talking about sourcing.

"He's the oldest Catholic I know. He makes the Pope look like a sacrilegious heathen. He's probably old enough to have met Jesus, so who knows what his deal is?"

"He did seem really God-focused."

"You met him?" West paused before starting the car.

"Briefly."

West's movements slowed down, though he tried to act uninterested.

"Why?"

"Nothing. Just weird. Does he know you're Lawrence's daughter?" West looked in the rearview mirror and locked the car doors.

"He does now. Why?"

"Nothing. Just...there is a lot of tense speculation about how he died. People think it was a setup. Half my unit thinks Azezel might have done it to take over Lawrence's covens. The other half think the Starvaski family did it to make Azezel look guilty so *they'd* get the covens. Lawrence had the most lucrative covens. So…" West looked out the side mirrors intensely before shifting the car to drive. "I think it's strange that Lawrence would never mention a daughter, and then all of a sudden end up dead in his brother's house, when everyone knows he was blood bound him. So it couldn't have been Eshmael who killed him—and some people think there was a girl and a guy leaving the house. No one credible, but still…" West drove, staring out the window like he wasn't saying he thought she'd been at the crime scene and had caused a shit-ton of confusion because they'd left and reported nothing.

"I told him what happened." Katie wondered if letting West know he was on to something was a smart choice or not.

"What did he say?"

"That Larry was with God now. And hopefully we wouldn't see him any time soon. Or something creepy like that."

"Larry? That's…cute."

"Shut up. That's what I knew him as. Larry, the ice cream shop owner."

"This is getting bizarre." West relaxed in his seat.

"You don't know the half of it."

"It's cool. You don't have to tell me. I just wanted to make sure I wasn't driving a fugitive around in my car. That would have done hell to my career—and lifespan. I thought I was going to have to drive like hell to the next underground city." West looked over at her, and she truly felt like they were friends.

It wasn't like she hadn't thought of him as a friend before, but she was starting to see what Tristan meant by West weaseling into everything. He had a way of becoming something without asking consent. He was like Zuri. They intruded into her personal space so abruptly that it felt natural.

West caught her staring. "Don't look at me like that. My heart belongs to someone else, kid."

Katie rolled her eyes. "Don't make a mountain out of a mole hill."

"You sound like my grandmother. *And* you're wearing that damn sweater again," West teased as he drove up the streets to the car lift that would take them into Boise.

Katie had a thing or two to say about his unkempt hair and ever-growing facial hair. It wasn't until Lucinda called her phone again and Katie slipped it back into her pocket that she remembered she had more issues than she needed.

"My...well, in a nutshell she's like my mom because I don't have one, but not really because we've never really said that—but anyway," Katie started.

"Why is everything in your life so complicated? Don't you have anything normal about you?"

"One—rude. Two—I was pretty normal back in the day. I was even on a swim team. And three—don't interrupt."

He waved her on.

"So I haven't talked to her in a while because she kind of flipped out on me and called me a useless, helpless junkie."

"Damn, Fake-Mama."

"West."

"Sorry. Go on."

"So she called today. Actually she's called me every day for two months, but I let it go to voicemail because…I was doing better. You know, day by day. I just wanted to focus on everything but rock-bottom. So I accidentally picked up today and she wants me to go to her Christmas party and I don't really want to go but—is this avoidance? It is, right?"

West bit his lip. "It depends. Do you not want to be around her because you're afraid she's going to tear you down? Or is it because you don't want to apologize for whatever you've done to piss her off?"

"I did. I mean, I was there and sitting in the intervention circle spilling my guts. I was apologizing and telling them stuff I hadn't even told myself. And then *she* got angry—who does that? I was seconds from running out the door and sucking off the first person I saw—I know. I heard it. Too late to take it back."

West laughed louder than an accidental dirty joke deserved. "Sounds like you're mad."

"Maybe." Katie stared out the window. Rush hour was always the worst. She watched a girl put on mascara in the car next to her. They locked eyes, and Katie smiled, making the girl double-take.

"Do you know her?" West nodded his head and waved.

"Oh, god, no, but now she's for sure weirded out." Katie was right. The girl made sure not to look in their direction again.

"I think you're avoiding her for good and bad reasons."

Katie sat up straight, hoping he'd tell her not to go to the party.

"She sounds like a lot of baggage. Like someone who dumps their *stuff* on you at inappropriate times. But you also seem mad. And you're that person who hides how mad they are until they explode."

"Am not."

"How many times have you talked to her?"

"Touché," Katie said.

"Just go—be quiet, let me finish. Here's the plan: go and sort out the stuff you need to. If it's too much and you feel ambushed, then leave. It's as simple as that. You don't need people in your life who are going to abuse you."

"She doesn't. She would never. I've known her like…my entire life."

"Those are usually the people who do the most damage. You don't see it. They don't see it. They do it for love, and next thing you know you're stuck in this place where you can't move forward and, if you stay still, you'll combust." West eyed her pointedly.

Katie didn't know if she felt like Lucinda was that kind of person, but he was right about the plan.

"If it gets really bad, call me. I'll come pick you up and we'll figure it out from there."

"I can handle my own stuff, you know."

"Says the girl who nearly killed a man."

Katie closed her eyes. It still hurt when he did that, brought up Emanuel. Thirty-two years old. Not married but engaged. Had one son, who was going to turn three in four months, and a really big family—four sisters and five brothers, to be exact.

West had researched it for her, said it was important she knew exactly what she took away from him.

"Truth hurts," West said. "I don't say that just to make you feel bad. I say it to remind you that you can't do it all on you own. None of us can. We can try, but if you can't admit you need help, you end up doing something stupid."

Katie nodded and turned on the radio. She got it. But she was good on the talking for now.

17
Merry Freaking Christmas

T HE NEXT TIME Katie saw West was just a few days later when they all met up at a restaurant called Latin Fever. It would be the last time they saw each other before Christmas. Mariam and Salem were going to spend the holidays with their family, Zuri mentioned being completely wrapped in mistletoe with her boyfriend Hugh, and West and Tristan were working through Christmas Eve.

Katie made her way to the restaurant, only getting lost three times because Zuri was notorious for giving shoddy directions. The more wrong streets she turned down, the more nervous she got being alone in the Burrow, a place that was growing more and more anxious.

When she found the restaurant, Tristan was outside waiting, and he smiled when he saw her. He waved in that weird way *"friends"* wave at each other, but then stopped because he probably realized friends don't really wave like that—like he was nervously saying hello to a date.

"You read way too much into everything," he said. "You make it awkward."

"*I* make it awkward? You should have seen that wave." Katie smiled, pulling in her thoughts. She wanted to lean in and hug him, but they hadn't gotten to that level yet. In fact, she couldn't remember the last time she'd felt his skin next to hers. His bare arm and firm hands had never looked so tempting to touch…

"Everyone is already inside."

Katie cleared her throat.

He eyed her suspiciously and held the door open for her. Loud Spanish music greeted her. "And in case you're wondering, I'm holding the door open because I'm a decent person. Not because I'm hoping to score some points."

Katie laughed. It never failed—they were always in the weird friend lane.

Her mouth would have watered if she was still into spicy foods. The restaurant was classier than she was used to. There was a large dance floor in the middle, and a few people salsa dancing off-beat. She could tell by their smiles and the way they laughed that they were either really bad and having fun or really good and a little drunk.

"Kat," Zuri called, waving.

"That's how friends wave," she said to Tristan, waving back.

He smiled and shook his head, pulling out a seat for her. "Still just being decent," he murmured.

Katie sat down. Mariam and Salem were too busy arguing over the menu to notice, and West sketched on a notepad.

"I'm starving, but the twins won't let anyone else see the menu," Zuri sighed.

"Don't call us that," Salem said. "We have names."

Zuri stuck out her tongue and smiled at Katie. "You look nice," she said with a wink.

Katie blushed. She *had* put in a little extra effort. She'd done it to be noticed—by Tristan, mainly—so she shouldn't have felt embarrassed, but she did.

"Nice to see you in something other than that sweater." West called over a waiter.

"Don't call him over. I haven't even looked at the menu," Zuri said.

"You always get the same thing. Hell, they always do this, and you always order chicken and rice with salsa on the side."

"Maybe I want something else." Zuri's silver hair swung around her cheeks.

"That's what you say. That's what you *always* say. But you don't and life will be easier as soon as you admit it."

Zuri looked at everything but West. "I didn't know you felt so strongly about the chicken."

"I don't." West ordered some food and drinks. The loud

muted trumpets sounded more edgy and out of control rather than bright and catchy.

While they waited, West handed Tristan the sketchpad. They were going to play the drawing game again. Katie didn't know the name of it, but she liked it.

Tristan drew a round thing that looked like an orange.

West looked at the drawing and then to Tristan. "Fail."

"You wrote *square*. What am I supposed to draw?" Tristan moved to a new sheet and sketched down a word.

"Anything but an orange," West said.

Tristan handed Katie the sketchpad. "It's not an orange. It's a circle."

Katie looked at the sketchpad.

Honey pot.

She felt the corners of her mouth curl. She dared to look at Tristan. He raised his eyebrows and tapped her on the nose with the pencil.

By the time the food had arrived and they'd eaten, Mariam and Salem had argued over which dish was best, why it was best, and whether the restaurant had any attributes at all. The blood at this restaurant was better than other fusion restaurants, and Katie was enjoying the last sip in her glass when Zuri and West's voices grew louder.

"Because it's stupid," West said.

Zuri faked a laugh. "Yes, to a vampire, equality *is* stupid. It's hard to see others as equals when you have to look down to find them."

"Just because I don't believe in this Seven crap doesn't mean I don't think everyone is equal."

"Then tell me, what do you believe?"

West sucked his teeth. "Why is this dinner conversation?"

Salem and Mariam groaned in unison.

Mariam raised her hand in a plea. "Can we not do this? You two will never see eye to eye on it."

"No." Zuri sat taller in her chair. "Let him tell us why he believes The Seven are crap. Why *their* speeches on equality are so different from his own."

"Zuri." West's face scrunched up in annoyance. "We live equally now. What is wrong with that? What is wrong with accepting that fundamentally we *are* different? When I see you, I see you for who you are—the essence of you. I don't care about what you're made of, but I respect that you are a witch. That your needs are different than mine."

"Oh. And they are." Zuri's laugh had a bite that West took personally.

"Yes, they *are*. I'm not made weak by my past and present because *I* see a future and will outlive half of us at this damn table."

Katie glanced at Mariam and Salem. Like Katie, their eyes were alert.

Tristan cleared his throat. "I think it's safe to say The Seven cause more problems than they are trying to solve. Look at the guy at the community center. He tried to kill a bunch of kids."

"He was a fanatic," Zuri shot back.

"Was he?" Salem spoke up, though Mariam elbowed him. "He's not the only one who believes that we are living like sewer rats. Five guys left our pack last month saying how they can't follow a leader who answers to slave masters. They were completely bought on it. It's not a secret that other packs are losing members to this group."

Zuri shook her head. "But can't you see there is truth to it? We are forced to live underground."

West squinted like he had a headache. "No one *forces* us. There are thousands, if not more, who live top-side. Gray City is a safe place, Zuri. How can you not see that? Wasn't it witches who created the underground cities? Aren't witches the ones who hexed the humans and guardians?"

"I am not my council," Zuri growled.

"No, but you could have been. You could actually be doing something with the power you have, but you're not, are you? Why even be gifted with something you're going to waste on festivals and fashion?" West stared her down.

"Don't pretend like you know everything I do or don't do."

"Just like you to sweep everything under the rug. We all know you have incredible powers. We all know the council has been begging you to join for years. We all know you do nothing and have no actual ambition for anything except—"

The entire restaurant went dark, and a spotlight lit up their table.

"What's going on?" Katie looked between everyone else at the table. West and Zuri still glowered like two lions gearing up for a fight over the last scrap of a zebra carcass.

Mariam smiled apologetically. "Sorry, Kat. If we had given you warning, you would have been a flight risk."

Katie looked around the table as the band on stage began playing music. A man approached her from the darkness.

"What the hell?" Katie said out of the corner of her mouth.

"Take one for the team," Salem whispered.

The man held out his hand. "There is a special lady here to celebrate a very special night with us." He said something else in Spanish, and Katie had no idea what he was saying or why he wanted her to get up. Applause erupted across the restaurant, and Tristan moved his chair, giving Katie the room to get out of her seat.

"Tristan!" she hissed, aware that everyone in the restaurant was staring at her.

The mysterious man spoke again. "I've got a message for you, darling." Katie gave him her hand and cast a murderous look across her giggling table. He kissed her hand, and Katie swore Tristan's smile wavered. The man pulled her to the middle of the room, and she heard her table scream in unison over the music.

"Happy birthday, Kat!"

Katie's face burned red, and her eyes bulged as the restaurant clapped louder and the man started singing in Spanish and dancing—forcing her to do the worst salsa she'd ever done in her life. She caught a few words in the song, things like *irresistible* and *love* and *your beauty*. However, her two years of Spanish during her normal human days was the worst of her subjects.

She relaxed, because what else can you do when a song seems to be going on for more than the allotted polite thirty seconds you have to embarrass someone? She let him guide her on the dance floor and hoped she looked half as good as he did.

When the song ended, he got down on one knee and all the women swooned. She might have joined them—he oozed charm and was probably the suavest man she'd ever have in front of her on one knee while speaking the smoothest of Spanish—but having a spotlight shining down on her and the attention of all the people in the restaurant left her with little motivation to swoon.

"Happy birthday," he said, kissing her hand again.

Katie thanked him and tried to walk calmly back to her seat as the lights returned and the band went back to gently playing.

"I will murder all of you in your sleep," Katie said.

Each and every one of them cried with laughter.

Katie held back her own laugh and threatened to toss the cake that was delivered to their table free of charge. "Take one for the team? Only half the team is going to eat this." If anything, at least West and Zuri seemed to have stopped fighting and were enjoying a good laugh.

Amongst it all, she felt like she was flying high in the sky. Whether it was the dancing or the fact that she was surrounded by people who liked her—actually wanted her around, craziness and all—she felt like, for once, she was winning.

After "the team" devoured the cake, they got up to leave the restaurant, and Katie received a wink from the band singer as she crossed the floor to the exit.

Next on the agenda was a karaoke bar. Katie had never been to an actual karaoke bar in her life, let alone sang in front of more people than her reflection in the mirror. She prayed that taking one for the team meant she was exempt from singing alone and revealing the dying-cats quality of her singing voice.

Mariam was the first to sing, and contrary to her usual deep voice, her singing voice was higher pitched, smooth and mesmerizing.

"That's not fair," Katie said as Mariam sat back down. She was still getting applause from a few tables. "You should be paid for that performance."

Mariam waved Katie off, but hunger pawed behind her eyes. "I wish. But singing will make Salem hate me for all eternity. Besides I love cooking with my brother. It's the only thing better than being on stage."

Katie watched Salem on stage; he was possibly a worse singer than Katie. He and Mariam were so different for people who looked the same. Katie laughed as he held out a long note, most likely offending everyone in a two-block radius.

Her eyes found Tristan standing next to West at the bar, drinking what Katie thought was his third *alcoholic* drink. She couldn't help but feel nervous. The last time he drank, he'd sent them both to a dark place she never wanted to go again. But despite her reservations, Tristan wasn't the same as he had been back then. He and West were having fun together. It was a glimpse into what things might have been like between them before he left. He laughed, and his face was more open than it had been for a while. It was beautiful, how free he looked. She could even feel his wall threatening to crumble down with the next laugh. The parts of him that slipped out warmed her.

A few people sang, but only one stood out, a guy with green-frosted tips and green eyebrows. He set out to rap but ended up crying. The announcer took the microphone from him, and Katie was surprised to hear the next name.

"Tristan Vaun—Vauntgard?" he said, looking up and back down at the paper to make sure he'd said the name right.

She looked over at Tristan, who was still laughing. Katie told Zuri there was no way he was going to get up there—and ate her words when he chugged the rest of his drink and made his way to the stage.

"Oh, this should be good," Zuri laughed.

Tristan looked through the book quickly and picked out a song before taking the mike.

Katie's mouth flopped down to the floor. She stared at *her* Tristan on stage with a mike in hand doing some weird thing with his mouth. Were they mouth exercises? She held back a giggle. *This* was unreal. She blinked, still waiting for reality to kick in as West sat in the chair next to her instead of Zuri.

The title flashed on the screen behind him: *My Best Friend by Weezer.* Katie had never heard the song before, but her heart fell to the floor, joining her mouth, when he pointed at her.

"This one is for Katalina Kitty Kat."

Katie blinked. He had to be drunk out of his mind—and he was good. His voice was smooth and had that man-charm that guys either had or didn't. However, the song he chose was far more impressive than how he sang it. She caught things like how she brought light to his dark, how seeing her face made him happy inside, how he *needed* her, how he'd never leave her, how he felt her pain when she cried—and of course over and over that he loved her.

The words filled her heart with the kind of happiness that hurt. It hurt so much she cried. But she pretended her tears were tears of laughter, a product of the air guitar solo he completely invested himself in. She laughed and she cried, knowing neither Zuri nor West bought that it was all because Tristan was both uncharacteristically good at singing and amusing.

As the song died to an end, he held out those perfect notes full of literal love and then leaned into the microphone, staring at her directly. "And I didn't say all that because I'm drunk."

They all clapped. His was the best performance in the bar— definitely the best.

Her heart drummed hard in her chest as he walked toward her and bent slightly, leaning his face into hers. "I said it because I'm decent," he said with a smile, and Katie's body ached, wanting to touch him, hug him, hold onto him—anything. But he moved away, sitting in the only empty seat between Salem and West.

Katie didn't have to sing. Everyone agreed that making her salsa dance in a restaurant full of people while being serenaded for a fake birthday had been enough for one day. It neared eleven-thirty when they left the bar. Katie had only gotten her dad to agree to her staying out until midnight. And that was only because she'd called him every hour, sent him a text every thirty minutes, and to her biggest annoyance, because her can-do-no-wrong sponsor West was with her.

Zuri was the last to come out of the bar, and she looked a little less sparkly than usual. "Don't forget. New Year's Eve at my place. You all swore. Even if it's only for a little." She eyed Katie, who'd already said she'd have to leave early because there was no way her dad would let her stay out past midnight, even if it was New Year's.

"Maybe," West said.

"What do you mean *maybe*? This is tradition. You don't say *maybe* to tradition." Zuri walked past West and linked arms with Mariam.

"I am now." West hadn't drank much alcohol, but a dark look settled on his face—that kind of looseness that came with letting go of inhibitions glinted in his eyes.

Katie locked eyes with Tristan and he shrugged, but she heard clearly in her head, *"Stay out of it."*

He looked away and pulled the rest of his thoughts with him. Thoughts that had lingered on her legs in her jeans. Katie blushed, glad they were all walking again.

"I don't get why he has to be childish about everything. Then he wonders why…" Zuri said quietly to Mariam, but everyone could hear her.

"*Why* what, Zuri?" West said. There was a dangerous cut to his voice when he said her name. Like it pained him.

She sighed, exasperated. "Nothing."

"Let it go," Salem said. He tried to get West to look at some graffiti art on a building they passed.

"No. *Why* what, Zuri? You brought it up. Let's talk about it. God forbid our friends know what we do behind closed doors when your boyfriend is MIA."

Zuri's face flushed, and she walked faster. "Shut up, West."

"No. I'm tired of your shit. Do you know what it's like for me? To stand here wanting you. Wanting all of you. Not just the *you* who gets lonely or the *you* who gets sad."

Zuri let go of Mariam and tried to pull West in the other direction, but he didn't budge. "West, this is why. *This* is why. Look at you. You're yelling at me in the middle of the street."

"Because you won't listen to me anywhere else. You think this is embarrassing? Try being the rebound who fell in love."

"What does that even mean?" Zuri yelled.

"Tell me. Who should I be? Who am I supposed to be to make you love me? Because clearly I'm not good enough, I'm not smart enough, I'm not man enough. So tell me, who the fuck am I supposed to be, Zuri?"

"What did you expect? You don't even think species should mix. How can I love someone who doesn't think I'm an equal?"

"That's politics, not my life. You're the one telling me that it won't work, then using me when your warlock walks out on you. Does *he* treat you like an equal?"

Zuri's voice burned with rage. "He's everything you're not. He's not some little boy with his tail between his legs because things don't go his way."

"So why come back to me? Apparently you *like* the tail between my legs."

Blood rushed to Zuri's face. "He's going to ask me to marry him. And I'm going to say *yes*. Happy New Year and Merry Freaking Christmas!" she yelled. Her eyes were wide, and Katie felt something she'd never felt in Gray City: a breeze, rolling between them all. It swirled around Zuri and West, yet neither of them flinched.

West's eyes turned to stone. He stood there, quiet, with Zuri's words still bouncing off all of them like an echo in the breeze.

Even Katie's heart ached for him. She had grown used to their weird secret love, but it was going to end now. Right here in the street for everyone close enough to hear. There was no taking it back. Not with it splattered all across the Burrow.

West moved and everyone's eyes were glued to him, but he only saw Zuri. He reached into his shirt, grabbing at a black cord around his neck. "You want your heart back?" He unclasped one of two necklaces, threw it onto the sidewalk, and walked away.

Zuri stared at it, her eyes wide and blank. The wind stopped.

"Uh…" Tristan looked between West and Katie.

"I'll get home. Go ahead. I'm fine. I'll just call my dad to pick me up," Katie said, nodding. If anyone knew what it felt like to be publicly humiliated and dumped by their not-so-official girlfriend, it was Tristan. Katie burned, wondering if it had looked like this to Allison when she'd done the same thing to Tristan last year. Katie thought she was the only one crazy enough to tear down someone she loved out of hurt and anger.

Salem picked up the necklace and gave it to Zuri. "Okay, enough street drama for one night. Let's get out of here before people start throwing money at us."

Zuri's face was empty, but she laughed and gripped the necklace between her fingers.

"Are you sure you're okay to get home?" Zuri asked, breathing like she'd just ran around the block.

"Yeah. Yeah." Katie tried to think of what she could say, but she didn't think there was anything that would make Zuri feel anything other than angry or regretful.

"Don't forget the party," Zuri said, taking a deep breath and walking away.

"Zuri—" Katie started.

"You better get going, it's late." Zuri waved and told Mariam at least three times that she was fine to walk home alone.

Katie said her goodbyes to Mariam and Salem and called her dad to meet her at the nearest elevator. When she was in the car with him, he asked her how the night had gone. Despite hoping that West wasn't as broken-hearted as he'd looked, she could only see Tristan, standing on stage and singing *I love you* over and over.

∼18∼

Past the Point of No Return

KATIE DIDN'T HAVE a dress to wear for Lucinda's Christmas party. She didn't even know what kind of dress she should wear. *Family and friends?* That could mean anything with Lucinda. Calling Allison was out of the question. Katie didn't know her new number or think Allison would pick up if she did—and Zuri probably wasn't in the mood to shop or talk. She normally texted Katie at random times of the night, but all had been quiet on that front after her and West's relationship had exploded on the street.

Since Katie's dad had the weekends off now, she dragged him to the mall and made him sit in a chair while she decided everything she wore looked horrible or worse than horrible. So much time in Gray City had made her a little paler and the fact that it was winter and the sun was always hidden behind thick cloud cover didn't help.

The day was long and without hope, until her dad suggested she watch while he got a burger from his favorite burger place downtown. While she listened to him shovel in fries, her eyes were graced by the perfect dress.

It hung in the window of a little boutique, simple and deep purple. It didn't have frills or look like she was trying to go to a job interview, and it wasn't sexy or lusty. It was soft and kind of magical. It had that spark she was used to seeing in Gray City. Katie eyed the sign suspiciously.

Lilly's Closet. It was normal enough, but there was no doubt these clothes were probably more than what the eye could glean.

While her dad finished his burger, she tried on the dress and bought it, along with a pair of silver heels. Her dad was so relieved that she had a bag in her hand he didn't ask about how much it cost or where the money had come from. But he had to have known.

Christmas Eve came a lot sooner than it had the year before, like the days were passing by and she'd somehow used up all the time. She spent her days with her dad doing actual things. They went to movies, and she helped him with projects he'd picked up around the house while she'd been at Burberry—upgrading the kitchen, adding a back deck to the patio. Most of the time she spent laughing at him when he fell down, exhausted, while she still had the energy of a work ox. It was good to be outside, even though the snow was building up and the wind was bitter. Being with her dad was nice, and for once they had conversations that didn't make him look at her like she was that strung-out girl covering her eyes from the car headlights.

⁘

Katie ran her hands over her new dress. It was so soft. She let it fall gracefully from her fingertips and back onto the hanger. She sat on her bed and dried her hair.

She hadn't seen Tristan in a week, and the last time she'd seen him, the meeting had been brief as he'd been on his way to his new station. She was starting to feel comfortable with his job. It wasn't like what she'd thought before. He didn't spend his days chasing people down to kill. He spent his days answering noise disturbances and studying to be a new recruit trainer. Tristan—*a teacher*. He'd said he'd decided on it because of her. He felt like he'd taught her so much, and she would probably be his worst student ever. Compared to her, any other students would be a breeze.

Katie couldn't wrap her mind around how focused and driven he was. In such a sort amount of time, he had gotten back on his path and was zooming straight ahead. It inspired her to work harder too because she didn't want to get left behind.

She looked at herself in the mirror. She didn't know how to do her hair. Usually Allison helped her with stuff like this. This was the first time it would be all up to her. *Family and friends,* she reminded herself. She ditched the makeup and left her hair down for once. The curls were freshly conditioned so they had a shine and she didn't trust herself to be able to do anything besides a messy bun.

She met her dad downstairs. He had on a nice, collared shirt and a sweater vest. Katie snorted. He tugged on one of her curls and told her he was bringing sexy back. He even hinted that he might find himself a pretty lady who liked his sweater vest. Katie laughed but wondered if he was trying to find a way to tell her he was starting to date.

They drove to Lucinda's, and she geared herself up for seeing Lucinda for the first time since the intervention.

When they rang the bell, Brian answered.

"Hey, Mr. Watts. Katie, haven't seen you in years." He smiled and let them in.

"It's been like a month."

"When you go from every day to never, it feels like years. I haven't seen Allison in decades. I think she died."

"Don't make jokes like that, Brian." Lucinda moved to give Katie a hug, and Katie wondered if Lucinda felt the tension in her arms.

"Don't start, Mom. We're at a party." Brian waved Katie toward the dining room.

"We'll chat later, sweetie," Lucinda said, looking a little sad, but it was hard to look sad in a party dress as shimmery as hers.

Though Lucinda had said family and friends, it was hard to tell the difference between this year and any other. There were people everywhere, and the same faces looked up from playing cards as she entered the dining room. Everyone was there except Tristan and Allison. Michael, Christi, Ethan, Allan, and Jenn. They waved at Katie as if they'd seen her just the other day, as if she hadn't fallen off the face of the earth and climbed her way back, only to hide out underground.

"Hey, Watts. It's been a while. We're playing poker and trying to get Brian to drink. We wanna see if we can get another episode of *Family Drama*. Want to be dealt in?"

"I'll watch." Katie smiled. It was strange. She didn't really dislike them like she'd thought she had. Well, Ethan—he was still the weird kid who she'd never said more than three words to in her whole life.

Michael looked at her again. "Your boobs look nice. You can sit next to me if you want."

Katie glared at Michael—maybe she did dislike him a little. She took the seat next to Christi instead.

"So I hear you're at a school in Gray City?" Christi put her cards on the table. "I'm out." She turned her face, and Katie saw the scar. It didn't look so bad, but it was definitely going to be there for the rest of her life.

"Yep. You'll never guess what I'm studying."

"If it has anything to do with hamsters, I'm going to give myself to the Mother and join a nunnery."

A smile stretched across Katie's face. "Would you like to swear that on a Bible?"

"You're not serious?"

"*Well,* it's veterinarian studies. We don't have hamsters—but that's something can be arranged."

Christi nodded. "All right, I'll admit. I did *not* see that coming." She took a drink of what smelled like hot cocoa. They chatted a little before Katie excused herself from Michael eyeing her boobs.

"I know you'll be back. Jenn's boobs will keep me company till then."

Katie heard something smack, and Michael scream. Even after everything, they hadn't changed much, and she didn't know if she found that comforting, tiresome, or worrisome.

Her feet took her to Tristan's room, though she'd never intended to go there. She took in the smell. There was nothing more comforting than the faint smell of Tristan. She sat on the bed. The room wasn't as empty as it used to be. A pile of paperwork and books sat piled on the desk, his jacket hung on the chair, and a stick of deodorant lay in the middle of his bed next to her hand. Sure, it was sparse for any normal guy's room, but Tristan leaving things about—it meant he'd made himself at home.

Katie knew he didn't stay here most nights. When he was on duty, he stayed in some dorms in Gray City. He wouldn't be off until around eleven tonight, and Katie knew he wouldn't show up here if the party was still going on. Her phone buzzed and she smiled, seeing Tristan's name.

West isn't actually there, is he? Tristan texted.

Katie rolled her eyes. Why did West always find a way to get under Tristan's skin and why did Tristan let him?

Yes. We even invited all of SA. This party is raging.

Katie lay back on his bed, imagining what it would feel like if he were lying next to her. She'd give anything just to see him. But she couldn't tell him that. She couldn't make it harder than it already was.

Buzz.

Meet me outside your house. Midnight. I have to tell you something.

Katie texted him back and waited, but he never replied. The last time he'd had something to tell her, he'd rejoined the Patrol. Not bad news, but not good news either. Meeting her in the middle of the night meant big news.

"Grrrr," she growled. Why did he do that? He was the worst, but she smiled anyway, wishing the next four hours would zoom by.

They didn't.

It was the longest four hours of her life, especially when Lucinda pulled her aside and had a crying session and apologized for storming out on Katie and all things she'd said. Katie apologized for how things went and for not answering her calls, but it was all Katie could do to keep from getting swept up in the emotions. She was in a house full of pulses; losing control would turn this party into a scene straight out of *Dracula*, the uncut, rated-D-for-death version.

She spent a good hour watching her dad drink more eggnog than he should have and shamelessly flirt with a woman Katie didn't know.

Katie had to smile. He was kind of charming—well, up until the next glass of eggnog. Then he was embarrassing. But the woman didn't seem to notice and laughed along with every cheesy joke like it was the first time she'd ever heard them.

Go, Dad.

Around eleven-thirty, Katie really started getting into gear. She'd made her rounds to say goodnight and wish a few people Merry Christmas. Not surprisingly, Brian and Christi were missing. Katie went to collect her dad, but he was dead asleep in the guest bedroom sans sweater vest. Katie snuck out, even though the party was still going strong, and made her way home.

Snow drifted down, and she pulled her coat around her. It was rare that the cold got to her, but a bone-chilling wind danced around her hair and nipped at her.

As she neared her house, she saw him sitting on her front porch still wearing his uniform. She watched him, wanting to take him in before letting him know she was there. The way he sat, relaxed and like he owned every bit of space around him, made her yearn to wrap her arms around his broad chest, place her head on his shoulders, and take in his warm smell.

She called his name, even as his gaze found her.

She was glad her dad was passed out drunk at Lucinda's house. His eyes, bright against the black of his uniform, spoke to her in ways his words couldn't.

She faltered. They were full of something she'd seen just a few times but knew so well it set off sparks in her stomach and warmed her blood. She smiled and unlocked the door.

"How was the party?" he asked.

"Long," she said, unsure why her breath caught in her throat. She closed the door and took off her coat.

He didn't say anything. Tristan grabbed her hand and laced his fingers between hers, pulling her away from the door and toward his body.

She didn't move away. They could apologize for being careless when the sun was high in the sky and things seemed clearer. For now, she let him pull her up to her room and wrap his arms around her once the door closed.

"If you tell me to, I'll stop."

Katie said nothing, but tightened her grip around him.

He pulled away just enough to look down at her mouth.

She parted her lips and kissed him. It was sweet, warm, and she felt it in places that fuzzed her mind. His hands ran over her back and over her hips. She trailed her fingers over the side of his face and then down his chest. It didn't matter that her hands never left his body; it wasn't enough. She needed to make up for all the lost time.

He slid up her dress and slowly dragged his fingertips over her stomach.

She gasped, her mind full of him—his smell, his warmth, his love.

"If you tell me not to, I won't."

Katie felt an electric burn travel from between her legs up into her throat. They moved backward until they were on top of the bed. He pulled off his shirt. Katie slid under the covers and pulled off her dress, her bare skin tense on the cool sheets.

He slid under the sheet with her, and they both removed the rest of their clothes.

In his eyes, she saw clarity.

The silence sat between them, but never had she understood him better. His hands found her, and he moved on top of her slowly, full of nervousness and lust. The weight of him was both overwhelming and right.

They found each other, and she knew, no matter what tomorrow brought, she wouldn't regret this moment. She'd never regret that it was him or that it was now. Time stopped and they lost themselves in each other.

⋅⋅⋅

"Stop laughing." He smiled from ear to ear. They lay opposite of each other shy—ridiculously shy.

"I can't help it. If I stop, I'll burst." Katie rolled back and forth, giddy and high as a kite.

He laughed, rubbing his hands over his face. "You're such a—you're perfect."

"What were you going to tell me?" she asked, not even caring about how frustrated with anticipation she was.

Tristan laughed, and an evil grin slid across his face. "Merry Christmas."

They laughed and play-fought until his hands touching her bare body erased the laughter, leaving just the bliss.

Katie never felt more alive.

Her hair had messed and knotted around her pillow. Tristan wrapped a curl around his finger. The way his eyes darted ever so slightly, taking her in under the sunlight, and the curve of his muscle in the morning light made her stomach jump again in delight—he was perfect.

He was here, in her bed, loving her openly and fully. All of her. Not a thought in his mind said otherwise, no hesitation, no regret—

He smiled. *"I don't think there is any other way. Not with you. No matter how far away you are, how you feel about me, or how many times you walk away from me. I'll love you. Like this."* His blue eyes shined clear as water. "Always."

⋅౭ℛ౨౨⋅

It was true what they said—when someone's done it, they get a bounce to their step. She couldn't shake it. She felt *different*. Not life-changing different, but every now and again she'd do something ordinary, like the dishes, and he'd pop into her mind. In-between her thighs would burn with a kind of lust she'd never felt before.

He'd pop up in her mind at the most random times, and a warm zing of pleasure would hit her. It was worse when she saw him. She'd immediately think about the way he had touched her, and then he'd think about it and look at her with those eyes.

Those eyes.

She thanked the heavens and the stars and all the gods she could think of that no one noticed the bounce in her step or the way he smiled that goofy grin when he looked at her.

Sex was written all over their faces and bodies, and she was thankful no one bothered to take the time to see it. It was the best and most terrifyingly amazing Christmas of her life.

She counted down the days until New Year's Eve. He had to work through Zuri's party and would meet her at Lucinda's house at nine. Their short conversations resumed friendship status but constantly drifted into the gray area where neither was sure if it was okay to cross the line again. It was silly really. They'd done the most intimate thing two people could do, yet they still tiptoed around each other like a pair of giggling middle-schoolers. In the back of her mind, she knew they needed to redefine what they were or at least admit that sex was off the table until they *could* figure it out.

New Year's Eve finally arrived; however, it was still Friday and SA, as Roger said the previous week, "must live on." Elma still had her cat, which even Katie could tell was a miracle. Queenie was down to what Katie thought was probably her regular size, the definition of hourglass. The kind of thick curviness that belonged in a pinup magazine. The kind that would have been on the front cover and the envy of all women.

Jeffry spoke for the first time in a while (and Katie was also glad that he had finally stopped staring at her like it would make her disappear). "I joined a pottery club." He grabbed a bag from under his chair and pulled out a bunch of bowls he'd made for everyone. They all had names, except Katie's said "*New Girl*," but she liked it anyway.

Katie made sure to put it down with care as they stood up and chanted another motivational poster. This time it was a drawn picture of tribal hippos that she was sure Roger had made because, like all the others, it didn't quite make sense.

Katie elbowed West as he gave the chant a halfhearted go. It was her first time seeing him since karaoke night, and he definitely looked like he didn't want to talk about it, think about it, or even be reminded of it—so Katie made sure to keep the conversation light as they headed out the door.

"Any New Year's resolutions? Maybe you should pick up something like Jeffry. You could do basket weaving."

West opened his car and tossed his bowl in the backseat. "Need a ride home?"

"No, I'm going to Zuri's…" Katie pointed down the street as if Zuri lived just a few doors down.

"I'll walk with you then. I'm meeting my partner down that way."

"You work New Year's Eve?" Katie asked.

West took her bowl and looked it over. "Yup. Picked up some extra shifts. Staying busy. You don't have to pretend like you didn't see what happened." He gave the bowl back to her. "Mine's better."

Katie was relieved. "Well, it's the respectable thing to do."

"Since when are you respectable?" he said. "Or is that your new resolution?"

Katie furrowed her brows and stuck out her tongue.

"Yeah, real respectable."

They walked in silence for a while until reaching the river that separated the vampire district and the Burrow. Crossing the bridge was one of the worst parts about going to and from the vampire district. The water was black. Only lights from the bridge lamps reflected off the underground river. She wondered what the current was like or what kind of animals lived in it. She never wanted to know, of course, because it was terrifying to think of being in water where you couldn't tell the bottom from the top.

When she moved to the middle of the bridge, West spoke. "It doesn't matter what you are, does it?"

"What?" Katie watched as two boys leaned over the side of the bridge, talking as if it weren't the most dangerous thing in the world.

"No matter what you are or who you are. Love sucks."

"Not all the time."

"Yeah, a twelve-year-old would say that."

Katie side-eyed him. "It'll get better. One day at a time."

West sighed and changed the subject. "Work is crazy. We've been assigned to the Burrow to find all those missing people from the summer. Do you know how annoying it is to walk around looking for a clue on where a missing human might be?"

"No clue." Katie eyed the black river.

"My partner is worthless. He can't follow a lead to save his life, and I'm almost sure The Seven has something to do with it. But it's like trying to infiltrate Fort Knox. Anyone we find connected with The Seven all say the same thing. They don't know anything beyond the propaganda they keep littering the streets with."

"Maybe it's not them."

"What do you know?"

Katie punched West's arm.

"You're just like T. Are words not a thing you can use? So quick to violence. You two deserve each other."

Katie blushed. As far as he knew, they weren't together—unless Tristan had told him they'd had sex. Katie's eyes grew wide, and she stared straight ahead.

"What? You think I wouldn't have figured it out? A guy doesn't come to work smiling, especially on Christmas. Just don't tell him I figured it out. He thinks he's unreadable."

Katie walked faster.

"Come on. It's not like—wait, why are you so defensive?"

"Shut up, West."

"You guys did the bump-and-grind, didn't you?"

Katie punched him again. Hard.

West laughed, his face lighting up for the first time. "Oh, shit. You totally did."

Katie cursed herself. "Not cool, West. Not cool."

"You're such a girl. Fine." West left the topic alone and said nothing else except when he wished her a happy new year as they reached the front of Zuri's brownstone.

Katie climbed up the stairs, wondering if Zuri was already engaged and if she would have to pretend to be happy for her even though West was walking down the street, broken-hearted and clearly aching.

Katie knocked, but there was no answer. She tried the door,

knowing that Zuri was probably in one of her magical fits, yelling at the cat or getting things ready for the party.

When the door opened, Katie was met with silence. Everything was…dead. There was no other way to explain it. Zuri's apartment was always alive. Even when she was distracted, things hovered or itched to move. Now, they were so still that they had become the kind of ordinary Katie was not accustomed to.

"Zuri?" Katie called. She stepped inside. Even Sylvester was gone or hiding. Katie ducked her head around the large plant blocking the living room and saw her.

Curled up on the ground next to the window was Zuri's tiny body. "Zuri?" Katie ran over to her. She could hear the panic in her own voice. Her heart pounded. Zuri didn't move. She was alive, but she wasn't responding. Katie turned her over and saw her face. It was bruised and bloody.

Katie threw open the window and screamed West's name at the top of her lungs. She hoped he was still close enough to hear her. She knelt back down next to Zuri and looked around the apartment—there were no other pulses as loud as hers. No one else was there.

Zuri opened an eye.

"What happened, Zuri? What happened?" Katie reached out to her, but Zuri shook her head. There were tears in her eyes as she cradled herself. Her hair was jet-black and she looked…dim. The sparkle that had always been behind her eyes was gone.

Katie panicked. She didn't know what to do. She pulled out her phone, thinking to call the emergency line she'd saved in there from the Burberry emergency numbers packet they'd given her. But she was supposed to call a special line for witches and she didn't have that. She never thought she'd need it.

She found the one for vampires, thinking maybe they could give her the right number or send help, but she didn't have to call. West came through the door.

"What…" His voice dropped, and he disappeared and reappeared next to Zuri. He looked at her face, and she cried. Her sobs were quiet and soft, and Katie shook, not knowing what kind of evil would do this. "Go get a cloth and warm water," West said, quiet but stern.

Katie left them, searching the bathroom for some hand towels, hydrogen peroxide, or any type of healing ointment. She grabbed a mixing bowl from the kitchen and filled it with warm water. If only she'd stopped by a cafe for a drink. She'd thought she'd do it after the party. There was no way she'd try and heal Zuri now; she might all but leave her lifeless if she tried without being fully charged. Katie found what looked like a healing salve in one of the cupboards next to the bowls and brought it back to the living room.

West had moved Zuri to the couch and was kneeling in front of her. Katie set the bowl down on the table, and he soaked the hand towel in water. He slowly wiped Zuri's face until the blood was gone.

Katie sat next to Zuri and held her hand. She wished she

knew what to do. Allison would have known what to do and say.

Zuri looked down. "He took—he wasn't going to ask me to—he took my power. He took my power. I can barely feel…" She stopped, and West held her as she sobbed.

Katie looked at Zuri's black hair and everything in the apartment. Her magic was gone. "Hugh?" Katie said, needing to confirm what she thought, needing to know who to blame.

Zuri nodded as West rocked her in his arms. His voice was calm and soft, but in his eyes, Katie saw him shatter into a million little pieces. "Shhh. You're safe now. I'm here."

Zuri shook her head, sobbing into him.

Katie sat there, wishing she knew who to call and how to find this guy so she could make him pay. If only she'd been there earlier, she could have fought him off. She'd have killed him.

Katie went into the kitchen, looking for tea or coffee. Something to make for Zuri, because how do you make your friend feel better after she just got beat up by her boyfriend? She found some tea she'd never had before but the box read "calming" in Zuri's handwriting. She boiled some water in a turquoise pot she remembered used to whistle and scream until Zuri told it to shut up.

When she brought the tea out for Zuri, she was gone. West sat on the couch with his head in his hands.

"Where's Zuri?" A light ruffle sounded in Zuri's bedroom. "Never mind." Katie sat next to West and sighed. "I'll call Mariam and Salem and tell them the party is canceled. What should I say?"

West shrugged.

After a while, Katie went out into the hallway and called Mariam. She didn't want to lie, but she didn't want to exactly say something that was only Zuri's to tell. So she settled on saying Zuri didn't feel well. To Katie's relief, Mariam bought it and said she saw it coming, given Zuri and West's big blow-up before Christmas.

When she got off the phone, West and Zuri came out of the apartment. Zuri wore a baseball cap, and her hair pooled around her face darkly. She grabbed Katie's hand and squeezed it before going down the stairs.

"She's going to stay at my place for a while. I have to stay at the dorms anyway," West said, not making eye contact. Katie waited until he looked up. The way the light crumbled behind his eyes was nothing compared to the other night.

"Call me if she needs anything. Or…I don't know just call me and let me know how she is?"

West nodded, and Katie followed him out into the streets. She hugged Zuri, feeling her frailness, and stood in front of the brownstone, watching as West walked her down the street.

.ര ഉ.

Katie didn't know if there was any way to smile after seeing Zuri's face like that. She sat on Lucinda's couch, telling everyone she was just concerned about a sick friend. It was the truth—in a way—but it wasn't until Tristan came at nine that she felt like she could escape the glances in her direction.

"I heard." Tristan emptied a puzzle he'd found on the breakfast table. He liked puzzles. Katie couldn't really stand the beginning or the end of a puzzle; she preferred getting lost in the middle.

"He took her magic."

Tristan frowned. "I can't say I didn't see that coming."

"What does that mean?" Katie looked at Tristan.

"He's a warlock. And he was older, right? Only young warlocks date young witches—it's because they've already got a lot of power. Zuri had a lot of power for a young witch. What else would he want with her?"

Katie had read a lot about witches in her history class at Burberry. Witches grew into their power, getting more powerful the more they aged; they also lived separate from each other because, whether they wanted to or not, the more powerful witch always took the power of the weaker one. Warlocks, on the other hand, were very powerful at a young age and lost their power as they grew older. Around thirty, they started seeing huge drop-offs in their power until around their sixties when they either used the rest to do something spectacular or slowly deteriorated into something the books called a *clepta*. Which Katie later learned meant thief in Latin.

"Or, as guardians call them, omitters."

Katie thought back to Glock, the omitter who'd wanted to take more of her memories. The one who'd talked to her even though no one else heard him.

"Or they steal powers from witches. I can't imagine an older witch would let a warlock get that close to steal their magic, but a young girl hell-bent on doing nothing with the amount of power she has? I don't know how she got it, but I do know she was a walking target."

"Why…" Katie couldn't finish the question.

"You can't save someone from themselves. She had to have known she was a walking target, yet she let him right in. Some part of her either didn't want to believe what he wanted or didn't care."

Tristan kept searching for end pieces to the puzzle.

Katie shook her head. "That doesn't mean he can do this and get away with it. What do I do? She's my friend. How can I…" Katie slumped in the booth. Tristan grabbed her hand and ran his thumb across her skin.

"Witches have their own set of laws. But you can be there for her if she wants you there. Learn from my mistakes. Don't do like I did and berate her every day with questions." A sly smile stretched across his face, and Katie let out a small laugh.

He let his fingers slide between hers, and a rush of his thoughts hit her—all wanting more than to be sitting across from her and touching her fingers. Katie looked up, scared and thrilled to look into his eyes, letting his longing to kiss her lips sweep her off to lusty places.

He moved to sit next to her, his face getting closer to hers.

"We should talk about that," Katie said. Though as his

thoughts penetrated her mind, she couldn't help ignore her own rationale.

"Why talk about it when we can kiss?" His lips found hers.

The moment was lost as Lucinda called out to them. "Come watch the ball drop."

There was nothing more unsexy than Lucinda calling their names while they were thinking the most tempting thoughts about each other, while they were kissing each other, while his hand was sliding up her thigh.

"It's only ten," Tristan yelled back, just as annoyed as Katie.

Lucinda called back. "Well, yeah. We're going to watch the ball drop live. New York is two hours ahead."

"I know that," Tristan yelled, wondering why Lucinda was so weird.

"Then why are you confused? Hurry up. You're going to miss it."

Katie threw her head back, giving up.

Tristan let go of her thigh. "I don't care about the stupid ball." His voice neared a whine that surprised both himself and Katie.

"Shut up!" Will hissed from the living room. "Look. Look." There was an urgency to his voice that bordered on hysterical. Both Katie and Tristan got up from the table.

It wasn't until they heard Will say, "They're changing in front of everyone. Oh. My. God. They're shapeshifting," that they both ran.

19

THE NEW YEAR

KATIE COULDN'T BELIEVE her eyes. Hundreds of werewolves were in the middle of Times Square, transforming on TV.

It had to be a joke—except it wasn't.

No one in the room said anything. Her dad sat, staring at the TV and then her. Will was up, holding a phone that rang nonstop in his hand, and Lucinda and Brian just gaped at the TV.

Why would they expose themselves like that? They were endangering the existence of them all. The footage changed to a green screen. A man Katie now knew to be lower than scum appeared. Hugh smiled softly and looked directly into the camera.

"Hello, ladies and gentlemen. You've spent your whole lives thinking you are the superior species on this Earth. You've spent your whole lives believing you are alone. You call yourselves the human race as if this is a competition in which you can win. In all scenarios, you are our prey. The food we eat. The lesser of the races. This is just a taste of what lies in the darkness. We're breaking the chains. We're done hiding." He looked at his watch and back to the camera and smiled. "See you in the new year."

The footage went back to Times Square. People screamed and ran from wolves, but like a ripple effect, they all began falling to the ground. Until there was nothing but silence and massive beasts running through the bodies, howling.

"Oh. My. God," Katie said. "Are they…" She looked at her dad and screamed as he opened his mouth and fell back in his chair. Will dropped to the ground, and Lucinda and Brian slumped in their seats.

"They aren't dead," Tristan said, his voice panicked in a way that let Katie know he didn't know what was happening either.

Tristan's phone rang, and he picked up. He spoke fast and relayed what was happening on their end. Katie listened to their pulses and, for once, found solace in the fact that she could hear them loud and clear in her mind. They weren't dead. But what was happening?

"They're calling me in. I don't know if the werewolves are trying to start a war but—"

"That man on the TV—that was Hugh. That was the guy who stole Zuri's powers," Katie said. "It's not werewolves. At least, it's not just them."

"No werewolf would follow a witch. They can't."

Katie was stuck standing in the middle of the room. "Then what is happening?"

Tristan stumbled on his words. "Are you sure? Are you absolutely sure that's the same guy?"

Katie nodded, and Tristan was on the phone again. "Officer Kane? The guy who made the statement. That was Hugh…" He looked at Katie for a last name, but she shook her head. "He's a warlock. Not a werewolf—wait, what?"

The voice on the other end spoke too fast for Katie to hear, but Tristan began to waver. Her terror rose every second. Tristan hung up the phone, and his arm dropped to his side.

"The Council of Witches is gone. Not just in this city—in all of them." He gripped the phone tighter. "I won't leave you here. Not like this."

Katie felt her own limbs go numb. "You have to go. It's more important that you go instead of sitting here with me. We have no idea what's going on. When they wake up—" Katie made sure to think *when* and not *if* "—we'll need to know what's happening."

Tristan pressed his forehead on hers and let her feel his resolve. He wasn't going to leave. Deep down, they both knew that whatever was happening was going to change everything.

Minutes ticked by as they watched the footage of people lying on the ground and distant howls—until Will's phone rang. They jumped and stared at it as if Satan himself was calling.

Tristan went to the phone and looked at the name. "It's Jim Heckler." Tristan answered.

"Will? What the hell happened? Did you see the TV? I feel like I got knocked out with a bat."

"He's still out," Tristan said.

"Who is this?" Jim's voice was both angry and scared.

"That doesn't matter. You're awake...you woke up," Tristan murmured and hung up the phone. She knew exactly what he meant.

They were going to wake up.

Katie watched as the people in Times Square started to wake up. Some were injured and unable to move because they'd been trampled while others fled. The news had come back, and the newscasters were in a frenzy.

Katie changed to different news stations, but it was the same. Some were asleep at their desk and waking up in a panic. Some hadn't seen the footage and were watching it live on TV via playback. Everyone else was gone. Gone where, Katie didn't know. All they'd left were empty desks and rolling cameras.

One woman stayed. She was from a local station. She reported that it might be Judgment Day and they'd just witnessed demons walking the Earth.

It took fifteen minutes for Katie's dad to wake up. She clutched onto him. Lucinda, Brian, and Will were only seconds behind him. Katie and Tristan answered their questions as best they could, but ultimately, neither of them knew how to verbalize exactly what they were thinking.

They weren't safe anymore.

Nobody was.

Tristan finally left after Katie convinced him that his job was more important than her comfort. She was scared out of her mind, but more troubling than that were the questions, the long wait for answers.

As New Year's Day dawned, answers came, but they weren't the ones she needed or wanted. According to Will, all able-bodied adult guardians were being called into Gray City. They were supposed to protect the peace at all cost. They had no idea what the witches and werewolves were planning—or if their powers were even effective against witches—so a red alert went into effect.

By lunch, Will was called back into his level-0 position and Lucinda was called shortly after to take over a position at the school for some of the teachers leaving to join the ranks.

Katie desperately needed to know about Allison. Was she going to be sent back to school with the rest of her class or was she staying in the accelerated program? Lucinda called everyone she knew. It took two hours, but she finally got word that Allison's unit was being fast-tracked to join the force.

By evening, Katie's throat simmered on low. Everyone she knew was in Gray City doing something. Even if it didn't matter or wasn't helping, they were doing something. She needed to do something. Watching the news and listening to Lucinda rattle off questions and repeat that she did have clearance for some information drove Katie crazy—and did nothing for her throat.

For two days she sat and waited, watching the same footage

over and over, looking for new clues, trying to link the witches to the werewolves—trying to remember what little she knew about The Seven.

On the morning of the third day, news came. It was barely past one a.m. when the first rumor started—there had been a purge in Beijing. But there was no real footage, not on the news at least. Katie dug around online, but every time she found a lead, the site had either taken it down or the page wouldn't load. She did find, however, another rumor saying there was no real evidence that the purge was even of real paranormals, but instead that the mass graves were a cover-up of a cleansing of terrorists and prisoners.

By the time her dad came home at four with more pizza and beer, new footage broke. Cairo.

Mobs of people killed each other in the streets, and there was no certainty that they were even paranormal.

Cairo was the first city to film the death of a vampire and send it out for the world to witness. A man, with rope tied around his neck, was dragged out of his home and into the sun-lit street.

Katie watched him scream and turn to ash on primetime television. How did they even know what he was?

When her dad was on his fourth beer after lunch, the military celebrated over the collected heads of werewolves still dripping with blood. Bodies, broken and bloodied, piled up over the hours. Bodies and mass graves—and blood. Cairo wanted the world to know they had answered.

Religious leaders said the only way back into God's good grace was to purge. Occult enthusiasts were invited to talk about the origins and defenses against the supernatural.

No one ever talked about peace or living in harmony.

People were afraid to send their children to school. They were afraid to go out after dusk, and they watched the windows. The New Years incident was now called The Blackout. Tens of thousands of people died due to plane and car crashes all over the world—and according to the news, the number was still growing. They, of course, blamed the blackout on whoever lurked in the dark.

Katie felt it in Boise. The silence and the tension. She never stopped watching the news, terrified she'd miss something—or worse, that there would be something to miss. It was becoming clear that the only safe place for her was Gray City.

⋆⊹⊱⋆

Any time Tristan could spare, he was with her. He'd turn off the TV and tell her nothing good ever came from waiting for the worst. On the fourth day since the blackout, he came to her with only two hours to spare before his next shift started. It was pitch-dark outside and more silent than ever. They sat in the living room while her dad drilled Tristan with questions he couldn't answer.

"I told you. I don't know. I just know the witches are involved."

"How did I not know witches existed? I feel like—I feel like…"

— 344 —

"You were hexed," Katie said for the fifteen-millionth time.

"But how is that possible? To hex us all?"

"They're witches," Katie said for the twenty-millionth time.

Her dad grunted. It had been the hardest part for him, knowing that he'd been left out of the biggest deception of all time. He, an ex-guardian, who was supposed to be the keeper of the biggest secret of all time.

Katie's phone buzzed. She and Tristan looked down at West's name glowing bright on the screen.

Tristan scoffed as Katie answered the phone.

"Hey, kid. I got a call from Roger. Everyone wants to call a meeting. Something about the entire world knowing they exist and some New Year's freak show has them on edge."

They weren't the only ones. She heard it in West's voice. He sounded just like she felt—terrified of what was to come. The world had stopped and no one dared move it. If darkness was true horror, than being out in the daylight was a reminder that the dark was coming.

"When?" Katie was already up and headed to her room. She grabbed her purse and emptied it of her wallet, pens, paper, and things she'd once counted as useful. Instinctively, she grabbed the beautiful wooden box Tristan had given her just a year ago.

"In thirty minutes?" West paused, and she heard him swallowing down a drink. "Can you hear them?"

Katie nodded. "Yeah." The pulses were worse, thumping and colliding with each other in her mind. She grabbed her knives in their soft sheaths and put one in each pocket.

"Have Tristan bring you. Last thing we need is you tweaking out on camera." West laughed, but it was tight.

"See you in thirty." Katie hung up and tied her hair back in a ponytail. As she came down the stairs, Tristan was by the door, putting on his black jacket. "Why do I feel like this?" Her body shook with nerves. She felt like as soon as she stepped out of the house, the world would crumble. It was five o' clock in the morning and maybe no one was awake—or awake, but too terrified to look out their windows, lest a monster snatch them.

"Because we aren't safe up here. Not right now. What you feel is their fear—our fear. Fear makes you see things that aren't there, hear things that were never said. Makes weakness stronger. I've never met a coward I felt safe around."

Katie grabbed her black hoodie and tied up her shoes. "I need to tell my dad I'm going." She could hear him flipping through the television channels. He hadn't slept well in days. He was waiting, too.

"What are you doing up there?" her dad shouted. "Why did it get quiet?"

"You're such a creeper," Katie said, walking into the living room.

He took in their clothes and her purse. "Where the hell do you two think you're going?" He was alert, but his eyes were heavy with bags.

"To a meeting. Dad—don't. Let me talk. I can't stay here. It's not safe. We have to go underground. That's the only safe haven we have, and all this anxiety is getting in my head. I spent the last hour listening to the neighbor's cat sitting on our porch."

"What? Katie...Jesus..." He ran a hand over his tired face. "Can't you wait until morning?"

"Dad." Katie stared at him. "I'm the thing everyone is afraid of in the dark—besides, everyone is meeting *now*. If I don't show up, Sugar is going to fixate and everyone will be pissed at me, and they need me. I need them." She hadn't realized how true that was. She needed them. They were her crazy little rocks. Completely jacked up and painted weird colors, but steady and there for her. The first ones to cheer her on when she'd made it only six days.

"I'll drive you."

"It's better if we run," Tristan said.

"We'll attract less attention," Katie added.

"You call me when you get there. Stay together." He pulled out his phone. "Keep your phone on. I'll be able to see where you are. After the meeting, go to your school and stay there. It may be safer for you there, but don't be fooled. It's not safe. Times like this, people get wound-up and the slightest nudge will set them off. Don't trust anyone. I'll call the school so they expect you. Use the nearest elevator." He got up and walked over to the small corner desk where he kept his papers. He rustled through the drawers and pulled out two small spray canisters. "This is bear mace. It will also put down a werewolf. This stuff is like acid to anyone's eyes—you don't even have to be close. Use it, even if you think you can walk away." He handed them to both her and Tristan.

She heard Tristan thinking they'd be to the nearest elevator before three minutes could go by, but he kept quiet and took the mace.

"Let's leave from the back," Tristan said.

They went to the backyard, and she hugged her dad. "When the sun comes out, come see me at school." She left out that she didn't feel like he was safe alone. The witches had put the guardians asleep, too. They thought of them as humans, and to be completely honest, so did everyone else she knew—the annoying humans who thought they had control in Gray City.

She climbed onto Tristan's back.

"Hold on tight." He gagged and tugged at her death grip on his neck. "Not that tight."

"Sorry." Katie breathed out the nerves.

Her dad looked at them and opened his mouth.

Katie cut him off before he protested. "I'll text you in three minutes when we get to the elevator. And I'll call you when we get to the meeting."

"See you later." Tristan wiggled his mace. "Thanks." He opened the door, and Katie glanced back at her dad one more time before shutting her eyes.

In a flash, the streets were blurred and houses blended with buildings and Katie's mind fogged. He'd gotten faster than the last time—or so she thought. She stopped thinking and squeezed her eyes shut before she choked on her spleen.

They stopped in front of Larry's old ice cream shop, and Katie fumbled with the keys. She barely made it inside and to the elevator in the back before plopping down onto the ground.

She breathed in through her nose and fought back the nausea. It was a strange feeling. "How do you do that?"

"We've been through that, Katalina." He looked around the back until he found a small piece of paper pinned to the wall. He pressed some numbers on the keypad and they descended— quicker than she liked.

"It's just not natural," Katie breathed. She texted her dad before they left the elevator. *Told you running was faster.*

If Boise was a dead zone, Gray City was a buzzing hive of bees. More cars, more shops full of people, and more spinning hotel doors with more people going in than out. The Burrow was packed.

Katie was surprised they couldn't hear the level of crowd noise before the elevators had opened.

"Everyone is here and awake." Katie looked around. They had to keep walking on the street to avoid being an obstruction in the flowing crowd.

"Yeah." Tristan grabbed her hand and held it tight.

They waded through the crowds and the tension. Some people were visibly terrified; others chatted frantically about The Seven. *Where were they? Why did they leave? Who gave them the right to expose us?* However, the question that seemed to ring above all the voices over and over was: *What now?*

The closer they got to the vampire district, the thinner the crowds got, but it was still busy and bustling. Katie wished they had taken an elevator deeper in town. The amount of time they spent trying to pass people just to get to the bridge left her with only ten minutes to get to the meeting.

Every now and again, Tristan would look at her and they'd hold eye contact, understanding that they both felt the uneasy excitement of the crowd and that, no matter what, they wouldn't let go of each other.

They made it to the community center with only a few minutes to spare, and Katie was, first and foremost, confused by all the lights. The building always moped with abandonment when she went to her meetings. Now, vampires bustled in and out, mainly women and children.

West held the door open for a young woman and a little girl with red hair and pigtails. As Katie and Tristan walked up, he raised his eyebrows. "It's crazy out here."

"Yeah. The Burrow is jam-packed with people." Tristan nodded at the community center. "What's going on here?"

"The second floor is a daycare. They're usually closed when we're here. There's only like five kids, but they've all got hot moms." West checked his watch. "Let's not keep Sugar waiting, Kat. *You* can hang out in the lobby and watch TV. Should only be an hour."

They went inside and saw some of the mothers standing by the TV, talking and half-watching the news. She left Tristan and followed West through the double doors of their meeting room. She had to squeeze past the anxiety just to fit in the room.

Queenie yelled at Elma, who was missing Oscar, the cat; Roger tried to get Jeffry to sit down; and everyone else, including

Sugar was stone-silent. The kind of silent Katie got when the pulses pounded in her ears.

"Queenie, it's all right," West said, sitting in his chair.

"It's not. How many cats is she going to kill before she gets it together?"

"I didn't kill him. I told you. I'm not lying. He ran away. I'm not lying." Elma's face was streaked with tears, and she shook deep to her bones.

"I believe you," Katie said, not sure what else to say. Maybe being believed was more important than the truth. "I believe you," she said again with more confidence.

"Me too." West smiled, but his eyes were preoccupied with something none of them could see.

Roger finally got Jeffry to sit down, and he took a few breaths before looking into all their eyes. "I know today feels worse than yesterday and the day before that and the day before that. I know it feels worse than New Year's Day. It's all the waiting and the questioning. I don't know what's going to happen now either, but I know this." He smiled, and his calm seemed to drift onto all of them. "If we stick together, we can make anything better."

There was a nodding consensus, and Katie had to admit to herself she found him, this—all of the crazy—comforting.

"Okay," Elma said after some quiet. "I killed him. But really it was an accident. I was watching repeat footage of Cairo, and all I could think was 'oh my god' and then Oscar was getting snappy and I tried to pet him. And then I saw *Him* on the screen making it sound like *I* was a part of that chaos and I—I couldn't take it. I don't want them to know."

Queenie rubbed Elma's back. "Sorry I yelled, honey. I feel the same way."

"Why?" Melvin leaned back in his chair, fingering his Hitler-stache. "What's the worst that could happen? People know we exist. They're just going to want to be like us or avoid us. Look at the guardians. They know we exist and they're human."

"They also can't be touched by us," Jeffry said, staring at the floor.

Everyone turned their head to the door. They had all heard what Katie heard.

The scream. It was on the TV. Tristan called to her, but she, like everyone else, was already up and running to the lobby.

"As they are running from the last of the fumes in the station they—Oh my god. Oh. My. God—She's burning—She's—She's turning to dust."

Katie couldn't believe her eyes. It was live footage from New York. All across the screen, she saw people running from Grand Central Station. A thick gas rolled from the building, out the doors and windows. The windows had been shot out, and people were gunned down in the streets—bodies falling, bodies burning. Katie heard crying, and though the sounds weren't coming from her, her own face was wet. The reporter was silent. The unrelenting rounds of gunfire echoed in the air and mangled with the screams and military thunder.

Three wolves emerged from the windows, running away from the carnage, but a heavy gun pumped shots into their bodies so fast and hard, Katie knew they were dead before they hit the ground.

The footage cut to two news anchors sitting at their desk, silent and in shock. The crying turned to sobbing and Tristan changed the channel to a different news station. On Channel Six News, they covered the same footage. It had been happening for forty-five minutes before they knew. Bodies were stacked upon bodies, and what looked like ash was all that was left of the vampires who had fled from the gas. Katie's phone buzzed and she answered.

"Dad?"

"Where are you? I'm going to come get you."

"Dad...they're murdering people. Dad—in New York—how?" she cried.

"Where are you?" His voice dropped in and out as the signal weakened.

Katie couldn't stop staring the footage. They showed an aerial shot, and if she hadn't seen it with her own eyes, she would have never believed it possible. Not in America. Not in New York. Not the US government massacring people as they ran for their lives. Innocent people. People like her.

"We have to get out," Tristan whispered, grabbing her hand and staring in shock at the TV.

"I'm still at the meeting, Dad. We're watching it on TV."

"Get out of the city—"

The line dropped. She tried to call back, but the call wouldn't connect. She tried to send a text message, but each attempt failed.

West turned to the local news channel. A woman screamed as they watched military tanks roll down the streets and open fire as dawn approached. From the sky, it looked like rats running from pockets of fire. Katie recognized the Knitting Factory as one of the main focal points. Gas rolled from the building.

Tristan gripped her hand. He pulled her straight toward the door, but they both stopped. Thunder rolled into the room and shook the windows.

They stared at each other, frozen in disbelief. A bomb.

When the second bomb hit, they felt it rumble and shake the walls.

"The children!" A woman ran for the stairway.

"We have to get out!" Queenie screamed and ran for the door. She stopped when they all heard the screams and another bomb.

The sound deafened Katie. Something had hit the building next to them—or across the street. The lights flickered. West and Tristan turned off the lights and the TV.

"Get down." West waved for everyone to get away from the windows as the women came back downstairs with their children and an older lady.

"We can't stay here," Jeffry said, his breath racing. Shouting and what sounded like heavy machinery grew louder. "Is there a back door? Or windows in the back we can get out of?"

Roger shook his head, maybe the calmest of them all.

The voices grew louder.

Footsteps thundered past their building, and everyone stopped, still as dead air. No one dared to breathe.

Katie's heart pounded in her chest, and tears streaked her face. She hadn't told her dad she loved him. Tristan grabbed her hand, and his terror spilled out of him. She knelt down next to West, watching dark figures move past the windows. Bullet casings clanked on the ground, each one striking half a second before a scream.

Queenie grabbed Katie's other hand. She hadn't realized how bad she was shaking until Queenie steadied her.

They waited in the dark. The children buried their faces in their mothers. They were so still, like terrified dolls—like they were already dead. Katie held back a sob. It was only a matter of time until they might be.

Marching—running—shouting—the thunder of explosions. The cadence of death. It was never-ending.

"We have to get to the Alcove," Tristan said.

West nodded. "There will be a defense line four blocks from here. That's the evacuation line."

Roger shook his head. "They could be deeper in the district than that."

Tristan grimaced. "They aren't."

"How do you know?" Roger whispered, a slight bit of hope in his voice.

"Because the guardians don't know about those elevators."

BAM. The doors shook.

They all ducked as light shined directly on the windows. Katie looked to the steps and around the room for a place to hide. Roger rushed to the mothers and signaled for them to follow him to a small closet where they could put the children. Whispers and little muffled cries quieted as Roger closed the door.

Thud.

The doors banged again, and she could hear the stone and metal giving way. She looked at Tristan, wishing she could say something—anything—to make this moment not be their last. He cupped her face, and she saw the fear in his eyes. The terror she'd only seen once before, when she was bleeding out on Lucinda's couch. West moved next to them and pulled out his iron coin. He whispered what sounded like a prayer, and Tristan let go of her hand.

"Tristan!" Katie hissed.

Thud.

"I love you. Forever. In this life and any other." Tristan kissed her, and she cried through it, ruining what would probably be their last kiss.

The doors were going to give way soon.

Elma and Sugar ran up the stairs with Jeffry.

"You should all go upstairs and hide. In the closets. In the cupboards. Survive." Roger corralled the rest of their group, but Melvin and Queenie stayed behind.

"Whether the blood runs or the ash falls…" West gave Katie a brief smile before standing up.

"…the darkness will always rise." Tristan stood up, never taking his eyes away from Katie. *"Forever."*

THUD.

"I need blood." Tristan looked to West.

West nodded slowly. "Only you are strong enough to take the door. I can grab a guy."

Katie shook her head. He was going to source. "No!" she yelled as much as a whisper allowed.

Tristan's voice edged into her mind and silenced her. *"I've already fought my demon. And I won."*

Tristan opened the door. Shouts of confusion erupted from the outside as West disappeared and reappeared with a man's limp body. Tristan slammed the door shut again and, without hesitation, ripped the soldier's vest and sunk his teeth into his neck.

Blood filled her nostrils as she watched the body fight and jerk. She turned away. The fear coursing though her veins trumped any craving she had for the blood on Tristan's lips. He didn't stop until every drop was gone.

The soldiers outside regrouped.

THUD.

Katie braced herself.

"Stay down, Katalina. No matter what happens. Stay down." Tristan's eyes glowed silver, and she watched as he and West faded to black. Before her eyes, they were nothing more than shadows.

Katie moved to the couch and dragged it in front of the closet door where the children were. Queenie and Roger helped her stack up furniture in front of it. If bullets were going to fly, at least they might not hit the children.

Roger grabbed her and pulled her and Queenie to hide behind the couch.

THUD.

Tristan opened the door, and West closed it behind him. Katie screamed his name until she was filled with his fear, his loneliness, and his anger.

The Black Void. Katie hadn't felt it for nearly a year. The place he kept all of the darkness, the parts of himself he couldn't forgive. The parts he hated. He welcomed it.

She smelled the blood first. It was right there with them in the room. She heard their screams second. Men screaming like animals, men screaming in ways no living being should ever be made to scream.

They all stared at the door, listening as bullets fired.

Pop. Pop. Pop.

Each round grew more panicked than the last. She'd felt the release of his strength. It was desperate to be free and hungry. It was thirstier for blood than she'd ever been. Thirsty for pain and anger. It was everything she feared, and it was loose, no longer bound inside of Tristan, but out and in control of him. Katie held her breath until there was nothing but silence and the pounding of Tristan's rage in her ears.

West opened the door. "We've got to get out now!" he yelled, loud enough for the people upstairs to hear him and start running down. Katie's hands shook, but she jumped up and pushed the couch away from the closet door. Roger and Queenie were on the same page, pushing the furniture out of the way and pulling the children out of the closet.

"We can run to the evacuation point," Roger said, quickly grabbing two kids. Queenie and a mother grabbed two little girls, and Katie, without a second thought picked up the last girl with the pigtails. The girl wrapped her arms around Katie so tight, Katie choked. The little girl only let go when her mother pulled her out of Katie's arms.

"Let's go!" West waved them out the door.

Katie was met with a blast of fresh blood. It was everywhere. She blocked the girl's view and took in the bodies. They weren't whole. Not anymore. Arms, legs, and heads were sprawled around Tristan.

He stood, breathing through his teeth and clenching his fists. He grabbed the little girl from a woman and one from Queenie. "Put her on my back," he said through a ragged breath.

Queenie hesitated, and one of the mothers screamed when she looked at Tristan, covered in blood with his blue eyes glinting with silver on her child.

West took the little girl. "It's okay. He's going to take you to safety. Your mom will be right behind you. Are you scared?"

The little girl nodded. She was terrified.

"So am I." He helped her hold onto Tristan, and then they were gone.

West grabbed the two boys from Roger. He gripped them and told them to close their eyes and hold on tight. "Stick to the shadows. The evacuation line isn't far. Don't stop." He was gone, a blur in the light and then nothing.

The rest of them ran. Katie, Elma, and the blond-haired woman took off running across the street. They didn't look back. They didn't stop. It was simple: run as fast as you can.

They made it a block, and she knew where they were headed—toward the fighting. There were more soldiers. Easily fifty or more far ahead. Roger grabbed onto her hand and yanked her back so hard her head smacked into a wall. Gunshots fired, and the woman in front of Katie dropped to the ground. She didn't get up.

Katie beat down the terror threatening to split her mind in two. She moved backward and tripped. Roger caught her and put his hand over her mouth as she looked down. She stood over the body of a little boy.

He was a little older than the kids they'd been with, but his face was blank except for the hole in his eye. She couldn't take her eyes off of him until Roger pulled her down an alley.

Katie ran faster than she'd ever had in her life, not thinking about the puddles that shouldn't exist in a city without rain.

One minute Queenie was in front of them, then she was gone. Katie kept running, feeling something blur past her. Shadows grabbed them from the dark of the alley. A hand reached out and grabbed her and picked up speed. Light burst and blurred as they ran past screams and bullets. The sounds growled and roared until they were distant again. Whoever carried her put her down and left again. All she knew was, it hadn't been Tristan.

Katie searched for the others, gasping for breath but steady.

People were everywhere, climbing into trucks and standing, wide-eyed and covered in blood. One man kept screaming the same name over and over: "Amelia! Amelia!"

She saw Queenie and Melvin. She ran to them and saw Roger running toward her. Her eyes darted to the children, three of them smeared with blood, the blood that was on Tristan. Their mothers pushed away a woman with gauze, and Katie saw the little girl who had clutched on to her, standing alone, searching. One of the mothers locked eyes with Katie and grabbed the little girl's hand. Katie shook her head. It was all she could do, but the woman understood.

The little girl's mother was gone. Dead. Katie turned away. Queenie covered her mouth, her head shaking back and forth. Where was the rest of the group? Where was Elma and Jeffry and Sugar?

"Look at me, kid." West shook her. "Look at me. Not yet. Not yet—you hear me?"

Katie focused on West and pushed everything else to the back of her mind.

"You have to get on the truck. It'll take you to the Alcove. I'm going to get Zuri. She's still at my apartment. You have to get on the truck."

Katie shook her head. She wasn't going anywhere without Tristan. She'd die with him right here in the streets before she'd leave without him.

"Kat. Get on the damn truck." West gripped her arm tight, but she shoved him off just as she saw Tristan.

Covered in blood, but still there. He carried an older woman with a hole in her leg. A man in a black uniform wearing a red patch with a cross on his arm took her from him.

Tristan locked eyes with Katie.

"Retreat!" yelled voices.

Shadows appeared, turning back into men and women. They were covered in blood. Some dropped to their knees; some fell into the arms of others.

"Retreat!"

West let go of Katie, and they looked down the road. In the floodlights, the shadows bounced here and there. A few soldiers were falling, but most were not. They had changed out their assault rifles for shotguns.

The shadows dropped to the ground. They pulled back. Katie saw it as if it were a few feet away and not at least three hundred yards from her. They were gunned down in the street as the soldiers advanced.

Katie looked at all the people around her, panicked and running to the trucks, trying to fit even though there was no room. Patrol officers directed people further down the street to the next evacuation sight.

"There's a tank!" someone yelled.

"Zuri," West breathed, his eyes wide and taking in what Katie realized was hopelessness.

"Go," Tristan said.

West was gone before Katie's next breath.

She reached out to Tristan. There wasn't much time left.

She heard the trucks screeching down the streets as they were ordered to go. People ran after them, screaming, because they knew, just like Katie, that they were going to die. There wasn't enough time to get to another evacuation post. There wasn't enough time for the trucks to get to the Alcove without the military there to follow. The military had tanks. All the Patrol had were scared, bloodied, and beaten people.

Katie's eyes grew wide as Tristan's thoughts mimicked hers— except there was something else there. Resolve.

"No," Katie said.

He wasn't going to leave with her. He was going to stay and fight until there was no fight left in him.

Let go, Katie heard in her head. He was chanting it to himself.

"Let go?" As soon as the words left her mouth, she tasted the poison. "No. No, Tristan."

"Be brave." Azezel had told her. *"Tell him to let go."* Katie wasn't going to be brave. She wasn't going to let him go. Katie grabbed onto Tristan; he held her hand, and in his squeeze, she felt his apology.

He turned and ran toward the fighting. Katie screamed so hard people parted as she ran after him.

"Tristan!" she screamed as his body disappeared from view. "Tristan!"

✤ 20 ✤

THE ONE

KATIE RAN. SHE knew he was already gone and the fighting was at least three hundred yards away from where she was, but she kept running, her eyes trained on the bouncing shadows—until the screams started.

First, they were just in her head, but the others must have heard them because they stared back at the attack as they ran. Shadows appeared in front of her, all backing away from where they had come. The screams of men being torn limb from limb filled the air. She saw it this time.

The soldiers scattered and regrouped like a school of fish being attacked by an invisible shark. They started shooting each other, and Katie tasted the blood as if it were splattering across her face and not Tristan's. His strength shook her body. How easy it was for him to pull an arm from a man and to step on the chest of another and completely obliterate it. It went on until the screams and chaotic shooting were the only sounds around them.

The men were no longer soldiers. They were frightened boys fighting in the darkness.

"The tank stopped. They stopped," a man said behind Katie. He wore a Patrol uniform.

He was right—it had stopped. But Katie blinked, unsure she saw it right. The turret moved, the barrel slowly aiming directly at the group of soldiers. There were at least a hundred of them, swarming and shooting at each other as Tristan went in and out, weaving them into a ball of chaos.

"Tristan!" she screamed and ran toward him.

The tank stopped moving.

"Tristan!" Her voice broke as the tank fired.

Katie screamed so hard nothing came out. The impact blew past her, and a chunk of cement knocked her off her feet. Her body grated against the ground, and her skin peeled. The ringing in her ears drowned out everything.

He was there. She could feel his body burning. His throat scorched. His bones exposed. A man in a patrol uniform grabbed her. He lifted her up and pulled her back. She screamed and scratched at him widely.

She was going to get to Tristan and drag his body away from there even if she was gunned down doing it.

As the smoke cleared, she felt his throat sooth. She tasted the blood like it was going down her own throat and straight into her veins. Her bones ached with sensitivity, and she burned with the stretching of new flesh.

The man let her go, and she fell to the ground, looking at exactly what made him drop her.

Tristan climbed out of a stack of bodies. His clothes were burned, his hair had been singed off his head, and his skin was blackened, but he climbed out and walked toward the tank. Katie watched as he healed, his bones disappearing as new muscle and flesh covered it.

The soldiers behind the tank began to back up, and the tank rolled backward. As they retreated, shouted orders erupted behind her.

Tristan stopped walking, and it felt like forever until he turned around. Katie scrambled up, and her feet pounded harder on the pavement than they ever had. By the time she collided into him, she couldn't breathe. She wrapped her arms around his neck. She held on, choking on air.

He grabbed onto her legs hoisting her up and ran toward the Alcove.

The streets and the people blurred, but she heard their voices.

"What is he?"

"How did he survive that?"

"Savior."

Tristan stopped when they reached the blackness between the city and the Alcove. He fell to his knees and wailed. The Black Void enveloped them. He had killed all those men. Men following orders. Whether they were on the wrong side or not, they'd still been men. Men that he'd butchered and ripped apart. He had become the demon whose only hunger was destruction itself.

Katie held onto him and rocked him back and forth. It was true. No matter what she wanted to tell him. No matter how much she wanted to say there was no choice or that he'd done the right thing to save all their lives, she knew that what he felt was also true.

He screamed and sobbed, holding onto her, and she didn't let go. Not here in the darkness, where he might slip away and never come back. She clutched onto him and let him mourn all the men he'd killed and the part of his soul that had died with them.

21

THE ALCOVE

T HEY WALKED TO the Alcove. Tristan steeled himself, and Katie knew nothing she could say was going to fix either one of them. Instead, she looked around.

The passage through the tunnel wasn't like before. Before it was dark and barren. Now, she saw for miles ahead—trucks, cars, and people, all moving in different directions. Lights from the trucks bounced off, creating a yellow hue on the thick rock that arched around them. As the road curved, she saw the opening—the Alcove.

People walked beside the road as trucks drove back into the tunnel—probably out to find more survivors. Katie and Tristan walked on the side of the road for an hour, listening to cries and words of comfort, hearing heavy footfalls and sounds full of disbelief.

Tristan signaled for her to follow a large crowd of people down a road that led to the manor—a place she didn't even recognize now that light poured out from every window and people were walking through the gates and into the large front doors.

Katie stopped. She had never realized how big it was before. She had only seen one building, but now the lights on the grounds were burning bright and she saw five or six different wings attached to the main house.

They walked down the street and to the front door, where a frail, older woman wearing a black dress with a high collar looked up from her clipboard.

"You," she spat, looking at Tristan. "I should have known when the kitchen window was broken. The blood on the lambskin. Your name was all over it. What in God's name happened to your clothes?"

"Enough." Tristan stared past her, but when their eyes met, she scowled.

"You can have your old room. I trust you know where that is. Unless you want to stay in the dungeons." She turned away from him and looked at Katie.

The woman was old, possibly in her seventies. There was a kind of recollection in her eyes as she studied Katie. "Lady Borsa, your rooms have been prepared. I will show them to you directly."

The woman called out to a man dressed in a black tuxedo. He too was old. He bowed to Katie and listened to the set of instructions the woman rattled off.

"Borsa? I'm…"

"Forgive me, madame, for speaking frankly, but if I am correct, you are Katalina Borsa. This house belongs to you. Yes?"

"Technically, yes, but—"

"Then this house is, and forever will be, yours until you die—no matter who leads the coven." The woman paused and snapped at a woman who was apparently taking too long directing people to their rooms. "I belong to the house. I belong to you. We all do. Please take a moment to get yourself together. You have a house to run."

"Jedidah…" Tristan said, still holding onto Katie's hand.

"Your rooms are to the right, boy."

"Tristan," Katie corrected.

"I'll show her the damn room." Tristan pulled Katie inside and up the three flights of stairs.

Jedidah was there before they were. "You'll do no such thing. I wouldn't even let you in this house except for the fact that you belong to this family."

"Back off, bone sack."

The woman didn't seem phased. "Lady Borsa, I urge you to be careful. He would destroy this whole house if he could. We spent three months rebuilding what *you* destroyed. I won't let you punch any more holes in my walls."

"Ms. Jedidah?" Katie said, watching Tristan grip the banister.

"Jedidah, Lady Borsa. I have no titles where you are concerned," she said.

"Can we just go to the room? Please?" Katie felt herself losing sight of the end. She still saw the little boy's blank face. She still heard the screams. Not to mention the entire house smelled like blood.

She cleared her throat.

Jedidah nodded and led Katie up another flight of stairs and down the left to two double doors. She pulled out a set of keys and opened it. Before her was a sitting room, and bright light shone through the window—the garden.

Jedidah waved her to another room. "This is the head of house's private quarters. I will close and lock the doors when you leave and make sure they are only opened to you when you return. This is your bed chambers—and Lord Borsa had the study moved to the other side of the bedroom, so the washing chambers are now to the right of the front door. I will bring your clothes. I didn't have much to go on besides a pair of clothes one of the maids found in the downstairs washroom." There was a twitch in her eye, but Jedidah smiled none the less. "So the closet has clothes that should fit. Any concerns, please let me know and we will..." Jedidah trailed off as reality sunk in. "Gertrude is decent enough with a needle, only sharp object she possesses."

They all looked out the window. The world was different now. What the hell did clothes matter?

"It's fine." Katie wanted to be alone with Tristan. "Someone else can have the room. I'll stay with Tristan."

Jedidah put her hand over her mouth as if Katie had slapped her and called her a foul name.

"Lady Borsa, only the head of house uses this room."

"Well, I don't want to use the same bed as Larry. That's weird."

Jedidah looked even more appalled. "We would never suggest you use any bed other than your own. I urge you to really think about what you are asking."

Katie shook her head. "You keep saying 'head of house.' I'm not that. I'm not the head of any family or a coven leader. Just give the room to Azezel."

Jedidah shook her head. "Azezel is not the head of this house. The house is yours. I will burn this room to the ground if you wish. We can shut the doors and seal them with cement. But I cannot permit anyone who is not the owner of this house to reside in this chamber."

"Fine," Katie said exasperated. All she wanted now was for her to leave. "Is there a phone I can use?"

Jedidah gestured to the bedroom. "It's through the room into the study." Jedidah pulled out her keys and ushered them to the bedroom door. "I know I am wasting the air that I breathe, but I feel obliged to inform you that you should keep *guests* to the sitting room area only."

Katie didn't let go of Tristan's hand, and Jedidah conceded. When she opened the door, Katie first saw a glow reflecting off of mirrors and dancing on the crystal chandelier overhead. Second, she saw the paintings. Paintings of people she knew or had seen. Her mom, Tristan, his father. Her. There were others, but Katie focused on the ones of her.

"Lord Borsa painted all of the paintings that hang on the walls of Hill Crest Manor. But the most important he keeps in here and in his study." Jedidah opened the door to the study, and Katie immediately found the phone and called her dad's cell.

Nothing.

She called Lucinda's landline, and it didn't connect. She called, hung up, and dialed the number three more times until it connected.

"Will?" Lucinda's voice was frantic.

"It's me. Tristan and I are safe," Katie said, not knowing how much was safe to say over the phone. "Can you tell my dad?"

"Oh, Katie." Lucinda cried, and Katie heard yelling in the background.

"Katie? Katie?" Her dad's voice was clear and cut straight through her heart.

"I'm safe. We're both safe."

"Okay. God. I saw the TV. The military is all over our neighborhood. I can't get to you. You're okay? Tristan?"

"Yeah. Are you?"

"For now. The president is supposed to give a speech. Our council won't admit it, but we know it was us who gave away the locations of the cities and entry points. The first city to fall was New York, where the council headquarters are."

"Dad…" Katie wanted to tell him everything she saw but it was too much.

"Are you sure you are safe?"

"Yeah. What about Will?"

"Will and Allison…are still missing."

Katie gripped the phone. They could be alive. They were alive. "I'm gonna go. Tell Lucinda Tristan's with me. We're safe." Katie promised to call at least three times a day and hung up the phone. She sat in the chair by the desk. There were so many people she knew who were in Gray City, and she had no idea if they were alive or not.

She breathed deep, her face pressed into her hands.

They were alive.

They were alive.

They had to be alive.

She stood up, realizing Tristan and Jedidah were in the sitting room. She heard Jedidah threatening Tristan, but she could tell he was far away and not caring.

Katie looked at the walls covered with books and saw more pictures of her mother dancing in-between bookcases. There was one of Katie, a photograph of her in a purple dress with a familiar up-do. It was the same picture that hung on the wall at her house. Under the picture was a midnight blue blanket folded neatly on a shelf. Katie picked it up and knew immediately that it was the quilt he'd promised to bring her the day he'd died. It was soft and embroidered with a little person blowing stars into the sky.

Katie collapsed onto the floor and cried into herself.

Will.

Allison.

Mercedes.

Mariam.

Salem.

Would she ever see them again? West wasn't back yet. Did he find Zuri? Were they okay?

Elma.

Jeffry.

Sugar.

The little girl's mom.

The boy with the bullet hole in his eye.

And countless others. They were all dead. Gunned down in the street. She was glad Tristan tore them apart limb from limb. She was glad he'd made them feel an ounce of the terror they had unleashed on them. She hoped it had been painful. She hoped it had been long-lasting and agonizing. She hoped they were still alive and dying slowly, staring up at the gray ceiling, knowing they'd never see the sky again.

⋅ఴఴⴰ⋅

Katie coaxed Tristan to take a bath, and she had to directly tell Jedidah to find him some of Lawrence's old clothes to distribute out to people who needed new clothing. She informed Katie that the people already had their own clothes, that that was what a safe house was for. She did, however, begrudgingly give

Tristan a black shirt that had belonged to Lawrence and brown-and-black-striped pants that were probably from the sixties.

Katie washed up after Tristan, and they both went to the main hall, where cries echoed throughout the cloud of silence. The hall was full of people. They were all searching for something. An answer. A loved one. A reason why.

Every time the door opened, every head in the hall would look up. Someone would scream and run, and they'd clutch onto each other. Others would start a new round of crying.

Tristan sat next to her, and she knew he was looking for West. They both were. He belonged to Lawrence's family, and he should have been here by now.

While they waited, they hear murmurs of *the savior*. The boy who'd been struck down by a missile and still sent the military running. *The one* who'd torn them limb from limb.

Tristan put his head in his hands, and Katie held onto him, saying he was more than that. That they'd all be dead if it weren't for him—until saying nothing was all she could think of.

The door opened, and Katie looked up instinctively. She jerked Tristan's hand and pointed. It was West. Everyone in the great hall looked to the door, but this time their eyes did not fall—there was a witch behind him.

Katie and Tristan raced down the stairs, pushing through the tension and savoring their own relief.

Jedidah was there in front of West. "No witch has ever stepped foot in a Borsa House and never will." Jedidah's eyes were blank.

"It's okay," Katie said. People stared at her as if she had no right to declare what was right or wrong.

"Lady Borsa…"

Katie ignored the murmurs. "She's with me."

Zuri stood behind West. Her black hair cut into her face. This wasn't the Zuri Katie knew. The girl she'd met not that long ago was gone, buried somewhere deep down in her nearly black eyes.

"Lady Borsa…"

"Stop calling me that. Just call me Katie. The witch is with me. She'll be in my room. No more questions, no more arguing. That's it. You said I own the damn house, so move."

Katie grabbed West and pulled him and Zuri toward the stairs.

Jedidah nodded, staring down at the floor with a glare that would have Katie looking over her shoulder for days—if they lived that long.

"You can't let her stay here. No one outside of the race can stay with the coven. It's against nature," said a woman with wide, darting eyes.

Katie looked around. The woman wasn't the only one looking at Zuri with a kind of boiling hysteria that threatened to spill over and burn them all. Katie was asking these people to accept something that was apparently more impossible than the mass genocide happening in the city they once called home.

"You're asking them to give up control on the only thing they have left." Tristan's voice was in her mind. *"Tell them she'll stay in your room until you talk with Azezel."*

Katie took in their eyes. She had no choice. They were hungry for revenge, and she wasn't going to give them a reason to try and take it out on a powerless girl. She looked at West, and she hoped her eyes begged for forgiveness.

"She's staying in my room until I speak with Azezel. He'll decide what to do from there."

West grimaced and held Zuri closer, following Katie back up the stairs. When they were back behind closed doors, West glared at Katie. "What the hell was that?"

Tristan stood in front of her. "Don't. I told her to say it. It was that or watch you fight off a mob of people who have nothing left to lose."

Zuri stared at the glow in the window from the garden below. "I deserve it. This is—he used my power. Without it, the hex they lifted off the humans would have been impossible." She stared at her hands like they weren't her own. West held her and quieted her cries.

"You can have the bedroom. I—I don't think we have food. I don't even think there are ovens or anything. I'll ask around," Katie said, not knowing who she'd ask. She'd pissed off the lady in charge, and to be honest, she had no idea what she was doing. Her head pounded with Zuri's pulse, and Katie went to the small balcony, finding solace in the large bone-white tree with glowing blue leaves.

"Listen to me, Katalina," Tristan said behind her. "You have to act the part, or else these people are going to freak out, tear themselves apart, and take us down with them."

"Then you do it," Katie said honestly. "I don't know how. I don't know the rules. I don't know anything besides what I saw out there. I just know that we are moments away from being found and hunted down like animals."

"They can't find us. Even if they make it to the dead zone, only special patrol teams can see in that kind of darkness and they are well-trained. Their only job is to patrol and kill what doesn't belong. Soldiers would be taken out before they can get far enough, and if they *do* get far enough, they'll blow the tunnel and seal the exit. We're safe here—from everyone but ourselves."

Katie shook her head and cried.

Elma.

Jeffry.

Sugar.

The little girl's mom.

The boy with the bullet hole in his eye.

Will.

Allison.

Mariam.

Salem.

Mercedes.

She saw their faces over and over. She'd thought she'd hit rock-bottom before… She hadn't known what Hell really was.

"Do it for them. Everyone in this manor has an Elma. They have a Jeffery and a Cookie."

"Sugar," Katie snapped. She didn't mean to. "I'm sorry."

He leaned his head against hers. She listened to his breathing. The world was falling down around them. Violence wasn't something people did; it was something they became. But they were still here. Still together. That counted for something. They had to keep trying, keep living. Especially for those who had been slain in the streets. For those still missing.

"Everyone has lost someone," Tristan said. "But I haven't lost you. Maybe that makes me lucky or maybe I should feel guilty, but I don't. I feel like you. We have to make it count. We have to keep going and hold on to what little we have. Right now we have the manor and, with it, our safety."

Katie nodded. They both turned when they heard the doors of her room open and close. It was Jedidah.

Jedidah turned on the lights in the dark room and looked at Katie on the balcony and nodded.

Tristan cursed Jedidah under his breath. Katie remembered he'd told her he stayed here when his parents had first died—that Lawrence had told him he couldn't see Katie anymore and he'd freaked out and gone postal, so Lawrence had sent him to the manor in New York. Katie was starting to understand the hate between Jedidah and Tristan.

Katie squeezed his hand. "I better see what she wants."

"That old sack of bones can wait."

"Tristan…" Katie whispered. She didn't need to make an enemy of the woman with keys to her room.

"She's technically your slave, Katalina. She couldn't touch you if she wanted to."

Katie's hand twitched as she touched the balcony door.

"She's a slave to the family. It is what it is. Don't—"

Katie opened the door and spoke to Jedidah straight out. "I can't be a slave owner. You're free. The whole staff is free. I set you free. Or whatever. *This* is too much."

Jedidah looked between Tristan and Katie. "Permit me to speak frankly."

Katie nodded. "Speak however you what. I don't own you."

"No, little girl. You don't. *You* don't own me anymore than I own the sun. You are a blip on the map. I belong to this house. I own this house as the house owns me. We are one. Do you understand that?"

Katie blinked.

"Sit down." Jedidah pointed to the sofa. "Sit." Her voice was curt, and Katie sat—slowly. She might not own the woman, but the woman didn't own her either. "Did you know I pulled your father out from between the legs of his mother? I beat his father before that. The little, fat thief was always stealing food out of the kitchens. Never in my life—and it has been a long one—have I seen a witch in a Borsa house. Never in my life have I been burdened with a head of house as incompetent as you—shut up, boy." Jedidah cut Tristan a dangerous look.

"Listen to me, girl. I will call you Lady Borsa because anything else is offensive, if not an insult to the entire Borsa line. You will refer to me as Jedidah and all the other house staff by their first names only. The rooms are as assigned. Azezel will stay in the green room, and you will stay in the family room, as the head of house always does. The late Lord Borsa passed this house to you and not the next coven leader. For whatever reason, it is as it stands and you will follow protocol—I'm not done." Jedidah held up her hand.

"You will not destroy this house. The people downstairs have suffered a great tragedy. They are looking for leadership and safety. If you cannot provide leadership, you will provide them safety by not defying the very laws we live by. Next, I will conduct the house in the way it is to be conducted. If you can trust me to help you, I will. We cannot work against each other. I will do whatever I can for this house. I have and will until the day I die and that will not be in the near future." Jedidah waited for a reply.

Katie glanced at Tristan. "Sorry for thinking you were my slave."

"If you will allow me to speak frankly once more." Jedidah eyed Tristan.

"Not if it's about him. Look, I'm listening. I don't know what to do, but you do. So do it. I won't fight it. Except Tristan stays with me in my room and Zuri stays, too, until Azezel gets here." Katie had a feeling that Azezel was more fair-minded than Jedidah.

She bowed her head. "Lady Borsa. If that is all."

"Do you really have to call me that?"

Jedidah cut her a look.

"Okay. That's it." Katie pulled her feet up and looked at them. Her shoes were soaked through with blood and dirt.

"If I may…" Jedidah paused before leaving. "It is by luck of birth that until now you have never seen true hate. The hate that takes pleasure in watching you lose everything worth having. The hate that takes comfort in your suffering and salivates at the thought of causing more.

"But there is another kind that is much worse. The kind of hate that just watches. The hate that does nothing, that feels nothing." Jedidah looked between both of them, her eyes softer than they had been since Katie met her just a few short hours ago. "The only way to overcome it is to live on, as I have. To find love when it seems lost. To build what others have destroyed. Don't try to understand it. Don't try to rationalize it. There are no winners in war—only the damned."

"War." Katie said the word like she had been running from it. "War takes two sides."

"No, Lady Borsa. It does not. I will bring Azezel when he arrives." Jedidah excused herself.

.୧୧୬୭.

It was almost time for sunset, and Katie heard the change in the air as *he* walked in. She stood at the top of the stairs with Tristan as Azezel and a large group of injured arrived.

Jedidah stood next to him, directing the injured to the west wing and those healthy enough to be taken to their rooms where harvested blood and clean clothes awaited. Jedidah then pointed toward the top of the stairs at Katie, and Azezel's eyes followed.

Azezel waved a patrolman to follow him as he came up the stairs. "What is the update from the other houses?"

"The numbers are still coming in, sir. Last update was an hour ago. The Starvaski house hasn't shown up yet."

Azezel paused. "Some of them had to have made it out of the Burrow."

"I asked around, sir. None of the Starvaski patrolmen showed up for work today."

Azezel clenched his fists.

Tristan spoke as Katie heard his thoughts form. "They left with The Seven. So the kidnappings, the D-ranges last year…it was them. They didn't just want to be head of the coven. They wanted to use the coven as an army."

Azezel nodded. "You're quick, boy." He turned his attention back to the patrolman behind him. "Send word to each house to get a party together to go and harvest blood. We'll need it."

"Sir." The patrolman bowed his head and hurried down the stairs, collecting other patrolmen and women as he went out the door.

"I understand you have a witch in the house?" Azezel said, beckoning Katie to her room. When they were inside, he walked directly to the balcony, taking in the glow.

"She has nowhere else to go. We can't—"

Azezel held up his hand. "For now, out of sight, out of mind. The people in the great hall will clear out to their rooms soon. Only nobility stay in the main house, and they will not question what I have said." He looked at her and then at the bedroom door where Zuri and West still were. "But keep it that way. She will starve before it becomes a problem."

"We'll find something," Katie said, not liking the way he seemed to own the room, probably more than she ever would. Maybe she should give it to him—get out of this mess while she still could.

Azezel turned to Tristan. "Finally. A boy to put to the face that haunts me. What is your name?"

Tristan's expression moved into a neutral state. Katie heard him study Azezel. His mannerisms, his posture, and the way his eyes darted over Tristan, sizing him up. "Tristan."

Azezel waited.

"Vauntgard."

Azezel nodded. "You look just like Ivan. Even the way you regard me suspiciously now. I am not your enemy, boy. I have seen what your father fought so hard to hide all his life. Your strength does not frighten me."

"I won't do it again," Tristan said, thinking miles ahead of Katie. In her mind, she saw his fears. She heard him thinking about his father and the words, *Don't ever let them use you.*

"I'm not asking you to."

"You asked her to." Tristan's face was still calm and unreadable.

Azezel sighed. "I didn't. I simply told her what God showed me. If he has plans for you, that is his design alone. I am no more than a messenger."

"Then why didn't you warn people?" Katie's mind reeled. If what he'd seen was Tristan going berserk on a military, why hadn't he warned them?

"It was not for me to tell. If God has a plan, it is not for me to thwart it."

"People are dead because of you." Katie put her head between her hands and tried to squeeze the crazy out. Her mind spun. The killings—all the killings could have been stopped. They could have evacuated an entire city. Children were dead in the street, mothers, fathers, and friends. Katie didn't know if she'd ever see Will, Allison, Mercedes, Mariam, or Salem again...

"I told you once. My gift is not a parlor trick. I am not some witch bedazzled with glamour and cheeky riddles. I see what God shows me. I risked enough telling you what I did to save the people I did."

"*Tristan* saved us, not you," Katie spat, astonished that Azezel would try to take credit for something he hadn't even been there for.

"No, little girl. God did. He planted the seed."

Katie shook her head, seeing their faces. So many dead faces. The puddles and bodies she ran through and over.

Tristan stood, still and passive, while this man went on, trying to rationalize it, trying to take credit.

"*Shhh,*" Tristan's voice whispered in her mind. "*It's okay. He's not the enemy, Katalina. He's someone who just lost hundreds, if not thousands, of people in his coven. Let it go.*"

Katie breathed back some of the hysteria, but the faces kept flashing like movie stills. The way her head had smacked against the wall when Roger had pulled her back, stealing her away from a bullet that had had her name on it. Her body slamming to the ground when they'd shot that missile at Tristan.

Azezel went back to the balcony door. He stared out into the garden. "I understand your anger—but you must hide it. Save it. This war has just begun. You are the next Borsa. This house belongs to you. Though I am their leader, this is their house and you are the symbol of safety. They all know you are just a girl. But if you are strong, they can find it in themselves to be stronger, too."

Katie blinked back tears. That wasn't fair. She grabbed the iron necklace and ran her thumb over it, like she had done a thousand times since West had given it to her. It helped take the edge off of Zuri's thumping pulse.

How was she supposed to be brave for others when she couldn't even be brave for herself? How could she become who others looked to for solace? She was a recovering junkie who was doing all she could, in this moment, to quiet the thirst. How was she supposed to help other people? She couldn't even help her friends, who were probably dead. Each and every one of them.

Katie sobbed. It came out loud, ugly, and desperate. She imagined, by the looks on their faces, that she sounded like an animal drowning in black murky water. Screams mixed in with shouts. She bent over her stomach in knots and pain because she couldn't catch her breath.

She heard Azezel rattling off in Spanish—prayers or curses—and crossed the room. She couldn't stop. It was like lightning and thunder struck and shook her entire body.

"I expect you to get back to work before the night is over," Azezel said to Tristan before leaving the room.

Katie collapsed onto the floor, coughing and crying. Tristan sat down and rubbed her back, looking at her with a sad and pitiful face.

༝༜ 22 ༡༠

A New Tomorrow

TRISTAN HELD KATIE in the dark room. The only soft light came from the garden's pulsing glow, weak like a heartbeat. She was faintly aware of West coming and speaking with Tristan before leaving. She was faintly aware of the low, strung-out crying as people filled up the rooms on the third and fourth floor. It wasn't until Jedidah was rubbing her face with a cloth that Katie knew she was no longer in the sitting room, but in the bathroom.

"That's right. You are still alive and amongst the living. Come back."

Katie sucked in a breath. "Where is Tristan?"

"I sent him to the dining room to drink. He looks horrible. Also, it's improper for a boy to be in the washroom with you. I won't allow it. I won't."

Katie sat in silence.

"The president is giving a speech in an hour. You can watch it in the sitting room. Or in the Great Hall. Many of us will be in the Great Hall."

"You want me to go and be brave for the people?" Katie said, her tongue dry and her eyes heavy.

"No. The lady can do what she wants." Jedidah held Katie's hands. They were surprisingly warm and strong for a woman who claimed to be older than Lawrence's father. "However…" She looked at Katie. "It is better to suffer in the arms of many than none." Jedidah stood up and began to brush Katie's hair. It was a strange thing, to have someone brushing her hair. Such a simple, kind thing when just hours ago she thought she was going to die and be another body on the ground.

"Don't you have other things to do?" Katie said sheepishly. Her senses were coming back to her, and she burned, embarrassed.

"Not when the head of the house is having a breakdown," Jedidah said, but then added. "My lady."

Katie sat in silence until Jedidah had brushed the knots out of her hair and fixed it in a tight bun. "If that is all, I'll be in the kitchen checking on Gertrude. She can't tell a broom from a ladle."

Katie stood up as well. She met Tristan in the sitting room, and he held out his hand, kissing Katie and hugging her so tight she stopped breathing. "I have to go," he said.

Katie knew it was inevitable. He couldn't stay here while the rest of his squad was out working. "Where will you be?" Katie asked.

Tristan shrugged. "I don't know yet. Wherever my team was assigned to." He kissed her again. "When my shift is over, I'll come back here. I promise."

Katie nodded and let him go. She memorized every inch of his face. His hair was still shorter than it had been before it'd been singed off, but his eyes were that crystal-clear blue she had grown to love and lose herself in. His hands lingered on her waist as his eyes darted across her face, too.

They wouldn't say it—why it was so important to remember every minuscule detail. Not aloud and not to themselves. They just did it.

She watched him leave, breathed deep as he let her follow his thoughts all the way down the staircase and out the door before eclipsing to places their minds couldn't meet.

Katie smacked her chest, trying to slow her heartbeat. She had to remind herself that she wasn't alone. She still had him, and that was more than what a lot of people could even hope for. She walked over to the bedroom and opened the door. She listened to Zuri's quiet, sleeping breaths for a moment before crossing the room to the study to call her dad again.

Hearing his voice and wanting to just see him made her knees buckle. It took a lot for her to hang up the phone and gather enough nerve to leave the room.

⋆ৎ৩৯⋆

The house staff still moved faster than ever. They were running to and from rooms, some shouting orders at others, but they all stopped to bow briefly when they saw Katie. She bowed back, feeling in the way and useless. She watched from the stairs as a few servants set up a large, flat, white screen along one of the long walls leading to the library. A man moved back and forth with a projector until a shorter woman gave him a satisfied nod. They ran the cables to it, and the man plugged in speakers as the woman turned everything on.

A loud voice filled the entire hall. Katie covered her ears and heard a few surprised screams. Jedidah appeared from nowhere and slapped the man in the back of the head, making him drop and apologize profusely. Katie ran down the stairs and stopped Jedidah from whacking the man a third time.

"It was just an accident." Katie unplugged the speakers. She found the speaker remote and turned it all the way down before plugging them back in.

"It should be on channel seven," Katie told the woman holding the cable box remote. The woman fumbled and found the channel.

On the wall for all of them to see the military marching through the streets of Boise as ash fell from the sky. It must have been repeat footage of just after the attack.

Katie turned up the sound.

"...Eye witness reports say that some have been torn from their homes for questioning. Many people are wondering if the price of safety from a people who have stayed hidden for so long is worth the massacre we are witnessing on our own streets."

Katie couldn't believe it. It hadn't snowed since a few days before Christmas, but right there in the middle of downtown was a pile of it. But it wasn't snow; it was the ashes of vampires who had either tried to run or been dragged out to burn. How many people had been murdered in the country? In the world, even? Who was going to stop a mass genocide when there was no one against it?

"Up next: The president will speak on the horrors we have witnessed today. Tom, I think it's safe to say, not everyone in America agrees with what has happened."

"No, Sophie. But it's safe to say, the threat is real. People all over the world were put to sleep for fifteen minutes. Some still haven't woken up. They could have stayed in hiding, but they decided to threaten our lives instead. We had to answer with something."

Katie looked behind her as people started to fill the hall. They poured in, watching the newscasters on the wall. They all waited as more footage was shown and the clock counted down to the top of the hour.

The president stood tall and solemn before them. His voice filled the room.

"My fellow Americans...we are at war. Today, I come to you with a heavy heart and a strong conviction. Recent events have shown us that the

belief we were safe in our communities and homes…is false. The enemy is at our doorsteps, and they have threatened our freedom, our safety, and that of our children as well. Well, we have answered. For the protection of our families—our species—I have authorized…"

The screen went black, and Katie looked at the projector, thinking someone had unplugged it, until the screen flashed bright again and gasps filled the room.

Hugh was on the TV, frowning at them all.

"Hello again. I am sorry to have to interrupt our president, but I have a message for those of us who escaped being slaughtered in the streets today. On News Year's Eve night, we gave the people of the world a gift—we woke them up. We believed it was time for all races to live as one, to cohabitate this world in harmony…but they answered our call by murdering our children like rats in a sewer. How many of you are still waiting to find the ones you love? How many of you know you never will?"

Katie looked around the room. Everyone had lost someone. She saw it in their eyes. She saw it in the way they nodded at Hugh's words.

"The guardians who were meant to protect our secret opened the doors to our homes where our loved ones slept. I say to hell with our secret keepers, we can guard ourselves. To hell with peace in a world that wants us dead. My brethren, wolves, children of the shadow, you don't have to like me, but you do have to choose. Will you let them keep us apart? Keep us in chains? Or will we stand together?"

Katie looked around the room. Everyone stared at Hugh, completely engrossed in his message. This was the man who'd beaten Zuri. The man who stolen her power and sent the world to hell on New Year's Eve. But in their eyes, she didn't sense the hatred they should have for him. Worst of all—in this moment, given everything, she didn't sense it in herself.

ᴀᴄᴋɴᴏᴡʟᴇᴅɢᴇᴍᴇɴᴛꜱ

This book shook me to my core and it took a lot of support to get through it. I first want to thank my husband for getting the through the tough parts and reminding me not to pull any punches just because I was scared. I have to give a huge hug again to my cover designer Kim. She brought Zuri to life and the cover is all I dreamed of. My copy editor Rebecca Ann, fix all my flaws and made this book shine with perfection.

Of course and this list is so long, but my early readers who took a leap of faith and held Katie's hand until the end.

And of course, I owe you the biggest thank you of all for going on yet another adventure with me and making it to the end. Also—this year was tough on Katie but I hope it wasn't to rough on you.

CPSIA information can be obtained
at www.ICGtesting.com
Printed in the USA
LVHW01s1548220418
574433LV00003BA/528/P

9 780997 710311